K.A Richardson

I've Been Watching You

K A Richardson

Praise for K A Richardson

'KA Richardson has the writing talent and story-telling skills to be with us a long while. I can't wait to see what she brings us next!' – *Howard Linskey, author of No Name Lane, Behind Dead Eyes, and the David Blake series.*

'A great follow on from With Deadly Intent with no punches pulled. This one is a must read.' *Sheila Quigley, best-selling author of the Seahills Series and Holy Island Trilogy.*

'KA Richardson writes with such knowledge, it's like watching an episode of Silent Witness.' *Tara Lyons, author of In The Shadows and co-author of The Caller.*

'KA Richardson is a brilliant Northern writer. She's created some of my favourite characters and her writing sings. LOVE LOVE LOVE IT.' *Eileen Wharton, award winning author of Blanket of Blood.*

'A truly talented writer taking the reader on a thrilling roller coaster of riveting suspense.' *Jayne Tomlinson, Branch Manager, Darlington Building Society.*

'With her attention to detail and her impassioned prose, KA Richardson is a fresh and exciting voice in the crime fiction genre.' *Ian Ayris, author of Abide With Me and April Skies.*

'KA Richardson writes a compelling story with characters to care about.' *Victoria Watson, Elementary V Watson.*

K.A Richardson

First published in 2016 by Bloodhound Books

www.bloodhoundbooks.com

ISBN 978-0-9955111-2-5

For my husband, Peter, and my mum, Jeannet, without their support writing wouldn't be possible.

Prologue

4th November 2008, 2320 hours - A field outside Durham, UK

He'd been watching her for weeks. It was finally time.

The only sound cutting through the darkness was the occasional hoot of an owl.

He strained, listening.

The damp soil was cold against his cheek as he lay there, feigning injury. He knew how it looked; the white mountain bike on the ground beside him, stark in the moonlight.

It looked as he had planned it would.

Stiffening, he heard her trainers slapping softly against the tarmac as she approached. He heard her pace change from steady to faltering and eventually to a walk. He pictured her pulling the headphones from her ears and looking at the gate in surprise. Tensed and ready, he almost jumped as she said, 'Oh my God. Sir, are you alright?'

He waited, not moving a muscle, his eyes closed. A soft squelching sounded as she stepped into the mud at the edge of the field.

'Crap,' she muttered as she cautiously moved closer.

His hand gripped the knife concealed underneath him as his erection strained painfully against the zip of his trousers. His stomach churned with butterflies – this was going to be good.

He felt the touch of her hand on the arm of his jacket, and ready for action, he jumped to his feet with the agility of a gymnast. The faint moonlight glinted on the knife in his hand and he heard her gasp as she turned to run.

But it was too late.

He grabbed her, the knife to her throat in a movement that was controlled; more so than he thought it would be. Adrenaline pumped through his veins as the look of pained surprise on her face turned to fear.

Swiftly, he brought his fist around and allowed it to connect with the side of her face, knocking her to the ground. Kneeling down, he pushed the blade into her stomach - the motion slow and controlled, and he smiled in the moonlight as she groaned in pain.

Calm now, he pulled the cable ties from his pocket and secured her hands. Then he used them to drag her deeper into the darkness of the field, took a moment to close the gate, and chuckled as she screamed and struggled against the bonds.

'I've been watching you,' he whispered, kneeling beside her, watching the fear on her face intensify as he unzipped his fly, pulled the condom free from its packaging and slid it down his length.

He hadn't even touched her yet, but he felt shivers ripple down his spine at the thought of the things to come.

Chapter One
28th May, 0910 hours, Present Day – Newstead Residential Home, Sunderland

Pausing at the door, John Whitworth felt his mouth harden in anticipation. He hated this place. Always had.

Ever since they had brought his wife Eve here six years ago, he'd endured that smell that only hospitals and care homes could produce. He'd had to cope with the anaemic walls and musty furniture. He had wanted his wife to stay at home, but it just wasn't practical. He couldn't afford not to work, and she needed full-time care. Most of his pay cheque went on paying for her single room and board in the place that had now become his own personal hell.

He felt his teeth grit as he pressed his index finger onto the door buzzer. Ever careful, the home required that the front door be permanently locked and all visitors were expected to sign in on entry: security measures to keep the sane people out and the insane people in.

A half-smile flitted over his lips –anyone actually wanting to break in would have to be nuts. It was full of men and women of varying ages, in different stages of illness that was not likely to be cured. Many of them wore sodden or stained clothing with drool hanging in the corner of their mouths like an icicle ready to drop but never quite getting the momentum. *A tad harsh?* Maybe, but it was how he felt. If he ever got to the stage when someone wanted to put him in this home … *That will never happen. I won't let it. I'll end it all myself before I get stuck in a shithole like this.*

As the door clicked open he readied his sympathy face. He always made sure his facade never slipped in here. And sympathy was always the way forward when faced with a room full of blithering idiots.

He signed his name in the visitor book. *Same sad table, same cheap pen. Nothing ever changes.*

Resuming his false smile, he followed the carer down the corridor. The years had not been kind to Betty Sanders: her wide

3

hips swung from side to side as she walked, less of a sashay and more of a waddle. Her thunderous thighs rubbed together with every step, causing her trousers to edge upwards on the inside seam and making the inner leg appear shorter than the outer. The tight-fitting, faded tunic screamed of too many biscuits eaten at the residents' break times. He wondered if the residents actually got to eat any. Betty's untidy hair was swept up, a kind of messy grey birds nest, her wrinkled face well-tanned, presumably from holidays. It looked more like old leather than a healthy sun-kissed glow.

The only thing Betty had going for her was her eyes: piercing, intelligent, blue. The kind of eyes a man could look at and know she would take no crap from anyone.

For a moment John wondered whether there was a Mr Sanders at home, waiting for her with dinner on the table. *Aye; dinner for three, just for her.* He smirked to himself at the thought.

But it was only for a moment.

As they neared the door to his wife's room, he forgot all about Betty. His breath stuck in his throat as he waited for *that* look - the look Eve always gave him through her stupor as he entered the room. The look of fear mildly disguised with defiance. He couldn't hurt her in here. Not physically, anyway. But still he knew she was petrified. She knew everything of him, but she couldn't say it. Her illness was now so far gone it was unlikely she even recollected a lot of the bad stuff. Her speech was down to the odd groan and grunt.

But he knew she always remembered him; he could tell by her eyes.

He felt his heart thud as he saw the fear fade to resignation. He was here again, and there wasn't a damn thing she could do about it.

28th May, 1005 hours – CSI Department, Sunderland City Centre Depot

Ben Cassidy had juggled her force folder, a bag of evidence and her camera case up the stairs to the office. With a complete lack of grace, she dumped the lot onto her desk, pulled the fingerprint lifts from the pocket of her combats and sat down with a sigh.

Other than her, the office was empty. She was on day shift with Craig Simpson, who was still out fixing up all the jobs he could before the mid-shift came in at 11 a.m. Ben also knew he was more than aware she had to leave early; he'd already picked up her slack by radioing her and telling her to get back to the nick to put her jobs through Socard, the forensic database used internally by the police.

She smiled to herself as she pulled out her scene notes to transfer over to the computer system – today was her daughter's first report day. At a few months off five years old, Grace was an absolute gem of a child, even at the worst of times. She had started reception the previous September and had settled into it straight away.

Ben already knew how adorable Grace was, had loved her with all her being since the moment she had been put into her arms, but she was eager to hear what the teachers thought of her. Ben and her aunt Aoife had taught Grace well from very early on. She was advanced on her reading and writing, but also on her maths and science - well past the average levels for most children her age. It hadn't taken the school long to pop Grace into some of the year one classes to help her advance.

This meeting was to discuss what would happen at the start of the new term in September – and Ben was more excited than Grace was. Trying her best to focus on the job at hand, she cracked on with transferring the information over to the computer.

Hearing a huffing sound in the corridor, she turned, looking towards the door. Her eyes widened as Cass McKay entered the room with about as much elegance as a pet elephant. Which was not entirely her fault – her large, pregnant tummy protruded outwards, making her movements jerky and undignified.

'Cass! I thought you were on maternity. What on earth are you doing here?' asked Ben, jumping up and pulling her into a bear hug, barely able to get her arms round Cass's belly.

'Damn baby wants to hurry up and come out. I've been lugging this round for nine months now. She was due out yesterday but she's holding her ground. I'm convinced she's doing it on purpose too. She keeps giving me Braxton Hicks, getting me to the point I think it's real and then stopping,' grumbled Cass, pulling up a chair and lowering herself down slowly. 'As to what I'm doing here, I couldn't stay inside. Am sick to death of being at home, cooped up in the cottage with only Ollie to keep me company. There's only so many times you can have a conversation with the dog before you think you're going crazy. Alex keeps going to work, which is fine: he has to work or he won't get as much paternity, but seriously, I can't even get over the stile to take Ollie for a walk. I'm bored shitless. So today I figured I'd pop in and see how things are going with you. You've been flying solo for, like, two months now, right?'

Ben smiled and nodded. Cass had been the reason she had opted to transfer into the CSI Department. In the year and a half since Cass had been kidnapped so much had changed. Ben had been sick of working just to pay the bills, and with the redundancies being offered, the CSI team had found themselves one person short. Cass had encouraged Ben to apply, giving her all the help she needed, and Ben had been offered the job six months ago. After a nine-week intensive training course, she had been mentored at the Ryhope station with Cass as her supervisor, and then transferred into the busier station in the city centre.

'It's flown by. I can barely remember being on front office now. It's funny how quickly we settle into something new. Can you believe I start my Introduction to Digital Forensics course tomorrow? How's married life?'

Cass rolled her eyes. 'Alex is fussing over me like a mother hen, even more so now I've gone off on leave. He's doing everything in the house, driving me if I need to go anywhere. It's damned annoying.' Her comments, however, were contradicted by the contented smile on her face. 'Tomorrow? That's come around quick. How's Grace finding school?'

'She loves it. I've a meeting with her teacher today. I can't wait to see what she has to say – Grace is growing up so fast!'

'I hear they do that,' grinned Cass. 'I'm gonna leave you to your Socard for a sec, need to pop up and see Alex and Ali. Feels weird having him down here too. The secondment came up just at the right time for him. What time are you leaving? I can give you a lift if you don't have the car with you.'

'Ali's so much like Alex. He ran point on an assault I had last week in the town, handled himself the way Alex does. You sure about the lift?'

At Cass's nod, Ben added, 'That's great, thanks. I'll cancel the taxi I've got booked. Aoife has the car today. She had some appointment or other after she'd taken Grace to school.'

Cass grimaced as she used the back of the chair to pull herself up. 'I'm the size of a bloody house,' she grumbled as she made her way down the corridor.

Ben grinned to herself; despite it being nearly five years ago, that was one feeling she remembered all too well. Grabbing the SD card from her camera, she headed next door to the photography room to write off her Write Once Read Many disc for the photos she'd taken earlier. The WORM was then retained by the Photography Department as the original and copies were made for use from that one by the officer dealing, and the courts. Once the disc was written, Ben selected the ones she would print if later requested, glancing at each one in sequence and marking them on the order form that got sent off with the WORM disc.

She really did enjoy forensic work, even if it made her sad at times. Like today; the job she was in the process of writing up was a break in to an allotment – didn't sound all that sad, but people could be so cruel and nasty at times.

The victim was a man in his seventies, Arthur Phelps. He kept pigeons on his allotment, and had gained quite the reputation for breeding excellent racers. The offender, obviously someone from the same racing circles, had broken into the allotment and killed all of Arthur's twenty-four pigeons, bar one. The one left alive had two broken wings, and Arthur had had no choice but to kill his last pigeon himself. He had been devastated when Ben got there; it was heart-breaking to watch a man cry over the loss of something so dear to him. Ben wanted to tell him something that would make him feel a little better before she left. Luckily, Arthur was one of the few allotment keepers who had a pristine sanctuary – he'd recently glossed his keep doors, and Ben had managed to lift fingerprints from them and had cast footwear marks from the soil outside, and the offender had dropped a tool which could offer DNA for comparison. Rarely was evidence obtained from an allotment, but Ben had been pleased with the result. Maybe there was a chance to find out who would want to hurt Arthur, and to get him a little peace of mind.

The look on his face was definitely not one she would forget in a hurry. He had been so pleased she had found something that he shook her hand for about five minutes straight when she explained it all to him. So far, in her limited experience, it was days like these that made it all worthwhile.

Ben finished prepping the evidence to send off, and tidied her desk. She heard Cass's huffing again in the corridor, grabbed her bag and carefully locked the CSI office behind her.

28ᵗʰ May, 1150 hours – St Mary's Catholic First School, Sunderland.
'Ah, Miss Cassidy. The teachers are all waiting in the main hall. I believe you're seeing Mrs Muztachs.'

Ben nodded and followed David Goodfellow, the head of the school, to the hall. She smiled to herself, it didn't matter where in the world your school was, there was something about its main hall that reeked of assembly and prayer, especially in a Catholic school like this one. Mr Goodfellow broke off as they entered, side-tracked by an argument starting between two children.

She was glad the meetings weren't being held in the gym. Ben shivered as she remembered her last visit to that part of the school. It had only been a couple of months before Grace had started, when Ben had been called there for work. Some scrote had broken in and sliced his femoral artery climbing over the broken glass. He was obviously a junky looking for something to hock for his next fix and he'd passed out in the gymnasium before bleeding out. By the time the gym teacher had realised the next day, it was too late. The kids in the first gym class had seen the body. The man had been dead a while. There was blood spatter over the walls and a pool had been congealing beneath him. The teacher had ushered the kids out, but they were deeply distressed by the sight.

Glancing around the room Ben made eye contact with Mrs Muztachs and wove her way through the tables to her destination. Grace turned in her seat, rising to her knees. Her eyes were sparkling brightly, and she beamed quite possibly the biggest smile Ben had ever seen. It almost knocked her to her knees. *God, I love this child.*

Bending, she planted a kiss on her daughter's forehead.

'Hi, Gracey, you having a good day?'

Grace nodded and sat back down, turning her attention to her teacher with a solemn look.

'Hi, Ben.' Mrs Muztachs shook Ben's hand. 'I'm so glad you could make it today. I know it was short notice.'

At Ben's nod, the teacher continued. 'Grace is polite, has a smile for everyone, shares willingly – seriously, I could go on and on but I know how pressed for time we are. She's great at reading and her writing is coming along nicely. I'd like to suggest that we push her into the year two class for reading in September. We don't want her to become bored. It will be challenging for her and she may require a little additional help at home, but we will make sure you're equipped with everything you would need. She's a little chatterbox – especially in maths. We often have to remind her to be quiet in class but that's not too much of a problem as yet. We'll just keep an eye on her.'

It was a long speech, but Ben was grinning widely. Aware of Grace staring up at her, she said, 'What do you think, Grace? Would you like to move into a new class after the summer holidays so you can learn more things?'

Grace nodded, looking thoughtful. 'I wouldn't see my friends in class any more would I? I would have to make new friends?'

'You would still see them in your other lessons, sweetheart, but you'll make new friends too. You could still play together at break-times and lunchtime though, and you can still ask Alice over to play like you do now. If you want to think about it and talk to me at home though, I'm sure Mrs Muztachs will give us a few days to think it over?'

'Of course. You two can take as long as you need to make your minds up. If you decide you want to stay where you are, Grace, and your mum agrees, then that's absolutely fine too.'

Grace frowned, something she did often when she was processing her thoughts. She was very grown up for a four-year-old, weighing things up rather than just rushing in and doing them like most children. Her brown eyes, with their long, dark lashes, blinked slowly, and eventually her mouth widened into a smile.

'Can we ask Aunty Aoife when we get home, please, Mummy? We could sit at the table and have some ice-cream. Strawberry is my favourite.'

'Well, I can't see why we shouldn't have some ice-cream when Aunty Aoife gets home. This is a very big decision, and I'm sure the ice-cream will help us all decide what to do.' Ben winked at Grace with a grin. Grace could take or leave sweets and crisps, much preferring an apple or a Satsuma; but when it came to strawberry ice-cream she was lost.

'Perfect,' said Mrs Muztachs. 'Here are the preliminary school reports. You'll notice Grace is marked as good in every subject except PE. This isn't because she is bad at PE; she's on a par with other children her age. PE doesn't really have an exceptional category until the children get older and choose to excel in one sport or another. If you decide to move her up next year, she will move on the first day of the new term. I'm actually head of year two next year so Grace would still be learning with me if she moves.'

'That's brill; thank you so much, Mrs Muztachs. I'll take the reports home, and I presume if I have any questions it's alright for me to email or ring you?'

'Of course. It's been a pleasure meeting with you again. Grace, you enjoy your ice-cream, OK?'

Grace nodded as she clambered down from her chair.

Ben took hold of her daughter's hand and ignored the shudder that passed down her spine as she turned and saw the door to the gym next door. The blood really had got everywhere in the room, she didn't even have to close her eyes to remember it. It had looked like some kind of horrific murder had taken place. She'd never look at the gym in the same way again. The poor kids that had found the body had ended up needing counselling.

Her train of thought was interrupted by Grace saying 'Mummy, do I have to go back to class now or is it home time?'

'No, you don't have to go to class. The teachers have a training afternoon. We'll have to pop to Asda on our way home though; I think you ate all of the ice-cream last week when Alice came over. Which one should we buy?'

Grace cocked her head to one side again. 'Well, you like vanilla, and Aunty Aoife likes chocolate so could we get one of the 'poltan ones, please?'

'You mean Neapolitan? The one with the three colours inside?'

'Yes please, Mummy, the 'napoltan one will be perfect. Am I allowed a teddy wafer too? And strawberry sauce? And sprinkles?'

'We'll see how many pennies I have when we get there, OK? If I have enough pennies then yes; if not we'll have to have the toffee sauce we already have at home.'

Grace started skipping as they walked out of the school gates. One bonus in choosing to live close to the school was that you didn't have far to go to get home. Ben and Aoife lived in the same house, had done since Ben had moved back in after telling her aunt she was pregnant.

Accepting without question, Aoife had decorated Ben's room and prepped what became the nursery, and eventually decorated it with the pink fairy design Grace had begged for on her last birthday.

It made Ben happy being back with her Aunt, she liked the company. And it suited Aoife too: she had been considering selling before Ben had moved back. The house was too big for one person to clatter about in.

Ben was glad to have the afternoon off. With the way the CSI shifts worked she sometimes felt like she hardly saw Grace or Aoife. But she was back at work tomorrow, and if today's number of jobs had been anything to go by, it would prove to be a busy one.

Chapter Two
28th May, 1320 hours – Sunderland Royal Hospital

Aoife O'Byrne sat in the car, her face ashen. Her brown eyes were troubled, almost on the verge of dropping the tears she knew were hiding there but weren't quite ready to show, and her curly grey hair was turning frizzy with the dampness in the air.

How the hell am I supposed to deal with this?

She had Ben and Grace to think about. She didn't have time to be ill, especially with something like this. Did this even qualify as ill? She actually felt fine.

Maybe it's a mistake. Doctors get things wrong all the time, if the news is anything to believe. Maybe they're wrong this time too.

But she knew in her heart they weren't wrong. A single tear spilled over and trickled down her cheek. Not one for crying, she immediately felt embarrassed and swiped at it with the back of her hand.

This just wasn't fair.

It's not supposed to be like this.

She'd gone for the tests without telling anyone, firmly believing the lump in her breast was just a fatty deposit. She'd winced as they had clamped her breast between two metal plates and taken the mammogram. She had still believed it would be nothing. And last week she'd attended for the biopsy, which, until twenty minutes previously, she had also thought would be nothing.

In the space of twenty minutes the oncologist had put this belief to rest and shattered her whole world with a single word.

Cancer.

Her eyes filled again, and for a moment she didn't care anymore, couldn't fight the waves of emotion. She sat in the driver's seat, held her head in her hands and sobbed, her body heaving and her eyes finally opening the gates to the flood of tears.

This sucks. What the hell am I going to do?

28th May, 1410 hours – Tunstall, Sunderland City Centre

He adjusted the screen, staring at it, willing her to turn around. And turn she did. He felt himself harden as she stood before him, all dressed up in lace lingerie. She had no idea he was watching, of course; that was the joy of the hidden digital camera seamlessly sending the footage straight to his computer. It would never be found, never had been before.

He wondered who she was dressing up for this time. Whether they would be meeting elsewhere or whether she would bring him to her bedroom and whore herself out, like the last time. He had been watching her for only a few days but she had already had several men back to the room.

Maybe she's a hooker?

There was much more to do before he could implement his plan. At this early stage there was no guarantee it would even be her. Pressing and holding the Alt key on his keyboard, he hit the tab key, the screen instantly jumping to the next image. This room was younger-looking, less sophisticated. She had been an easy mark. Sweet, innocent, a student just looking for new friends. Sighing, he realised she wasn't there.

He tabbed again. The screen turned darker. The curtains in the room were drawn and a form was wrapped up tightly in the duvet. He watched for a moment, imagined how easy it would be to sneak in and use the bed to his full advantage. It was one of the older-style metal frames, with spindles for a headboard and bed knobs at each side. Perfect for securing a person's hands to. He could almost feel the plastic cable ties beneath his fingers. Breathing slowly, he calmed his thoughts.

It's not the right time.

Not yet.

He flicked to the final screen and his eyes narrowed, his brow furrowing in concentration as he leaned in towards the screen. There was someone there. But it wasn't her. The man was dressed in black, a scarf covering his features. Instinctively he froze as the man's eyes stared straight into the camera lens, and for a moment he thought it had been found. His breath escaped in a small whoosh as the figure turned and began tipping out drawers onto the bed, selecting small items of jewellery and filling his pockets. Within minutes the figure had gone, the room now completely upturned.

He smiled to himself. He would get to see her reaction when she walked into that room, saw all her precious things had been taken. The timing couldn't have been better. This would quite likely help him decide who he would have. He checked the clock in the corner of the screen; it was time to make nice and head to his day job. Routine itself was as important as changing it.

As he jumped on the metro a few minutes later, he acknowledged that he liked the city. Cities normally held appeal for the obvious reason – lots of choice, anonymity. But this city was different from the others he'd been to. The last North East one he'd stayed in had been Durham, and that had been years before. It had been nice enough, but a little too small for his liking. A person could get lost in Sunderland if they felt the need, and it was easy to make contacts; hell, he even liked the football team.

He glanced around the carriage. Not one person made eye contact. He could make them all witnesses to something terrible and none of them would even remember his face.

Not today though. Today was about remaining invisible. He lowered his eyes back down to the *Echo* he had in his hand, taking in the headlines.

A soft smile spread across his lips. No one ever knew who he was.

Not really.

Half the time even he didn't know.

And that was just how he liked it.

28th May, 1810 hours – Sunderland University Campus

Jacob Tulley stood at the podium in the empty lecture hall and sighed. Where the hell were the students? He'd had pretty much full capacity of applicants, the date had been arranged and the lecture hall booked for the summer ahead. He had spent hours prepping his lecture material. Today was intended to be mainly ice-breaking and running over the various aspects of the Introduction to Digital Forensics course.

But nobody was here.

Muttering under his breath, he logged out of the computer, grabbed his walking cane and made his way up the steps to the door. Just as he reached for the handle the door flew open towards him. Losing his balance from the impact, he felt his leg give and he sank to his knee, bracing himself with his right arm. His leg burned and for a moment he was transported back in time.

The sandstorm was raging around him, the sharp granules hitting his skin like needles pricking. He couldn't hear a thing for the howling of the wind. As the storm suddenly stopped as fast as it had begun, he paused, surprised by the silence. He flung his hand upright with the fist clenched. A simple command for his team: Stop!

He didn't know quite what he had seen, or even sensed, but something had caused his hairs to stand to attention. The air stilled around them. Even before anything happened he found himself yelling 'Get down!' The air around them exploded and he felt something hit his leg and lower back, but he was focussed on his men and barely even noticed.

He saw a set of vacant eyes staring out from what used to be his friend's face on the ground in front of him. He remembered someone grabbing the scruff of his jacket, pulling him backwards.

And then, nothing but darkness.

Grimacing, he pulled himself back to the present and purposely slowed his breathing. The flashbacks didn't happen often any more. The cognitive behavioural therapy he'd gone through after his treatment kept them at bay. But when they did happen, they knocked him for six. Conscious of the fact he was on the floor and grinding his teeth, he looked up to see the shocked face of the cleaner, her ID badge stark against her tunic, showing the name Clarice.

'Oh my God. I'm so sorry. Sir, are you OK? Let me help you up.'

He swiped her hand away. 'I can manage.'

Adjusting his weight, he pulled himself to his feet, leaning heavily on his stick as he stood straight. His leg was already aching like a bitch. Later it would stiffen and he would have to work to get it looser again. Any slight slip caused him to go backwards in his recovery. He would have to phone his physiotherapist and get booked in for a couple of sessions. It was always the same.

Groaning inwardly, he focused on being in the here and now, and not the there and then. Glancing at Clarice again, he noticed the sorrow on her face. Her brown eyes shone brightly, standing out from her dark skin and styled black hair. He pegged her as about twenty years old, but wasn't quite sure. For a moment, he actually thought she might cry. To her mind she had just knocked over a disabled man who had then snapped at her. Feeling like a complete heel, he knew he had to say something.

'I'm sorry. I didn't mean to be ungrateful. As you can see, I'm fine.'

She nodded. 'I'm sorry for knocking you over. I thought the hall was empty and ready to be cleaned. I shouldn't have barrelled through like that.'

'Empty? It's the 29th, isn't it? I have the hall booked for my lectures until the summer break. Though as you can see, nobody has turned up.'

'It's the 28th,' she said quietly.

She looks like she thinks I'm going to phase out again.

Jacob tried to reassure her that he wouldn't. 'The 28th? I got my days wrong then.' He made his way through the open door, then glanced back with a wide smile, 'Thanks, Clarice. Sorry again for the bad reaction. Don't work too hard.'

Clarice felt her face grow warm as she took in the transformation. When he was on the floor, his face had contorted, looking stern and clouded with the storm battling inside his mind. But when he

17

smiled - wow. She almost felt the need to put her hand to her throat to still the pounding in her heart. Wait until she told Gill about this guy - it would be worth signing up to his classes just to ogle him every week.

As the door closed behind him, Clarice smiled back. Maybe this cleaning job wouldn't be too bad after all. She made her way down to the podium with her vacuum cleaner and plugged it in. She was about to switch it on when she noticed the pile of paperwork on the desk.

'Digital forensics? He teaches digital forensics. I should've known - he looked like an IT geek,' she muttered to herself. Normally the cleaners were told not to move papers left behind in the lecture halls, but she knew there were classes in there tomorrow morning: she was one of the students on the Business Development course starting at 9 a.m. Her tutor was a stalwart, old-school lecturer who had a habit of dumping anything left behind by other people into the bin so that it wasn't in his way. Deciding it would be a help not a hindrance on this occasion, she gathered up the papers and placed them neatly inside the small cupboard at the base of the podium. *I'll just pop in tomorrow when my five o'clock lecture finishes.*

Jacob had made his way out to his car, and once inside he sat for a moment, his head resting on the steering wheel. It had been months since his last flashback. He had thought he might finally be getting past it all, hoped he would one day be back to normal.

His leg would never heal properly, the shrapnel from the blast had caused so much damage that he'd needed several bouts of surgery, extensive physiotherapy, and the threat of life in a wheelchair to push him to the point he was at now.

There was a time the doctors had told him he would never walk again. But he had refused to give up, and his sister, TJ, had supported him. He smiled as he thought about her. She'd been devastated when he came home from the hospital, and he had become her personal mission. She hadn't left him alone for more than a day, pushing him constantly, reiterating that his life wasn't over even when the military had discharged him. When he had started the CBT, she had rapidly become one of his tools for dealing with the flashbacks.

Feeling a sudden need to hear her voice, he pulled his mobile from his pocket and hit speed dial number one. Her voice filled his head as the call diverted to voicemail and waiting for the beep, he left his message. 'Sis, it's me. Hit me back when you get a sec.'

His blood pressure now returning to manageable levels, he started the car and headed for home.

28th May, 2310 hours – Tunstall, Sunderland City Centre

Rewinding, he zoomed in on the screen. She was undressing, readying herself for bed. Her plain white underwear was stark against her contrasting skin. Almost as if she knew he was watching, she slowly undid her bra. He grew hard, using his hand to adjust himself. She was teasing him; it couldn't be anything else.

As she bent to remove her pants, he pulled himself free of the constraints of his clothing.

His hand working hard, he suddenly realised with the utmost clarity that she was the one. She had been put there in that room just for him. He would start making plans to have her. It was easier now than it had been when he first started, all those years ago. Technology made selection so much faster.

A frown marred his face momentarily: it used to be that there was a reason for choosing; now it seemed that the more time passed, the more he would settle for any small sign. Like her teasing him.

Clearing his mind, he focused on her image and continued. When the orgasm came it wasn't as powerful as he wanted it to be.

But it would be. When he had her it would finally be like the first time all over again.

He tucked himself back away, and checked his watch.

I've Been Watching You

It was time to do some reconnaissance.

Chapter Three
29th May, 1730 hours - Sunderland University Campus

Ben was nervous. It wasn't a feeling she was accustomed to, but the thought of starting a university course with a bunch of people she didn't know and probably out-aged by a gazillion years was daunting.

At this stage she didn't even know if she was doing the right thing. The only thing she knew of digital forensics was what she had learned in her forensic training course, and she wasn't that great with technology as a whole. What had possessed her to opt for this particular course when the funding opportunity came up at work she would never know.

But here she was.

She had arrived at the lecture hall exceptionally early, not wanting to be the last one in, the one everyone turned to look at as she walked down the aisle. She didn't really want to be the first one in either, but Aoife always said that to grow as a person you had to learn to bite the bullet and crack on with whatever life threw at you. So Ben gave herself a shake, and pushed open the door to the hall. Feigning confidence, she strode towards the front row. She was halfway down the stairs when she heard someone curse behind her.

A man.

She hadn't heard anyone else come in; didn't know if he had been there already or had followed her in.

Ben tried to swallow, her mouth dry and her tongue suddenly feeling too big for her mouth. She felt fear claw at her insides like a cat caught in a trap, trying to climb out. She paused, counting slowly in her head, picturing Grace's face in her mind. It calmed her breathing and finally she felt herself release the breath she was holding.

'Excuse me, I need to get past,' came the chocolaty-smooth voice from behind her. Slowly, she turned to look at the person speaking.

Jacob was a sight to behold, especially when he stood two steps higher: he was already tall, and his broad shoulders and muscled arms were only emphasised by the semi-fitted woollen jumper. His fair hair had that tousled, just-got-out-of-bed look that people paid a fortune in salons to get; but Ben was pretty sure he literally had just got out of bed.

She found herself staring, wondering who he was. Jacob watched in amusement as her gaze didn't falter.

Jacob was used to this effect - it happened regularly. TJ actually called it the 'Tulley Effect'.

They all had the same reaction until they saw the stick and his limp. Then they all backed off, none of them wanting a cripple for a date or whatever. It had got to the stage now where he waited for the expression to change. Their eyes would widen and their faces would take on the expression of mild horror. He tried to just brush it off. So he wasn't attractive any more, it wasn't the end of the world.

Only it was, really. He was lonely. He wanted what other people had. But he knew he'd never get it. How would he ever be sure the woman loved him for him, and not out of sympathy for his injuries?

Every time he saw 'the look', he felt a little more of him die inside, a little more of his wall get built up. Blocking people out was easier than letting them in. It hurt to let them in.

For once, though, he didn't want to see this woman's expression change. He stared back for a moment, taking in the red curls tied back in a loose pony tail, and the faint freckles covering her nose. She was dressed like most students in a fitted T-shirt and jeans, functional jacket unzipped. Definitely nothing special about her clothing, but there was something special about her.

Her green eyes held a hint of vulnerability, and for a second he felt like he had been punched in the gut. He felt his breath leave his lungs with a slow whoosh, and, realising he was the one staring now, he broke eye contact.

Leaning hard on his stick, he bypassed her and made his way to the podium. He felt sadness as he limped down the last few steps, and for a moment he wanted to turn around and see if her face had changed. But he didn't.

Ben followed him down the steps, first with her eyes then physically. Pulling into the front row she sat, her brow knitting together in a frown. *What the hell was that about?* For just a minute, he'd held her gaze. And she'd felt like she had seen into his soul, and he into hers.

In the echoing silence of the lecture hall, they both jumped as the door opened suddenly. The stairs vibrated with footsteps, and she felt the breeze as the young black girl rushed down.

'I'm sorry, sir. I had to move your papers last night; the lecturer in this morning would have binned them. They're just in the cupboard, though,' she explained, her cheeks reddening as Jacob glanced up at her.

'Thanks, Clarice, that was thoughtful.'

Ben had to grin: the poor girl was virtually swooning at his feet. She wondered if he knew he had that effect on her, and concentrated on him. If anything, he looked uncomfortable.

So he does know. And he doesn't like the attention.

Clarice made her way back out of the hall as the other students started filtering in. Ben heard the gasps of the few girls registered on the course, and the groans of the guys as they sat in the rows behind her. It was going to be interesting, watching how Jacob took to the attention. If there was one thing she had learned to do well, it was read people. She watched as Jacob's eyes shuttered. He looked uncomfortable and she wondered why he chose to lecture, and why he didn't handle the attention well when it was obviously something that happened regularly.

Maybe he's got a jealous wife at home or something.

No, it wasn't that. She hadn't noticed a ring when talking to him on the steps and her eyes had a habit of automatically checking. So that meant he must be one of those guys who genuinely didn't believe he was attractive.

But how can he not know he looks like some kind of model from a catalogue?

There was more to Jacob Tulley than met the eye. Maybe she should find out what it was. But no: as much as she liked understanding people, and what made them tick, getting to know Jacob would mean him getting to know her. He would find out about her past. Her breath held in her lungs in panic.

She couldn't do it.

She couldn't face the disgust that would cover his face when he found out, if he saw the scars covering her body. Talking herself out of getting to know him was easy. She'd done it so many times over the years, she'd lost count.

It's best if I just leave him to it. It's really none of my business anyway.

A wave of sadness washed over her. Even after all these years, despite her best efforts at moving on, the man who'd attacked her still had a hold over her. And no matter how much therapy she went through, she knew he would always be lurking there in the back of her mind.

Lurking yes, but not controlling. I control who I am, what I do. And I am strong enough to do that alone.

Satisfied with the mantra taught to her by her counsellor, she returned her focus to the lesson.

29th May, 2135 hours - O'Byrne residence, Sunderland

Aoife looked up from her newspaper, as Ben entered the kitchen. She looked her niece up and down for a moment. She'd decided earlier that for now, everything would be as it was before her appointment. She would tell Ben; just not yet.

She couldn't. It just felt too raw.

Opting for normality, she said, 'You met someone tonight. A man. I can see it in your eyes.'

24

Smiling, Ben shook her head. Wandering over she planted an affectionate kiss on the top of her aunt's head. 'You're incorrigible, Aoife. You say that every time I come in. Maybe one day it will be true.'

Aoife glanced at her sharply; there was something different in Ben's tone tonight. It wasn't as light as it normally was when she asked that question: a standing joke between the two.

Ben opened the fridge and peered inside, 'Did you happen to make me some tea? I'm Hank Marvin.'

'You'll not find it in there. Try the oven; it's already warm for you. How was the lecture?'

'Mmm, chicken and mash, my favourite.' Ben sniffed in appreciation, plucking a forkful and placing it into her mouth as she hunted the cupboard for the salt. Her mouth full, she answered Aoife. 'Lecture was good, ice-breaker and intro. It's gonna be an interesting course. Just hope I can keep up OK. I'm gonna have to go to the library tomorrow – Jacob's given us a reading list as long as my arm and I can't afford them all.'

'Jacob?' asked Aoife shrewdly, her eyes honing in on the faint flush spreading across Ben's cheeks as she spoke his name.

Well, well. Who'd have thunk it. I don't think I've ever seen her blush over a boy before.

Resolving not to push, Aoife filed the information in the back of her mind, giving Ben a quick, innocent grin.

'The lecturer,' replied Ben, rolling her eyes. 'Grace go down OK?'

The change in subject wasn't smooth but Aoife chose to ignore it, nodding instead. 'Doesn't she always? She still needs her goodnight kiss, though.'

Aoife watched in satisfaction as her niece ate, then when she'd finished, Ben kissed her aunt again. 'Loves you,' she whispered against her hair.

'Loves you too, sweetheart. Sweet dreams.'

Aoife felt her heart swell to twice its size.

She'd looked after Ben ever since her parents had died in a car accident when she was ten. She had held her as she cried into the night, and had been there for every event since. She watched Ben leave the kitchen, and felt her face turn downwards. This was the first time in eight years Aoife had seen light in Ben's eyes. The spark of attraction. It worried her. Was Ben really ready to move on? In her shoes, Aoife wasn't sure she would be ready. Some days she wondered how Ben managed at all, how she was strong enough. Having Grace made it easier, she knew; but still. She sighed: part of being a parent was letting one's children find their own way. It didn't matter that Ben wasn't actually her daughter: she was the daughter of her heart and that was what counted.

Knowing Ben would be listening from Grace's room, she wandered through the downstairs, checking the windows and doors were all locked. It was the same routine every night. Ben knew Aoife did it, and Aoife knew Ben had to recheck it all herself half an hour later. It helped put her mind at ease.

Aoife wandered up to her room and settled into the large bed, the patchwork quilt visible with the glow of the street lights outside. She switched on the antique lamp on the table beside her, picked up her book and opened it. Frowning as the words swam before her eyes, she put it back down. Tonight wasn't a night for reading. She needed to think.

Clicking the lamp off, she tugged the quilt tightly round her shoulders. In the darkness, she listened, and finally heard Ben padding down the stairs.

How was she supposed to tell her? She had always been a big believer in honesty. She had never lied to Ben about anything.

But this just felt too big. It would crush her.

Hell, it's crushing me. How am I supposed to deal with this?

Feeling her eyes fill again, she fought the tears back. Crying never did anyone any good. Besides, if she started again she might never stop.

Aoife swallowed hard, the lump in her throat barely even letting any air past. The weight of the doctor's diagnosis played on her mind, refusing to let her settle. She pulled herself into a sitting position and closed her eyes.

Placing her palms together, she touched her nose with her thumbs, and, for the first time in years, she prayed.

30th May, 0810 hours - Thompson residence, Sunderland

'Clarice, are you actually going to school today? Get up, lazy pants, you're gonna be late.'

Gill Thompson pulled the duvet down off Clarice with a sharp tug.

'What're you doing? Leave me alone, I'm sleepy,' groaned Clarice, feeling for the duvet.

'I don't need to remind you that you are at school at nine. The agreement with your mother is that you go to school. Now get up or I'll phone her and tell her you're skiving just `cos you're tired. You need to be quick if you want a lift: I'm setting off in twenty minutes.'

Gill didn't mean it for a moment - they had the same routine every morning. She would never tell Bernie, Clarice's mum, that she was skipping school, because Clarice never did.

She smiled down at her as Clarice finally squeezed her eyes open and grinned back. 'Go away, Gill, I need to get ready.' She threw a pillow as her friend made her way out of the room. She knew how lucky she was. Clarice had got into some trouble a couple of years before. The crowd she had been hanging around with encouraged her to take cocaine for the first time. The second and third times she hadn't needed as much encouragement, and soon she was hooked. She'd finally had her eyes opened when she stole money from her mum, the mum who had three other kids in the house and couldn't afford to even pay for a tin of beans to feed them with, thanks to Clarice. It had shocked her, scared the hell out of her, even, and she had promised to get clean.

Her mother, out of desperation, had contacted her friend Gill, who worked at an outreach place for troubled kids. There was nowhere else Bernie would have turned - and Gill, being Gill, had agreed to take Clarice in to live with her, helping her get clean and then letting her stay while she completed her uni course. Gill had helped her fill in the forms to get the cleaning job at the uni too, firmly believing that routine would help get her past the drug use and wild ways. And it was working, even if she did need a kick up the butt on a morning.

In fifteen minutes, Clarice was downstairs fully dressed with a light covering of make-up on her face. She grabbed the prepared toast off the plate in the kitchen and picked up her satchel before heading out of the door with Gill.

Pulling the car up in front of the uni, Gill said, 'You OK to make your own way home tonight? I don't know what time I'll be done at the centre. There's a million and one things to do today, and new clients to prep for. You can meet me there tonight if you want, or you can pop straight home. There's chicken in the fridge for tea.'

'I've got an essay to start researching - we were given it yesterday and I want to get started so I'm not rushing at the last minute. Gonna head to the library when I'm done with lectures. I'll text you this afternoon and let you know if that's OK?'

Gill nodded. 'If you're still at the library when I'm finished, I'll pick you up.'

'Gill,' Clarice paused, suddenly looking a little emotional. 'Thank you. I wouldn't be here doing all this if it wasn't for you. I just wanted you to know that I'm grateful. I know you didn't have to do any of it.'

'You're welcome. Now get out of the car before you make me late,' Gill's blue eyes shone a little brighter as Clarice grinned back at her. She tried to hide her emotion but she knew that Clarice would have seen it.

Clarice had told her that she had made a pact when going through the counselling for her addiction, to always let her family know how precious they were. Clarice had kept that promise by telling Gill, and the rest of them, regularly. And every time, Gill choked with emotion.

Not a day went by when she wasn't thankful for how it had all turned out with Clarice. Gill knew how it could easily go in the opposite direction. She'd seen it so many times with kids who just walked the wrong path and then couldn't get onto the right path no matter how much they tried. Sure, Clarice needed guidance at times; but she was a good kid, determined to make amends for her wrongs. Gill knew she sent her mum money every time she got her student loan payment. Clarice worked part-time to pay her way and manage, but all the spare cash went to her mum.

Being the oldest in a single-parent family was never easy; Gill had had that pleasure herself. But it was nice to see Clarice accepting some responsibility and wanting to take care of her mum and siblings. She grinned to herself as she sat in the car watching her friend's daughter make her way into the lecture theatre.

Clarice had no idea that her mum had never touched the money, splitting it between all four of the children in savings accounts. One day they would all be informed, but it wasn't Gill's job to tell Clarice. Even when Bernie had been skint, she'd always put money in those accounts, never touching it no matter how hard things got. She would go without tights, to make sure the kids were fed, and if she could only afford to put 50p in each account that week then that's what she did.

All the kids would be surprised when they were handed their account books, but it wouldn't be until they needed it. Bernie had always called it their rainy-day fund. Speaking of which, dark clouds had filled the sky, and the first drops were hitting Gill's windscreen.

She gave a deep sigh; she hated the rain. It always made the kids in the Outreach centre misbehave – something to do with the confines of four walls no doubt.

Chapter Four
30th May, 0845 hours - Sunderland University campus

It hadn't taken him long to find out where she studied. Hacking the university systems was a virtual piece of cake for someone with his skills. He'd found out which degree she was studying for and which buildings her classes were held in, even had a copy of her class schedule.

Yes, she was perfect. It wasn't the first time he had pursued a black woman, but she wasn't his usual choice. There was just something about her curves, her innocent white underwear. The others had paled into comparison. Clarice Fielding was definitely the one.

He sat outside the campus building, watching as she jumped out of the car and wandered up the steps to the entrance. He really liked this part - the cameras were essential. They helped him build a profile of the woman that would become his. She was young, yes, but definitely womanly. He'd only seen breasts like hers on one of his victims. Smiling, he let himself remember - she had been the fourth. Her body lithe and graceful, but her large breasts most memorable. He hadn't been able to resist leaving his mark on them.

Criss cross marks with his sharp knife. Marking her as his.

No one else would ever have had her, even if she'd survived. He remembered that there hadn't been a great deal of media attention surrounding her murder. Darkness flooded his mind, he hadn't actually *checked*. He had been picked up on a DUI charge days later, and, deemed a flight risk, he'd been locked up for a few weeks. When he'd gotten out the news had all died down, and he had been focussing on where to settle.

But he still remembered, would never forget her. The way her skin had glowed in the moonlight, the tears on her cheeks as she had begged him to stop and the feel of her as she'd wrapped around him. She had begged before the end, her eyes pleading with him to stop hurting her and to let her die. There was definitely no way she had survived.

He had slid the knife into her stomach, carefully paying attention as her eyes had widened. Not surprise, just painful acceptance.

He had stood over her as she bled into the soil surrounding her body, watching as the blood mingled into the soil like a battlefield of old. He saw the horror on her face as he had whispered those words. The words he always whispered.

'I've been watching you.'

Frowning now, he made the decision to check. It wouldn't do for someone to be out there who could identify him.

30th May, 1210 hours – Sunderland Outreach Centre

'Gill, go and ask Brian to phone the police. He's in his office. James is on one.' Stanley Hubbard's was softly spoken, but there was an undertone of frustration. 'That kid's gonna be the death of me.'

Nodding, Gill made her way down the corridor, leaving Stan to head back into the games room where James was pulling at a large picture that was still just about bolted to the wall. Chairs were upturned, and the few youths remaining in the room had congregated in a corner to watch the action.

'Connor, Liam and Titch, head out to the tuck shop. Now, please.' The three boys groaned but left the room. All the kids at the centre had a lot of respect for Stan. He'd been there for all of them when Scott Anderson, their friend, had been murdered. Stan was trained in counselling, and though the kids had a tough-guy exterior, Scott's death had hit them all hard. Stan had been at the centre now for a several years, on and off, his contract casual initially. He had been offered a permanent position when the funding had become available a few months before. And he was good at dealing with the kids.

A few weeks previously, James's mum had passed away from a drug overdose, and the child was beside himself. To his fourteen year old mind, everyone he cared for ended up leaving him. So why should he behave?

'James, I want you to listen to me. Brian is on the phone to the police. We can't tolerate this kind of behaviour. I want to help you, but you need to stop destroying things and listen.'

James paused from tugging at the picture frame, and half turned his head. His eyes were wild, and they made Stan think of a fox caught in a trap. This kid needed to vent, he needed something to pull him from his grief and into reality. An idea started to form, one he would need to speak with Brian about, but he already suspected Brian would agree. The centre was all about improving life for the kids, and the more ways they had to do that the better.

'Listen, when you're done at the station, I want you to come back here. I'm going to set something up that'll help you get some of this anger out. Will you do that, James? Will you come back here?'

The boy finally stopped pulling at the picture, glanced round at Stan with sorrow mixing with the anger in his eyes, and nodded slowly. His energy spent for the time being, he righted one of the chairs, and sat down, looking at the floor.

Stan pulled a chair up beside James. It was one of those occasions where words were not needed.

30th May, 1310 hours - Sunderland Outreach Centre

Ben pulled up outside the centre, applied the handbrake and made her way inside.

'Excuse me, I'm looking for a Gill Thompson?'

She directed her question at a young lad, loitering by the wall at the entrance. His gaze narrowed as he looked at her. 'You're 5-O right? Your pal just took Speedy away. What're you doing here?'

His hostility made Ben pause, 'I'm not 5-O - I work in forensics. I'm just here to take some photos, love, that's all. Nothing exciting. If you don't know where Gill is, I can ask someone inside.'

'Forensics? That's like the CSI shit off the telly, right?'

At her nod, he continued, 'So you've seen like dead bodies and shit? Is it true what they say? That they stink and still make noises when they're dead?'

Seeing genuine interest hidden beneath his prickly exterior, Ben nodded again. 'Some smell, some don't. But yes, they can make noises when they're dead. It's caused by a build-up of gas.'

He smiled at her, his dimples giving him the appearance of a cheeky kid, not the thug he had first portrayed. 'They fart? That's what you mean right.' His grin widened, obviously tickled by the thought of dead bodies farting.

With a little guarded respect in his eyes, he flicked his head towards the door. 'Gill's probably in her office. Second door on the left as you go in.'

'Thanks,' replied Ben as she made her way inside.

Entering the room, her eyes widened a little. Gills office was *not* what Ben expected. There was no one inside for a start, but she couldn't move without looking around first. There were posters on the wall promoting positivity and life changes. Her gaze settled on one in particular, it was an oversized print of the poem 'Don't Quit'. That poem had seen her through a lot of tough times, its lyrics providing her with a push whenever Aoife wasn't around. The desk was strewn with fluffy pens, bright coloured sticky note pads, and a bright pink stapler. Ben didn't think she had ever seen such an abundance of colour in one room.

She jumped as Gill bustled in past her.

'Rory said he'd directed you to my office, I'm Gill. You must be the crime scene investigator? Rob mentioned you would be popping by. If you'd like to follow me, I'll show you the damage.'

Following her lead, Ben ended up in what looked like a classroom. A somewhat dishevelled and broken classroom - two windows were smashed, furniture lay on its side, and one of the pictures on the wall hung lop-sided.

'He's a good kid really. Speedy ... sorry, I mean James. He lost his mum recently. He started acting out and ended up here. Stan, one of my colleagues, has been trying to get through to him, but it's slow going. Brian, the boss, has to play by the book so we had to phone the police when he kicked off. We aren't pressing charges though, but hopefully a few hours in the cells will help James see he can't act out here.'

'You do a lot of good here. I've read a few articles in the Echo. How long have you worked here?'

'I've been here about two years now. It's nice to make a difference, you know?'

'Yeah I know what you mean,' Ben thought for a moment before adding, 'I help run an online support group for women who have been raped. We use a lot of the positivity stuff from your office to help women cope, helping them realise that what happened isn't their fault. It's not easy at times: we have to refer a lot to other agencies, but we make a difference. It helps.'

Obviously surprised, Ben saw Gill's expression soften. 'Sounds like a tough thing to do. I council troubled teens which is tough, but I can only imagine what that would be like. The kids here, some things in their pasts and presents can't be changed. But we're here to help them in any way we can. It can be hard when they don't want to accept the help you offer. But it's all personal choice. I get the feeling you don't tell many people about the support group?'

Ben shook her head, 'In conversation, no, but sometimes I meet people who might need to know the group exists – and I thought you'd probably understand. Is this the only damage that needs photographing?'

'Yeah just the one room.'

Hearing Stan shout for her from down the corridor, Gill added, 'I'll leave you to it. Give me a wave when you're done. I'll be in the craft room at the end of the corridor.'

30th May, 1640 hours – Sunderland Outreach Centre

PC Rob Winters watched James scowl in his direction as his police car pulled up outside the centre. Rob had let him stew in a cell for a couple of hours on request of Brian, and given the kid a stern talking to about destruction of property.

Curious as to why Brian had wanted James dropping back off at the centre, Rob followed the youth inside.

'Brian, Stan,' he greeted as he found them in the exercise room. His eyes widened as he noticed the boxing ring now being erected in the centre of the room.

Stan was matter-of-fact in his explanation. 'Had this going spare in the store room at the gym I part own. Figured the lads could use some training, help them get rid of some of that pent up energy.'

'You're gonna teach them to box?' asked Rob.

'Not me personally. Ricardo, one of the fellas from the gym has agreed though. Boxing's great, teaches discipline and keeps the body active. Seems like the lads are looking forward to it. They'll be allocated ring time when they've done what work needs doing.'

'Ah, an incentive for them to work. I like it. As the local beat officer here, I wouldn't mind being involved somehow if there's anything I can do? My jobs all about being involved in the local community. I boxed my way through college. I'll be a tad rusty, but am happy to help if you can use me.'

Stan smiled. 'I'm sure we can find you something to do.'

'Great, keep me updated on what's happening, and I'll work something around my shifts. I'd love to help on police time, but I can't see the sergeant going for that.'

Stan grinned back, 'Nope, guess not. I'll drop you an email though, Rob. Thanks.'

1st June, 1720 hours - Newstead Residential Home, Sunderland

John was pissed off.

It had taken him almost an hour to travel a fifteen minute journey - all because some stupid woman had seen fit to break down and block the road. He felt his blood boil; women should know their place. They should know to check their cars, or at the very least ask their men to check them.

His wife had always known. He'd taught her. Right from the start she had known to have his tea ready at 5 p.m. on the dot, known to get the car serviced every six months and tell him if anything was wrong and she'd known if she didn't tell him, then there would be trouble. Hitting her didn't make him feel like a man. He'd never had a problem feeling like a man, he knew his place.

Always had.

Way above the position of any mere woman. But hitting her had helped teach her that she was so far below him she could taste dirt quite comfortably. He made sure their son, Matthew never saw though. He didn't want his son seeing all the things he'd experienced as a child. As right as it was to show a woman her place, he would teach his own son the right way - slowly and patiently - not by hammering the point home with every whore passing through the house.

When Eve had told him she was pregnant, he'd seen the fear in her eyes, the belief that he would hurt her for getting pregnant. She couldn't have been more wrong. For the nine months she carried their son, he never laid a hand on her. He would never hurt his own child, the one person to whom he could pass along everything his father had taught him. He would never let anything happen to a child of his.

He was a better father than his own had been.

John had been removed from his father's care at eight years old, placed into what would become the first of many foster homes.

He'd thrown himself into studying, finding an early infinity for computers and using them as an escape for the constant abuse and hatred in the children's homes. Focussing on the computing, he had built his resume and now worked as a mobile nerd, attending and fixing people's home computers daily, as well as those brought into the store.

But he'd never forgotten the lessons his father had taught him in those early years.

John's mother had left when he was four: disappearing into the night without a word, leaving him behind. His father had moved straight on - bringing in different women until he found one that stayed past the next morning. A woman who knew her place, directly beneath his dad. Social services had done their best to keep him away, restrict his contact. But he had resisted, running away often and finally returning when he turned sixteen.

John frowned to himself. That's when it had all changed. He'd arrived at the house and walked in, expecting some kind of reunion. Instead he had found his father dead in his tatty old armchair, an empty bottle of whiskey at his side. He'd spent his teens imaging some kind of reunion where he would be welcomed back into the fold with open arms, and in one visit his dreams had been squashed. John had been devastated, and somewhat relieved all at the same time. He'd never had any illusions regarding his father, but he was family. As soon as the funeral was over he had started searching, looking for someone to fill the void.

It hadn't taken long for him to meet Eve.

Releasing the tension in his frown, his cheeks relaxed as his wrinkles subsided. It was time to play nice. Nobody could know the anger simmering beneath like a volcano sleeping softly.

Nobody except Eve.

And there wasn't a whole lot she could do about it.

He waited until the nurse left them alone, him sitting by his wife's bedside. Clicking the bedroom door shut, he smiled widely as her eyes flashed through fear to acceptance. The zip of his trousers sounded as loudly as the crack of a gun in the small room. He held the smile in place as he pulled her head down towards him, feeling her gag as he thrust in and out.

It never took him long to finish, the fear of someone walking in a constant worry to him, but she was his wife. And in this home or not, she would perform her wifely duties.

She couldn't tell anyone. Wouldn't have even if she could. She knew her place.

Chapter Five
1st June, 1910 hours - Police Gymnasium, Sunderland HQ

Jacob grimaced as he kept a steady pace on the treadmill. His hands kept him steady on the handles and finally, he felt himself falter as the throbbing in his leg increased.

He turned the machine off, gingerly stepping down and testing the strength as he reached for his stick. His leg was burning; the fall had definitely set him back. It had been six months since his last surgery, when the surgeon had advised him that this was 'as good as it would get.' The four hour operation had tightened the muscles around the tissue and tendon damage, ultimately giving him more support. But he still needed the stick, always would.

His back had healed, the shrapnel left behind melding to muscle and becoming part of him.

But not his leg.

He remembered TJ at his side at the hospital, holding his arm as he struggled out of the wheelchair for the first time after being flown back from Afghanistan. She'd been by his side, supporting his weight as he had walked the required number of steps before collapsing at the end.

The first surgery had helped give him back the ability to bend and straighten his leg, though at that point they figured the chair was a permanent addition to his life. The second was designed to strengthen his tendons but he had overdone the physiotherapy, over stretching as his body tried its best to heal. Dogged determination had seen him through the next two surgeries.

Jacob paused by the full length mirror, normally used by people sparring or completing their self-defence and take down courses. The gym was empty apart from him. Everyone else either progressing onto their shift or home after.

Slowly, he lowered the waist of his track suit bottoms, past his shorts to his knees and turned, the back of his leg now visible over his shoulder. His mouth straightened as he took in the first long ragged scar. It was ugly, winding up his leg like a snake. Some of his muscle mass had been removed, either by the original shrapnel shards or by the subsequent surgeries, leaving his leg deformed and looking more like the twisted trunk of a tree. Secondary and tertiary scarring marred the surrounding areas and for a moment he almost felt sick.

It was so much a part of him that he rarely looked at it any more, hating it with all his heart. It wasn't a war wound. It wasn't a survivor wound. It was only proof that he had survived when half of his team hadn't.

Proof he'd led them into a situation that had ended with three of them dying.

Proof that he shouldn't be alive today.

The medal they had given him on his return sat at the bottom of a drawer hidden in the dark. He was no damn hero. He didn't deserve any medals.

What he did deserve though was the pain. It forced him to remember. Not a day passed when he didn't feel guilty for being there. TJ had helped turn that guilt into something else. Though even she knew it was still there, lingering beneath the surface. She had pushed him into digital forensics, knowing that whilst his hands were suited to war, his brain was suited to a more technical path.

And he'd done a lot of good, he knew that. Through examining computers, laptops and phones, he'd been responsible for bringing down murderers and paedophiles alike, but knowing it just helped stop the guilt from taking over. It didn't make it go away.

He sighed as he pulled the waistband back up. It was how it was.

He didn't have to like it. But he was damn sure he would learn to accept it.

One day.

Focussing on his own eyes in the mirror, he slowed his breathing, seeing past his exterior like the therapist had taught him to. He allowed himself to see his vulnerability, his humanity.

It was OK to feel guilty. It was OK to still hurt. It was normal to feel the things he was feeling.

Calmer now, he pulled his phone from his pocket and hit the speed dial.

'Hey sis, it's me. Long day - you wanna meet for Mexican? My treat?'

1st June, 2000 hours – Desperado's Restaurant, Sunderland City Centre
'So what's been so tough about today?' TJ asked, reaching for nacho's just placed down by the waitress.

'I dunno. I'm probably just over analysing things.'

Jacob's eyes were troubled as he looked over at his sister.

Identical eyes met his gaze, grey with small flecks of green. They both had their mum's eyes, and stood out because of them. TJ was younger than him, only by a couple of years, but still. She'd always been the responsible one though. When their parents had been killed, several years before he had joined the army, TJ had stepped up. Only sixteen at the time, she had managed to fit cleaning house, and cooking tea into her daily routine around college. He had kept the garden tidy, and done all the DIY. They had pulled each other through the grief.

He still remembered how hurt she'd appeared to be when he left to enlist. Their parents had died and he had chosen to leave her, opting to defend his country rather than look after his sister. She had only been eighteen. But as hurt as she'd felt, she'd never once blamed him, understanding he needed to deal with things himself. TJ had wrapped herself up in college, getting her degree and then her masters. She had been working on her PhD for the last couple of years.

'You do have a habit of doing that, bro. What's happened since your flash the other day?'

Jacob felt himself blush as the image of a freckled red-head popped into his mind. He thought he had gotten away with it, but TJ was too adept at noticing his subtle changes.

'You met someone? Who? Where?'

'I didn't, not exactly anyway.' He knew he had to continue. 'She's a student.'

TJ's eyes widened, 'Aren't there rules against fraternising with students?'

Jacob coughed into his coke, 'I'm not fraternising. She is a student, a mature student if you must know. I barely even spoke to her.' Uncomfortable now under her scrutiny, he added, 'Nothing happened. Nothing's going to happen. Like she'd go near *here* anyway with this damn stick.' His hand swept in a downward motion indicating to his legs, and his eyes had filled with just enough despair to make them darken.

'Bro, how many times do I need to tell you that the right woman won't see your stick? Or your scars? I get that you hate your stick, I really do, but you need it. You'll always need it. If that's all people see then they're not worth having in your life.'

Jacob frowned. He knew what she said made sense, but he struggled to accept it as truth. Nobody had ever *not* seen his stick since he'd started walking again. Why should she be any different?

He knew TJ understood him more than anyone else, but even she had told him to his face that he was as pig-headed as they came.

TJ knew he hammered his frustrations out at the gym. He always had. And now he was wasting time trying to rebuild muscles that couldn't be rebuilt. Suddenly she decided she would quite like to meet the person who had grabbed her brothers attention, student or not. His next class was scheduled for 5th June. Sometimes her brother needed a nudge in the right direction, and it usually fell to her to give him it. She needed to meet the girl who had Jacob all a-fluster, and make sure she wasn't going to break his heart.

But, Jacob didn't need to know she would attend the Uni.

She gave him an innocent grin, changing the subject and asking how his class had gone.

2nd June, 0915 hours – Tunstall, Sunderland City Centre
He'd watched as she had gotten dressed that morning: her dark brown skin glistening with the remaining dampness from her shower. He had seen the older woman enter the room, handing Clarice a large pile of clothing.

He had felt a shiver pass down his spine as she had bent over, putting the clothes away in the bottom drawer.

He could almost taste her - he would taste her.

Years before he had surprised his victims, jumping out on them, or using the old 'man off the bike trick'. Now he knew it was easier to get to know them a little first. Not much, not enough so they would tell people about him at any rate. But enough so they felt comfortable. It made the rush even better - the moment when they realised he wasn't the nice guy they thought he was. To be fair he had never actually been a nice guy. That was a fallacy, all part of the elaborate person that was him. There was no one else like him, he knew that.

He could tell just looking at her that she would be the type to please.

His background checks had been fruitful - she had a history of drug use. With that history she no doubt had a reputation for sleeping around. For a millisecond he wondered if he had made the right choice, there was a chance she was damaged goods. That someone else had gotten there first. And that was something he couldn't entertain. He needed the rush, the fear as he forced them to do his bidding.

Frowning, he acknowledged that it was harder now to get that feeling. The first three women had been but fumbles in the dark, but number four, now she had been special. He had left his mark. Made her beg right up to the end. No one had compared to her, not yet anyway. He was pretty sure Clarice would though.

He pushed the niggle of doubt aside - he would soon put her in her place. He'd watched her for days now - knew she would take some training. She'd be defiant at first, angry even. But she would learn.

They all learned in the end.

Smiling he picked up his books and put them into his newly purchased backpack. He smoothed his now blond locks into a geeky style, the temporary hair dye making him look years younger. Using the mirror in the hall, he applied the clear lens nerd glasses over his blue eyes, perching them on his nose. The false goatee, and modern clothing finished off the look and he was satisfied. He would blend in with the rest of the geeky business study students.

He didn't stand out - even the lecturer would be unlikely to remember him if pressed.

Inserting himself onto the class register had been easy, obtaining a valid student number a little more difficult but definitely not rocket science. To all intents and purposes, his new identity, Gareth Chamberlain, was an average student who had been sick for the first few weeks of term due to an episode of 'mumps'. He had created false student reports using his own coded software, and had 'submitted' his assignments online for the period, altering the dates to make them appear as if they were submitted on time but had been lost in the system. Being technological was a blessing when it came to creating a new life.

He'd done it all over the UK, often claiming benefits whilst working, with transactions that were virtually untraceable, in most cases not even noticed. He had several identities to work with – all of them meticulously realistic, like the one he used now. He had so many in fact, that even he occasionally forgot who he really was. He worked when he wanted to, confident that skimming off the government would always top him up.

Clarice would remember him though, at least for the short time she would live. None of the others had survived - he supposed it was all down to strength. After he put them in their place, it was up to them to be strong enough to want to live. Plainly none of the others had wanted to.

He heard the beep outside - his taxi was here.

It was time for school.

2nd June, 1105 hours - CSI Department, Sunderland City Centre Depot
Ben had reworded the statement for the assault case four times so far. Deciding to take a break she popped the kettle on and made her way next door.

'Kev, I'm struggling with the statement for the assault outside Retox from a few weeks ago. Have you got a template of some kind you could maybe email me? The scene ended up being spread and I'm having trouble putting it into words without elaborating. I've only really had photo statements up until now.'

'I'll come give you a hand. It was the stabbing right? You consulted with Jason if memory serves?'

'Yeah that's the one. The images are loaded up if you wanna review. It ended up being three areas around the nightclub. There wasn't a whole lot of evidence like. It's more the logistics of what I did process wise.'

'I read your notes for that one - was gonna mention it in your PDR meeting next week. Considering that was one of the first major scenes you processed solo, you did an excellent job. Your photos were good quality too - you've been practising with the tripod and night-time shots and it shows. Use your notes to write the statement. Start at the first area, write what you did, the processes you used and what you recovered, then move onto the second bit. I'll have a read before you send it to the CPS.'

Ben felt her cheeks flush. She had never taken praise well, but was pleased her hard work had been noticed.

'How's the digital course going? You've got Tulley as your lecturer right?'

'Yeah. Seems great so far, think I'm going to find it tough going, like. I've already got six books at home to read. Popped to the library on my way in this morning. You know Jacob?'

'So do you, indirectly at least. He works in the forensics lab at the HQ building.'

'He works for the force? That's why his name sounded familiar.'

'I'm sure he will be able to offer you additional help when he realises. If you want, I can arrange an attachment for you. You could spend a day or two up at the lab, see it first hand? Might help some of the technical terminology sink in a little?'

'Would you mind? That'd be great thank you.'

They both looked up as Alex and Ali burst in through the door. Alex looked so much like his brother Ali that they could have been twins. Both had serious grey eyes, both had dark hair with a scattering of silver showing at the temples. Ali was a little taller and broader but no one could have mistaken them for anything but brothers.

'Cass's waters just broke. She's in labour. I'm going to be a dad.' Alex sounded shocked, as though the realisation had just sunk in.

'Cass asked us to let you know - I'm taking him to hospital. Give me your number, Ben, I'll ring you later,' added Ali with a grin.

Jotting her number down, Ben found herself smiling back. There was something infectious about the news. She almost wanted to be there with Cass. Deciding she would pop to the hospital later, she handed the paper over to Ali who promptly herded Alex out of the room to his car.

'That's come around so fast. Doesn't seem like two minutes since Cass was last at work. This month's gone in a flash,' said Kevin quietly. His eyes saddened, and lost in his thoughts, he stood and walked back to his office. Ben knew it had been just over eighteen months since his wife had died from cancer. She knew loss got easier with time, but sometimes Kev faded off without warning. It obviously still hurt much more than he let on to his staff.

Now that Ben had the structure for the statement, she managed to crack on and get it done without further issue. She entered Kevin's force number on the email system and hit send just as she was called on the radio.

Opting for the clearer phone line, she picked the receiver up and rang the control room.

'We've got a report of a sudden death in Pallion. Would you be free to attend? Sgt MacKenzie has cleared it as non-suspicious.'

'Yea no probs, LV. I should be there in around half an hour max. What's the log number?' It was second nature to use the short designation assigned to the control room personnel.

At the dispatchers reply, she plugged it into the force system and brought the incident details up on the screen. The dial tone rang in her ear as they hung up, and she replaced the receiver while scanning the information.

Pulling the info she needed, she grabbed a Tech 41, the form the CSIs used for contemporaneous notes, and noted down the address, name and date of birth of the deceased and the officer dealings collar number. The officer in charge of the case, or OIC was generally the cop dealing with the incident. Recognising the number, she knew this would be straight-forward. Martin Cottlethwaite, or Cotty as his colleagues called him, was as professional as they came. He was always polite and managed to build relationships with effortless ease both with victims and personnel attending. Even the local kids got on well with him, having a bit of banter when he was called to reports of antisocial behaviour.

In what seemed like minutes, she pulled up outside the address.

Cotty's colleague, a probationer named Sam, stood point outside.

'The body's upstairs, front bedroom,' he said, opening the front door to let her in.

As soon as the door opened, Ben heard the distraught wailing of what she thought was a female, though it was reminiscent of a barn owls screech in the dead of night. She steeled herself as she knocked at the living room door and walked inside.

The wailing turned out to be from a man who was sitting on the couch, his head in his hands sobbing loudly. He glanced up at Ben as she entered, completely oblivious to the streak of snot that he'd smeared across his cheek. A woman sat beside him silently rubbing his back. She was either a friend or relative. Ben guessed them both to be around mid-thirties.

Cotty looked up, and motioned her back towards the door.

'Steve,' he said softly, 'I need to take the CSI upstairs. I'll leave Sarah here with you.'

He didn't even get a reply.

Cotty didn't speak again until both he and Ben were on the landing at the top of the stairs.

'It's a suicide. Bit of a strange one as you'll see when you go in. We've already phoned the pathologist. It's Nigel Evans on call today - he should be about twenty minutes. The deceased is Joseph Wilkinson. He left a note.'

Cotty handed her the evidence bag with the paper inside. 'It's pretty brutal.'

Scanning, Ben took in the anger in the note. All of it directed at the man keening downstairs, blaming him for the suicide.

'Jesus. Has he read this?' she asked, her voice sounding strangely high-pitched - she'd never read anything so vindictive. Cotty wasn't wrong when he'd said brutal. In his letter, Joseph called the man downstairs every name under the sun, while stating he was doing this to get back at him for screwing his best friend in their bed and berating him both as a partner and a man.

Cotty nodded his answer, 'Can I leave you to crack on? Just give me a shout if you need anything.'

Waiting until he had gone back into the living room, Ben opened the bedroom door and went inside. The male was lying beside the radiator under the window. There was a plastic bag over his head and a tube leading from under the bag where his face was to an attachment on a large gas tank. Ben followed the outer edge of the room as she performed the visual examination.

Joseph's eyes were open, staring vacantly through the plastic. His hands had frozen in a contorted position at his sides, and his neatly ironed shirt and jeans were obviously freshly laundered. His face was set in a position of contorted pain, with his lips a pale shade of blue. His wax-like face had a grey pallor to it. This wasn't an attempt at suicide; this was planned and well thought out to the least detail.

Satisfied she had finished her first look, Ben started down the stairs and began her photography.

By the time Nigel Evans arrived, she was just finishing up.

'Don't think we've met?' he said as he met her in the hall. The pathologist extended his hand, gripping hers firmly for a moment as she introduced herself.

'Would you mind if I watch as you examine the body?' she asked.

'Not at all. If you have any questions please ask.'

Ben observed as Nigel worked his way round the body. Finally, her curiosity got the better of her and she asked, 'Why have his hands done that?'

'The tank contains helium. It's not lethal to humans as a gas, but what it does is it displaces the oxygen particles in the blood-stream, essentially suffocating the body. With the bag tied on his head he would have asphyxiated within a few minutes. Part of the process is the body then seizing, which causes the muscles to contract. And his hands have held the contraction.'

'Would it have hurt?'

'For the short time he was conscious, yes. But that wouldn't have been long,' replied Nigel, giving her a sympathetic smile.

By the time he had finished his brief examination, the undertakers could be heard speaking with Joseph's partner downstairs.

Ben packed up her things and made her way to the van. She hoped she'd be put down to do the post-mortem for that one. She'd heard from the other CSIs that Nigel was the one to be with in a PM, but she had yet to attend one he had been appointed to.

2nd June, 1535 hours – Sunderland University Campus

He could barely contain his boredom.

People actually want to come to school to learn this?

He'd been sitting in the stuffy lecture hall now for five hours, with the only respite being an hour break over the lunch period. The morning lectures had been on prevailing trends in business administration, the afternoon pertaining to ergonomics, and health and safety.

It was hardly genius material.

Most of the course students were female, Clarice one of them. If the course had been designed for male students, he had no doubt it would have been a lot more in depth. It was a scientifically proven fact that it was mostly women who chose to study such subjects. He figured it was because their brains didn't work the same as men's, which were far superior.

He'd watched Clarice as she had entered the hall, giggling with her group of friends as they made their way in and chose their seats about half way down the stairs. He was sitting behind them. He had arrived first and he hadn't a clue where their normal seating was, but he figured most people preferred the halfway point – not too close that you were considered a swot, and not too far back that you couldn't hear.

She had listened intently, making shorthand style notes as the lectures had progressed, pausing only to take sips from the Diet Coke bottle on the desk at her side.

He felt himself stir as she had put the bottle to her lips – one day soon that would be him. Listening intently, he heard the girls start whispering about their up-coming night out. It was booked for the 15th June starting in The Cavendish in the city centre and moving to Retox later.

Smiling, he wrote the date and venue down. The 15th would give him ample time to prepare. It appeared attending the class was a good idea.

Now he had the information he needed, he wouldn't need to go to any more of the droll lectures. In fact he could delete the whole persona if he wanted. From now on it would just be a case of monitoring her Facebook page, watching her in her room, and maybe even eventually getting to know her a little. He felt a slight flare of frustration, all that work creating the files at the university and no one had even checked if he was allowed to be in the lecture hall. There hadn't been a register taken.

As the lecturer wrapped up and told them to get themselves away for an early finish, he remained seated, watching as she threw her writing pad and pencil case into her bag. *Why doesn't she have a tablet? The world and his dog have a damn tablet nowadays. And she still works on paper?*

Joining the throng, he left the hall, following Clarice and her friends at a distance. He paused as they made their way into the glass fronted library, his falsified student ID card wouldn't get him past the swipe system and he hadn't bothered setting up the full student account so there was a chance the library wouldn't recognise him as a student. Opting not to risk it, he made his way in the opposite direction to ring a taxi.

He had plenty to be going on with for now.

Chapter Six
2ⁿᵈ June, 1810 hours – Maternity Ward, Sunderland Royal Hospital

Ben quietly knocked at the door labelled with Cass's name, not wanting to wake her if she was sleeping.

Alex opened the door, and smiled widely at her, gesturing her inside.

'Don't let the nurse see – they're pretty strict in here on only allowing two visitors at a time,' he whispered conspiratorially with a grin.

Cass was sitting up in bed. She looked tired, her hair mussed and frizzed, but she looked happy and had that contented glow about her.

She smiled widely at Ben, 'Come and meet Isobel Rose McKay.'

As Ben got to the side of the bed, Cass stretched her hands out, handing her a small bundle wrapped in a soft white blanket.

She took hold of Isobel gently, smiling down, suddenly filled with emotion. It reminded her of the day Grace had been born. For a second she let the warmth of the memory envelop her.

It had been September 12ᵗʰ, four and a half years earlier. The country had been in uproar about the rising price of fuel and Ben had stock piled, panicking in case she couldn't get to the hospital with anticipated strike action on her due date of the 3ʳᵈ. Grace though, had decided her due date was too soon, and had refused to make an appearance until nine whole days later. The north east was in the middle of a sudden flash heat wave, and Aoife had driven a sweating Ben to the hospital, as recommended by the midwife.

She barely remembered the birth itself. The human memory does an amazing job of blocking out the pain in exchange for the gift of the child. She had looked down on the baby's perfect features, and known that this child was her saving grace – it had been how her daughter had come to the name she had.

'She's absolutely beautiful,' said Ben softly, smiling back at Cass. 'And I love the name Isobel - is that one you guys just decided on? Or does it mean something?'

'Isobel is Alex's mum, Rose is mine. In fact the rest of the family are coming down shortly - you're the first to arrive. Ali just left to go pick them up.'

'Sweetie,' interrupted Rose Peters, Cass's mum, 'I'm gonna go down to the cafe with Roger to have a bite. Can I bring you something up?'

'No I'm good thanks, Mum, you guys take your time. Enjoy it.'

Ben watched as Rose patted her daughters arm with a smile of utter pride, then she and her husband left the room.

2nd June, 2010 hours – O'Byrne residence, Sunderland

Aoife had been sat in the rocking chair beside Grace's bed since she put her niece down over an hour earlier. The story had suddenly ceased as her voice had faltered a few sentences in, and Grace with the infinite wisdom of a four year old, had clambered out of bed and into Aoife's arms, wrapping herself around her Great Aunt and snuggling in, knowing instinctively that she needed comforting. Aoife had arranged for the chair to be transported over from Ben's childhood home in Ireland when her parents had died, and had held Ben in it back then whenever she had cried over missing her parents. When Grace had been born, Ben had taken to nursing in it, and they both used it to read the bedtime stories that Grace adored.

Today though, the rocking motion afforded Aoife little comfort.

She had struggled not to cry, managing to hold back the tears until Grace dropped off to sleep. And then the silent tears had fallen, wetting her sleeve as her arm held the child in place, using her legs to gently rock back and forth, letting the motion soothe her with each full sweep.

She'd cried for almost an hour, thinking about everything, wondering why it had happened to her, what she had done to deserve it.

Statistically, she was aware it could happen to anyone, she actually knew a couple of people who had been through it. But you always think you're invincible, always think it won't happen to you.

But it had.

Realising the time, Aoife moved position, placed the sleeping child into the bed and tucked her in. Leaving the room, she set the bath to fill, adding some bubbles for good measure.

She would speak to the consultant tomorrow; find out what the next steps were. And once she knew this, she would tell Ben.

Knowing her time of tears was over, at least for now, Aoife lowered herself into the hot, foam filled bath just as Ben came through the front door.

'Aoife?'

Ben's quietly raised voice echoed up the stairs.

'Up here, sweetie. Am just in the bath.'

'Cass's baby is as cute as a button,' sighed Ben, pushing open the door and sitting on the closed toilet seat.

Aoife smiled to herself, she'd brought Ben up to be comfortable and at ease at home. When she was a child she used to sit on the loo and chat to her aunt constantly, telling her all about school and what happened in her day. It got so it became normal for whoever wasn't in the bath to sit and chat to the other. Aoife liked to think of it as family time. Yes some people would think it was weird, but she had always thought it important to be approachable all the time with Ben. Having had no children of her own she had nothing to compare it to of course, but chatting just felt right.

'I bet she is, what have they called her?'

'Isobel Rose. What a lovely name huh? Almost makes me broody.'

'Glad it's only almost. One Grace is enough for your old aunt.'

Ben snorted with laughter, 'Old my arse. You act younger than me! Wasn't it only last week you were begging me to go paintballing with you and some of the girls from your reading group?'

Aoife smiled. 'Yeah, I guess you're right.'

They fell into a comfortable silence for a moment, and Aoife found herself wanting to tell Ben about the cancer, but the right words wouldn't come. How on earth did someone tell something like that?

Did they just sit down and say, 'I have something to tell you,' like they did in the movies? And proceed to blurt it out. Or should she be more subtle.

Aoife sighed. There really should be a manual out there, telling her how to deal with this. Explaining how to tell 'the-girl-who-was-almost-her-daughter' that she had breast cancer. And going on to explain how to tell a four year old. Imperceptibly, she shook her head.

She couldn't do this. Not right now.

'You wanna jump in after me? I'll go knock us up some omelettes for supper if you like?'

You, Aoife O'Byrne, are nothing but a coward. She needs to know.

The thought rang round her head as she clambered out of the bath, dried off and headed downstairs in her pyjamas to make the promised supper.

3rd June, 0910 hours – Digital Forensics Lab, Sunderland HQ

'Tulley, I've had a request from Kevin Lang, one of the forensic supervisors, asking if we can allow one of his CSIs to come over for a two day attachment. I was thinking of arranging it for the end of the week? That OK with you?'

Edward Franklin's voice boomed from the side of Jacob's desk, almost making him hit enter on the current copy job before he was ready. As big as the man was, his boss had an awful habit of sneaking up without announcement or noise. Jacob firmly believed it had to do with the five teenage daughters the man had: he would need to be stealthy to keep track of all the women in his home.

Fixing his smile in place, he made eye contact with his boss.

'Sure no problem, Ed, shall we say Wednesday and Thursday? That gives Lang a few days to let the CSI know and schedule in cover?'

'Sounds good to me. Can you let him know, I'm about to head over to Newcastle to speak with the Superintendent over there about where we spend our money. Exciting stuff. How's this one coming along?'

Jacob felt Ed lean in to stare over his shoulder.

'Just in the process of creating the acquisition copy to work on. Was just double checking there were no traps or delete codes written in when you came over. I'll crack on with it now.'

Jacob glanced up and saw Ed nod his head in satisfaction before he walked off. Ed was easy going; he let his team crack on with their work, which suited Jacob down to the ground.

This case wasn't a pleasant one – Jacob knew that the files would contain some hard core material. The computer had been seized from a prolific paedophile. In his opinion these were the hardest computers to work on. The generic key word searches and investigations into the slack space provided information and very often images that he would prefer not to see. But the evidence would help Ali's team build the full case to present to the CPS.

It took several hours, sometimes even longer, to create the acquisition or exact copy. His plan was to do that this morning before working on a couple of mobile phones relating to a completely separate incident this afternoon.

Before he forgot and got himself wrapped up in his world, he typed a short reply to Kevin accepting his CSI for attachment.

For a brief moment, he wondered who it would be, then shrugged his shoulders and turned back to the job at hand.

3rd June – 1110 hours – O'Byrne residence, Sunderland

Feeling like a coward, Aoife listened at the window as Ben started the car and left the driveway. Her niece had taken Grace to school, then returned home and started on some cleaning before deciding it was time to do a food shop. She'd asked Aoife, who normally went with her, but her aunt had declined, feigning a headache. She needed some time alone to think and decide how to tell Ben about the cancer. Once again, fear and doubt sent arguments spinning through her mind.

You have to tell her. She has a right to know.

Her conscience prickled at her. Why did this have to be so hard?

Aoife picked up the phone, and pulled the oncologist's card from her purse, punching in the number.

It was time to find out what happened next, how she could fight this.

3rd June, 1915 hours – Tunstall, Sunderland City Centre

He'd spent precious minutes sharpening his knife; grazing the edge up and down the section of stone from base to tip. He placed his finger against the blade, liking how smooth it felt as it cut through the top layer of his skin as if it were thin air.

It always made him horny, the touch of the blade on his skin, the cold metal causing tingles in places he never even knew existed. It was even more intense when the knife was against someone else's skin.

He let the shivers ripple down his spine as memories flooded his mind.

There had been quite a few now, the more recent blurring into one another, getting confused and making it so he couldn't see their faces. But he remembered the earlier ones. Especially *her*.

She had been the one he compared all the others to. She had been perfect. He remembered the glow of her breasts in the moonlight, how they had called out for him to touch them, to mark them as his. She was the only one he had ever marked. The first three had been girlfriends, women he had been seeing, sleeping with even. None of them had suspected the monster that lurked beneath.

He smiled as he remembered how tentative he had been at the start; how with each kill his confidence had increased until he had decided it was time to take someone unfamiliar to him. Over the years, he'd evolved; the interaction with his chosen victims making the whole thing easier in the end. *She* had been the only one he hadn't met first, and it had worked with her, but overall he preferred the personal touch. He smiled as he registered his thoughts. *Touch, I'll be touching soon enough.*

He half-wished now that he hadn't killed her though, longed for the feeling he had with her that hadn't been present during any of the others. If he'd let her live, he could have had that feeling again and again. He could have hidden away somewhere where no one would find her; she would have grown to love him, obey him.

This time would be different.

Clarice was younger, she was of a different race. It would make a difference.

It had to.

His smile faded as his thoughts strayed back to his father. The horrible man had made a point of giving him regular beatings, forcing him into submission like he'd done with the whores that passed through. He knew he was his father's son, but he also knew he had more control than his father had ever had. He'd never drown himself in a bottle like his old man.

It hadn't been easy for him as a child. He had been beaten into submission on more than one occasion, and though now he understood that kind of discipline was necessary, he hadn't really got it as a child.

His eyes grew darker as he recalled why he preferred open spaces. His father had been drunk, the latest floozy crying in the corner after refusing to accommodate his father. It had been her fault, the useless bitch. If she hadn't argued when his father had pushed her towards the stairs, then he wouldn't have even been noticed. He had just gotten in from school and was in the process of taking his coat off, already knowing from the weeping that he needed to keep out of the way.

The woman had clawed at his father's face as he pushed her up the stairs, enraging him.

He had watched from behind the safety of the coats hanging on the wall as his father had raised his fist and beaten her, dragging her by the hair back to the base of the stairs then hitting her again. In desperation, she had grabbed his leg, begged him to help get his father off her.

He hadn't even seen his father's fist until it had collided with his face, knocking his head into the wall. He'd watched, dazed, as she scrambled away from them, leaving him to his fate with a father who was now blinded by uncontrollable rage, kicking and punching his son as if everything wrong in life was his fault, before dragging him by one foot to the cupboard under the stairs.

Without hesitation, his old man had flung him inside, locked the door and left him there crying in the dark. His fingers still showed the small scars from scratching at the door as the day had turned to night. Thirst had caused his tongue to swell in his mouth and he had believed he would never be let out.

His father had released him the next morning, throwing a dirty rag at him and telling him to clean the crusted blood from his face, pretending that nothing had happened.

He'd gone through years of his father blaming him every time the latest bit of skirt had left him, hitting out at him when anything went wrong, or even when he was just majorly pissed off. And with each beating he had grown more resilient, tougher. Until one day he'd had enough. He'd just turned sixteen and the only thing he'd received in recognition of his coming of age had been a beating that broke two ribs and a collar bone.

Lacing his father's whiskey bottle with the crushed up remnants of every pill he had found in the house had been easy. He'd hidden in the hallway, watching as his father drank the last of the bottle and eventually fallen asleep. He didn't move as vomit appeared at the sides of his father's mouth, a lengthy seizure caused him to bite his tongue, and blood dripped down his chin. He watched as his father's eyes finally turned glass-like and his heart pumped for the last time.

Only once his dad was dead did he stir, gathering his meagre belongings together, taking the small amount of cash from his father's wallet, and leaving the home he grew up in.

His father was a mean drunk who lost control of the things that should have been important to him. He'd deserved everything he'd got.

Not him though. He liked control.

And getting the feeling back when he killed Clarice, the feeling he had felt with *her*, would restore the balance and put him back in control. He just knew that when he found it again he would be able to stop, finally rest and start to live.

Chapter Seven

4th June, 1200 hours – Newstead Residential Home, Sunderland
Something was wrong.

John had pulled up outside the care home, Matthew sitting in the back seat of the car playing on his PSP; there was an ambulance and a police car outside the home. *If she's gone and fallen out of her chair again then she deserves whatever pain she's going to be in. Damned stupid woman. Never did listen when I said sit up straight.*

He jumped from the car and made his way to the door, fake concern evident on his face. He wished Eve was still at home.

Smirking to himself, John acknowledged if she was still at home she wouldn't be alive. He would have killed her; the failed attempt six years ago would have become a reality. It was that attempt that had brought her to this home, and had been the cause of her illness.

Complications in her brain from a head injury meant she couldn't walk unaided. It had caused irreparable damage to her front cortex, so he'd been told anyway, which had affected her capacity for speech, movement and memory.

If it hadn't been for Eve's sister, Carolyn, arriving at the address mere seconds after he had pushed her down the stairs, John would have finished the job.

Worthless piece of shit. Eve deserves everything that happens to her.

Still bitter about Carolyn, he purposely timed their visits to Eve so they never coincided. The interfering bitch had never liked him anyway, had always blamed him for Eve 'falling' down the stairs, yelling at him and saying it was his entire fault.

It damn well was not my fault. If she hadn't run the bath too hot then I wouldn't have lost my temper. It was her fault, everything is always her fault.

Carolyn was always surrounded by a melee of people though. He had initially thought he could teach her a lesson or two, but it was like she knew. In the days after Eve had been put in the home, Carolyn was never alone, and made a point of avoiding him. Whether she could prove it or not, he knew she thought he was responsible for hurting her sister.

She had tried to make a case for custody of Matthew, claiming John had been unstable throughout his marriage to Eve. Saying Eve had confided in her about on-going abuse. The courts had agreed with her to a point. She could provide a stable home environment for Matthew, but John was still awarded overall custody as the boy's father. And John made sure he never had to speak to Carolyn. Matthew stayed with his aunt and cousins every weekend. She would arrive at the house and beep her horn, and Matthew would go out. Though the older his son got, the less he wanted to go, at least that's how it seemed to John.

He was confident it wouldn't be much longer before Matthew made his own decisions about visiting his aunt. He grinned to himself again, acknowledging it might have a little to do with what he taught his son about women. Matthew had been taught from an early age that his aunt was a waste of space, yet John still found he asked to visit.

John painted himself as the model husband and father. And he was very careful.

Steeling himself once more at the entrance, he pressed the buzzer and asked for entry.

It was a few minutes before Ann Caffrey, one of the members of staff hustled John and Matthew through the door.

'Is everything OK, Ann? I saw the police car and ambulance outside?'

Putting patient confidentiality aside, she whispered back conspiratorially, 'Oh it's all fine. Turns out Mrs Francis's son, the one who just got out of prison, has stolen all her jewellery. The daughter is beside herself, ended up having a panic attack. Family dynamics these days, Mr Whitworth.'

Pathetic.

'How're you doing, Matthew? We haven't seen you in a couple of weeks,'

'Busy with homework,' muttered the boy, his attention focussed on what he was doing on the handheld computer.

John placed his hand on his son's back as they followed Ann to his wife's room, and for once, he didn't even notice Eve's expression.

Eve however, noticed his; she saw the thunder clouds hiding behind the sunshine of his smile to the staff, and she understood. This was going to hurt. She didn't know how, but she knew he would hurt her. Like always, he'd send her precious son to the coke machine in the lounge, then he'd do something.

Unable to help herself, Eve felt the warmth of her own urine soaking through her pants into the cushion on the chair. Fear was a terrible thing.

As Ann turned to leave, she forced a loud grunt out, waiting as the nurse turned back around and knelt in front of her.

Eve stared into the eyes of her favourite nurse, and diverted her eyes downwards, grunting again. Ann realised the problem straight away.

'Mr Whitworth, if you and Matthew would care to just step outside for five minutes, you wife needs some personal care. I'll call you back in when we are done.'

John felt his anger start to simmer.

Who the hell did she think she was? Ordering him out of the room like he was nothing more than a child, someone to do her bidding.

He'd seen the wet stain spreading on the cushion, knew his wife had pissed herself yet again. He didn't care that the doctors had told him it was a symptom of being seated constantly, that her bladder had been weakened by the lack of muscle use. He was convinced she did it on purpose.

She should still be able to hold it in. She was taught to hold it in when she first moved in. Bathroom breaks were on my terms not hers. And now that damn nurse lets her go in the chair? In front of me?

He felt his teeth gritting together as he stood in the corridor, his hands shoved deep in his pockets. He needed to get a grip. It wouldn't do to lose it here. He would make Ann pay for her insolence, but not here where people could see, where reports could be made. His breath made a hissing sound as he inhaled deeply, drawing in the breath through his jaw, locked in position with his anger. Trying to rein it back in, he glanced at Matthew who had slid to the floor, his eyes still on the game.

Now he had time to think about what he could do to Ann – wipe her savings? Put her in trouble with the tax man? It was definitely something to look into.

Nobody spoke to him like that and got away with it.

4th June, 2335 hours – Thompson residence, Sunderland

He'd waited for the darkness to finally fall before approaching the house.

He hated the summer months. It was hard to work in the daylight with people showing nerve and being as nosy as they were. He much preferred the winter months in which to carry out his observations.

Frowning to himself, he acknowledged the time between each had slowly been decreasing. There was a time when he had left a year between each, taking time to watch and research. This time though, it had only been a few months.

He knew he'd been careless last time too. He had left the cable ties at the scene instead of removing them. Granted, he had worn gloves through the assault, but he was still concerned his DNA might have been located. He remembered the article he had read a month back in one of the forensic journals, about how the labs now only needed a few loci to help identify someone, even when there were mixed DNA profiles.

He sighed to himself, his DNA might well be on file, he couldn't afford any more slip-ups. Melding into the shadows at the back of the house, he watched Clarice through her bedroom window. She was sitting at her desk, intently reading something with her head resting on one hand.

His only intent had been making sure she was at home. And she was.

It was time to start implementing stage two of his plan.

As silently as he had arrived, he left the shrubs and returned to his own home.

It took seconds for the screen to load with the camera image from her room. Obtaining her IP address had been easy, hacking in using his tablet when he was hidden in the bushes.

Now it was time to start talking, let her get to know him a little. Falsifying a Facebook account was a piece of cake. Reaching out with a friend request equally so. Minor details about what course he was studying applied to the relevant section, he hit send and sat back to wait for a reply.

He knew when she realised what a nice guy he was, she would want to meet up. And he could be very nice, when he wanted to be.

5th June, 0500 hours – Frederick Street, Sunderland
John sat in the driver's seat of the old car, picked up for parts from the local scrap yard, the front bumper facing the way he figured Ann Caffrey would go to work. The car was so ancient it barely even worked. He'd had to tow it to the garage he leased a couple of streets from his home address and tinker with it just to get the engine to fire. But, being from a scrap yard, it was virtually untraceable. He'd paid cash, stating it was for parts.

Being an IT consultant by trade meant it had been child's play hacking into the records held by the nursing home. He'd already been in several times over the years making sure there was nothing on Eve's records to indicate any problems. Finding the staff details was just as easy and a quick search on Google maps had shown him the street she lived on in all its glory thanks to the street view function. Living only a couple of blocks from the home meant she was likely to walk to work.

A quick check on the rota showed she was due to start at 5.30 a.m.

John had ensured he would be there in plenty of time. He'd left Matthew tucked under his duvet sound asleep. He felt a moment of pride. His son was a good sleeper. He'd be in bed now until 8 a.m. when John would wake him for school. Matthew was a good student too, studied hard, listened to his dad. He would go far, that boy. John would do everything in his power to provide him with all the opportunities. He was already into computers like his old man, and at nearly eleven years old, he was already writing gaming codes and learning how the background stuff worked. John had no doubts his son would one day surpass his dad's own talents.

John had been stewing over Ann Caffrey's attitude all night, his anger increasing from a steady simmer to boiling point. Too pissed off to sleep, he'd focussed his attention on painting the small Warcraft figurines that formed part of his collection. It took concentration, each separate piece requiring intricate and detailed work to get it to look exactly the same as the original character. He liked the control it gave him, and he was good at it.

Eve had always hated his hobby. In the beginning she'd said it was childish for a grown man to paint figures. John had soon proved to her he was no child. That beating had been one of the first. She had never mentioned the figures again.

A movement to his right caught his eye, and he watched as Ann locked her front door, and stepped out from the porch into the dull light of the morning. For a supposed summer month, it had been insanely wet, and a chill hung in the air. If he didn't know better he'd have thought it was autumn. He smirked as she slipped a little on one of the wet steps, catching herself on the banister.

Turning the key, John started the car, letting the engine idle for a moment as he gauged which route she was going to take.

He ignored the rattle from the engine and the second she

angled her walking to head towards the road, he pulled out from the parking spot.

Dozy cow hasn't even noticed me behind her.

As Ann stepped into the road, John revved the engine and his foot pushed hard on the accelerator.

He smiled. The engine roared to life as the car lurched forward.

Ann barely even managed to turn as the car bumper hit her legs with a satisfying crunch, sending her head crashing into his windscreen which instantly shattered. He heard the thud as she hit the floor, the double thud as both sets of wheels flashed over her body and John glanced in the rear view mirror as he sped off smiling with satisfaction as he realised the street was still deserted.

The adrenaline rush took him by surprise, and he felt a bubble of laughter rise from his stomach and escape.

That was fun.

Dumping the car a few streets over, he climbed back into his own car which he'd parked there the night before, and he made his way home.

Now he would be able to sleep. He was sure of it.

5th June, 0710 hours - CSI Department, Sunderland City Centre Depot
Ben stretched and rubbed her eyes. She had only been at work for ten minutes and already she wished it was home time.

Grace had woken in the night, crying and running a fever. In a matter of minutes she had thrown up in both her own bed and Bens. So Ben had bathed her daughter, given her a little calpol, and remade the beds, before putting Grace back down and softly rubbing a finger along her hairline until she had fallen asleep. She'd seemed a little perkier when Ben had left for work but she had to be kept off school anyway. They always recommended a day or two off after a bout of sickness in case it was contagious.

Ben had left Grace and Aoife planning what they would watch through their unscheduled 'sofa-day'.

Sighing, she got to her feet and clicked the kettle on. Another coffee was definitely required. She heard a burst of static from her radio and turned the volume up as she stirred the hot brew.

'7916 Cassidy, come in, over.'

She pressed her finger on the speech button and replied, 'Yeah go ahead, LV.'

'Ben, we've had a report of a fatal hit and run. The offending vehicle was recovered a few streets away and has just been uplifted to SL Motorbods for exam but DI McKay is asking if you would be free to attend the scene? It's log 201 of today if you want to have a quick read?'

'No probs, LV, I should be there in about fifteen minutes.'

Ben took a gulp of her coffee, burning her mouth and swallowing hard. The heat brought tears to her eyes as it travelled down her throat.

'Shit,' she muttered to herself, feeling the roof of her mouth start to blister a little.

'You OK, Ben?' came Kev's voice from behind her.

'Yeah I'm OK, just burnt my mouth on my coffee. Am just about to head out to a fatal RTC. I saw on the rota we're thin on the ground today? Do you want me to leave the vehicle ' til tomorrow? LV said it's been uplifted to SL Motorbods. They'll have it in the forensic bay so it can wait if need be.'

'I heard. I'll pitch in and go do the scene if you don't mind heading to SLs for the vehicle? I have a meeting in a couple of hours, don't want to get too caught up before then,' said Kev.

Ben nodded. 'OK no probs. I'll head over there in a minute.'

'Finish your coffee first, you look tired today.' Kev winked and then left the office.

5th June, 0740 hours – SL Motorbods, Sunderland

Pulling the handbrake up on the van, Ben yawned and rubbed her eyes. She felt like she needed a dunk in a cold shower. The tiredness was making her a little groggy. Some idiot had seen fit to pull out on her on route to the garage too, causing her to slam the brakes on. She'd heard anything not bolted down lurch in the back of the van, and she wasn't looking forward to opening the side door.

She pulled her mobile out of her pocket and checked the screen. She was always a little worried when Grace was off school, but the screen saver smiled up at her with no messages showing.

Ben turned to open the door, and jumped as she saw Eddie Conlan's face grinning at her through the window.

'Hey, Eddie,' she said. 'How's you this miserable morning?'

'Morning, Ben. Saw that nutter on the roundabout. You OK?'

'You saw that? Complete arsehole. Nearly smacked into the side of him when he undertook like that.'

'I'd have liked to have seen his face if you had though. They all think they're the bees' knees 'til they see the police badge.'

Ben yawned again. 'Sorry, Eddie. Long night.'

Eddie waggled his eyebrows in response, his Bluetooth headset jiggling at the side of his head as he grinned. 'Oo aye? Nudge nudge, wink wink. Say no more.'

'Not like that,' Ben said quickly. 'Grace was up at daft o'clock being sick. Makes for a long one when you've got to change two sets of bedding through the night.'

'Aw bless her little cottons. It's awful when they're poorly. Joey was up with something similar a couple of weeks ago. Elise and I were both zombies that day.'

'How is Elise? Expecting again I hear? Congratulations, Eddie.'

'Yeah. Took all these years to happen so it makes sense that having more is gonna be in quick succession. Doc says it's twins this time. Dunno how we're gonna manage with two babies and a toddler, but I'm sure we will.' His grin was wide and infectious, and Ben couldn't help but smile back.

'You're here for the one that hit the lady down on Frederick Street right? I've put it in the forensic bay for you. White with one sugar?'

'Better make it white with two today: think I need the rush.'

Eddie left her and headed to the small, but well-equipped staff kitchen to the rear of the main office.

Ben made her way over to the forensic bay, and did a quick once around the exterior of the vehicle. It was an old car, and the paintwork was faded in places from too many years sat in the British sunshine. The front bumper was distorted from the impact, and the windscreen was shattered, a clump of hair and blood visible in the centre. It definitely looked like the vehicle had collided with someone.

She looked up as Eddie entered, handing her a steaming mug of what smelled suspiciously like freshly brewed coffee. Ben groaned as she inhaled that wonderful scent that only the fresh stuff gives off.

'It's the good stuff. They opened a new Starbucks around the corner. Treated the lads to one of their machines as a thank you for their work over Christmas. Best darn thing I ever bought. That blend's the new fair-trade one from Guatemala, has just a hint of cinnamon hiding in the background.'

'You give me coffee like this and I'll never leave,' threatened Ben with a smile as she blew the surface of the coffee and took a small, cautious sip. 'Mmm that's fantastic. Thanks, Eddie.'

'You know where the kitchen is if you want more. I've got a shout for a vehicle broken down on the A19 – might not be back before you leave.'

'No probs, love. Take care and drive safe.'

She turned back round, took another sip of coffee, and placed it on the side next to her camera case. Giving her head a shake, she put herself in the zone, and started the external photographs.

5th June, 2055 hours – Sunderland University Campus

TJ cracked open the door to the lecture hall, and stepped inside silently. She huddled against the wall for a moment, contemplating. Dressed in a tailored trouser suit, she acknowledged to herself she would look pretty out of place if she sat down. One of the non-perks of reconnaissance after finishing work she supposed. The job in the estate agents wasn't the best, but it was paying for her doctorate.

Her grey eyes narrowed as she focussed in on the class. Jacob was at the front of the room, standing at the podium, and the students who were peppered throughout the different seating levels, had already started putting their things in their bags, obviously happy that he was wrapping up.

She stood to one side, allowing them to egress as she waited for him to notice her. It gave her the perfect vantage point and she leaned forward as she watched a girl who was sitting near the front. Her red hair was loose, curls flowing down her back but clipped at the top with a silver slide. Without even needing to see any interaction, TJ knew instinctively that she was the one who had her brother all a fluster.

Jacob packed up his papers and looked up, as TJ made her way down the stairs.

He glanced over at Ben, smiling as she made eye contact despite the initial flash of panic. *What's TJ doing here?*

Ben's cheeks flushed, as she stood and made her way down to the podium.

He flashed a warning look towards TJ, who'd paused mid-way down the stairs, her face curving into a smile, obviously enjoying his discomfort.

'It's Ben, right?' he asked, disarming her shyness with his demeanour.

'Yeah. I only found out the other day that we both work for North East Police. My boss has requested an attachment for me and I just wondered whether the request had made its way to you yet?'

'I sent the acceptance back the other day. You're booked to come over the day after tomorrow. Hadn't Kevin passed the message on?'

'No, but to be honest it's been manic busy today and he was on rest days yesterday. It probably slipped his mind. That's great, thanks, Jacob.'

'No problem. I'll see you then.'

Jacob's words sounded way to prim and proper. He found himself shaking his head as he watched Ben head past TJ on the stairs, and by the time TJ reached him, smiling gleefully, he knew she had overheard the exchange.

'Hadn't he passed the message on?' mocked TJ in a posh voice, grimacing as he jokingly punched her in the arm.

'She's pretty,' she said shrewdly, holding her arms out in surrender as he glared at her.

'Don't go there, sis, she's a student.'

'Nope. She's a colleague, you work together. That means you already had relationship status before meeting here. So the fact she's a student is beside the point.'

Jacob sighed; he knew her logic couldn't be argued with. Lord knew he'd tried enough over the years.

'So how long do you two have working up close and personal?'

He looked at his sister with what he hoped was his sternest parental stare, and failed miserably as he caught the sparkle of laughter in her eyes.

'Two days. Are we done here? Think we can go get some food now?'

He knew his tone sounded exasperated but he didn't need ribbing right now. On TJs nod, he gathered his stuff together and followed her back up the stairs.

Wow, that smile. TJ's right, Ben is really pretty, Maybe...

Pushing the thoughts back, he sighed. *She wouldn't like me anyway.*

5th June, 2120 hours – O'Byrne residence, Sunderland

5th June, 2120 hours – O'Byrne residence, Sunderland

As Ben entered the house, she had the feeling that something was very wrong. She couldn't put her finger on it. It wasn't often she had feelings like that, not anymore. They had been more prevalent when she was younger but she had grown out of believing intuition was a thing to be acted on.

That belief was challenged today, though. The lead-like feeling had started in her gut a few days ago and had been increasing in weight ever since. Even the medication she took for the increased bile production hadn't stopped the severe indigestion.

You just need to relax.

Berating herself didn't help either though. She shook her head as she wandered in through the front door, latching it behind her and locking it with the key. As she took her coat off, Aoife came from the kitchen and into the hall.

She looks so tired lately. I wish she would tell me what's bugging her. This last week she's aged about ten years.

Resolving to get to the bottom of it, Ben smiled at her aunt and quietly said two words.

'Family Meeting.'

Aoife, knowing it was finally time, nodded slowly and followed Ben through to the kitchen. Stalling, she made them both a brew, setting the steaming cups on the table and sitting down.

She couldn't even speak, the lump in her throat felt so big it hurt to breathe. Taking a hint from Ben's arsenal for dealing with difficult situations, she pictured Grace in her mind, smiling widely.

It didn't work.

Aoife's eyes filled with tears as she stared at the girl who wasn't her daughter but who was in her heart, and unable to help herself she started to sob.

Aoife saw Bens concern as her niece knelt in front of her and pulled her close, and she dropped her head to Ben's shoulder as her body shook with wracking sobs. She heard Ben's breath catch, and knew she was crying too. It provided little comfort and Aoife felt guilty that she was responsible.

After a few minutes, Aoife allayed her crying to a series of hiccups, still holding her niece tightly.

Ben's voice sounded muffled as she finally asked her aunt what was wrong.

Aoife took a deep breath, holding Ben's at arms' length so she could make eye contact whilst she told her.

'I've been wanting to tell you this for days. It's just been so hard, I didn't want to upset you with everything you have on your plate at the moment.'

Ben visibly straightened her back, and stretched her shoulders, as if steeling herself for what was to come.

Aoife's voice broke, but she managed to get the words out.

'I have cancer.'

'No,' whispered Ben, the colour draining from her face. 'How bad? You're fighting it, right? Aoife? Please.'

Ben's voice was shocked, her fear permeated the air in the kitchen, and it felt thick and clogged with emotion. The overwhelming ache Aoife hadn't been able to shake, suddenly faded, there was no way this was going to beat her. She wouldn't let it. She had a family, damn it. A family who needed her.

Steadying herself further, she gave Ben the full details.

'I have an appointment to see my consultant tomorrow but I think I'll be scheduled in shortly to have the lump removed. From what I understand, this tells the surgeon how bad it is and how best to treat it. It's usually radiotherapy, or chemotherapy. Sometimes it's both. He said the lump is small, only about three centimetres in diameter, so he's hopeful.'

'How long have you known?' Ben paused, she was obviously hurt that her aunt hadn't told her before now. 'Why didn't you tell me you had a lump?'

'I found the lump a couple of months ago. But I only found out it was cancer last week. The day of your meeting at the school. And I didn't tell you because I thought it was nothing. I didn't want you to worry. I'm sorry.'

Ben shook her head. 'I knew it. I knew something was wrong. I've had a bad feeling all week. Aoife, what can I do? You know I'll help. I can reduce my hours at work, you won't be able to look after Grace as much, and...'

'Now you wait just a minute.' Aoife was instantly annoyed. 'Don't you dare go writing me off yet, young lady. I am perfectly capable of carrying on as we are for the time being. The consultant said he will go over the ins and outs of the treatment plan tomorrow. I was going to ask if you would come with me, if you wouldn't mind that is.'

'Of course I will,' Ben pulled her aunt back into a tight hug, 'I'm sorry, I didn't mean to imply I was writing you off. I'm just worried. I love you.'

'We are going to get through this, Ben. You and me, we can cope with anything as long as we have each other's support. You taught me that.'

Aoife felt Ben plant a soft kiss on her forehead, and knew she understood as she asked, 'What happens now?'

'Now, you get your dinner which is in the microwave. You check on that wonderful baby asleep upstairs, and we deal with the cancer tomorrow. I will not let either of us dwell on the bad here. My consultant is positive, and it's the only way I want to be. I should've told you earlier but that can't be helped now. It's going to take a lot more than a lump in my boob to take me away from my family. And if fate doesn't like that, well he can stick it up his arse.'

Ben couldn't help but smile at her aunt; the sudden burst of angry determination had brought out her strong Irish accent and it was a rare occasion when Aoife used cuss words. She was glad to see her aunt's fighting spirit coming out. *I can't believe she didn't tell me.*

It was hard to stay positive but she knew her aunt needed her. Aoife didn't deserve cancer, nobody did.

The uneasy feeling in her stomach settled down, as if knowing what was wrong helped make it a little lighter. Everything was going to be OK. It had to be.

Chapter Eight
6th June, 0700 hours – Tunstall, Sunderland City Centre

He sat in front of the computer screens, focussing on the images in front of him. He knew Clarice was the one, but he still hadn't been able to stop watching the others. It gave him a buzz watching the women when he knew they didn't even know, would never think for a second that a camera had been installed.

Maybe when he was finished with Clarice he should have one of the others. Or maybe he should have one of them first, a starter course of sorts.

With a mild frown, he shook his head.

No.

Nothing would detract from her. It all had to be perfect this time.

He entered in the disconnection codes for the other four cameras, the screens suddenly going dark before he could change his mind.

He had already decided where he would take her, the perfect location for their rendezvous. It had been Clarice's carer who had provided the answer. A simple virus installed on the computers at the Outreach centre, an interceptor on the line as they had called the engineer and he was set to go. Fixing the virus had been easy, installing a couple of cameras also simple. The override for the alarm system had been harder but even that had been no real issue. He actually had access to several potential locations, but he knew this one would work the best. There was something about the Outreach Centre that made this personal. And personal was always good. He knew he wouldn't stick around for long afterwards.

Noting the positivity posters on the wall of the carer's office, he shuddered in disgust.

We'll see how positive you are afterwards.

Most of the preparation work was done. He was ready.

Now he just had a couple more days to wait until D-Day; he smiled, D-Day was an apt description. D for Die. He had a little more time to watch her in her room, doing the things young women did when they thought no-one was watching.

He was pleased she didn't have a boyfriend. He hadn't had to watch someone else defiling her – she was his now.

And it would be his pleasure to show her where women stood in his life.

The lopsided grin passed over his face, his scar glowing eerily in the ebbing light of his computer screens. The feeling of power made him harden instantly.

As he watched her pull herself out of bed and stretch gracefully, he pulled himself free from his trousers, and slowly worked his hand up and down.

This was going to feel so good.

6th June, 1035 hours – Oncology Department, Sunderland Royal Hospital
'Mrs O'Byrne?' the nurse smiled softly as she motioned for Ben and Aoife to follow her through to the consultant's room.

He stood as they entered, his checked shirt freshly ironed with crisp creases, and his warm smile extending down his arm as he took Aoife's hand and shook it, using his other hand at the small of her back, guiding her to the seat in front of the large oak table.

Aoife sat in the chair beside Ben, barely even daring to breath. Ben's hand on her knee was a silent but strong message of support. She put her hand over the top and squeezed gently.

'How are you coping? It's not easy I know,' said the consultant.

His voice was smooth, disarming; Aoife felt a little of her overwhelming desire to run fade. She was here to get sorted. She would not run away or bury her head in the sand, as much as she might want to.

'I'm OK. Still finding it a little hard to believe if I'm honest. I want you to be truthful with me Dr Carmichael, don't sugar-coat it, OK?'

'OK,' Arthur Carmichael leaned back in his chair, crossing one leg over the other, leaving his body language open. He was plainly experienced in dealing with patients. 'At this stage we need to schedule in surgery to start, preferably as soon as possible. I actually have a cancellation tomorrow, if that's not too soon for you. The nurse will see you after we're done here and perform a pre-op assessment. What I'm hoping is that a lumpectomy will suffice. Do you know what that is?'

At her nod, he continued, 'From the scan last week it doesn't appear to have spread to the lymph nodes and as you know it's roughly three centimetres in diameter. The surgery will take out the lump and a margin of flesh from around the lump. This will then be sent to the pathology lab for testing which will ascertain whether the margin is clear of cancer cells. We'll then know what stage we are dealing with and can prepare your treatment plan. We caught this early thanks to your diligence with your breast checks. I'm hopeful for the outcome here.'

Aoife coughed a little, it was what she had expected after she had spent time researching, but it still scared the hell out of her.

'Will I have to stay in hospital long?'

'You should be out the day after surgery all being well. After the surgery though, you will need to take it easy for a few weeks, no lifting whatsoever using your left arm, so that means no housework, no driving, nothing that could constitute work, OK?'

Aoife nodded again, glancing at Ben to see if she had any questions.

Ben shook her head, her hand now holding her aunts tightly.

Forcing a smile, her aunt added, 'Well I guess it's time to see the nurse for the pre-op.'

6th June, 1605 hours – CSI Department, Sunderland City Centre Depot

'Jacob? It's Ben from Sunderland depot,' Ben held the phone to her ear, chewing her bottom lip. She didn't know how this would look, being scheduled for an attachment was no light thing, but it was important she was at the hospital with Grace when Aoife came out of surgery.

'Hi, how are you?' His voice sounded gruff, and if she was honest with herself, a little sexy.

'I'm OK. Listen I know I'm due at HQ in the morning at 9 a.m. which is fine, but my aunt has just been diagnosed with breast cancer and has her surgery tomorrow afternoon, and I've got my little girl to pick up from school and have to get to the hospital. It'll mean that I have to leave early but I completely understand if you feel you need to cancel my attachment and reschedule, or cancel completely if you see this as a –'

'Whoa, slow down,' interrupted Jacob. Ben could almost hear him smile down the phone, fully aware she had been babbling.

'It's fine, Ben. I'm not a monster you know. If you need to get away you get away, end of. Are you sure you can still come in prior to picking the bairn up from school? If your aunt needs you beforehand then we can reschedule for next week. It's entirely up to you.'

'No I should be OK, Jacob, thank you. I just need to get away mid-afternoon. The day after should be OK too; I've arranged for one of the other mums to pick Grace up from school and keep her until I finish work. We'll go get my aunt after that, providing she's fine to be released.'

'OK, if you're sure, Ben. Don't worry if plans change. We can work around them. Sounds like you're having a bit of a tough time at the moment.'

Ben sighed down the phone, 'Like you wouldn't believe. Thanks again, Jacob, I'll see you in the morning.'

7th June, 0115 hours – Whitworth residence, Sunderland
John felt his eyes blur as he stared at the screen. He hadn't been surprised to realise there were sites dedicated to appeasing the morbid curiosity surrounding death and murder. There were in

fact, dedicated sites showing the brutality of the bodies before the police had arrived and cordoned them all off, restricting views. It really was fascinating stuff.

He just couldn't see his way to going to bed yet. He felt a need to learn more, to perfect whichever was the most effective method for the next time. He had barely slept since killing Ann Caffrey, and tonight was not going to be any different.

His son was still staying at Carolyn's house, leaving him free to be on the internet all day if he wanted. Killing played on his mind, he found himself replaying kill methods in his head, acting out every method he had found with victims who were faceless, nameless shapes. On the rare occasion he managed to sleep, his dreams were filled with bloodshed and vacant eyes staring at him.

He needed to see it for himself. It was growing stronger, almost out of control.

He hadn't even been to work today. He had phoned his boss and told him in a monotone voice that he was sick.

And he knew he was.

It was no longer about putting his wife in her place, or any other woman for that matter. Now it was all about killing one, a very special one. The one of his choosing.

He pulled his coat over his shoulders, and left the house.

Chapter Nine
7th June, 0850 hours – Digital Forensics Lab, Sunderland HQ

Ben turned the key to the side entrance door at HQ and made her way inside. She'd been in plenty of times before, liaising with the submissions team as well as those in the photography and chemical labs. She knew the place inside out: its drab walls in need of a lick of paint, the carpets worn along the routes most used. The corridors were adorned with posters about Domestic Violence, latest police campaigns, and union issues. It had always been that way, was the same in the smaller stations too.

She paused at the door to the digital forensics office, taking a deep breath. *Get a grip already. Getting so nervous all the time is just plain silly.* Pushing her shoulders back, she opened the door and entered.

The office was combined with the lab: with one end of the room fully kitted out with screens and the gadgets the technicians used to recover the data required from seized items. She felt herself grin – it was most definitely not as hi-tech as the TV portrayed in the American cop dramas. But then reality never was. She had often had a giggle to herself watching the CSI shows where the forensics personnel entered scenes wearing high heels, their flowing locks left loose in a way that would contaminate any evidence picked up, and magically got an ident within minutes.

Spotting Jacob working on something at the end of the office, she made her way down.

'Ben, hi,' he greeted, glancing up from the screen for a moment, 'just give me a sec, and I'll be with you.'

Walking around the desk, she stood behind him, watching the computer screen.

'The computer was seized from the house of a drug runner. I've created the two exact copies I need. This one's the working copy. I've already catalogued the disk contents and I'm just setting up a keyword list to look for related files.' He spoke quietly, concentrating on typing onto the black square in the middle of the screen.

'The keyword list checks the slack space and the unallocated areas right?' asked Ben, pulling a chair over and sitting down.

Jacob looked over at her again, his eye brows raised.

'Someone been reading from the book-list I take it?'

Ben felt her cheeks turn pink as she nodded. 'Yeah I got most of them from the library. I'm not technically-minded at all, figured I'd need a good head start.'

'Not technically-minded? And you chose a digital forensics intro course; why exactly? Not that I'm complaining mind you. It just seems a little strange you would choose to do something you don't know a great deal about.'

I should have known he would ask.

Giving herself a virtual shake was easy: it was something she did regularly now. Now was as good a time as any to mention the support group.

'I assist in the running of an online support group for women who have been raped. We were hacked last year and some of our members ended up getting abusive emails. I guess the interest started around that time. At the time, I'd also just finished my training course for the CSI job and that piqued it a little further. When the funding came up through the Education Bursary for Police Staff, I thought it would be a good time to explore more.'

'Support group? Did you set it up using secure server information and limit the administrators?'

'I didn't set it up. I only assist with the running now 'cos I was an active member for years. It was one of those progression things. I have full administrator status but don't have the knowledge to check the security aspects.'

Jacob's eyes narrowed. *A member for years? What did that mean?*

'Give me the web address later and I'll have a look at it for you. It wouldn't be good for someone to get access to info like email addresses and the like. There's people out there who can glean everything about a person just by getting a couple of bits of information.'

A little startled, Ben nodded, 'Thanks, Jacob. It only allows you access into the forum area with registration though.'

Suddenly uncomfortable, she wondered why she had told him about the group. She could have answered his question sufficiently with the info she had received on the training course. Realising she had managed to avoid the unasked question of *why* she was a member in the first place, she took in a slow breath. Hardly anyone knew that answer.

She pulled herself back into the conversation to catch the tail end of Jacob's sentence.

'.....time do you have to get away?'

Thinking on her feet she answered, 'about half two at the latest if that's OK?'

'No problem. What time's your aunts surgery scheduled for?'

'As far as I know it's scheduled for 2 p.m. She's going to ring me as she goes down to theatre. I need to be there when she's brought back up to the ward.'

'Must be hard for you. I can't imagine how it must feel.'

Ben was glad he hadn't said he knew how she felt. That sentence always grated on her. Nobody but you knows how you feel, and you wouldn't expect people to know.

'It's a bit weird to be honest. She found out last week and didn't tell me until yesterday. I guess it's still sinking in a little.'

'She left it a week to tell you? Why?' Suddenly conscious he seemed nosy, he added, 'Sorry I'm being intrusive. You don't have to answer that.'

'No, you're not, it's fine. Honest. She didn't want to worry me, didn't know how to tell me. I guess I'd have been the same in that situation.'

'Suppose the old adage of everyone handling things differently would apply. I don't know how I'd deal with something like that either. Sounds to me like your aunt needed to work things out herself before involving you. What's her prognosis?'

'Good according to her consultant. He thinks she'll be fine.'

Jacob nodded. 'Bit of a slog to get there though. How's your daughter taking it all? Your aunt will be her great aunt right?'

'Yeah, Grace is only four so we haven't told her too much, just that Aoife is ill and needs something bad taken away. She seems to be coping OK at the minute, but that might change after the hospital. She's never really been around ill people, actually she hasn't stepped foot in hospital since she was born. But she's a good kid, mature for her age. She'll ask questions if something bothers her.'

Seeing Ben's eyes light up talking about her daughter, Jacob found himself staring back, letting her green eyes draw him into their exotic depths. For a moment he almost forgot where he was. He coughed a little, forcing his gaze back to the computer screen.

What the hell? I've never met anyone like her. I wanted to dive into those eyes and never come back out.

It was disturbing, and made him uncomfortable. The next two days was going to be tough, he needed to maintain a professional distance. He hadn't been with a woman since he had returned from Afghanistan.

Because they'd run screaming from my scars.

The thought had been there since his return, festering in his mind and making him feel as though he was the most unattractive man ever. No matter how much TJ tried to tell him to open up, he'd never been able to.

Women deserve a man who can look after them. I can barely even look after myself any more.

Pushing the desolation and depression back, he plastered his false smile on his face and quietly told Ben to make herself a coffee. She was there to learn, there wouldn't be anything more.

He could not let himself be attracted to her.

7th June, 1140 hours – Tunstall, Sunderland City Centre

He sat back from the computer screens, waiting for her response. He had made contact with Clarice the day before and they'd been messaging constantly since. She thought she was getting to know someone on her course, someone who may well turn out to be attracted to her. He had started by asking her for lesson notes, indicating he had been ill and would be off class this week. After a little coaxing she had agreed, sending him the information last night and promising to send more this morning.

It had taken time to get her to start opening up, but now she was messaging him replies instantly. He hadn't even needed to check her Facebook information today – she had already told him she had a night out planned for the 16th. He had replied, telling her he was out with his friends and they should plan to meet up.

And that's when she had sent her mobile number.

Stupid bitch – women were so fickle. Slightest bit of attention and they believed someone was genuinely interested in them.

It was so pathetic it bordered on the ridiculous. Laying the groundwork to teach his lessons was necessary, but he hated how they always presumed he gave a damn.

He would show her just how little he cared when he had her in the centre, begging him not to kill her, saying she would do anything if he would just let her live, promising she wouldn't tell.

He smiled. They always said the same things.

Not that it mattered. No-one ever told. Because no-one ever lived.

Bringing up his internet explorer, he put the terms rape, 2008, Durham into the search engine, and hit enter.

The first hit was the right one. Clicking on it, he started to read. He shuffled in his seat, adjusting himself as the memories of *her* flooded through his mind. She had been the only one who hadn't promised not to tell, accepting early on that she wouldn't be alive to tell the tale.

As he read through the news report, his eyes widened.

'The victim, as yet unnamed, was taken to the University Hospital of Durham where they treated her for extensive injuries and serious sexual assault. Her condition at this time is critical. Anyone with any information is asked to contact either the local police force or Crime Stoppers.'

Sitting back he had to fight the sudden surge of panic. Treatment for injuries? Meaning she had been alive when they took her to the hospital? How in the hell could he have left her alive? He had watched as her blood soaked into the soil around her, listened to her raspy breaths as she fought to delay the inevitable. His knife had needed cleaning after being plunged deep into her stomach. She'd barely even been breathing even as he left.

The surge of anger surprised him. He swiped his hand across the computer desk, sending two screens crashing to the floor along with a cold mug of stagnant coffee. It splashed up onto his bare foot, and he looked down in confusion.

How was it possible that she had survived and he hadn't known? Maybe she had died later? What if she had woken up and told the police who had done it? He hadn't worn any kind of disguise back in those days, not caring as his victims didn't live to tell the tale. Hell, he only wore them now when he was prepping, never during the actual teachings.

Scanning through the rest of the article, he was disappointed to see there was no links to other articles relating to the attack. Going back to the search engine, he tried some of the other sites but the information was pretty much standard. As he passed over the progressing dates, it moved from being popular news to less popular and eventually petered off.

Focussed now, he took himself to the registrar's website. Jumping up from the chair, he pulled his precious box down from the shelf to his right. It was still meticulous, fully ordered. Retrieving the fourth envelope in, he read the name and date on the front. He had never bothered learning their names at the time; instead he'd written them down in case he ever needed them for reference.

He entered the date into the search engine, and found a more recent article, dated a year after the assault.

'*After surviving the horrific attack of a year ago, the victim, who wishes to remain anonymous has finally recovered from her injuries but no doubt the scars run deep. She refused to comment to this reporter when approached, but we are to assume she is still dealing with the traumatic after effects of such an awful event. It's a year later and the police have not made any arrests – the attacker remains at large. We encourage women everywhere to remain vigilant in the face of such events, and recommend that if you have been the victim of a rape, you make sure you report it and get some support. A list of agencies is outlined below.*'

He curled his fist into a ball, pulled back and punched the computer screen hard. An ink stain effect immediately spread across half of it, obscuring the offending article from view.

Intent now, he double checked the rest of the victims in his box. She was the only one, the only one who had lived.

How could I have been so stupid? How could I not have known? She knows me! She will have told the police all about me, gave them my description. And what if I left something behind?

Struggling to calm himself down, he felt his breath flare his nostrils as he inhaled and exhaled sharply. It had been years. If the police had anything on him, then he would have been approached by now. Slowly, his breathing calmed and he noticed the mess now surrounding him. It was time to get some new equipment. He would take care of Clarice first, she would definitely *not* survive. Then he would look into where Bree was now.

He would pay her another visit, and this time she also would definitely *not* live to tell the tale.

7th June, 1725 hours – Sunderland Royal Hospital

Ben watched as Grace sat on the floor in front of her with a colouring book and crayons. She had gotten a lot better at staying inside the lines, and Ben felt a sudden wave of pride wash over her. Her daughter was truly the best thing in her life. Shuffling in her seat, she realised she was clenching and unclenching her hands.

Waiting was hell.

Surely it shouldn't take this long to take something out. What if something's gone wrong? What if it was bigger than they thought?

Ben argued with herself in her head, was still doing so in fact when the surgeon finally approached, his green scrubs stark against the cream walls of the corridor outside the recovery room.

Smiling at her, he put her at ease. 'She's come through fine.' He glanced down at Grace who was looking up at him expectantly before continuing, 'She's going to be sore for a few weeks, but it looks like it hadn't spread. I'm confident we got it all.'

Ben nodded, a little too choked up to speak straight away. 'Can we see her?'

'She's still in recovery, but she'll be taken back to her room in the next ten minutes. Why don't you and Grace head upstairs and meet her there?'

He looked down again as Grace tugged at the leg of his trousers. Smiling, he bent down to her level.

'Did you take the bad thing out of my Aunty Aoife?'

'I sure did, sweetheart. Your aunty is going to be fine. But you might have to help her for a few weeks. She's going to be a little bit sore.'

Grace nodded solemnly, 'Like when I fall over and hurt my knee. Will the bad thing come back?'

He glanced up at Ben, 'Bright kid isn't she,' he said softly, his eye brows raised. Turning his attention back to Grace, he added, 'I don't think so. My magic hands took it all away.'

At this Grace looked at him with a little disbelief. 'You don't have magic hands.'

'Sure I do. Watch.'

He asked Ben for a coin which she duly handed over. Holding both hands out, he asked Grace which hand the coin was in. She picked one and looked astonished when it wasn't there. He opened the other palm and grinned as her face looked confused. The coin wasn't there either. He reached over to her ear, and appeared to pull the coin from there, handing it to her.

'Mummy, did you see that? He really does have magic hands.'

'He sure does. Come on, Gracey, let's go upstairs and wait for Aoife. Thank you, Doctor,' she took his hand for a moment, then released it, and bent to pack up the colouring things into the bag Grace had brought with her.

When Aoife was wheeled into her room a little later, Grace was sitting on one of the oversized chairs reading with her LeapPad. Ben had been pacing by the window, but seeing her aunt, she stopped, watching as the nurses put her back into her bed.

Aoife felt groggy; her chest was throbbing but the morphine they had given her in the recovery room kept actual pain at bay. All in all she didn't feel too bad. But she was thirsty.

'Could I trouble you for a cup of tea please?' she asked one of the nurses, her voice sounding like she had sandpaper caught in her throat.

Nodding and smiling, the smaller of the two nurses left the room. The other nurse plumped up her pillows and showed her how to use the bed movement remote. In moments, Aoife was sitting up, a steaming brew on the table beside her.

'How're you feeling?' asked Ben, finally getting to the bedside and taking her aunts hand. Aoife patted the back of her hand. Her niece had always been empathic, understanding other people's pain and providing silent support. When she was a child, Aoife had often thought Ben would end up in nursing.

'I'm fine, love, very thirsty and a little spacey off the drugs, but I'm OK. Dr Carmichael said he got it all out. He's coming round later to go over the next stage of treatment.'

'I loves you, you know,' whispered Ben, raising her aunt's hand to her lips and kissing it softly.

'I loves you too, you know,' replied her aunt, using her thumb to rub her niece's thumb in response.

Deciding she wanted to be in on the love too, Grace carefully climbed up the side of the bed and said she loved them both. She was so careful not to touch her aunt, not wanting to cause her any pain.

'If you come round the other side, I can give you a cuddle,' said Aoife with a grin.

The smile on Grace's face lit up the room, and she clambered down, then up the other side, and snuggled into the crook of Aoife's arm.

7ᵗʰ June, 1940 hours – Newstead Residential Home, Sunderland
John pulled up into the car park. He hadn't stopped smiling for three days.

It had felt so good to kill that interfering busy-body. He wondered how it was that he hadn't done something like that in the past. Every time he pictured her head hitting his windscreen he felt the buzz of adrenaline, the rush of knowing he had been responsible.

If that stupid bitch of a sister hadn't come in at precisely the wrong time, I would have done it back then too. Then Eve would have been the first.

He felt a little like the release he had been chasing for years had finally arrived. He didn't remember ever feeling so liberated. He wanted it to continue.

He only wished he'd done it from a closer, more personal standpoint. He wished he had watched her die.

He knew he would have to be careful though. The last thing Matthew needed was for him to get caught. He was at an impressionable age. It wouldn't do for someone to undo all of his hard work with the boy. John would have to consider things very carefully. If he did it again, it would have to be someone with no links to him, nothing to point the finger of blame in his direction.

It would take much more research than he done so far, and was something he would look into later.

Pulling himself from the car, he made his way inside only to be faced with a picture of Ann Caffrey smiling out from the lobby, a vase of flowers at the side. Letting the wave of emotion flow over him, he smiled the first genuine smile he'd done in forever.

Pressing the buzzer, he composed himself, pushing the euphoria back a little.

After a few minutes, the door opened and he came face to face with Betty.

'Mr Whitworth, come on through. It's good you're here. Your wife has been upset. We lost one of our members of staff the other day. Car accident. Eve loved Ann. It's hit her hard.'

You mean I hit her hard! He almost smirked at the thought.

Betty's voice had sounded even more rough than normal, the choke of tears suddenly threatening her composure.

'Sorry. We all loved Ann,' she added by way of explanation.

'I'm so sorry for your loss.' His words were smooth, and fell from his lips like leaves from a tree in autumn. 'A car accident you say? That's just awful.'

'Whoever hit her just drove off. How could someone do that, Mr Whitworth, hit someone with their car and just drive away?'

'I suppose it takes allsorts to make up the world, Betty. Who's to say why a person would do such a thing?' His words were laced with sarcastic undertones. He knew perfectly well why people would do such things.

'Your wife is in her bed. She hasn't stopped crying since she was informed.'

His stomach actually felt like it contained a swarm of agitated butterflies. She would know it was him. The second he walked in she would know. And she would also know it was all her fault.

Closing the door, he walked around the bed and faced his wife.

Eve looked up at him, and for the first time in her life, her eyes showed anger not fear. She would get him for killing Ann. She didn't know how she knew it was him, but she did, and she had every intention of making him pay. Her body might not be willing, but her mind was. She would *make* someone understand.

She could see John's surprise, and she knew well that his anger would be simmering beneath the surface.

Her husband grabbed her hair roughly, bending in so close she could smell the faint whiff of the breath mint he'd eaten hours before.

'You know your place, Eve. Don't even think that *you* could outsmart *me*. You're nothing but a pathetic woman. Matthew agrees, he didn't even want to come and see you today. I had to take him to your sister's early just so he didn't have to come.'

Her anger flickered, then rekindled. This was the first step on her road to defiance. She had to do something. Had to stop her son from turning into his father, had to get revenge for her lovely sweet Ann.

He went to unzip his pants. Eve clamped her jaw shut. She couldn't do much, but she knew how to piss him off.

He shook his head as she kept her jaw shut, and grabbed her face hard, his bony fingers digging into her cheeks.

'Open your mouth, Eve. You know your place,'

Gritting her teeth together she kept it closed, watching as eventually he let her go and sat down beside her, staring at her in contempt.

Inside her mind she laughed at him. It was a small victory, but it was a victory none the less.

7th June, 0715 hours – Newstead Residential Home, Sunderland

John was tired. He felt like his mind was spread thin, like jam over too much bread, and his thoughts were clogged with images of death and pain. It had been ages since he'd slept well, and it showed. Heavy purple bags sat under his bloodshot eyes. For once, he was glad Matthew was at Carolyn's for a few nights. He felt like he needed the break, not that it would end up being that way.

He'd had the phone call from the home at 6 a.m. – his wife had fallen out of bed and hit her head. He'd arrived as the carers were stemming the bleeding from her temple, the red liquid covering the side of her face. Because of the drugs she was on, her blood was thin, and took a while to clot properly. She had already been upset, but the moment he walked in she'd pretty much started climbing the walls, non-literally of course, and as they loaded her into the waiting ambulance, she was hysterical.

Irritation simmered beneath the surface. He'd gone to bed too late to deal with a crisis this early in the morning. Pushing his car into gear, he followed the ambulance out of the car park.

It was going to be a long day.

Chapter Ten
8th June, 1010 hours – The Bridges Shopping Centre, Sunderland

He sat in the cafe nursing a luke-warm cappuccino, watching the people pass by without a care in the world. He could sit here all day, had on many occasions now in fact. He found it calming, retaining anonymity whilst observing everyday people going about their mundane lives.

There was a reason for him to be in the mall today, though. Clarice had told him she was going shopping with her friends. He was in the prime position to watch, knowing that many of the students shopped in places like Primark, Top Shop and River Island. This particular cafe was the only one with a 240 degree view. By sitting here, he could see the three corridors lined with shops, leading to the central point – the food court.

He'd been there for almost an hour now: the waitress glancing over at him periodically to see if she would have chance to get a better tip by offering him a refill. He already had the tip put aside in his pocket - always tipped the people who earned the least in unfulfilling jobs.

He felt a shiver pass down his spine. She was here. Somewhere. He just knew it.

As Clarice came into view, approaching the large doorway to Primark with two other girls, his skin started to prickle with anticipation. Dressed in leggings with a flowing low cut top, she looked irresistible. She'd agreed to meet him in a couple of hours, to pass over the class notes in person. And as much as he wanted to just take her then, make her his; he knew he had to take the notes and leave.

It wasn't time yet.

When he left he would text her, say how beautiful she had looked. Girls loved to believe flattery, even when it was false. They were such vain creatures.

He decided it was time he bought some supplies. He would go for value over quality, heading into the pound shop for a pack of cable ties. He'd bet his last penny that Clarice was a fighter. And he wanted her to be. The harder they fought, the harder they fell when they finally accepted their fate. And it was such a turn on, watching them struggle against the bonds with gaffer tape stuck across their loud mouths.

As he handed over the money to the waitress, he smiled, more of a grimace really, the scar at the side of his mouth distorting his features.

The waitress smiled back, but then shivered at the cold feeling that spread suddenly through her from her very bones. It was a large tip, one from anyone else she would have happily pocketed, but the coins in her hand felt ... unpleasant. She made sure he wasn't watching, and put them in the charity box beside the till instead.

8th June, 1050 hours - Digital Forensics Lab, Sunderland HQ

His proximity was unnerving. Ben felt more flustered than she had felt in forever. *What the hell is wrong with me?* Jacob's leg was so close to hers she could feel his body heat radiating outwards and into the padding on the outside of her thigh. She could hear the pounding of her pulse in her ears, rhythmic, like the sound of a drum, and she wondered if it was possible at all that he could hear it too. She glanced at him sideways, a brief look, catching his face set in utter concentration as he told her what he was doing with the mobile phone. She'd actually zoned out about five minutes back.

He was too close.

She couldn't do this, he would know. And she didn't understand it anyway. Confused, Ben pushed her chair back.

'You OK?' he asked, turning a little on the swivel seat to look at her. The blue of his eyes darkened, and she thought he saw attraction, but it was instantly masked so she figured she'd probably imagined it. She knew her own expression had responded, saw the flicker of a response in his face. Having him so close to her was encouraging thoughts she really shouldn't be having. The seconds stretched out as she didn't respond to his question, their eyes locked on each other.

Ben had to move. If she didn't move she risked leaning in and kissing him. *Kissing him? Where had that come from?* Now it took all her energy trying not to think about how that would feel. She really had to move. Pushing the chair back she stood, breaking eye contact after what seemed like an eternity.

'Bathroom,' she said, aware he was still staring.

Jacob didn't trust himself to speak. He watched as she strode down the office, her hips swaying gently, and her backside … *Whoa! Get a grip! She's not a piece of meat.* He frowned to himself. That moment had him wanting to grab her arms and pull her in, lock his lips to hers and never let her go. He felt his body betray his thoughts that it couldn't happen. Thank goodness he only had to do this for the rest of the day.

Groaning out loud now, he knew 'the rest of the day' would be the longest rest of the day ever. It was a long time until 5 p.m. Pulling the job allocation sheet from the file at his side, he marked up a few more jobs. If he was busy and focussed he wouldn't be thinking about her.

Yeah right.

8th June, 1410 hours - Digital Forensics Lab, Sunderland HQ

The day was dragging. Jacob was hot and bothered, and not from the dodgy heating system in the station. Ben couldn't sit still, she was up and down constantly and it was unnerving him. Making a flash decision, he decided it was time for a field trip.

'Come on, let's go do a house call,' he said, grabbing his coat off the rack behind his desk, and his stick from its place by the wall.

'A house call?' asked Ben, her voice a little startled. 'Digital do house calls?'

'On occasion, yeah. The POLSA team have just done a house search, some big-wig in the organised crime family. They're wanting his system seized but think it might be booby trapped if they disconnect. We'll go have a look and see if that's the case, and if it's not then they will get one of the CSIs in to disconnect and label it up for transportation. It's not something we do regularly, but it gets us out of the office for an hour.'

Ben nodded as she followed him out. She watched as he limped in front of her. She'd been wondering what had happened to him since she had first seen him in the class room.

Settling into the passenger seat of his automatic-control Skoda, she decided to bite the bullet and just ask.

'Were you injured?'

Her voice sounded small to her ears, and for a moment she wondered whether he had actually heard her. She opened her mouth to ask again, then clamped it shut as he answered.

'Are you always so outspoken?' Realising how exasperated he sounded, he forced himself to relax. She didn't even know the impact she was having on him, how could she? Naturally she was curious. He glanced at her sideways, and responded again. 'Sorry, I'm a bit snappy today.'

'Time of the month?' she joked lightly, 'It's fine. I'm just nosy. I learnt a long time ago that if you don't ask you don't get. Sometimes I ask when I shouldn't and develop a severe case of foot in mouth syndrome. You don't have to answer if you don't want to.'

'No it's OK, I shouldn't have snapped like that. Yes, I was injured. I used to serve in the army, paratrooper regiment. I was on assignment in Afghanistan with my team when an IED went off.'

His voice was curt and to the point, and Ben felt like an idiot. She had absolutely no right asking what had happened, putting him in a position where he felt he had to answer. She wasn't stupid, had seen the pain spear through his grey eyes prior to him answering.

Knowing she had been the cause of that pain made her feel even worse.

'I shouldn't have asked. I'm sorry if I upset you.'

'I'm not upset. It's just … well, if I'm honest, no one's ever come straight out and just asked what happened. You threw me. You're pretty direct, Cassidy.' His grin softened the use of her surname.

Ben felt her face flush. His tone had lightened, almost on the verge of being teasing.

'That's down to Aoife. She brought me up to always ask questions. Grace is starting to do the same too. Maybe I need to learn when not to put my foot in my mouth though,'

'You didn't. It's fine, honest, if anything it's refreshing. Normally women run screaming when how I came to limp comes into conversation.'

Now it was Ben's eyes that narrowed in on him, his expression hadn't changed, his face still neutral, but the slight tick at the side of his jaw told her more than he intended her to know. *He believes that. He thinks he's not attractive. What the hell? Has he even looked in the mirror?*

'Well maybe the women who run screaming aren't the women you should have in your life. We all have scars; lord knows I do at any rate. It helps define us into the people we are. Other people should either accept that or leave well enough alone in my opinion.'

'You sound like my sister,' he said, giving her a quick grin. 'TJ's always saying exactly the same thing.'

'TJ? Is that the woman in the suit who was in the lecture hall the other day? Sounds like a wise woman to me.'

'Teresa Jane. She's always been called TJ. Yeah that's her. She decided to surprise me with a late supper. Wise maybe, but she can be a pain in the ass. All she ever goes on about is seeing past the damn leg and into the future.'

'Well maybe it's time you did that. You can't live in the past, and you can't let the past define your future. We're all the people we are, scars, limps and all. I think living is about accepting that we aren't perfect, nobody is. Surely it's more about accepting the good with the bad and just living?'

Her words pierced straight into his heart like an arrow, and not even thinking, he pulled the car over and turned to face her.

'You really believe that don't you? That everyone is different and has a right to be? That the past doesn't define us? But, what if it *does* define us. If I hadn't been injured I'd never have gone into digital forensics, I wouldn't be working for the police. I'd still be working the rounds in whichever country I was dispatched to with a team of men and women at my side.'

'And you don't have that now? You could look at it another way. If you hadn't been injured you wouldn't be working in digital forensics,'

He looked a little puzzled, 'That's what I just said?'

'Jacob, you're good at what you do. You're a natural teacher who has the ability to dumb down the intricate knowledge for people like me who don't have a clue. You work with a close-knit team, people who see the worst parts of humanity and still maintain the kind of working relationship that people only get when dealing with stressful situations. Getting injured serving your country is awful; the things you saw were no doubt awful too, but that career paved the way for where you are now, for *who* you are now. Don't minimise that by undermining the person it led you to become.'

It was a long speech, and Ben felt like she had maybe gone too far. But she had worked so hard not to let her past get in the way of her future that she just couldn't abide it when people thought what they did was a waste. She saw it all the time, the cleaner in the police station, the young lasses whose houses she visited as a CSI. Ben firmly believed you made your own life, and if you weren't happy with it only you could change it. She had told herself that so many times over the years that it had become her personal mantra.

She took in a deep breath as Jacob replied, 'You do sound just like TJ. I don't mean to undermine what I do now, and I know I work with a good team, the best in fact. I enjoy my work and I'm good at it, and you're right. Maybe I should stop focussing so much on the things I can't change, and start looking at the things I can. Like the fact I'll never walk without a stick, but at least I'm walking. Right?'

Ben heard the hesitation in his voice; saw the uncertainty in his eyes. 'Nobody said it was easy, Jacob.' Without her even realising, her hand had drifted and settled itself on his upper thigh, providing comfort and reassurance instinctively.

She felt her skin tingle at the heat from his, and she couldn't help but want to keep her hand there forever. She was caught in his gaze, her own eyes widening like the proverbial deer caught in the headlights. He shifted position, and she panicked.

Tearing her gaze from his she looked down, pulled her hand back from his leg and grasped it with her other one, her fingers moving together as the nerves took over.

'What just happened?' he asked softly, a little confused by her reaction. *Did I misread that look? I thought I saw a spark, but now she's pulled back. I must have been wrong. Shit.* Ben sat wringing her hands together like he had just made the biggest mistake ever.

'Nothing. Nothing happened. I erm, well I may have given you the wrong impression. I'm not interested in a relationship, or whatever, I was just.... erm, well.....' her voice trailed off into silence.

'Relationship? Hell, Ben, all I did was look at you. I wasn't asking for anything else. I barely know you, for Christ's sake.' Even as the words left his mouth, he felt the hurt. The realisation that she accepted his injury as part of him must have made him lose his marbles for a moment. Granted he hadn't asked for a relationship, but for a second he had wanted nothing more than to kiss her. And it appeared she knew that and didn't agree.

Ben heard the hurt in his tone, and kicked herself for being the cause. The truth was being so close to him, having such a real conversation had touched her heart. She had seen his eyes flash with want, and she wanted him too. And that scared the shit out of her. Despite her belief that the past doesn't define you, with her it sometimes did. No matter how hard she tried to get away from it, she was reminded of it every single day. But it didn't give her the right to hurt the man sitting beside her. She had just sat there and preached at him, and he had taken in what she said just to have her shoot him down. *Smart Ben, really smart. Tell him. Now.*

'I'm sorry. I'm good at preaching about leaving the past in the past but sometimes I don't listen to my own advice. I didn't mean to hurt you, Jacob.'

'You didn't hurt me. I mean, we barely know each other, Ben. Sure I think you're attractive, you have the most gorgeous eyes I've ever seen, but I wasn't implying that we should jump into bed together or anything. What you said made sense, that's all, and for a moment I thought maybe you meant you were interested in me. I was wrong, and that's OK. I misread you. I'm the one that should be apologising.'

His outburst was heartfelt, honest, and Ben paused for a second, letting his words sink in. *He thinks I'm attractive? Me?*

'You don't need to apologise, Jacob. This is awkward. Look, you read me right, OK? I do think you're attractive. But I have … issues … and I haven't yet dealt with them fully. It scares me to think there might be something between us. It's...' she paused, considering how much to actually say in a car in the middle of a busy street to this man she barely knew, 'Look, maybe we could go for a drink or something. Talk properly. I don't think it's appropriate to talk here at work.'

Jacob felt his jaw drop. *Did she just ask me out?* He nodded slowly. 'A drink. To talk. When?' He felt his stomach turn a somersault. It had been years since he'd had a drink with a woman.

'Tonight, if you're free? I put Grace down at 730 p.m. and I'll need to make sure Aoife is home and settled. And I can't stay long. Maybe it would just be best if you came to mine instead of us going out? It was a spur of the moment offer, I didn't really think about the other stuff.'

'Your place at 830 p.m. then?'

Ben heard her heart pounding in her ears again. *What the hell am I doing?* She hadn't invited a boy back to Aoife's in forever, and granted Jacob was way more than a boy, but still. Even as she flashed a quick smile at Jacob and nodded, she groaned inside. Aoife was going to have her life over this one. She'd never live it down.

Jacob pressed down on the accelerator and pulled the car off from the kerb. He fought to stop the boyish grin spreading across his face.

I'm going for a drink with a woman; TJ will never let me live this one down.

8th June, 1535 hours - Sunderland University Campus
He stood in the shadows beside the library and waited, knowing Clarice was due to finish her lesson at 3 p.m. and had agreed to meet him for a coffee and to go over the notes from the lectures he had 'missed'. He was excited. It felt good to get so close, so personal. It would make it even more fun when he finally had her in his grasp tomorrow.

It would be perfect.

His mind wandered back to the one that got away, Bree. Frowning he acknowledged it was a little harder than he had thought it would be to locate her. She definitely was no longer on the voters roll for County Durham. He'd decided earlier he would look into her location after he had finished with the delectable Clarice.

As she approached, tentatively smiling at him, he had to fight the urge to take her there and then. She was too trusting, too gullible. He would enjoy teaching her to be careful who she trusted. Not that it mattered really, she trusted him.

And that would prove to be her biggest mistake yet.

It had taken him many years to get comfortable in his routine. Even if he searched endlessly for that one feeling he was looking for, even if no one had competed yet, he had managed to establish his own way of doing things, a natural order with which to progress. It started with them getting comfortable enough to let their guard down, and then he taught them how much of a mistake this was. His father had taught him that lesson, and he felt duty-bound to teach others. And teach he would, another day, not today.

Plastering the fake smile on his face, he waved in acknowledgement and made his way to meet her. The scar always caused questions of course. How had he gotten it? And Clarice was no different.

As soon as they were seated in the secluded booth in the pub across the road, she had asked. Expecting it made it easier to rein his temper in, keep it under control. *She has no right to ask.*

But he held back, giving her the answer she was waiting for. 'I fell off my bike when I was eight. The scar's been there ever since.'

A complete lie.

The scar had been caused by his father. He'd taken affront to something he had said. He'd been around fourteen at the time. His father had grabbed the first thing to hand, the damn whiskey bottle, and thrown it so hard it had split his lip and cheek on impact. He remembered staring at his father, believing in that moment that he was going to die, that his own father would kill him. But as it had happened, his dad had calmed down, throwing him a rag and telling him to wipe up the blood. There were no stitches though, no offer of medical assistance. So the wound had healed slowly, crusting to a jagged scab and eventually a scar.

There was no need for other people to know that though. They had no right to know. He was the only person left alive who knew what had happened that day. He re-focussed on the conversation as she replied.

'Aw nightmare. I fell off mine too when I was a kid. Scarred my knee. Was it just Business Enterprise that you needed the notes for? That's all I've brought with me today, but if you need the rest I can scan them and email you a copy later tonight if you like.'

Her voice was smooth, the hint of a local accent coming through. He liked doing this. Interacting together. He was good at it too. There had been a time when despite his eagerness to keep the company of women, he'd found them hard to talk to. He used to stammer and almost felt his cheeks warm at the memory, but after years of practise, he was now adept at pretending to listen, and the women were so naive that they firmly believed he gave a rat's ass.

Which naturally he didn't.

Ordering another coffee, he let the charade continue.

8th June, 2020 hours - O'Byrne residence, Sunderland

Aoife hadn't stopped smiling since Ben had told her that Jacob was coming over. She was settled on the sofa, blanket on her lap and everything within easy reach, but she had purposefully left her glasses in the kitchen. It wouldn't hurt to stick her head in a bit later and see how they were doing, and the glasses gave her the perfect excuse. Ben had asked him back to the house! Miracles would never cease.

She'd done her best to extract more information, but Ben had her mouth firmly closed. It had to mean something though. Something had happened today that Ben felt needed further exploration. Something she wasn't ready to tell her aunt.

Cocking her head to one side, Aoife heard Ben pottering around upstairs. Grinning again, she realised she was trying to find something to wear. A small part of her was worried. She didn't know this man; maybe he wouldn't be right for Ben. Or just maybe he would.

Hearing a small knock at the front door, Aoife couldn't resist getting up to answer it.

Her gaze travelled up from his feet, past his stick and finally settled on his smile.

'You must be Aoife?' His voice gave away his nerves, and she nodded and smiled, granting him access.

'And you're Jacob. Pleased to meet you. Come on through to the kitchen. I'll let Ben know you're here.'

Jacob followed her down the hallway and into the kitchen. He smiled at the pictures attached to the fridge with an array of bright magnets.

'Grace's I presume?' he asked, his polite tone making him wonder what on earth he was doing here. He almost felt like he had been summoned to the head teacher's office. Aoife was grinning at him, knowing she had somehow managed to make him uncomfortable. She flicked the on switch of the kettle and used her right arm to set out some cups.

Deciding to give him even more of the heebie jeebies, she asked, 'So what are your intentions with my niece?'

The look of horror on his face was too much and she broke down in a fit of giggles. 'I'm only messing with you, Jacob. Don't look so nervous. Ben is quite capable of making her own choices. It's been a long time since she brought someone home though.'

Aoife's words hung heavy in the air - she might have been joking but he sensed a slight undertone, something hiding behind her words that he didn't quite understand yet.

He was still thinking about how to respond, when Ben pushed open the kitchen door, her face hidden behind a pile of washing. 'Put the kettle down and step away from the counter, Aoife. I said I'd make you some tea in a second.'

She lugged the pile past Jacob without noticing him, and plonked the clothing in a pile in the laundry room at the back of the kitchen.

'I'm quite capable of making my own tea,' responded Aoife, then added cheekily, 'Besides, I wasn't making it for *me*. I was making it for Jacob.'

'Well, Jacob's not here yet so go and sit yourself back down, I'll bring the tea in ....' Ben's voice trailed off as she turned around and came face to face with Jacob, who was sitting at the table grinning from ear to ear at the exchange.

'Aoife O'Byrne, you are incorrigible. Out. Now,' she added guiding her aunt back to the living room.

'You didn't tell me he was so good-looking,' whispered her aunt, letting Ben arrange the blanket on her lap.

As she turned to leave the room, Aoife added, 'Ben. You're OK, right? You're ready for this? It's been a long time and I know how hard it's been for you. If it's not right, or he says something to upset you, you just call me, OK? Even without the use of my arm, I'll knock his block off if he hurts you.'

Ben's expression softened at her aunts words. Turning back, she knelt before the only person who knew her secrets, the only person she truly trusted.

'I honestly don't know, Aoife. But it's been eight years. Surely I must be ready to at least be friends with a man. I have to at least give it a chance, right?'

'Course you do, girl, I just don't want to see you get hurt again. When you told me about the night you conceived Grace, I wanted to find that man and punch him on the nose. Getting you drunk and taking advantage like that. He's lucky I didn't find him. I just don't want something like that to happen again.'

'I know, Aoife, neither do I. And it won't. What're your first impressions? Do you think Jacob would do something like that?'

Without hesitating, Aoife shook her head. 'That boy was so nervous *I* almost started stuttering. He seems nice. But take it slow, sweetheart, OK? There's no rush for these things. If it's meant to be then it will be. Que sera sera and all that.'

'I promise. Now, I'm going to go and talk to the guy in the kitchen, if he hasn't turned tail and ran already.'

Ben gave her aunt a quick cuddle, before getting back to her feet and heading into the kitchen.

'You and your aunt seem close. Have you always lived with her?' Jacob sat at the well-loved table in the kitchen nursing his tea. He got the impression from her absence and by Aoife's guarded comments that there was something he didn't know about Ben, and not normally intrusive, he had a feeling it was something he needed to know.

'Pretty much. My mum and dad died in a car accident when I was ten. Aoife took me in, she raised me. I moved away for a short time years ago, but came back when I fell pregnant.'

Ben was doing her best to keep her nerves at bay, having him here, in her home, made it feel as though the walls of the large kitchen were closing in on her. She felt a little like she was suffocating. *That's just the nerves talking. You calm yourself down right now – this man is a nice guy, he does not need to see you in the middle of a panic attack. Breathe.*

'Are you OK? You've gone a little pale.'

His words barely penetrated the mist now swirling in front of her eyes. She tried to focus on Grace's face, the way she had been taught. But it eluded her, mingling with the swirling as her breath hitched and seemed to stop in her throat. Panic now. She couldn't breathe; felt black curtains threatening to close in on her from the sides of her vision.

Jacob recognised the symptoms immediately. In the hospital after his return, many of the soldiers had panic attacks, a result of the sudden change from foreign lands and threats to relative normality, and the time to actually allow the memories of what they'd seen to enter their minds. He got to his feet, cursing the stiffness in his leg, and grimaced as he kneeled in front of her. He took her face in his hands, looking into her eyes, and spoke slowly, calmly. He mentioned Grace and Aoife's names several times, keeping his tone neutral, none threatening.

Ben tried to grab hold of something solid in her mind, one thing that could pull her from this haze and calm her pounding heart. The image of Grace was still swirling around, giggling a hairs breadth from her grasp. The suddenly there was something solid, a set of grey eyes looking like islands in the middle of the ocean, and she grabbed hold of them, concentrating as they drew her in. She felt her breathing start to slow, saw the mist start to unfurl and slowly disappear. And as her eyes eventually refocused, she realised Jacob was knelt in front of her, felt the warmth of his hands on her cheeks. He kept talking for a couple of minutes, helping her keep focussed enough to calm herself.

'How did you do that?' she finally asked, her voice a quiet whisper. 'Nobody's ever managed to calm me down before when I've had one that bad. I normally have to pull myself out of it. Or be sedated, whichever works.'

'In the hospital when I returned from Afghanistan, there were a lot of guys holding a lot of memories. Normal life isn't all it's cracked up to be, especially when you've seen war first hand. Sometimes it would get too much and the panic would set in. I was in there for quite a long time, I'd watch the nurses calm people and eventually I was the only one in the room when a guy called Paul started to panic. I couldn't leave him like that. I just did what I'd seen the nurses do is all.'

His voice was still calm, neutral even, but his leg was starting to throb. He couldn't help but grimace as a wave of cramp passed through his thigh.

'I need to get up. Would you mind helping me to my feet? My leg has seized.' His teeth were gritting together as pain pulsed through the top of his leg.

Ben stood, then bent beside him, offering him her shoulder for support. He gasped as his leg straightened and the pain ebbed to a high dose of pins and needles. Still leaning on her for support, he flexed and bent his leg, his face taut as eventually it returned to its relatively normal state.

As he sat back down, he glanced up at Ben.

'Does it happen often? The panic attacks?'

Just as Ben was about to answer, the kitchen door opened and a sleepy four year old walked in.

'Mammy, I'm thirsty,' she grumbled, rubbing her tired eyes. They widened as she saw Jacob sat at the table. Curious now, and suddenly much more awake, she wandered round the table and stood in front of him, looking up at him.

'What's your name?' she asked, holding her hand out solemnly for him to shake. He hid a grin as he shook her hand.

'Jacob. And you must be Grace.'

She nodded, then added, 'Why are you in our house?'

Startled he looked at Ben.

She was smiling widely. Deciding to intervene, she stood and grabbed hold of Grace, spinning her in a big circle, causing her to gasp and loudly say, 'Mammy, put me down!'

'You, young lady, are out of bed when you're supposed to be in it. Jacob is a friend of Mammy's. Another day you can talk to him properly but right now, it's time for you to go back to bed.' She kissed Grace on the end of her nose and lowered her back down to the floor. Ben poured a small cup of juice and took her daughters hand.

'I'll be back in a second, I'll just go put her back down.'

'I'll take her,' said Aoife suddenly from the doorway. She smiled innocently at Ben and Jacob, holding her hand out for Grace who skipped over.

'Will you read me another story, Aunty Aoife? I'm not very tired,' asked Grace hopefully as she was led back into the hall. Ben didn't hear her aunts answer, but she knew it would be a while before Aoife came back down the stairs.

'You know she's been outside the door for ages, right?' groaned Ben with a shrug of her shoulders.

110

Jacob felt his mouth curve in response. 'Yeah, she sure has. She's just worried about you I guess. Doesn't want you to get hurt. Mums are like that.'

Ben smiled back, acknowledging silently his meaningful slip. Aoife had always acted like her mother, and though she sometimes missed her parents, she was always grateful her aunt had been there to step up.

'Would you like another tea? Maybe a glass of wine?' asked Ben. She was surprised to realise she suddenly felt more at ease with him being there, the kitchen stretching back to its normal size and any residual panic ebbing back into the recesses of her mind.

'Tea would be great thanks.' Jacob also felt more relaxed, settling back into the chair and stretching his leg out in front of him. There was definitely something about learning about each other that promoted comfort.

'So, panic attacks?' asked Jacob, as his hands closed round the cup minutes later.

Ben frowned, her head cocking to one side.

Can I do this? I barely know him. I never tell anyone about this stuff. Even Cass doesn't know and she's pretty much my best friend.

Acknowledging silently that she'd been building up to it provided her with some comfort. She'd told two people about the support group in the last week, which in itself was almost unheard of.

She pushed her emotion aside, and answered. 'Eight years ago I was raped.'

Jacob leaned back in his chair. 'I'm sorry, Ben. I shouldn't have asked.'

'Actually, it's fine. It's not something that generally comes up in conversation; in fact, it's not something I tend to tell people at all. Even Cass doesn't know, and she's practically my best friend. But maybe it's time to start telling people. I've only ever discussed it with Aoife, and my counsellor of course. But part of healing is accepting, and that's the thing I've always had trouble with.'

'Well if you don't want to tell me you don't have to. I don't want to push you into it. It's your story, only you can decide if you're ready.'

'I was twenty one. I'd moved out and was living in Durham city and working for the police down there. I used to run, not that you'd know that by looking at me now.' Ben's voice held a hint of nostalgia, almost as though it was a happier time. And it had been. At twenty one, the world couldn't touch you, you were invincible. Until the world *did* touch you anyway, then it all changed. 'It was late and I'd been running on one of the roads outside the city centre. Don't know if you know Durham, but it's pretty unique. A large bustling city, then all of a sudden there's rural farm land everywhere.'

At his nod, she continued. 'Anyway, it was dark and as I turned the bend I saw a man lying unconscious, just beyond the gate to a field. I stopped and asked if he was OK.'

Pausing, she frowned. 'You know I must've been pretty damn stupid. What kind of woman stops to check on someone when it's dark and you're in the middle of nowhere? It's the stuff horror movies are made of.'

'You're not stupid. You cared was all.'

Jacobs reply was swift, and she gave him a sad smile in response.

Her mind flooded with a melee of thoughts: *It almost feels normal to be discussing this with him, for the first time it's like I'm just talking about something that happened, not something that's still happening.*

Ben took in a deep breath and carried on. 'I didn't see the knife until it was too late. He jumped up, and stabbed me in the stomach. I remember thinking that it couldn't really be happening, that I must be dreaming. He tied my hands, and I screamed. At least I think I did. He put tape over my mouth and dragged me further into the field, out of view of the road.'

Jacob's heart almost stopped beating. He didn't know if she realised how matter of fact she sounded, but her story had him hypnotised. *How does someone go through that and come out normal at the other end?*

'I don't actually remember a lot about the rape itself. It's like it all melded into one action. I remember the pain and knowing I was going to die. My stomach was already burning, and I was so scared. I just kept thinking that when he was done, maybe he'd let me go. When he got off me, he wouldn't stop staring. I'll never forget his eyes. Even in the moonlight I could see them. They were empty, like I was looking into a black hole.'

Ben's voice had lowered to a whisper, and her eyes were troubled.

'You don't have to say anymore, Ben.' Jacob had his hand on her thigh as he looked at her, tortured and caught in the memory while trying to stay detached enough to talk.

'I want to. I need to. There has to come a day when I can talk about this without feeling this way right?'

'I dunno, Ben. Sometimes it's harder to remember. Sometimes it's better just to *not* remember.'

She inhaled deeply, putting her hand on top of his. Her connection to the real world re-established, she focussed on telling the rest. 'When he was done, he ... hurt me. Left me for dead. And I would have been too, if it hadn't been for the farmer. It was just starting to get light, and I remember hearing the sound of a tractor. The farmer thought I was dead, but I think I must have groaned or something ˈcos he almost fell over then covered me with his jacket and told me he was getting help. I think I passed out at that point. Aoife said I was unconscious for six days. They didn't catch him.'

Ben finally breathed a soft sigh of relief. It hadn't been as bad this time. It had taken her months to tell her counsellor, Amelia Griffiths. Talking on the forum was different. It was anonymous. But in counselling she'd had her doubts that she'd ever be able to tell it all. She frowned again, remembering the things she hadn't said. She'd made no mention to Amelia about the scars. Only Aoife knew about those. Criss-cross marks across both her breasts, the smaller straight scars from the knife wounds, the faint bite marks on her shoulders. Sometimes the scars were harder to think about than the actual rape.

She took in a steadying breath and made eye-contact with Jacob. He looked troubled, shocked and a little green around the gills. Preparing for the rest of the conversation, she silently got up and put the kettle back on. More tea was definitely required.

8th June, 2350 hours – O'Byrne residence, Sunderland

As Jacob said his goodbyes at the door, he felt completely drained. He was pleased she trusted him enough to tell him her story, but at the same time what she'd been through beggared belief. Not that he doubted it had happened, but that kind of stuff happened to *victims*, and the last thing that he would ever have thought Ben was, was a victim.

He surprised himself by leaning in and kissing her on the cheek while they stood on the front porch. It had seemed like the right thing to do, and she had smiled at him in response. He could see how tired she was, how much it had taken out of her to control her emotion as she'd told him.

Jacob raised his hand, giving her a wave as he started the engine and pulled away from the house. Now out of view, he frowned.

She trusted me. She told me all of that despite the fact it must have hurt her like hell to do it.

Anger simmered beneath the surface. They'd never caught the bastard. He knew if he ever got his hands on him, he wouldn't be quite so in control of his emotions.

He had some thinking to do and when he got home he set his music away and stretched before plugging in the settings on the treadmill.

8th June, 2355 hours – O'Byrne residence, Sunderland

'You told him.' Aoife's voice was matter of fact as she sat on the sofa looking up at Ben.

Ben nodded silently, and plonked herself down on the couch next to her aunt. 'I didn't even cry. It's the first time I've told anyone other than you. I thought it would be harder.'

Aoife moved position, and pulled Ben's head onto her shoulder. Ben shifted and snuggled in, for a moment remembering how her aunt used to do that on the chair she now used for Grace.

Planting a kiss on her forehead, Aoife said, 'Sometimes you don't realise the specific moment you start to deal with something horrible like what happened to you. You just do, and then it becomes easier to accept. I've seen small changes in you over the last year. You've grown more confident, it's only natural to believe that as you've grown into this wonderful, beautiful person, the bad stuff has eased.'

'But he's a guy. I guess I always figured when I told someone, it would be a friend or something.'

'You told the person who it was right for you to tell. It's that simple. Now, I think it must be time for bed. You look exhausted. Let's check the house together, then head upstairs.'

Ben looked up at her aunt. 'You really think it was the right thing to do? I work with Jacob, it's probably unprofessional.'

'Bugger that, love. At the end of the day, there's something between you two. Whether you're both ready to acknowledge that or not is irrelevant. He obviously wanted to know or he wouldn't have been here.'

Ben leaned in and placed a kiss on her aunts soft cheek, inhaling the hint of the lavender body cream she knew Aoife used. It was a smell she would always associate with her aunt. 'I loves you, Aoife.'

'I loves you too, now let's be off.'

Ben helped her aunt to her feet and kept hold of her hand as they checked the house together.

Chapter Eleven
9th June, 0910 hours – Whitworth residence, Sunderland

John had shipped Matthew out of the house and onto the school bus over half an hour ago. He should have left for work already, flexi-time was all very well but he had to work the late starts he took at another time. But he had managed to distract himself with the internet.

Google was a wonderful search engine. All he had done was enter the words, 'what's the best way to kill someone' and he had millions of hits return. He hadn't been able to get Ann out of his mind, the crunch as she hit the car replaying as if through a speaker constantly, the image of her crumpled body implanted in his brain.

He had to feel *that* again.

When he'd pushed Eve down the stairs, it had felt good, but this? This was great. He wished he'd gotten out of the car and looked at her face. John wanted to know what it looked like, what death looked like when it happened unexpectedly.

He had to do it again.

But who to do it to? It couldn't be someone close to him, someone who knew him, that would be too obvious. He wasn't a particular fan of cop shows, but even he knew if someone he knew died then he would be a suspect.

A stranger then. Someone not connected to him in any way.

But who?

This question now implanted in his mind, he gathered his things up and locked up the house. Research, that's what he needed to do. Even as he drove to work, he had images of crumpled bodies flooding his mind, and for the first in a long time, he felt alive.

9th June, 1405 hours –CSI Department, Sunderland City Centre Depot

Cass smiled at the front office clerk as she pushed the buggy through the doors and into the corridor that led to the CSI offices.

Just being out of the house was a godsend at the minute – the
parents and in-laws driving her nuts. It felt like she'd had no time
to herself since Isobel had been born. At a week old, her daughter
was as cute as a button, and was an excellent sleeper. But it didn't
stop Cass watching her constantly as she slept, terrified that
something would happen. It was a habit she was finding hard to
break, and deciding that she needed a little air, she'd wrapped the
baby up, popped her in the car seat, and driven to work.

She frowned a little as she felt her abdomen pull in protest
– there was still quite a bit of pain, but the doctor had said it was
to be expected. He'd also told her to take it easy, but he plainly
didn't have children – no mum could ever take it easy.

Pushing the buggy was a skill, and she turned the corner
into the CSI office as though she was an expert. Ben looked up
from the desk as Cass entered the room, and her eyes widened
both in shock and pleasure at seeing her friend.

'Cass! What're you doing here? Isn't it too soon to be out
of the house with Isobel yet?'

'I'm sick to death of being cooped up to be honest. His
mum's round constantly, my mum's round constantly. It's like
Piccadilly bloody station at my house! I just wanted an hour where
I wasn't with family.'

'You look a little pale. Are you sure you're OK being out
at present?' Ben frowned a little as she asked – she'd felt the same
when she'd had Grace. And had eventually been diagnosed with
Post-Natal Depression. *Is that what this is?*

Cass pouted, her face reminiscent of a moody teenager.
'I'm fine. Still a bit sore but that's no reason I have to stay house-
bound right?' She sighed before continuing, 'You're probably
right, I probably shouldn't be out yet. But I was going nuts there.
Alex is great, he's up doing night feeds and everything. And Isobel
is a dream. But I guess I just miss my independence. It feels like
my little cottage is over-run with people. It's so loud and all I want
to do is sleep for a while.'

Cass stopped talking when she realised her voice had gone up an octave and had started to sound desperate.

'Izzy's only a week old – if I feel this nutty now what's going to happen later? I don't know if I'm cut out for this.'

Cass's voice broke and tears started falling from her eyes.

Ben jumped from her seat and knelt in front of her friend, pulling her in close in a tight hug. 'Shhh, it's OK. What you're feeling is completely natural. I felt exactly the same when I had Grace. It's like all of a sudden there's this little, fragile person that depends on you, and all you want to do is wrap them in cotton wool and keep them all to yourself.'

She felt Cass sniff on her shoulder, and continued. 'You have to remember that the parents are just trying to help. This is all new for them too, and they both have their own way of doing things. Have you told Alex how you're feeling?'

'No, when he's not taking care of Izzy he's chatting to his mum or Ali. It feels like he's not even there sometimes, even though he is.'

'You need to sit and talk to him, Cass, how's he supposed to know what you're feeling if you don't tell him? Can I be honest with you?'

Cass pulled back and looked into Ben's eyes, 'Please.'

'Perhaps you need to speak to a doc too? I had feelings like this when I had Grace, I felt like I wasn't good enough, and that she would be better off without me. I felt like I was walking in the dark without a candle. I'd barely have enough energy to get washed and dressed. If it hadn't been for Aoife, I don't know what I would have done. Cass, what I'm trying to say is talk to someone before the baby blues turn into Post-Natal Depression. I mean you might be fine too, but it's worth speaking to someone, like your midwife.'

'I shouldn't be feeling like this, Ben. I'm so lucky; I have everything I could ever have dreamed of. But I'm so afraid something is going to happen to her. I sit and watch her every time she's asleep. I lie in bed listening to her breathe. I'm so scared, Ben.'

Cass dissolved into tears again, resting her head back on Ben's shoulder. After several minutes crying though, she pulled back, and looked slightly more relaxed.

'There are a lot of other women out there who feel the same as you, you know. When you get home I want you to tell Alex how you feel. When's your next home appointment?'

'Tomorrow morning,' replied Cass, wiping her hand over her eyes. A sudden rush of determination flashed over her teary eyes, 'You're right. I'll talk to Alex when I get home, and I'll tell the midwife tomorrow.' Her voice dropped to a shaky whisper, 'What if she thinks I'm nuts though?'

'She won't, Cass, I promise. If you like, I can come and sit with you for the appointment? I'm off tomorrow.'

Cass gave her head a shake, 'No, you've got enough going on at home. I can do this. Now though, I'm going to get a McDonalds, and I'm gonna head home, and tell some parents I need a little bit of space.'

'If ever you need anything you know where I am. You sure you're OK to drive? I can take you home if you like?'

'No, I'm OK honest,' Cass paused and took hold of Ben's hand. 'Thanks, Ben, you're a good friend.'

A little embarrassed, Ben replied, 'You're welcome. Now get that little bundle home to her moses basket. I'll pop up and see you over the next couple of days.'

Ben watched as Cass got to her feet and pushed Izzy out of the room. She waited a few more minutes, then picked up her mobile and selected Alex's name from the contact list.

'Alex, it's Ben. Listen, Cass has just been to the office with Izzy. I'm not wanting to interfere but you need to know what's going on ...'

After explaining the situation to Alex, Ben felt both relief and guilt. Cass was going to need a little help, and Alex was best placed to get her that help. Telling him meant that he was aware even if Cass got home and bottled out. Thoughtfully, she turned back to the computer and refocused her attention on inputting her scene notes.

9th June, 1430 hours – CSI Department, Sunderland City Centre Depot
Jacob paused outside the office door, listening as he heard sniffling from inside. He heard Ben softly tell someone that it was all OK, and for a minute he wondered what was going on.

A stab of guilt passed through him – it was rude to eavesdrop. But he'd come all this way to see Ben, believing they needed to carry on from their chat last night.

The conversation inside the office changed as he listened, and eventually he heard someone shuffle to their feet. *Shit, this is gonna look so bad.*

Using his stick, he limped round the corner out of sight. *I'm terrible! Can't believe I'm hiding. What am I, twelve?*

He waited a couple of minutes and walked back round to the office entrance. Ben was on the phone talking softly, and again he found himself listening.

I'm a bloody stalker is what I am. Pull yourself together and get in there.

As his train of thought ended, he forced himself to wander into the room, a faint flush on his cheeks the only give away that he wasn't wholly at ease.

'Hey,' he said, as Ben looked up.

He watched as a flash of desire passed over her face, masked by a smile.

'Hey back. You OK? What're you doing here?'

'I had a job round the corner and thought I'd pop in and say hi. You said last night you were on days today. Last shift?'

'Yeah I'm off after today for three whole days.'

'I erm, wondered if you fancied going out one night? Maybe for dinner or something?'

Ben froze, her breath caught in her throat. *He's asking me out! On a date! Holy crap, what do I say?*

Releasing her breath, she smiled. 'That'd be really nice, Jacob. Where did you fancy?'

'Honestly, I don't have a clue. I don't date much. There's a great Mexican in the city centre?'

'Desperado's? Yeah I know it. Sounds good. What time?'

Ben thought her voice sounded detached, a little like she was watching herself say it. It sounded polite, and aloof, and for a minute she thought she had scared him off. Her heart was pounding in her ears, and her stomach was turning somersaults. *A date? An actual date.*

Jacob smiled back. 'I could pick you up at say 7.30 p.m.? Would tomorrow be OK?'

'Can we make it Wednesday? Grace has a dance recital tomorrow and I don't think I'll be back in time?'

'Thursday is great. I'll see you then. Here's my mobile number in case something comes up.' He handed her his business card.

As Jacob left the room, Ben found herself grinning like the Cheshire cat. She plugged his number into her phone, and put the card in her purse. Inside her mind, she did a little jig. She hadn't had a proper date since well before the rape. Maybe she really was ready to start moving on.

10ᵗʰ June, 0605 hours – Tunstall, Sunderland City Centre

His eyes blurred as he stared at the computer screen. He'd been sat there for a while now, watching Clarice sleep. It would be so easy to have her now. His mouth went dry at the thought of how she would taste. He needed a release. Bringing himself to orgasm just wasn't going to cut it this time.

He grinned to himself as he pulled himself out of the leather computer chair, pulled on a pair of trousers and made his way to an address a couple of streets over.

Knocking on the door, he waited impatiently for an answer.

Finally a blurry eyed girl answered, obviously having just woken up.

Her eyes widened as she saw him standing there. Silently she opened the door to allow him access.

He knew where he was going, and made his way to the bedroom at the back of the hallway, not even noticing the dirt on the floor and the thread-bare bedclothes. He was there for one reason only, and he knew she would accommodate. She always did, the need for her next fix prevailing over any other emotion.

He didn't need to speak as she came into the room and knelt before him.

The rush of power was faint, but he still felt it, as she pulled down the zip to his trousers and took him inside her mouth.

He needed more though.

Pulling her to her feet, he twisted her round and flung her face down onto the bed. Yanking her pyjama bottoms down, he applied a condom and within seconds was buried deep inside her. Grabbing the hair at the nape of her neck, he yanked back hard, satisfaction seeping into his soul as she cried out in pain.

Huddling over her as he pounded, he put his hands round her throat and squeezed, hard.

Hearing her breath choking in her throat as she tried her best to inhale through the vice-like grip, his body shuddered. It wasn't anywhere near the scale he would feel when he finally had Clarice, but it was better than doing it himself.

He felt the woman's thin body go limp beneath him.

Dirty bitch. She loved it.

He discarded the used condom in a carrier bag lying on the floor, tucked himself back into his trousers and stood over her, staring. She wasn't a pretty girl. Her body was thin, undernourished, and he could see the ribs protruding outwards from her chest. She had yellowing bruises on the right hand side, indicating she had taken a beating in the not so distant past. Turning her over, he saw the black circles underneath her eyes, the gauntness to her cheeks. He placed two fingers against the bruises now covering her neck, checking for a pulse. It was still there; faint, but beating none-the-less. Pulling out his wallet, he peeled off two ten pound notes, threw them on the bed beside her and left.

Only six days to go now.

10th June, 1720 hours – Whitworth residence, Sunderland
'Matthew, tea's ready,' yelled John from the bottom of the stairs as he tore open the envelope in his hand. His son had, as usual, come in from school and made his way straight upstairs to his room to play on the computer games he loved so much. John had literally gotten in from work and put tea in the oven.

Getting no reply, and not hearing any sound from upstairs, John sighed, and pulled the letter out, flicking it open, as he started up the stairs. Seeing the title at the top of the page, he stopped. It read Angus, Marshall and Stead; the solicitors firm Carolyn used. Frowning, he read on.

Mr Whitworth,
We have had a formal request for full custody of Matthew Whitworth, date of birth 19.06.2005. Matthew himself has asked that he be allowed to remain with his aunt, Carolyn Fredericks. He indicated that he is suffering some emotional problems at the moment and that he had no intention of returning to your address at this time, advising that if he is taken there then he will just run away. Obviously we have concerns for Matthew because of this, and feel that it is best he remains where he is at the present time for his own safety and welfare. Whilst this letter is not saying in any way that full custody has been granted – this is something that will be discussed in depth at the hearing next week, for which you will receive a further letter. It is requested that you do not attend the Frederick's address without contacting either ourselves, or Carolyn directly to arrange for an access session.
Again, to clarify, you are allowed access to Matthew with permission, and this letter is merely a recommendation at this stage, but he was very upset

when we advised that he should initially return to you, and we feel that having him leave Carolyn's care at the present time would be detrimental to his health. He has seen a GP at Carolyn's surgery in regards to the way he is feeling at the present time, and the GP also recommended he remain where he is for the time being. As stated, we will be in contact shortly regarding initial hearing date for the full custody application by the Fredericks, and would recommend that you attain the services of your own solicitor unless you intend to represent yourself in this matter.

Sincerely,

TJT, on behalf of Angus, Marshall and Stead Solicitors

John stepped back down the two stairs and back into the hallway at the bottom, shock evident on his face.

My own son doesn't want to live with me?

John felt his fury simmering. How had he not seen this coming? Carolyn had had her claws in Matthew since Eve had gone into the home. His son had no more need of women like her in his life. And who the hell did that solicitors think they were? Advising him not to attend the address where his son was. They had no right!

What the hell do I do now though? Fuck it, I'm going to get my son. He needs to be with his father damn it!

Grabbing his car keys, John revved the engine and pulled off the driveway, his tyres squealing in protest. By the time he arrived at Carolyn's address, his anger filled the car like a thick mist. Leaving his keys in the ignition and the engine running, he jumped out and stormed up the path to the front door.

Lifting his fist he began banging loudly.

'Matthew! You come out of this house and speak to your father!'

He tried to control the tone of his voice, but failed miserably, his yells echoing down the street. Through the haze, he saw the curtains twitch in the window beside him, and froze as he saw his son staring back, fear in his eyes.

John took a step back, staring back at the eyes that were so like his own, but that were looking at him like he was some kind of monster.

He's afraid of me. I've never laid a hand on the boy, how can he be afraid?

The door opened a crack, the metal chain holding it at the required distance, and Carolyn peered out at him, her disdain evident.

'You were told to contact me if you wanted access, not just turn up screaming like a raving lunatic.'

Her voice was calm, her eyes determined.

'You've got no right to take my son. He's my boy, for God's sake,' replied John, maintaining his control despite wanting to punch the face of the woman in front of him.

'He asked to stay. He says all you do is fiddle with the computer and that you have been yelling and muttering at him. He told me you had no food in the fridge for two days. Someone needs to look after the child. With poor Eve still in the care-home, you'd think you'd care more for your son than your stupid computer contracts.'

'Who the hell do you think you are?' he hissed, bubbles of spit flying out between his pursed lips. He took another step towards the front door, he leaned in close. 'I will fight you with every fibre of my being. That boy is my *son*. He needs his father whether he realises it now or not. I will not allow a bitch like you to take over his upbringing.'

'Then I'll see you in court,' replied Carolyn curtly, before closing the door firmly in his face. He heard the latch click as she locked it for good measure. Now he had a choice, go home and prepare for the court case, or stay and kick off trying to get his son back, which was what he really wanted to do.

He wanted to make his sister-in-law pay: she obviously thought she was better than him. She'd always had that air of superiority, even when Eve had been put in the home; she'd interfered, not thinking him capable of looking after Matthew who was only four at the time. She needed bringing down a peg or two. And so did that damn solicitor! How dare they take money off people to remove children from where they belonged? Matthew belonged with him.

He glared at the house for a few seconds more, before turning and storming down the path back to his car. Slamming the door with such force he thought he might've damaged the hinges, he again revved the engine and sped down the street.

If she wants a bloody fight, she's got one. The ignorant bitch will pay, and so will the arseholes she's paying. How dare they!

Chapter Twelve
11ᵗʰ June, 1005 hours – Whitworth residence, Sunderland

John woke with a pounding headache. He had paced the house for hours the night before, thinking about what he needed to do now. Slowly a plan had begun to form.

First on his list was the solicitor – with him out of the picture, Carolyn would feel fear. And that's what he wanted, her to be so scared she was ready just to drop the case for fear of reprisal. She'd never be able to prove it was him; he'd make damn sure of that. And then, when she gave him Matthew back, he'd make her life a living hell. He'd wipe her bank accounts, blacken her credit file, put her into arrears with every bill she'd ever had. And eventually she would come crawling to him, begging him to help her. And he would take her in, ever the good brother-in-law.

Then she would learn what happened to people who tried to hurt him. She'd likely end up under the patio so to speak, but he'd enjoy getting her to that point. She would end up a shell of what she was now, and it would all be down to him.

Picking up the phone, he dialled the number at the top of the solicitor's letter.

Putting on his best phone voice, he spoke. 'Good morning. I wonder if you can help. I am after speaking to someone who signed this letter I have but unfortunately, I don't know the name. It's signed TJT?'

'OK, Sir, no problem. That would be Teresa-Jane Tulley. I can see if she's available if you would care to speak to her?'

'That's fine thank you, I'll be writing my reply. Thanks for your help.'

He smiled as he hung up the phone. Now he had her name and where she worked, it was time to find out the rest. Opening his laptop, he set to work.

11ᵗʰ June, 2005 hours – Desperado's Restaurant, Sunderland City Centre

'This is lovely. I've never been in before, have you?' asked Ben, taking a small sip from the glass of rosé in her hand. She'd looked around with interest when they had entered a few minutes ago, taking in the red and orange walls, the pictures of salamanders and sombreros and the astonishing collection of tequila bottles behind the bar. Whoever had designed the restaurant had done it well: mirrors were strategically placed to aid with lighting, tables were set to perfection and it was bustling with people.

'Yeah, a few times. Me and TJ eat out regularly and this is her favourite place.'

'It's great that you two are so close. Have you always been that way?'

Jacob nodded, 'Even before Mum and Dad died we were always like two peas in a pod. She's great. She's done so much for me. I can't imagine her ever not being there. She's pretty busy at the moment with her PhD and working for the solicitors, so we don't get together as often as we'd like. I probably see her twice a week at present.'

'Next time we go out, you'll have to invite her.' Realising what she'd said, she felt her cheeks colour. *Next time? We haven't even finished this time yet!*

Jacob just smiled. 'Definitely.'

Ben felt a hand on her arm as the waiter appeared beside them.

'Very sorry for the delay, your table is ready now if you'd like to follow me.'

11th June, 2059 hours - Angus, Marshall and Stead Solicitors, Sunderland

TJ locked the main door behind her with a soft click. She was always the first in the office and the last to leave. She was still at the stage in the law firm where she was trying to prove herself, and granted the partners had been giving her more cases to work, but she wanted it to get even better. She wanted the cases they didn't think they would win easily. She wanted something other than custody battles and property return requests.

Her PhD was well underway. Her research on the economy and impact of joblessness on the unemployed, and the laws governing the social implications of such things was not something she had initially opted for, but now she was working on it she realised how important it was to be instrumental in making the government understand that changes were required. It was slow going and difficult: it meant speaking to a lot of people who had suffered misfortune, getting their stories and understanding what they were going through.

She earned plenty to pay her bills, but already she knew she wanted to be able to work the pro bono cases more often, somehow change her law knowledge into something that could help even more people.

Double checking the door was locked, she turned and made her way to the small private car park at the rear of the offices.

John watched as she finally came round the side if the building. He could already feel the rage burning inside him. This bitch was responsible for Matthew wanting to leave him. He hated solicitors. The only person they did anything for was themselves, lining their already heavy pockets with the cash of people who had nothing better to do than to complain about other people.

He knew all too well that if Eve was capable, she would have put him through a divorce, or tried to at any rate. He never would have let it happen - women had no right putting men through that kind of humiliation - no right at all. And there should be punishment if they tried.

In that moment, he decided to change his plan. He wanted to see the fear in her eyes as he showed her where her place was, how far beneath his shoe she actually sat. Clicking open the car door, he grabbed the socket wrench from the passenger seat and strode over to her silently.

He watched as she reached her car and fumbled in her hand bag for her key.

His mind suddenly went blank, and he stopped, his face twisting into a grimace. Before he could doubt his decision, he raised the wrench above his head and swung it round hard. It connected with the side of TJ's face with a sickening crunch and she fell to her knees, dazed. Blood started pouring from the gash to the side of the head, and she looked up at John, confusion in her eyes.

'You shouldn't interfere in other people's business. I'm here to teach you that women have a place, and *that* is far below the superiority of men. Who do you think you are taking other people's lives in your hands, twisting the truth so that fathers don't have custody of their kids?'

He felt a sense of power unfurl in his stomach. This pathetic woman was kneeling before him, covered in blood from a wound caused by his own hand. She had no clue who he was, no clue why he was even there. Smiling now, he bent down and cupped her face in his hand roughly.

'You have been deemed not worthy. You will never do to another man, what you have done to me.'

With that statement in mind, John raised the wrench again and swung at her face. He heard a loud crack as it connected with the side of her face, shattering her cheek bone and jaw. She slumped to the floor with a soft whoosh of air.

John smiled as he bent down. The dim glow from the outside light in the car park was just bright enough to show the slow pool of blood forming on the Tarmac beneath her face. He *knew* he had hit her hard enough - there was no way any woman would survive a blow like that to her head. He was confident - it had said as much online, outlining the perfect angle from which to strike, explaining that the impact would likely cause swelling in the brain and eventually death.

He was sure there would be nobody around at this time of night to find her - her crumpled body would be discovered the next day by her colleagues and then the police would get involved. A niggle of doubt started to form - what if they could tell it was him? Working quicker now, he grabbed her handbag from beside her and pulled out the Radley purse. He opened it and removed the cash and cards, then flung it back down on the floor beside her. Reaching back into the bag, he pulled out her mobile phone and switched it off, placing it alongside the purse contents and into his pocket. Now the police would think it was a robbery.

Pleased with his actions, he made his way back to his car and got inside, the engine roaring to life as he turned the key. He didn't even glance at her as he pulled away from the street outside the car park.

TJ couldn't see much through the streams of blood covering her eyes. Her face was burning and she could feel her body wanting to pass out. Gritting her teeth together, she pulled a pen and notebook from her handbag and watched as the man walked to his car and got inside. The angle of the road was such that she would be able to see his registration plate as he pulled away. Angling the pen above the paper she watched. Her mind surprisingly clear, at least for the moment, she painstakingly jotted down the numbers she saw, ND13K. Before she could finish though, her mind went blank. She felt herself slipping, falling into darkness, and too tired to fight now, she let go.

11th June, 2115 hrs - Boxmania Gymnasium, Sunderland
Stan threw the heavy bag over his shoulder and left the gym. He'd had a long work out, slowly punching out the kinks in his neck and shoulders. His left cheek was a little tender and he opened his mouth and rotated his jaw from side to side. It had been a good match, taking on one of the featherweights who had been after some additional coaching for an upcoming match.

The road to his apartment was long, and usually deserted at this time of night. He heard a car squeal as it pulled away from the kerb a short way ahead, and went back to thinking.

Introducing the boxing ring at the centre was definitely one of his more fruitful plans. Brian had been patting him on the back ever since, but he knew what the kids needed. The ring was the perfect place for them to vent, and in the few days it had been up, the behaviour had dramatically improved, the lads in the centre wanting nothing more than to finish their work, then box.

It was a habit of his to know his neighbourhood; he knew what was going on where and with whom. He glanced at the rear of the solicitors as he always did when he passed – they'd had a break in a couple of months back, and since then he'd made a more conscious effort to check both that building and the other commercial ones in the street.

His steps slowed as he saw the crumpled form of a female on the floor. Dropping his gym bag, he made his way over to her and placed two fingers on her neck. Her pulse was thready and weak, pounding softly against his fingers like the soft swell of waves on sand. Careful not to touch anything else, he pulled his mobile from his pocket, pressed 141 followed by 999 and asked for the ambulance. Speaking softly, he advised them of the situation, hung up and picked up his bag. He didn't like attention, she was still alive and there was nothing more he could do for her. He could watch the events unfolding from his kitchen window if he hurried home.

11th June, 2145 hrs - Desperado's Restaurant, Sunderland City Centre
'That was fantastic,' said Ben, leaning back in her chair feeling stuffed. 'I can definitely see why this is TJ's favourite place. The enchiladas were cooked to perfection.'

'You have room for dessert?' asked Jacob, as he topped up Ben's wine glass with the sweet white she'd selected.

Ben shook her head slowly, 'Nope. I couldn't be any fuller if I tried. If I eat one more thing I may actually go pop.'

'Know how you feel. I was ...' Jacob was interrupted by his phone ringing. 'Jacob Tulley,' he said into the receiver after swiping the screen to answer. As he listened his face went pale, 'What? Where? ... OK, I'm on my way.'

'Sorry, Ben, I need to go. TJ's been in an accident. She's at the hospital.'

'I'll come with you.' Ben stood and made her way to the front desk to pay the bill, and within minutes they were in the car heading towards the Sunderland Royal.

Jacob stayed silent for the whole journey, his face taut with worry.

11ᵗʰ *June, 2200 hours – Sunderland Royal Hospital*

As they reached the hospital, Jacob parked in a disabled bay outside the Accident and Emergency ward, grabbed his stick and limped inside, Ben following closely.

She glanced around as they entered, taking in the three uniformed cops stood quietly to one side. She recognised one as Sergeant Harry Green and nodded at him as she followed Jacob to the reception.

'My name's Jacob Tulley, I believe you have my sister here? Someone just phoned me.'

'Jacob? My names Harry. Come sit down and we'll discuss what's happened.' Obviously having overheard Jacob, Harry had made his way over and interrupted. Ben saw the flash of sympathy on the face of the receptionist. This wasn't going to be good.

'Are you happy for Ben to sit with you?' asked Harry, his eyes flicking between the two. At Jacob's nod, he continued. 'Your sister was found in the car park to the rear of the solicitors. It would appear she was robbed. Whoever the offender is, he's given her a couple of good whacks round the head with something hard. The doctors have her in X-ray now.'

'A robbery? But I don't understand. TJ can take care of herself, she's done karate for years. She wouldn't have just let someone hit her.'

'It looks like she was surprised; the offender hit her from behind to the side of the head. We think he then hit her again while she was down. She's a smart girl your sister though. She managed to scribble a partial plate before she passed out.'

'Who's doing the scene?' interrupted Ben quietly.

'Craig I think. And it's being headed up by Ali McKay. He's at the scene now but when he gets here we'll head back to the nick. She's a strong one, Jacob. Am sure she will be fine.'

Jacob nodded slowly, his brow crinkled in concentration. *A robbery? Why the hell would someone want to rob TJ?*

'Mr Tulley?' asked a tired looking nurse, flashing him a brief but strained smile. It was obviously a busy night. He nodded at her silently, not quite trusting himself to speak just yet. 'If you'd like to follow me, I'll take you through to the family room. The doctor will be through to update you shortly.'

'Please, Nurse ...' he paused as he checked her name badge, 'Gina. TJ is my sister, we are very close. Please at least tell me if she's alive.' His voice threatened to break, fear running every scenario through his brain as he stood and waited for her to respond.

Despite her obvious tiredness, Gina nodded. 'She's alive. We think she has a head injury and some facial breakages, but the doctor will clarify in full when he comes through. She's not currently conscious, and we're not out of the woods yet, but trust me when I say Dr Stirling is the best there is. She's in good hands.' She placed her hand on his arm, a brief pat of comfort, then turned and led the way to the family room.

Not quite knowing what to do, Ben followed behind. If Jacob wanted her to leave he could just ask.

It took a moment for them to get seated; they were the only people inside the room. The walls were painted puce, and there were posters asking whether the NHS had provided a good service, and telling how to submit feedback. One corner held some tired and broken books and toys, and a couple of small tables were scattered with the remnants of magazines from years gone by.

Jacob sat rigidly, his back straight, his hands clenched on top of his legs. His eyes were troubled, like storm clouds rolling in on rough oceans. *What if she's not OK? What if she dies? God, please don't die, TJ.*

Feeling his pain, Ben placed a hand on top of his. 'I'm sure she'll pull through this, Jacob. From what you've told me, TJ is a strong person. You need to believe she'll be OK.'

Jacob took hold of Ben's hand and held it tightly. What she was saying made sense, but still, he was worried. He needed to see her himself, touch her hand and feel her pulse pound beneath his fingers. Visions of injured soldiers, crying and screaming in pain ran through his mind, and he felt himself starting to slip. *Not now.* His teeth ground in his mouth, and he tried to focus on his breathing. He did *not* need a PTSD flashback right now. But his mind didn't listen to his urgent plea.

He was in the base hospital. Unable to move his lower body, he was propped in bed by pillows. Screaming could be heard at the entrance, and suddenly four nurses ran inside, their faces terrified. They were followed by an Asian male carrying an AK47 rifle. Jacob couldn't move, couldn't save them. All he could do was watch as the man opened fire on the three nurses huddled together in the corner. He made no eye movement towards the one hidden beside his bed though, all he could do was hope the man finished him off and didn't look past him to see her. He stared at the man, feeling his hatred of these western people, and their healing methods. The man held his eye contact, raised his weapon and aimed it at the middle of his chest. As Jacob prepared for the gun to fire, he saw the man's eyes widen in surprise suddenly. Jacob watched as his eyes turned vacant, and the man's body slumped forward to the floor, a growing stain of red spreading over his back. Glancing at the door, he saw the armed response officer enter the room, sweeping the gun from side to side as he checked for further threats. He nodded at Jacob, and pulled the now sobbing nurse to her feet and led her away from the room, her colleagues slumped together with blood pooling, amalgamating, beneath their bodies.

The images started to fade, and Jacob focussed on Ben's words. She was telling him over and over that he was OK, and that TJ was going to be fine. He felt her thumb softly rubbing the back of his hand, just as he had done when he'd helped her through her panic attack. He felt his breathing slow back down, and realised that judging by the pain now pulsing in his jaw, he had been gnashing his teeth together throughout the episode.

'I'm OK, thank you.' He said the words quietly, his voice neutral.

'How often does it happen?'

'Depends. Usually maybe once every few months, but if I'm stressed they come more regularly. Doc says they might just disappear one day, or they might never go away.'

'You want to tell me about what you see when you go back there?'

'I do, but -' Jacob's sentence was interrupted as the door opened, and the doctor entered.

'Mr Tulley, I presume?' Dr Stirling held his hand out for Jacob to shake. He gave a quick nod to Ben, and continued. 'I believe in being straight to the point and not sugar-coating information. Your sister was assaulted by someone wielding a hard object; from the shape and colouration around the bruising I'd say something like a wrench. She has a bad concussion, fractured jaw and cheekbone and some severe bruising. She's just heading to surgery now where my colleague will put a metal plate inside her cheek to hold her bones in place whilst they heal. He will also apply some wire to her jaw to hold this in place. Obviously there are certain risks to surgery, but we are confident she will be fine given time. She will be in hospital for at least the next few days, so I don't know if you want to pop home and get her some toiletries and pyjamas. She'll be moved to a private room on the Ward 42 once she's out of recovery.'

Jacob let the information sink in. She was hurt, but she would be OK. 'Thanks, Doc, I'll pop to her flat now. How long will it be before she gets back to the ward?'

'I can't say as yet – the surgery itself isn't too complicated, it's something the surgeons perform relatively regularly. Try not to worry, Mr Tulley. You'll be seeing her soon enough.' And with that, he left the room just as he'd entered.

11th June, 2335 hours – O'Byrne residence, Sunderland

Ben stood and watched as Jacob's tail-lights turned the corner at
the bottom of the street as he made his way to TJ's house. He'd
already dropped Ben off at home, and she knew he would spend
the night at the hospital, waiting for TJ to come out of surgery and
then sitting with her through the night. He'd glared at the one
nurse who dared to suggest he head home and wait for them to
ring him on his mobile phone with an update. She'd smiled
knowingly, patted his arm, and left him in the waiting room with
Ben.

Opening the front door, Ben made her way inside with a
sigh.

'Ben, you're home earlier than I thought you would be.
Did you and Jacob not have a good evening?'

Looking at her aunt, she nodded with a soft smile. 'We
had a lovely meal, but TJ, Jacob's sister was attacked in the car park
of the place she works. We've been at the hospital the last couple
of hours.'

'Oh goodness, is the poor girl alright? What happened? Is
Jacob OK?'

'Whoa, lots of questions there. Let's have a cup of tea and
I'll tell you everything.'

'Now that sounds like a plan, I've just boiled the kettle.'

Ben followed Aoife into the kitchen and as her aunt
reached the bench, Ben cuddled her gently from behind. 'I loves
you, you know.'

'I loves you, too.' Aoife patted Ben's hand with a smile,
reaching for cups with her good hand. Ben kept hold, not wanting
to let her go, needing the closeness for a moment.

'You OK, sweetheart?' Aoife turned and looked at Ben,
studying her expression thoughtfully.

'Yeah, I'm OK. I just wish certain things didn't happen
sometimes is all. TJ getting attacked is awful. I mean, I see this all
the time at work, but I detach from it, don't let it affect me as a
person. When it happens to someone you know, it just makes it all

so real. I moved back here `cos I couldn't cope with Durham, kept constantly thinking *he* was out there somewhere looking for me. Is it naïve of me to have believed that it would be different here?'

'No it's not naïve, love. You just need to remember that there's a little bit of bad everywhere. But there's also a whole lot of good everywhere too. You've put things in place to stop anything like that happening to you again. That's all you can do, is do your best to be safe. It's all any of us can do.'

Ben reached for her tea and held the cup in both hands, leaning against the bench behind her. Her green eyes were thoughtful as she nodded slowly.

'I worry that something might happen to Gracey too. Sunderland's a big city. Maybe we'd be better living in the country somewhere?'

'You can't wrap the child in cotton wool. She's a good kid. She knows not to talk to strangers and anything else at her age would just make her scared. She has a good set of friends and she goes to a great school. You take her to the country and she loses out on all the things she should have as a child, friends who live close by, parks to play in. I think you need to stop worrying so much. You're doing a wonderful job of raising a confident, happy little girl. You can't change the bad things that the minority do – they'll always do it regardless, but you can focus on living life as best as you can.'

Aoife took a slurp of her tea. She didn't want Ben to move, would hardly see her or Grace if they did. And she knew in her heart that they both belonged where they were, at least for the time being. She'd think about looking for somewhere else if things worked out for Ben and Jacob, and call it intuition, but she already felt like it would. The two were well suited, even if they didn't see it yet. And as much as she knew that the future wasn't preordained, she just had a feeling that everything would work out fine.

Finishing her tea, Aoife pecked Ben on the cheek, and said, 'I'm heading up to bed now. There's a Victoria sponge in the

K.A Richardson

fridge, and some crispy cakes in the tin if you're peckish. Me and Grace did a little baking.'

Ben smiled after her, and downed the rest of her tea. She was too het up to sleep just yet. Making her way into the living room, she selected a book off the shelf and opened it. It was one Aoife had read recently, a classic Sherlock Holmes. She found herself drawn into the plot woven by Arthur Conan-Doyle, and pulled her knees to her chin as she sat on the sofa. Finally her eyes started to blur and tiredness seeped through her mind into her brain and made her realise it was bedtime. Glancing at the clock, she was surprised to see it read 02.02 a.m. Definitely time for bed now. She put the book on the table and checked the windows and doors before heading upstairs.

12th June, 0205 hours – Tunstall, Sunderland City Centre

Damn he wished that had been him. Though if it were, he knew he'd have done the job properly – he wouldn't have left her alive to tell her tale. The local news headlines were ablaze with an assault that had happened near the town centre, a female solicitor robbed and assaulted. The reporters had got hold of it quickly: it had happened earlier that night. He knew it would be front page in the print editions. According to the report, she wasn't dead so the story would fade past page two the day after, as was usually the way.

He would have done it better. Any fool could hit a woman with a 'metal object'. Doing what he did took skill, class even. He'd had a lot of practice, perfected his methods. And in all the time he'd been doing it, he'd never been caught. The box on his shelf held twelve envelopes now, the delectable Clarice would be thirteen. Unlucky for some, he smirked to himself. Thirteen was a good number and he liked it. He'd have to make this one extra special, maybe hint to the stupid cops, who were never wily enough to catch him, that this wasn't his first time. His smile

139

widened. Hell, he'd pretty much have to leave them a note saying this is number thirteen. They were so dense he didn't even know if they'd understand that. He'd had experience with cops - the various jobs he'd done had meant interacting with them on a fairly regular basis. He usually found that they were over-muscled idiots of less-than-average intelligence who couldn't solve a crime if you handed it to them on a plate.

Whoever had attacked the girl had guts though - CCTV all over the town centre meant the attacker could be picked up somewhere along the line. It would be mildly interesting to see the case progress. He nodded once as he added the headline to his favourites list - he'd keep an eye on it.

Feeling restless now, he flicked the screen over to Clarice's bedroom. He saw a lump wrapped up in the bedclothes and sighed. It was too late. She was already sleeping and likely wouldn't move until the next morning now. He hit sleep on his computer system and made his way into what usually stood as a spare room. Fastening the laces to his Nike Air Max trainers, he pulled his iPhone from his pocket and selected the playlist labelled 'running'. Setting the treadmill going, he hopped on and listened as the heavy rock from the likes of Rammstein and Drowning Pool filled his ears, his feet pounding as he found his rhythm. Now established, he increased the speed and focussed on the music, sweat slowly starting to pool at the small of his back. He'd be there for hours now. There was something freeing about being able to exercise whenever the need overtook him. He liked the control.

Chapter Thirteen
12th June, 0920 hours – ICU Ward, Sunderland Royal Hospital

Ali McKay made his way to the lift through the rabbit-warren of corridors in the hospital. The smell was almost overwhelming – that disinfectant used in hospitals the world over. A faint whiff of school-dinner type food drifted over from wherever the canteen was situated, adding to the nauseating scent. Ali frowned. Even through the standard hospital smells there was always an undertone of death and illness. It had always scared him as a child; he'd kicked up a fuss the size of Mount Everest on every occasion his mum had seen fit to take him there for treatment. Now it wasn't so much the fear but the memory of fear that bothered him. He'd been taken there when his dad had died, a final goodbye for a wife and gaggle of children too young to deal with such horror. He'd only ever stepped foot in hospitals when he absolutely had to since then.

In the lift, he felt his stomach stop churning and slowly return to normal. The ICU ward was on the sixth floor, and he was the only person in the lift. He hoped TJ was awake. He really needed to know if she'd seen her attacker. The CCTV was being examined by one of the uniforms, but it was arduous work and would take hours to get through footage from all the different camera angles. Then, if someone was identified as a suspect, the other cameras would have to be looked at for further intelligence anyway.

The lift dinged loudly. The automated voice told him politely that he had arrived at his destination. He walked down the corridor and buzzed at the door for entry. When a quiet-spoken female voice asked his identity, he pressed the button on the wall and answered.

'Detective Inspector McKay, North East Police. I'm here in relation to Teresa Tulley.'

The door beeped loudly and he made his way down the ward to TJ's side room. He'd attended late last night, had even sat with Jacob a while and chatted. TJ had still been unconscious after her surgery.

Reaching the door, he knocked softly, pushing the door open and glancing inside. TJ was propped in the bed, her eyes closed and the heart monitor to her side beeping it's declaration of life.

Jacob was asleep, his head resting on the side of the bed. His position didn't look comfortable. Ali didn't want to wake him, but he needed to know if TJ had woken up. He walked round the bed, and gently placed his hand on Jacob's arm.

Almost in slow motion, Jacob woke, grabbed Ali's hand and had him on his knees in a move that was so smooth that Ali almost doubted he had actually had his hand on Jacob's arm in the first place. He gasped as pain shot through his wrist.

Through gritted teeth, he said, 'Tulley, it's Ali. Now let me go.'

He watched as Jacob's eyes widened in shock, saw the recognition set in and then the horror as Jacob realised what the soldier in him had done. He let go of Ali's hand.

'I'm so sorry, Ali. Army background, PTSD. Sometimes I don't know what's real and what isn't. No excuses though, I shouldn't have grabbed you like that.'

'You're a good guy to have in your corner in a fight, Tulley. Don't worry about it – it's not the first time I've almost cried like a girl and no doubt it won't be the last. PTSD huh? Must make life tough.'

Jacob sighed. 'Sometimes, yeah. It's like one minute you're fine, just going about your daily business. Then the next day it's bam, you're back in Kandahar or Afghanistan or wherever, just for a second. But that second is as real in your mind as the one before.' He patted TJ's hand softly, 'She knows how to deal when I have an episode. Always has, even before she spoke with my counsellor and learned some of the calm techniques.'

'Did she wake up last night after I'd left?'

'No, she's been out since last night. The doc said her body needed time to process what had happened.'

'She's actually awake now.' TJ's voice was croaky and muffled, her facial movements restricted by the wire in her jaw. 'Need water.'

Jacob grabbed a plastic cup and filled it from the jug on the stand, popped in a straw and held it to TJ's lips. She sucked for a few seconds, and leaned back into the pillows.

'How come I'm here?' she asked, directing her gaze at Jacob.

'You were attacked last night. In the car-park at the solicitors. Do you remember anything?'

TJ's face paled to an even lighter shade. 'Attacked? By who?'

'That's what we're hoping you can tell us. I'm DI Ali McKay, North East Police. Can you tell me what happened from the time you left the office?'

TJ closed her eyes for a moment. 'It was late. I'd been working on the Ferguson case and everyone else had left ages before. I was the last to leave so I had to set the alarm. I locked the back door and walked to my car. That's ... pretty much all I remember.' Her face twisted into a grimace and she gasped. She looked to Jacob for help.

His nod was almost imperceptible as he got to his feet, grabbed his stick and left the room to find the nurse.

'If you remember anything else will you give me a call? My name's on this card. I'll leave you in peace, Miss Tulley,' said Ali as he went to leave.

'Wait. I heard him say something, I think he said that he was a father and we had wronged him. It's possible it's a client.'

'Anything else stand out about him?'

'His eyes. They were flat. Creepy looking. Kind of like sharks eyes.'

'Ok. If you remember anything else please call me, any time day or night. My mobile's always on.'

As Ali left the room Teresa groaned again: her face felt like she'd walked into a steam roller. The nurse followed Jacob back in, and injected some morphine into the cannula in TJ's hand, and before she knew it she was floating on a sea of clouds.

12th June, 1220 hours – Whitworth residence, Sunderland

John got out of bed and stretched, yawning loudly. That was the best he'd slept in forever. When he had got home it had been late, but he'd checked the headlines persistently until news of the attack had been forthcoming. He'd bookmarked the article and had read it multiple times through the night. He was still buzzing, his arm ached from the force with which he'd struck her head and when he closed his eyes he could still see the blood. Unfortunately, she'd survived, not died as he'd hoped. She wouldn't be the same though. He'd hit her with so much force that her mind would be addled – there was no way she'd be able to identify him.

Striding downstairs he popped the kettle on and checked his laptop. He already had a list of jobs outstanding –working from home as an IT technician meant people asked for his help whenever the need took them.

He loved computers. It gave him a sense of enjoyment knowing he could solve problems. What he didn't like was the fools who needed the IT support. Half of them didn't even know what the alt key was. He was glad he worked online and on the phone – if people could see his face when he dealt with those buffoons he'd end up getting the sack.

He checked the emails and organised them into a list, most urgent at the top. It was going to be a long afternoon, but he had enough time to reread the article. He brought up his bookmarks and had a quick scan. His stomach clenched in response to certain key words as he read: attack, injury, life-threatening. It felt good knowing he was the cause.

If that bitch hadn't stuck her nose into my business, then she wouldn't be lying in a hospital bed now.

Turning his attention back to the list of emails, he started work.

12ᵗʰ June, 1510 hours – Tunstall, Sunderland City Centre
It had been several days now since he had obtained the lesson notes off Clarice. It was approaching time to give them back to her so no one was any the wiser when she did not go home. No-one had seen his face and nothing would point towards him. He'd been into the town several times now to scope out the club where he knew she'd end up. There would definitely be no room for error.

Clicking open his fake social network profile, he typed her a quick message asking if they could meet up so he could give her the notes back. He signed it with a smiley face: unthreatening, docile, the norm. Even in his forties he could keep up with the youth of today. His boyish looks helped of course. Most people presumed him to be late twenties, maybe early thirties at a push.

He sat lost in thought for a moment, and was almost surprised when his computer pinged at him. One of the database searches for Bree had come back, and with a positive result no less. Grinning from ear to ear, he opened the report and scanned the information.

Well, well, wonders never cease. She's right here in sunny Sunderland. Although, she goes by a different name now. As soon as I'm done with Clarice I'll go looking, see how old Bree has been for all the years since we last met.

Now he knew she lived in Sunderland, and the name she was using, she'd be easy to trace. It'd be a piece of cake to find out where she was living, who she was shacked up with, and even better, it'd be simple to restore the balance. She would die as she should have all those years before. Momentarily, he wondered if her breasts were still as fantastic, whether they still bore his mark of possession. He felt himself growing hard just thinking about it.

Ruefully, he acknowledged the time and changed his train of thought. Within seconds he was soft, ready to leave the dark comfort of his computer room and head off to the day job. He quite enjoyed it really, had been doing it for some time in one form or another. Despite having access to all the money he could possibly want, sometimes it was nice to go and earn it for himself. This was one of those days. He grabbed his large black bag on his way past the living room, and threw his jacket inside.

Today is a good day.

12th June, 1935 hours – O'Byrne residence, Sunderland

'Mummy, you know the man who was here the other night? When can I meet him properly? You said I could.' Grace was lying in bed, propped up on her elbows staring at Ben.

Ben felt a rush of love – she knew every parent thought their child was special but hers really was. Even at just four, Grace was old beyond her years. She listened intently and picked things up from conversations that a lot of adults would miss.

'Soon. His sister TJ is poorly in hospital, remember? So he's probably going to be busy looking after her. And she needs him, doesn't she? There'll be plenty of time for you to meet him later. Do you think I should finish the story now?'

'Is TJ being a big girl? Like when I fell over and scraped my hand the other day. I didn't cry did I, Mammy? You said I was a big girl. Is TJ being big too and not crying?'

Ben sighed a little and put the book down. Grace was plainly too awake to go to sleep yet. Smiling at her daughter, she said, 'Come give mammy a cuddle, we'll sit on the chair and chat for ten more minutes but then it's bed time, OK?'

Grace flashed her the biggest smile and clambered out of bed and into Ben's waiting arms. She wiggled for a moment getting comfortable, and rested her head on her mum's shoulder.

Ben planted a kiss on her forehead, 'You, young lady, are spoilt rotten. Now, you asked about TJ. I'm sure TJ is being a big girl and not crying, just like you were when you fell down. Next question.'

'Where's my daddy?'

Ben froze in shock. Grace had never once asked about her father – where was this coming from? Hell, where was it going?

'You were brought to Mammy by the angels as a special gift. I was very sad, you see, and you were brought to help me smile again. Your Daddy wasn't from Sunderland, he was from very far away, and he left before I could tell him you were here. I didn't know where he went so I couldn't let him know.'

'You were lost, Mammy.' Grace's voice was very solemn as she said the words, so very grown up, and for a second Ben thought her heart might actually crack in two. Not trusting herself to speak, she nodded.

'Jacob is lost too. But we'll show him the way home won't we, Mammy?'

'Jacob's not lost, sweetheart. He's at the hospital with his sister, remember? He knows his way home.'

'No, he's lost. But we'll help him,' said Grace softly, snuggling further into Ben's shoulder.

Ben looked down and saw Grace's eyelids flutter softly. She was finally getting tired. Content though, Ben set the chair rocking back and forth. She'd put her to bed in a minute. She sat contemplating Grace's words. *Was Jacob lost? Has my little girl picked up on something so deep that most adults would miss it? Or was it just an innocent question from a four year old?*

She didn't even notice her own eyes closing, her mind going blank with the rocking motion as she dropped off to sleep.

The bedroom door suddenly clicked open, light from the landing flooding into the bedroom and she jerked awake, blinking her eyes furiously as they adjusted to the bright invasion. She was surprised to see Jacob's shadow filling the door frame.

'One second,' she whispered quietly, trying to manoeuvre herself so she could pick Grace up without waking her.

'Let me,' his voice was soft and he suddenly appeared in front of her. She felt his arms brush against her sides as he scooped her daughter up as though she weighed nothing more than a feather, and lowered her down onto her mattress. It was

147

only as Ben stood that she realised his stick was propped against the chair, and she watched as it went to topple, anticipating the clatter but unable to prevent it. In an equally smooth motion, though, he grabbed it and moved off as she stepped forward to tuck the light summer duvet round her daughter.

They left the bedroom and Ben closed the door with a click.

'Sorry to intrude, Aoife told me to come straight up.'

'It's fine,' her reply sounded false somehow, hollow. 'Cuppa?' she added brightly, doing her best to ignore the pounding in her chest. *What the hell is it about this guy that has me all to pot?*

'So, how's TJ?' asked Ben, handing him a steaming mug.

'Well she's already moaning about wanting to leave the hospital so not too bad. She has to keep the wire in her jaw for a few weeks, the plate in her cheek a bit longer. Her concussion is easing but they want to keep her in for observations again. Her blood pressure keeps dipping apparently, which is a side effect of concussion. I think they're doing it to stop her getting to her feet too. She was already making sounds about going back to work. The doctors have told her she needs at least two weeks off and she's spitting feathers.'

'Hard though, being cooped up in a hospital bed. Gives you too much time to think.'

'You're not wrong,' Jacob smiled at her. His smile suddenly turned into a frown though. 'She thinks the guy who did it is a client, or at least someone connected to a client. She didn't remember much when she woke up this morning but now she's said he told her she wasn't worthy, that she would be taught a lesson in where women should be, which is well below men apparently. Ali is treating it like a hate aggravated assault. She has to have injury photos taken tomorrow at the hospital.'

'Does she think it was hate related then? I might get asked to photograph – I'm on days tomorrow and I think we're a bit thin on the ground. She wouldn't mind would she?'

'Why would she mind?'

Before Ben could answer, a loud crash sounded in the living room, followed rapidly by a scream.

Ben was up and out of the kitchen door before Jacob had even realised she'd got up.

'Aoife? Are you OK? What the hell happened?' asked Ben, her voice shrill with panic as she saw her aunt on the sofa and took in the broken glass spread all over the floor, and the breeze now coming in through the hole in the window.

'I think I dropped off to sleep. Jesus, Mary and Joseph, I thought someone was breaking in. I screamed to scare them off.'

'What? Did you see anyone?' Ben walked to the window and peered out onto the driveway and the street beyond.

'No, love. Just heard the crash.'

Ben saw the stone lying on the floor by the TV and picked it up thoughtfully. 'The lights are all on, and there's the porch light outside which is also on. A burglar would be nuts to think he could get in here unnoticed using a brick. More than likely it was just kids playing silly beggars.' Her heart was pounding though, echoing loudly in her ears as she spoke the words with a calmness she didn't feel.

'This little lady must've woke up with the noise,' interrupted Jacob, holding a scared looking Grace on his hip as he leaned heavily on the one stick he was using to navigate. 'I found her in the hall.'

'Don't put her down, there's glass everywhere. It'll cut her feet to shreds. Let me get the dustpan,' fretted Aoife, heading into the kitchen.

'Grace, would you mind letting Jacob take you back upstairs while Mammy cleans up this mess? I'll be up in a minute, OK?'

Grace nodded silently, her small hands woven into the fabric of Jacob's shirt as she held on tightly. Aoife came back in and handed her the dust pan and brush.

'I'll ring the police while you do that. That was nice of Jacob, taking Grace back to bed.'

Ben ignored the comment and began to sweep. In no time at all she was tipping the fragments into the plastic bin. Aoife had disappeared into the kitchen, presumably to put the kettle on while she phoned the control room. Ben took the opportunity and made her way back upstairs.

Jacob was sitting in the rocking chair, Grace already asleep and snuggled into his shoulder. He smiled at Ben as she entered, 'Sorry. She fell asleep and I didn't know how to put her to bed without waking her from this position.'

This time, Ben scooped her up and placed her on the mattress, pulling the duvet up and kissing her on the forehead. 'She'll be full of questions tomorrow, but for now she'll sleep. Oh to be a child again, huh?'

'Do you have wood big enough to fit that window lying around anywhere? I can fix it up until it gets repaired tomorrow? Save you phoning repair guy out?'

Ben scrunched her eyes for a moment in concentration. 'Yeah, I think there's some plywood out in the garage. From memory, we used to put it on the grass under the tent when I camped in the garden as a kid.'

'Great. Where's the garage?'

'Outside the back through the kitchen. You sure you don't mind?'

'Positive,' replied Jacob, making his way back down the stairs.

Chapter Fourteen
13th June, 0840 hours – CSI Department, Sunderland City Centre Depot

'Hey, Ben,' said Ali, entering the CSI office with a grin. 'You busy? How'd your class go last night?'

Ben looked up from the carpet of paperwork concealing her desk and gestured towards it with her hand. 'Unfortunately busy, yea. Class was cancelled as Jacob couldn't get someone to cover. How can I help?'

'I know you have a personal connection to TJ and her brother. Would it be OK if you pop out to take some injury photos? I know it's a pain when they're not in the studio `cos the lighting and what not is unpredictable, but I could use some now and later photos? I've already mentioned it to Kevin and he's happy for you to attend if you're not too busy. He said you were on writing statements today.'

'It's fine, Ali. I don't mind at all. I'll pop over to the hospital later this morning – want me to print off your copy of the disc when I get back?'

'Please,' he said. 'Can I be cheeky and ask for your statement too? If I get it all at once it makes it easier to keep track of.'

As Ben nodded again, he stood from his position perched on the edge of the desk and thanked her before leaving the room.

Ben felt a little like a storm chaser when she was around Ali. It was like the guy had two settings, whirlwind and tornado. Everything he did was at full pelt. She quite often felt like she'd be left behind in a trail of dust if she ever had to keep up with everything the man did.

13th June, 1105 hours – Ward 42, Sunderland Royal Hospital

'Doc, I'm fine. I just want to go home.' TJ was fully aware she sounded like a whiny child but she had really had enough of lying in bed surrounded by the noises filling the hospital ward. The doctor was just about to reply when a loud clatter sounded from the doorway. Glancing round, they saw Ben manoeuvre around a nurse who was picking up utensils off the floor.

'What on earth is all this noise?' asked the doctor, making his way into the corridor to help her.

'Hey, TJ. I'm Ben. I've been asked to come and take some photos of your injuries. Is that OK?'

'Yeah, sure. Ben as in Jacob's Ben, right?' TJ's question was shrewd and she watched as Ben's cheeks flushed with colour.

'I ... erm, I know your brother, yes.'

'You *know* my brother?' TJ tried to inject a note of seriousness into her tone. *This was too easy!* Her wicked sense of humour was howling at the sight of Ben stumbling over fitting the flash gun to her camera as she thought about how to respond. 'I'm pulling your chain. Don't worry. Jacob's a big boy. He can take care of himself. It's nice to see him interested in someone to be honest. He likes you a lot.'

'He does?' Ben tried for a neutral tone and was horrified when she realised how corny her voice sounded. She was like the kid who just got told her school boy crush liked her back. She seriously needed to rein herself back a little. She barely knew him for goodness sake. 'Are you ready?' All business now, Ben smiled at TJ who nodded silently.

'I'll start by taking one of your face so just look straight ahead. Then I'll move to your injuries. You'll need to help me by holding the scale if you don't mind.'

Ben double checked the camera settings and set to work, covering all angles and injuries in a matter of minutes. 'You'll need to arrange to come down for some further photo's when you've had the wire and plate removed. It's just so we can show from start to finish.'

'Yeah, no problems. I'll have Jacob arrange something with you directly if that's OK?'

Ben nodded, her shyness finally leaving her. She bit her lip, wanting to ask TJ about the PTSD but not quite knowing where to start.

Intuitively though, TJ picked up on it. 'He's never violent, he loses himself in the visions sometimes but I've never known him lash out. He told me about your past, I hope you don't mind. Actually, in fairness to Jacob, he thought I was asleep at the time so he didn't *tell me* tell me.'

'That's not what I was going to say. I didn't think he would lash out for one moment. I was just going to ask how you bring him round? Is it just a case of talking to him or is there a special technique that you've learned?'

'It's pretty much the same as for your panic attacks to be honest – focus on breathing, talking calmly, and body contact helps so hold his hand or squeeze his arm. He can often prevent them himself now but it's worse when he's upset.'

'That's what he said. Sorry, I didn't mean to be intrusive.'

'It's not intrusive, Ben. You don't get if you don't ask.' TJ gazed at Ben thoughtfully. 'Don't hurt him, OK? He's got this major hang up. He thinks he's not attractive and that he can't look after a woman. It's not true, obviously, but it's how he feels. I've never been able to get him past that. But, I have a feeling you may.'

'I have no intention of hurting him. Truth be told, we both have issues. I don't even know where it's going yet, but I do like him. I guess time will tell if it grows into anything else.'

TJ nodded in response, then grimaced as her mouth tried to smile. 'Darn wires. Keep forgetting they're there then they pull at my face. It's the weirdest feeling.'

'I bet. Well, I'd best get off. Have a mile-long list of stuff to do today.'

TJ watched as Ben left the ward, her back straight and her camera case thrown over one shoulder, banging off her hip.

13th June, 1125 hours – *Whitworth residence, Sunderland*

John sat staring at the computer screen in front of him, his gaze focussed on the blinking mouse arrow without actually seeing it. He hadn't been able to sleep when he'd gotten in the night before.

His mind kept flashing over what had happened in the car park, replaying the events over and over.

His eyes were troubled and bloodshot. *What the hell have I done?*

After killing Ann, it had seemed like natural progression, moving onto someone else, the burn to see their face taking over almost to the point where it consumed him. But it hadn't given him what he wanted. He had seen fear in TJ's eyes as he swung the wrench round, but it wasn't fear he craved. He wanted the buzz he had felt as the car had hit Ann's legs, he wanted the satisfaction of hearing the thud as the car had impacted. Hurting TJ hadn't been the same. And she hadn't died.

The whole city was on alert now. A photofit of his description had been circulated through the news, and it kept flashing up on the news website he was hovering over at the present time. It looked nothing like him, and everything like him. *What the hell am I going to do? Why didn't I research properly – it was obvious there would be CCTV in the city centre.*

A little voice set up niggling in the back of his mind. *Murderer. You're going to get caught.*

It wasn't supposed to be like this. It was supposed to have been smooth sailing, get in, get it done, get out. He didn't know where this over-analysis had come from, but he didn't like it. The niggling voice grew louder, drowning out even the ring of the telephone.

What am I going to do now?

A sudden burst of anger caused him to swipe his arm across the table, sending the cold cup of coffee clattering to the ground, splashing brown liquid up the bottom of his trousers and the wall behind.

I'm never going to see Matthew again. No court would ever allow a murderer near a boy. *This is all Eve's fault. Damn her for not dying, for going into that fucking home. If she'd died in the first place none of this would have happened.*

His mouth set in a grim line as he pondered. Clarity followed a moment later - if Eve was to die now then balance would be restored. Matthew would crave his father's love and attention if his mother was no longer around. It would be difficult, harder than knocking someone down or hitting them with a wrench. All suspicion had to lead far away from him. A smile flittered across his lips - maybe it should point towards Carolyn. Maybe Matthew's aunt wouldn't be as innocent as she seemed. The courts would have to award him full custody if Matthew's aunt was accused of killing his mum.

Turning his head back to the laptop, his smile widened. Now he had a plan.

13th June, 1320 hours – Tunstall, Sunderland City Centre

He loaded up the screen as he threw the things he needed into his black bag. Time for one last look at Clarice - there was loads going on today and it would be his last chance for a while. Her time table showed she was on free time for the next couple of hours. It was more than he could hope that she'd be at home. It was getting closer to her night out, closer to the time when he would have her as his, taste the skin that smelled faintly of coconut, and touch the hair that shone so brightly in the sunshine.

She had no idea - was still flattered by his passing attention in fact. That was the trouble with women, they took everything to heart. He had sent her the occasional message, innocent comments that she would construe as being all about her. *Stupid cow hasn't even noticed I've not been in the classroom. She just keeps chatting and flirting. Like they all did. Every single one of them. Sidelong glances from the sides of their eyes, tiny smiles aimed just at me. She won't flirt once I have her though. She'll cry and beg for mercy. Like they all did.*

His brow furrowed as Clarice's bedroom came into focus, and then he grinned. She was lying on the bed face down, her head buried in some book or other. The camera angle caught the swell of her breasts as they were pushed up towards her chin, her neck lengthening as she stretched. His breath caught a little in his throat. She truly was divine. She would satisfy him, she had to. It didn't matter that he'd had to become more experimental with each one since Bree, that it was getting harder to achieve his goal with each one. Clarice was *different*. She was the one he had been watching for, he was certain of it.

He paused for a moment, staring at Clarice as memories flooded his mind. His first time with a woman hadn't been what he had expected. He'd lived with his father long enough to realise that women were playthings, but his father had decided he needed initiating early. Said a man should always know how to treat a woman, and then had proceeded to beat the crap out of whichever whore he had been with at the time. His father had beaten the teeth from her very mouth, and then called his son into the room.

He always thought his first time with a woman would be painful for her, had dreamt about hurting even back then. What he hadn't realised was that it could hurt him. He had entered the room apprehensively, expecting his father's fist at the side of his head. Instead the old man had been sitting in the dirty rocking chair by the window, his trousers round his ankles. The whore of the moment was tied to the bed. She alternated alcohol-fuelled tirades of abuse with pleas for release, all the while spraying spittle and blood from her smashed mouth. 'It's your turn, boy,' his father had sneered, 'if you can even get that wiener to stand up on its own.'

The whore had looked at him then, this mini me of the monster that had beaten her and hurt her, but that kept her fuelled with the vodka she preferred, and the crack she partook of on a daily basis. She had licked her blood covered tongue over her lips, and cackled at him loudly. 'He couldn't get it up if he tried, could you, sweetness?'

He remembered feeling calm as he approached the bed. He was scared, both of what his father would do if he did what he wanted to the whore, and of what he'd do if he didn't. He knew the basics, he was thirteen after all. But it wasn't the thought of sex that turned him on. Even back then, the sight of the blood covering the whore's mouth, the bruising to her jaw where his father had thumped her, this was what had turned him on.

Blanking out his father's evil leer, he knelt on the bed between her spread legs, raised his fist, and for the first time in his life, he felt pleasure. His father had ended up pulling him off the whore, not perturbed at all by the fact his son wanted to hurt her, not fuck her. His father had thrown him into the hall, then shut the door behind him as he went back to her.

But by then, the damage was done. If it hadn't been preordained by the constant abuse of his childhood, being let loose to vent his anger against his father's whore had taught him that he got pleasure from causing pain. His only regret at the time had been that the whore had lived. *But they don't live now.*

His eyes refocused on Clarice, and the present. *It's your turn, bitch.*

Chapter Fifteen
14th June, 0850 hours – Newstead Residential Home, Sunderland
John waited at the back of the building until the last staff member stubbed out her cigarette and entered through the insecure fire door. Most people knew the staff used this area as an ashtray, despite the rules that there was no smoking on the home's grounds.

He caught the door before it clicked shut, and silently made his way inside.

He'd already checked the staff list before he left the house, and knew that the home was on minimal staff today, many of them off sick with a nicely timed sickness bug. Which worked well in his favour. Fewer staff meant it was busier for them. At this time of day, they'd have served breakfast and would be slowly but surely doing the rounds across the two floors of residents. Personal care they called it. In reality it was wiping arses and cleaning dirty underwear.

It gave him the perfect opportunity to slip in unnoticed and start implementing his plan.

By the end of the day, Eve would be dead. Of this he was certain.

He made his way to boiler room, slipped inside and tucked himself into a corner to wait. Shift changeover was at 4 p.m. – that was when he would implement his plan. With the machines droning beside him and his mind finally at peace with the knowledge of what would make his whole situation better, John fell asleep.

14th June, 1320 hours – Tunstall, Sunderland City Centre
Touch-typing, he replied to Clarice's message on Facebook.

'Am good thanks. It's 2moro ur out in town isn't it? I'm out with some of the lads. Might see you out.'

The best laid plans required preparation; if she thought he was going to be out anyway, it would make it all the easier to lure her away. He'd been monitoring her conversations with friends about the upcoming night out, and knew they were planning to end up in Retox nightclub. He'd already scoped out the club, knew where the bouncers stood and where the CCTV blind spots were.

Her prompt reply made him smile: 'Yea starting in the Tannenbaum then going around the town. Cocktail hour in the Lucky Duck from 8 p.m. – u like cocktails?'

It couldn't be easier to plan a murder when the victim was sucking it up as much as Clarice was. He'd have her in his hands soon enough. And then he would make her pay for her stupidity. No self-respecting woman should throw herself at a man, hell a self-respecting woman shouldn't be throwing themselves at any one. Clarice was still young, still learning the ropes. He felt his scar pull as he smiled widely at the screen.

Not long now.

14ᵗʰ June, 1835 hours – Thompson residence, Sunderland

Clarice pulled her hair back into a ponytail and dragged a clean t-shirt over her head. She made her way into the kitchen where Gill was busily chopping carrots.

'Hey, sweetheart. Would you mind peeling those spuds for me?' asked Gill, nodding her head towards the pile of potatoes on the side.

'Sure. I'm going into town in the morning; need a new outfit for tomorrow night. Do you need anything getting?'

Clarice picked up the peeler and started removing the outer skin from the spuds, listening to the track playing quietly on the radio. She smiled a little; Bruno Mars singing about being lazy. It had been ages since she'd heard that song.

'I think I'm OK,' Gill began, then paused before adding, 'Actually could you get me a bag of those little cheesy biscuit things from the pound shop? And maybe some popcorn? Was thinking we might have a movie night on Monday if you're up for it?'

Clarice grinned widely. 'Wine and pizza?'

Gill nodded.

'You betcha. I'll sort some bits out. We haven't had movie night in ages!' Putting the peeler down, Clarice turned and grabbed Gill in a bear hug from behind. 'I love you, Gill. It'll be great! Who do you have a fancy for, then? The new Fast and Furious movie is out now, a bit of Vin Diesel and Paul Walker? Or there's the Hobbit movie – we haven't seen the latest instalment yet? Or there's even the old faithful classics like Dirty Dancing?'

'Why don't you choose a couple? You take care of the movies and I'll sort the food and wine? You did say you're on study day on Tuesday right? I don't want you getting drunk on a school night.'

'Yup, study day is Tuesday. I'm already well ahead though. The only assignment I've got at the minute is the one due in three weeks, and I've done all my prep and am about two thirds of the way through the write-up.'

'So where is it you're going tomorrow night, then?'

'We're starting at the Tannenbaum then doing the rounds. Think the plan is to end up in Retox. I don't want to be too late back though. Early class Monday morning.'

'Who you going with? People off your course?'

'Yeah. You remember Jess, with the short blonde hair? And you know Amy and Philippa. There'll be more turn up but those are the definites. We might even be meeting up with some of the boys off the course.'

The last comment was nonchalant, and Gill happened to look up at the same time as a faint blush passed over Clarice's cheeks. She narrowed her eyes thoughtfully.

'Boys, huh? Any particular boy you have your eye on?'

'Well, there is one guy I quite like. He's called Gareth. He's a mature student. We've been chatting.'

'Mature student? Just how mature are we talking?'

'I dunno, probably about thirty, I think. He's on my course.'

'Ok, well you know what I always say. And ring me if you need a lift home. I don't like the thought of you getting taxis on your own.'

'I know, Gill, if I can't be good be careful. If I don't get a cab with the other girls I'll give you a ring, but don't wait up, OK. Don't want you cursing me when you're tired at work on Monday.'

They both went back to their peeling, a comfortable silence between them as the radio finished with Bruno and moved onto the more classic Queen.

14th June, 1850 hours – Newstead Residential Home, Sunderland

John had woken a few hours back. Despite the noise of the machines, it had been the deepest sleep he'd had in forever. He'd scoped the home silently, hiding from staff in several of the rooms that were supposed to be kept locked. They were so rarely used that the staff never actually checked.

He felt his stomach grumble, and wished that he'd thought ahead and brought some food with him. Maybe once he was done he'd treat himself to a takeaway on the way home.

He grabbed the small bag he'd rested his head on, and searched through it. A towel, a thin cord, and even a knife just in case his plan didn't work. Zipping it shut once more, he quietly left the boiler room, and made his way to his wife's room. He knew she was last on the care register. Whoever was on duty would pop in at 7 p.m. to attend to her personal care, set the TV to whichever channel his wife wanted, and serve her a cup of tea and biscuits. They then wouldn't be back until 9 p.m. unless his wife buzzed for attention.

He felt the flutter of butterflies in his stomach – he was finally going to be rid of her, the bane of his life. The woman who had managed thus far to avoid the fate that he knew should have already occurred. Then he would get Matthew back and everything would be fine. He knew that Carolyn had been scheduled to visit Eve earlier that afternoon; it had been logged on the system as she had wanted to take Eve shopping to choose a birthday present for Matthew who was eleven in a few days.

He had Carolyn's earrings in his bag, earrings that had been left at his house many years before. They had her DNA on them. He knew how important DNA was; he'd watched the occasional cop show. He just needed to ensure that the earring was wrapped in the towel when he was done and the police would join the dots together.

He also had a couple of Carolyn's hairs, obtained earlier that morning as he discreetly 'broken' into her house using the key he had taken from Eve's keychain. He'd known Matthew would be at school, and that Carolyn worked mornings in a local shop. The hairbrush had been right there on the hall table, almost begging him to take it. So he had.

The final piece of the puzzle was a letter he had hand written that morning, crumpling the paper and fraying the creases, making it look like it had been written months before. The content was simple, it told Carolyn that he couldn't continue their affair, that it wasn't fair on Eve as they were still married. It said that as long as Eve was alive, they would never be able to be together and that she would just have to accept it, as Eve was his main concern and responsibility. It had sickened him writing it. As if *he* would ever shag an overweight, hormonal sack like that. But it served its purpose as evidence of a convincing motive for the terrible crime that 'Carolyn' was about to commit.

John reached Eve's room at a little after 7 p.m., peeking in the window on the door to see his wife propped up on the bed, some wildlife programme on the TV. He clicked open the door, and walked inside, smiling as his wife's eyes widened in shock.

Without him noticing, she managed to press the buzzer in her hand just as he approached. She knew he was there to hurt her, Carolyn had told her about the custody case before even applying, wanting to be sure Eve had no objections to her sister looking after her son. Eve's happy tears on hearing that Matthew would no longer be in the grips of her husband, had told Carolyn that she was doing the right thing.

She dropped the buzzer on the bed, her eyes wide in fear. *Hurry, please hurry.*

He thought she didn't remember everything. He thought she was stupid. But she wasn't - not now. She had been stupid staying for all those years; putting up with the beatings; accepting sex when he wanted it, even if she didn't, allowing Matthew to be parented by the monster that was his father. Now though, she had a counsellor who had been teaching her to communicate again, helping her. She was almost there too, almost at the point where her words would form as she wanted them to. And she'd had every intention of reporting the bastard she was married to as soon as she got the opportunity.

He strode towards her, knocking the buzzer from her hand, confident she hadn't pressed it. She was too stupid to believe he would kill her in the home, and too afraid.

But then the niggle of doubt he'd had in the back of his mind since the look she had given him after he'd killed Ann, took hold and grew bigger as he stared at his wife. Gone was the fear he was so used to seeing. Her eyes were suddenly full of defiance. He could hear loud and clear her silent scream of 'FUCK YOU'.

Taking a deep breath he advanced, he didn't care whether she was scared or whether she shouted at the top of her silent voice. He was there to kill her, to make sure Carolyn got the blame, and to get his son back. There was no way he would let his son be raised by a single woman, a boy needed his father. He should know, he'd missed *his* since the day he'd been taken into care.

John opened the bag and pulled out the towel, the one he'd removed from Carolyn's airing cupboard that very morning, the one that smelled of that ridiculous perfumed washing powder she used for all her clothes and linen.

'This is all your fault. If you'd just died in the first instance like you were supposed to then I wouldn't have to do this now. You should know though, this is Carolyn's towel. Covered in her hair. Your sister killed you, Eve, and your son will be with me for the rest of his life. He'll grieve with me over the death of his beloved mother, my wonderful wife. And the bond between father and son will grow strong once more.'

His voice was calm, his eyes flat, devoid of emotion as the need to kill took over. He placed the towel over Eve's face, pressing down hard, listening to her whimper as she tried her best to struggle.

Her body was weak, though. It didn't allow for much movement without help.

She felt her lungs burn as they struggled to inhale oxygen, felt searing pain in her face as her husband pressed down with all his might, and she thought of her son. Matthew's face filled her mind, his young, troubled eyes giving away the horrors he had seen as a child.

She had to hold on.

She had to be there for him. She couldn't let this monster raise her son. Mustering every bit of her strength, she flung her body to the side, gasping in air as she landed on the carpeted floor, pain shooting through her shoulder as something gave with a loud crack.

Before she knew it though, he was back. Straddled over her like John Wayne on his horse, placing the awful towel over her face again. She tried to scream, but all that escaped was a pitiful grunt. *I'm going to die. He's actually going to kill me.*

Neither of them heard the door click open.

John only realised someone was in the room with them when he felt huge muscular arms wrap around his torso, pinning his arms to his side, as a deep voice bellowed, 'Betty, call the police, NOW!'

He felt himself go weightless as the man-mountain pulled him away from Eve and a guttural scream rose in his throat. 'Noooo, she must die. Let me go.'

John struggled but it was useless; the man who held him was the only male carer in the home. He knew the man's sheer size had almost meant he didn't get employed at the home when he'd applied a few years ago. The manager initially imagined the residents would be afraid of him. But he'd won her over with his gentle charm, his manner with the patients and his willingness to help.

George Ashton was one of those rare gentle giants. The residents loved him, and he loved them right back. He read them newspapers and stories and regaled them with his hobbies of magic and singing. He was in short, the best fit the home could have asked for. And right now, they were lucky he was there.

He held John immobile, as though he weighed nothing more than a big bag of feathers, ignoring the primal screams coming from the man as he struggled against the vice that held him tightly.

Betty ran into the room suddenly, having called the police from the phone at the end of the corridor. Ignoring George and John, she made her way straight round the bed to Eve who was lying on the floor, tears streaming down her face.

'Shhh, it's alright, pet. You're safe now.' Betty pulled Eve into a sitting position and held her close, stroking her back as Eve wept. Betty didn't realise that Eve's tears were mostly joyous. *I'm alive. He can't hurt me anymore. Matthew will be safe.*

By the time the police arrived a few minutes later, John had stopped struggling and fallen silent. *This isn't how it's supposed to happen. This isn't fair.* John felt the handcuffs tighten around his wrists, and held his head high more out of defiance than anything else, as he was led out to the waiting police van. *Shit. What the hell am I going to do now?*

165

14ᵗʰ June, 2100 hours – Tulley residence, Sunderland

Jacob stretched his leg on the sofa, small beads of sweat on his forehead as he raised the leg and lowered it repeatedly. The physio exercises that kept the muscles in his leg from deteriorating were almost second nature.

He'd got back from the hospital over an hour ago, where TJ had happily informed him that she would be released tomorrow. He had frowned at that. Though the lacerations to her face were scabbing properly, the bruising stood out on his sister's still pale face. If he had his way he'd lock her in the hospital and leave her there where the world couldn't hurt her.

All the things he'd seen in his career, all the sights he'd viewed in his role with the police, and nothing had scared him as much as the thought his sister could have died. He'd spoken to Ali and Ben earlier in the day, and though the investigation was still progressing, he just felt helpless. The CCTV was being trawled through, and he knew they were following up the registration plate, but it didn't ease the knot sitting in his stomach.

Picking up on his tension, Ben had asked if he wanted some company this evening. He had declined, saying he needed to work through some stuff at home. Now he wished he had taken her up on it. His 2-bedroomed terrace in the city centre seemed too quiet tonight, even with his tunes blaring from the iPhone docking station on the mantle.

Making his way into the spare room, he glanced around the books on the shelves. His gaze was finally drawn to one on his 'to-read' shelf. He poured himself a coffee, grabbed a large bunch of the grapes from the fruit bowl, and lay down on the sofa. He hadn't even read the first chapter when his mind relaxed and he suddenly fell into a deep sleep.

The book fell from his chest, waking him enough for him to realise that he was sliding into sleep. The joys of military training; his body was capable of falling asleep when he needed the rest, wherever he was. He dozily recalled the time he had woken on a tree branch in the middle of the jungle, with a python slithering over his stomach. Luckily for him, the python had eaten recently: it had a bulge in its middle. It moved over his stomach as he lay still, then made its way down the trunk of the tree to the ground. And Jacob had just turned his head and gone back to sleep.

He gave a soft sigh and turned his face towards the sofa back and gave in to sleep.

14*14th June, 2305 hours – Major Incident Room, Sunderland City Centre Depot*

Ali reread the log for the second time. It was almost time to interview the suspect. He wasn't conducting the interview, one of the DC's was; but he had every intention of sitting in. An attempted murder in a care home? This was going to be a media nightmare. By the time Deena Davis, the CSI, had arrived at the home, the place was already swarming with reporters. At least one person had obviously seen fit to leak the story.

And those reporters would want to know what had happened, whether there was any negligence, how he had got inside after the visiting hours. He had some answers from the staff. The rest would depend on how much John Whitworth wanted to disclose.

Ali knew he hadn't yet asked for a solicitor, and that that could either be good or bad. Whitworth would either 'no comment' through the interview; open up and tell all; or ask for a brief when they sat down to interview.

Ali had already been to the hospital to see the victim, not that she could say much. He ran his hand through his hair, and sighed.

The staff had told him how she ended up in the home, it wasn't too much of a leap to wonder whether, given what had happened today, Whitworth might have tried to harm his wife before. Just a gut feeling of course, but still.

John Whitworth's bag had been booked into evidence, and as DC Charlie Quinn stood suddenly from her seat, Ali knew it was time to find out what had happened.

Chapter Sixteen
15th June, 1045 hours – Tunstall, Sunderland City Centre

It was almost time.

His excitement levels had been rising for days, and he'd dulled it a few times by wasting money on the dirty whore a few streets over. She'd asked him the last time not to be so rough, and he'd left her knowing what rough actually was. It'd take weeks for the bruising to heal. She was only lucky he didn't kill whores – they had a certain acceptance when things went wrong, anticipation that at any given moment with a john, their luck could change. That, and the fact they'd all been round the block more times than daft mick. There was no pleasure to be gained from killing someone who expected it to happen. It did nothing for him.

He'd checked his tablet this morning, making sure the software he needed was saved and ready to go. There would be no trail leading back to him, absolutely nothing to say he'd ever been chatting to Clarice. The University had been a bit of a bugger though. They'd upgraded their security systems in the last few days and it had taken him a good hour to write the code that provided him with a way through the new firewalls they'd installed. But he'd managed it, and now any record of Gareth Chamberlain was well and truly erased.

He would get away with it again, and this time he wouldn't have to move to another county. He had things to stay here for now and a life he quite enjoyed.

He'd just have to be exceptionally careful not to leave anything behind to incriminate him. Extra careful.

15th June, 1205 hours – Custody, Sunderland City Centre Depot

John had just been handed another sandwich and cup of lukewarm coffee through the sliding window of the large metal cell door. Looking at the bread, he was sure he could see mould. He'd heard custody cells weren't the nicest places. The stench from the toilet in the corner of the cell was powerful, and just when he

thought his nose had acclimatised, a fresh waft would fill the air.
Through the night there had been clanking doors, drunks yelling
and people talking in a dull drone that could still be heard even
through the heavy metal door.

It was a good job he'd slept in the boiler room, because
there was no hope of sleeping in this shithole. He stood and
walked the few feet over to the toilet, undid his trousers and had a
piss. He'd needed to for a while but had been resisting, knowing
from the last time that the piss sprayed out of the toilet bowl and
onto the wall at the back, making the smell even worse.

Zipping his trousers back up, he put his hands under his
shirt, and felt the thin nylon rope that was looped round his waist.
He'd had to take his belt off, even hand over his shoe laces and the
contents of his pockets, but they hadn't known about this rope.
He'd wanted to be prepared. The rope was his last-ditch attempt at
controlling the death of his wife. His brow furrowed in
disappointment. *The bitch is still alive. I'm here rotting in this cell and
she's living it up at the hospital with what, a broken arm maybe? This is
not how it's supposed to be.*

Knowing that it would be almost thirty minutes until the
window was opened on his cell again, he decided to make a new
plan. He didn't want to go to jail, didn't know if he could face it.
It was full of, well, criminals. And most of them a lot tougher than
he was. He'd be pond scum to them. He'd purposely asked for the
solicitor who handled his estate – an estate for an uncle he didn't
remember, but that who, knowing of John's existence, had left
everything he owned in trust. Not that it was much mind, but any
hand-outs had been welcome when he had first gone into business
for himself. He knew it would take them hours to travel up from
London, and it had given him time to consider his options.

Unhooking the thin rope from his waist, he started
looping the end into a large circle.

*15th June, 1240 hours – Major Incident Room, Sunderland City Centre
Depot*

Ali ran a hand over his eyes. He'd been in the nick pretty much solidly since last night, a quick hours kip and shower at some point in the wee hours his only break. The interview last night had consisted of total silence, Whitworth not disclosing anything. It had been decided to let him sleep on it, to contemplate his actions. They had locked him down in his cell, giving him a plastic cup of coffee and a sandwich.

Ali had actually watched through the sliding window of the cell door as the man meticulously removed the limp tomato and ate with methodical bites, chewing slowly before swallowing with a gulp. His eyes had been blank as they stared at the dirty looking grey floor of the 8ft by 6ft cell. He'd looked up as he had finished, and then said the fateful words. 'I want a solicitor. Mackie and Steepling from London. I'm already a client.'

It had taken the custody sergeant more than a couple of hours to contact the solicitors, and he'd been promptly informed that Mr Mackie himself would be making the trip up from London, and was expecting to land at the police station at around 4 p.m. It was a good delay tactic, Ali had to admit. Until then interviews couldn't be conducted. Not with Whitworth at any rate. Talking to the staff at the care home had been fruitful however. A couple of suspicious incidents now seemed linked to the prisoner in the cells, including the hit and run fatality on the 5th June. Staff had disclosed that the victim, Ann Caffrey, had been working closely with Eve, that she had expressed concerns about John in the past to her colleagues. It didn't mean John was responsible for Ann's death, Ali knew that, but it was still awfully convenient timing.

The phone's shrill ring interrupted his thoughts. He picked it up. 'McKay ... what? How the fuck did that happen? ... Shit ... I'll be right down.'

Ali pretty much ran down the two floors to the cells. He used his station key to unlock the entry doors then buzzed for entry. As the door clicked he pushed hard, the metal hinges screeching as the door slammed into the wall. He didn't even notice the plaster fall.

Striding past the custody desk and straight to cell M19, he pushed two uniformed cops out of the way.

'Shit.' He said again, as he saw John Whitworth lying on the floor, his eyes glassed and open, the noose still round his neck. This was not going to be a good day.

15th June, 1930 hours – CSI Department, Sunderland City Centre Depot
It was going to be a quiet night. The dayshift had gone home after a slow day. Even Craig who'd been on mid-shift had requested a little time off, not wanting to be sat twiddling his thumbs in the office for hours before home time. Which left Ben covering the late shift on her own.

Popping her tunes on quietly, she made a coffee and opened up Socard, intending to make a start on the bag of property at her feet. It was always the same on a slow shift. She had been informed by Kevin that the vans were all cleaned and stocked, and most of the store-room had been cleared. She had one measly bin bag of property to book through the system for destruction and that was it.

Reaching down, she grabbed the first piece of property. It was one of Cass's – a return from the Chem Lab. The label stuck to the front by the lab showed 'no fingerprints found' so the item was essentially useless. Inside the evidence bag was a plastic Asda carrier. It showed some yellow smears where it had been handled but Ben could see there was no visible ridge detail. She scanned the barcode onto Socard and marked it as disposed, then cut into the evidence bag and pulled it out, putting both into the other bin bag at her feet. When she'd finished she'd take it all down to the skip in the back yard.

It didn't take her long to empty the bag. For once, everything would be up to date. She turned in her chair, intending to stand, just as Ali walked in.

'Hey, Ben, just the person I wanted to see. You remember the assault at Retox the other week? Have you done your statement? I'm trying to put the file together and I don't seem to have it?'

Frowning, she replied, 'I sent it over to CPS last week. Need me to do you another copy?'

As he nodded, she continued, 'How's Cass and Alex? I've been a bit manic, haven't rang her.'

'Yeah she's fine. I think they're both pulling their hair out a little, to be honest. Cass's mum is still staying in the Hilton so is over every day, then our mum is down as well and staying in a bed and breakfast not far away. Guess it must feel a little like they're being pulled from one way to the other. I'd hate it.'

'Aw, bless them. I'll drop Cass a text later. Maybe we can meet for a coffee or something, get her away from it all.'

'I think she'd appreciate that. I can understand the mums though, Isobel is an absolute charmer. She smiled at me the other day, nearly knocked my socks off. I've got a photo on here somewhere,' he said pulling out his phone.

Frowning in consternation, he muttered, 'If I can find the stupid folder where the photos are kept. I hate technology. Here, you have a look.'

Ben took the phone with a grin, hit menu and brought up his images folder. Scrolling through the small number of photos, she smiled as she found the one he meant. Isobel was in his arms, the photo obviously taken by someone else, and her face was curved in innocent contentment. Ben didn't have the heart to tell him it was likely wind. Pressing a few buttons, she set the image as his wallpaper and screen saver.

Handing it back, she said, 'Press the button in the middle.'

Ali looked a little confused until Isobel's face shone at him. 'How'd you do that? Thanks, Ben.'

'For future reference, to access your pictures you just press the menu button, and go to the file named images. If you're ever stuck on how to do something just give me a shout.'

Nodding, Ali raised his behind off the desk he was resting on, and turned to leave the office. Glancing back, he thanked her again, and paused, wanting to say something but not quite knowing how.

'Tough day?' asked Ben quietly, taking in his body language, five o'clock shadow and crinkled clothing. He looked like he hadn't slept in a week. She could see he felt guilty. The talk of the suicide in the cells had spread around the nick like wildfire. It meant a major investigation, and staff were already preparing for interrogations and finger pointing.

'The toughest. Never lost one in the cells before.'

'You know it's not your fault right? PACE says custody don't have to search if they deem there is no risk of harm right? Did he present as suicidal?'

'No he didn't and I'm not sure they would have found the rope had they searched him to be honest. It was one of those really thin nylon ropes. But still, he killed himself in custody. It's opened a shit can full of worms. You know what this stuff is like when it hits the media. The police are accused of everything and sundry. The headlines will probably say he had the shit kicked out of him on arrest and was mistreated throughout.'

'As long as the custody officer did their job correctly, and it's all documented, I don't see what professional standards can do. They'll investigate `cos they have to, but try not to worry, Ali. There wasn't anything you could have done. If he wanted to kill himself he would have found a way. They always do if the intent is serious.'

'Yeah, I guess you're right. Thanks, Ben.'

Ali turned and left the office, his heavy footsteps fading as he made his way down the corridor. Ben sighed, sometimes bad days were bad days, and there was nothing you could do about it.

In what seemed like a few minutes, Ben had the rest of the property booked out for disposal. She was just about to pick it up and take it down when her radio burst to life.

'7916 Cassidy, come in, over.'

'Go ahead, LV.'

'Ben, if you're not busy, can you head down to the car park of the Sutton Arms in the town centre. There's been a few attempt break-ins to some vehicles down there. It's log 1215. Think most of the IPs are on scene.'

'Yea sure, LV. ETA around fifteen minutes.'

She listened as the radio dispatcher informed whichever cop was on scene that she was on route, grabbed the van keys off the hook by the door, locked up and left.

So much for a quiet night.

15th June, 2220 hours - CSI Department, Sunderland City Centre Depot
The job at the pub ended up being a complete waste of time. By the time she got there it was raining, and not just any rain, but that fine summer spray that drenches everything whilst barely even touching it. She had made quick work of the six cars that had been damaged, taking glass samples from the window frames and writing her notes in the van as thunder started to grumble in the distance. The cop had an arrest so the glass samples could be instrumental in linking the offender's clothing to the cars. She'd already told him to seize the kids clothing for forensic analysis. The rest would be up to him, and the CPS.

It had taken her all of half an hour to put the jobs through Socard and she stood to make herself a cuppa, almost tripping over the bag of property she'd done earlier. She moved it to one side, knowing she'd remember to take it to the bin when she left for home. Deciding to take her samples straight to the front office, she picked them up and wandered down the corridor.

The station was silent: few staff were working at that time of night, and most of them the 24/7 officers who worked on the next floor up. The front office clerks had packed up for the day hours before, and had she not worked out of the very same front office herself, she would have found the silence a little creepy. She pulled the key off the wall and opened the locked door to the transit store. As she placed the bags inside, something caught her eye. Turning the lock again, she walked over to the CCTV camera screens.

The CCTV had been installed in the station for years, but had been updated after Cass's kidnapping to cover all the rear yard and front entrance more fully, and with better night vision. Concentrating, she stared at the four screens, curious as to what it was that had grabbed her attention. She finally focussed on a darkly clothed figure, sidling up to the staff entrance door beside the front office. Her senses went into overdrive as he suddenly vanished from view and she heard the door slam in the corridor right outside the office.

Thinking on her feet, she grabbed the radio from the charger beside the screens and pressed the emergency button just as the male came into the office, furtively looking around. As his gaze focussed on her, his eyes narrowed and he took a step forward menacingly. His pupils had dilated to pin pricks, and the strip of skin she could see above the scarf and below his hat, was pasty, clammy and scattered with bad acne pockmarks.

'There's no money in here. This is just a front office.' She kept her tone neutral, holding her hands out in an attempt to placate the intruder.

'A front office with a petty cash box,' snarled the man, taking two more steps towards her. His hand was also out in front of him and she tried not to stare at the crowbar he held tightly.

'There's no cash in here. I'm sorry.'

Suddenly he lost it, shouting 'Fuck!' as he swept the metal tool across the table to his left, sending the screens and keyboards flying with a clatter.

He stopped again, his head cocked to one side, as he focussed his glare back on Ben, as though everything that had gone wrong was entirely her fault.

A sharp arrow of pure fear shot through her pounding heart. She knew that look. He was going to kill her.

Taking in a slow breath, she waited, not moving until he was right in front of her. He raised his arm with the intention of swinging the crowbar at her head, and still she waited, looking straight into his eyes. A guttural sound escaped from his mouth as the metal rod moved towards her, but all she could see was his tiny pupils like small black islands in a sea of pale blue. The bar moved almost as if in slow motion. It was centimetres from her when she finally leapt into action. Turning her body so her shoulder absorbed the blow instead of her head, she elbowed the man to the solar plexus, feeling his breath exit his body with a loud 'whoomph'. Pulling back, she grabbed the arm holding the crowbar and moved behind him taking the arm with her, her foot already moving to the rear of his knees to knock him from his feet. Using her strength, she pushed him to the floor, his left cheek impacting with the carpet, and his grunt muffled against the rough surface.

Through his grunt, she heard footsteps running down the corridor towards her, but they sounded as if they were in a tunnel, pounding feet just outside of her consciousness. She was panting, fear and adrenaline giving her the strength she needed to keep the man on the floor. Ali burst into the front office with several detectives at his side. They were expecting a fight, and they all paused in shock as they registered Ben sat on top of the suspect, his arm twisted behind him as he whimpered with pain.

'Ben, you can let go, we got this.'

Ali's soft voice penetrated through, but it was his hand on her arm that made her look up. She moved, allowing one of the DCs to take her place, silent as Ali led her from the room and into the small office behind the front desk window.

'Ben, you OK? Did he hurt you?' he asked softly, his hands on the top of her arms as he looked her up and down, checking her for signs of injury.

The adrenaline was starting to subside, and Ben felt herself start to shake. She focussed on keeping her breathing steady, staring at the poster on the wall behind Ali's back, reading the words over and over until she felt herself stop shaking.

'I'm OK,' she finally replied, 'He caught my shoulder with the crow bar, but I'm OK.'

'Let me see,' said Ali, gently trying to manoeuvre her.

Ben stepped away from him, 'I'm fine, Ali. Honest. He barely touched me.'

'You should still get it checked out. It might be worse than you think. We'll need some injury photo's doing too.'

'I'll get it sorted tomorrow, Ali. Do you need me to make my statement now?'

Ali frowned a little. He didn't quite know what had just happened but it was clear Ben did not want him touching her. Deciding to focus on finding out what had occurred, he put the other stuff to the back of his mind. There would be plenty of time for that later. Maybe Cass would know what's going on with Ben.

'What happened? How'd he get in?'

'I think he had a key. I was putting some stuff in the transit store and saw something on the CCTV. When I looked closer he was outside, and then the door slammed and he was in here. I think he's high or something. I told him there was no money in the front office and he just lost it. I had to restrain him, I didn't have a choice. He had a crowbar. Was going to hit me with it.'

'Hey, nobodies arguing with you, Ben. You did what you had to do, and might I add, you did it better than most cops would have. Where'd you learn those moves?'

'Self-defence training,' she replied. 'Not force provided,' she added as Ali raised his eye brows in question. He knew all too well that the police didn't provide forensic personnel with self-defence training, and it was something he campaigned for every time it came up in the yearly meetings.

Ben felt light-headed, her vision was swimming and she could see black spots. But she tried to ignore it, adding, 'Can I ring Kevin please? You're going to need a CSI here to take photos and I presume you'll be wanting me to make a statement. Although I couldn't do the photos anyway – conflict of interests I sup –'

She felt her sentence trail off at the end, saw the hoods of her eyes as they rolled back in her head, and thought 'shit' as the dizziness caused her to tilt.

Ben didn't want to wake up. She could feel someone stroking her cheek, telling her to open her eyes, but she didn't want to. Slowly she realised that there was something hard under her back, something rough and textured against her cheek, and she just knew she wasn't at home in bed. Forcing her eyes open, she saw Ali's concerned grey ones staring back.

She groaned as she tried to sit. 'I passed out didn't I?'

It was more of a statement than a question, and Ali nodded back.

'I've just phoned your aunt, told her I'll drop you off, or do you need a paramedic? We can take your statement tomorrow.'

He held his hand out to help her to her feet, and stood close in case she fell again. Ben felt her cheeks change to deep red. She was mortified. She had just passed out at work in front of pretty much the whole of the major incident team. *That could only happen to me! I take down a suspect then pass out for the sheer hell of it. What a complete numpty.*

'Ali, it's fine. Let me do my statement whilst it's all fresh in my mind. I don't need a medic. I'll ring Aoife now, and tell her I'll be back shortly.'

Standing aside to let her past, Ali followed her through, and tried not to eavesdrop as she made the phone call.

'Aoife it's me ... No I'm fine ... Aoife ... Aoife, stop OK. I'm going to give my statement then I'll be home I promise. I'm OK. Loves you.'

'Is your aunt OK? She was pretty upset when I spoke to her a moment ago.'

'She will be, as soon as I get home anyways,' said Ben, flashing Ali a quick but tight smile. 'Let's crack on, alright?'

15ᵗʰ June, 2315 hours – O'Byrne residence, Sunderland
Ben was home. Finally.

Giving the statement felt like it had taken forever, and it had been hard. Writing every last thing down and signing it off. It was almost like she had been transported to the past, though without quite as much of the trauma involved as the last time. It had actually felt good knowing she hadn't forgotten her training, that all those hours put in on the mat had actually accomplished something.

Reassuring Kevin that she was still fine to work her on-call that night was even harder, but she truly felt like she was fine. It hadn't been nice, thinking that some random stranger was going to attack her with a crowbar, that an offender had invaded the sanctity of the police station. But Ben was trying to look past all that. He had entered the station illegally, using keys someone had dropped outside. Whichever cop that was would be getting a rollocking, no doubt about that. She had just happened to be there.

She paused at the front door, her hand on the frame for a second as she laid her head on top. She suddenly felt so tired. She remembered feeling that way all those years ago, when the initial trauma and shock had worn off and she had been left on her own for the first time. She recalled feeling so utterly lonely, so desperately alone, despite Aoife being only rooms away. There were often still times when she closed her eyes, and all she could see was *him*. Standing over her, telling her he was watching. It had taken her so long to get to where she was now. It had been years of looking over her shoulder and struggling with paranoia and panic attacks. But she'd made it this far.

A scuffle with an offender was nothing compared to all that. Taking a deep breath, she pulled open the door, already knowing Aoife would be climbing the walls with worry.

'Hey, Aoife, I'm home,' she said, opening the door to the living room. Aoife wasn't in there, so Ben wandered through to the kitchen, again finding it empty.

Her heart swelled as she figured her aunt was upstairs with Grace. She was so grateful her aunt was there. If something had gone wrong today, Grace would have been looked after, she knew that. A lump grew in her throat and she forced it back down as she quietly opened Graces bedroom door. Grace was fast asleep, her dark curls spread over the pillow giving her an angelic appearance, and Aoife was sitting in the rocking chair holding a cuddly bunny. Her cheeks resembled a map, with rivers of tears running down to her chin, and she looked utterly devastated.

Ben knelt in front of her aunt, and pulled her close as Aoife started to sob.

'I don't ... know ... what I'd do.' Aoife stopped trying to speak, wrapped her good arm round Ben and held her so tight that for a moment she thought her ribs would break.

'I'm OK,' whispered Ben into her aunt's hair, inhaling the scent of lavender. 'Shh, I'm alright. Everything's OK.'

After a few minutes, an embarrassed Aoife pulled back.

'Sorry,' she whispered, 'It's just ...'

'Aoife, it's OK. I get it. But I'm alright, I promise. He didn't hurt me.'

Ben watched as she gave herself a shake, took Ben's hand to steady herself and pulled herself to her feet.

'We deserve a glass of wine. Come on, downstairs.'

'I'll have tea, Aoife, I'm on call tonight.'

'On call? They didn't even give you the night off?' Aoife's horror was written all over her face.

'They offered. I refused. I'm fine. It was a bit scary, but I'm fine.'

'Ali told me you kicked the intruder's arse?' Finally, a familiar twinkle appeared in her aunt's eye and Ben knew her aunt would be OK. Shock was a funny thing. She could only imagine how it must have felt having Ali call and explain what had happened. It wouldn't be natural to expect anything but the worst.

And she really was fine. *Even if my shoulder does hurt like a bitch.* She smiled to herself as she figured that if her shoulder hurt, then his stomach and shoulder would be hurting a lot more. *I must ring Davey and thank him again. If it wasn't for him persevering with me I'd never have been able to take that guy down.* Her martial arts instructor, David Cunningham, was one of the best in the business. He worked tournaments all over the world, and specialised in teaching women to handle themselves.

Chapter Seventeen
16th June, 0035 hours – Thompson residence, Sunderland

He found himself in the bushes again. And tonight the rain was falling heavily. His black summer jacket and combats already soaked through. The good thing though, was heavy rain made it darker. He liked the dark, needed it even. Especially tonight.

He'd watched her leave the house at eight on the dot to head into the town for her night out with the girls. She hadn't seen him, of course. No-one saw him unless he wanted them to. He'd already accessed her laptop from home and deleted all traces of him. Now he needed to check her room and make sure she hadn't been stupid enough to write about him in the journal he knew she kept.

He had watched from the shadows as her guardian had turned her bedroom light out almost an hour before. Even allowing time for someone to drop off, he was confident she would be sound asleep under the heavily floral bedding in the chintzy, feminine bedroom down the hall from Clarice's room. He had seen it when he installed the camera, had seen all the rooms in fact. He knew the layout inside, even what both women kept hidden at the bottom of their knicker drawers.

He smiled to himself at that thought. Knickers – it was such an old fashioned word. There had been a vast difference between the two drawers. Gill, the older one preferred high cut briefs, pretty and floral whilst maintaining comfort. And Clarice, his Clarice. Hers were functional, matching sets of plain knickers and bra's, but buried beneath the top layer he found the pot of gold. Matching sets of thongs and balcony bras, in bright colours and patterns.

He wondered when she wore them, whether it was for nights out like tonight. And he felt himself grow hard. It wouldn't be too long before he would find out.

Clarice had been chatting to him all night, he'd left the bar an hour before with the intention of doing his checks, but had said he would be back soon. He was confident that she would wait for him. Her friends were all very drunk by then anyway and dancing around their handbags. Clarice was more restrained, he had noticed, often ordering a coke instead of alcohol, but not telling her friends.

They wouldn't even recall him being there.

He smiled into the darkness. *Then again, neither will she.*

He'd told Clarice to meet him at the end of the road leading to the club at 1.30 a.m. – she had agreed. He was a nice guy, had offered to walk her home despite the rain, had even gone to his place to get an umbrella so she wouldn't get wet. At least, that's what he had told her.

He had been picturing her in his head all night, pulling on her sexy underwear, dressing up just for him, applying her make up so that he would be pleased. In reality he hated make-up. It made women look like the tramps they were, attracting the weak men like moths to a flame.

Not him though, he wasn't taken in by a sweep of mascara and a coating of lip gloss. All that meant was he had to try that little bit harder to make them understand that their place was not in this world. Girls like her, Clarice, they deserved to die.

He remembered his mother had liked make-up. Frowning he tried to conjure up her face in his mind. After losing everything, it seemed the best he could do.

But he couldn't do it. Maybe it had been too long. Or maybe he just hadn't cared enough to remember.

He stood, his head cocked to one side as he listened intently. *What did I just hear?*

Sometimes his hearing played tricks on him; years of being boxed around the head by his dad meant he suffered tinnitus and mild hearing impairments. He often had to strain to hear conversations, and had developed a habit of cocking his head to the side like a dog.

Appeased as he heard a man and woman pass by without noticing him, he emerged from the shadows and silently unlatched the window to Clarice's room. Entering, he held his pen torch in his teeth and checked the journal. It made mention of a guy she had met, been flirting with even, but it didn't mention his alias name. Flashing the torch around the room, he checked the university notes and files and was soon satisfied. There was nothing in here linking her to him. But he tore the page out just to be sure.

As quietly as he had entered, he climbed out of the window and closed it. There wasn't a whole lot he could do about the latch from outside, but it probably wouldn't even be noticed. *And if it is? Well, that's what gloves are for.*

16ᵗʰ June, 0130 hours – Alleyway near Retox Nightclub, Sunderland
He stood under the canopy of one of the long closed down pubs, a few hundred feet from the entrance to Retox. It was getting late and a steady stream of the less hard-core clubbers was exiting the club to make their way home or to the kebab shop. A few queued to pay the astronomical 'after midnight' entry fee to the club, but none of them saw him. He'd already observed one of the bouncers handing some substance or other to a party goer, spotting the young girl handing over a folded note in payment. If the bouncers knew he was there they would have alerted their colleague. But no-one did.

His light jacket was stuck to his skin and he felt uncomfortable.

And she was late.

His eyes glowered in the dark of the doorway. *Who the hell does she think she is? Making plans to see me then being late.*

For a moment he wondered whether she was worth it, whether he should just give up and pick one of the other four women he'd been watching at the start. He hated being kept waiting for anything.

He was about to step out of the doorway to leave, when she suddenly emerged down the steps of the club, gingerly taking each step as she used the hand rail to steady herself. Her heels weren't seven-inch wonders, but they were high enough, and she was plainly the type of girl who usually wore flats. She reached the pavement and looked up and down the street.

He could feel her asking herself what she was doing, arranging to meet a guy she hardly knew, faltering over her decision and thinking about whether she should go back inside. Pulling out his phone, he texted her before she changed her mind.

He saw her pull her mobile from the small clutch bag, and then stepped from the shadows, walking down the road towards her. As she looked up he waved, flashing his teeth as the right side of his mouth curved up in greeting.

'Did I mention earlier how great you look?' he said as he approached, popping the umbrella and holding it above her head. Might as well let her think he was a gentleman. At least for now.

He purposefully kept his gaze averted from the bouncers, and they ignored him completely. If they were asked to describe him, he was confident not one of them would even get his race right, let alone anything else.

He took hold of Clarice's hand with his own as they walked. He wanted to squeeze hard to watch her wince. But he resisted. There would be plenty of time for that later. He had all night. And as far as she knew, they were just going for a walk. They would end up at the Outreach Centre, and she would say she recognised it. Then he would strike; take her inside and out of reach of the community's prying eyes.

And she would wish she had never laid eyes on him.

16th June, 0150 hours – Sunderland Outreach Centre

Clarice was starting to regret leaving the club to meet Gareth. She hadn't even told her friends she was leaving. That was stupid. She was pretty sure he fancied her, but after tonight she definitely didn't like him back. The walk so far had consisted of his clammy hand holding hers and him trying to be funny when he plainly wasn't. Prior to actually spending time with him tonight, she'd thought he seemed nice, liked the attention he gave with his messages. But in reality he wasn't the guy she had been texting.

She felt a shiver pass down her spine – something wasn't right here.

She had to stop herself from bolting when he finally released her hand to put the umbrella down because the rain was finally easing up. She could hear the faint cracks of thunder as it approached from the sea, and despite it being near enough midsummer, she was cold. Wishing she had some ruby slippers so she could click them together and just be at home, she sighed and said, 'I'm really going to have to get home. Gill will be worried about me. I've had a lovely evening, though.'

His eyes narrowed as he looked at her, and she realised she was actually a little afraid. Of what she didn't know, but she didn't like it. Glancing around, she noticed the area was familiar.

It's the Outreach Centre! Shit, I'm miles from home. How the hell did I not notice that!

'I think I'll phone for a cab. We seem to have gone way off track.' Her voice sounded small to her ears, and when he didn't react she wondered if he'd actually heard her.

Stopping, she reached into the small clutch bag and felt around. She frowned, realising that both her purse and phone were missing.

What the hell? Where the fuck is my phone? Gill's gonna go spare.

'Problem?' asked Gareth smoothly, putting his hand into his pocket to reassure himself that her phone was in there with her purse. He felt the rectangular outline and smiled. Lifting them had been easy. He'd pretended to have an issue with the umbrella a while back, and she'd taken it from him to 'fix', handing him her bag as she did so.

'Can't find my phone,' muttered Clarice, her gaze still focussed on the inside of the bag as her hand scrabbled about.

It was the perfect opportunity.

Silently, he moved around her, and before she realised what was happening, he had his arm round her throat, squeezing tightly as her body went taut then relaxed. The sleeper hold had its desired effect and she slumped against him. She hadn't even managed to get out a scream, which boded well for him. The fewer people awake, the better.

Propping her beside the doorway to the centre, he unlocked it with his copy of the master key. He grabbed her shoulders and dragged her inside, aware that she wouldn't be incapacitated for very long. Letting go of her, he grinned as her head hit the hard floor with a thud. Locking the door behind him, he acknowledged that the rush of adrenaline he felt was strong. This one was definitely going to go well. He just knew it.

Tying her hands with cable ties, he used them to drag her down the corridor and into the office on the left. When he had started with his first victim, he had used rope. But rope allowed movement. He'd learned that cable ties didn't. Skin would cut and bleed and still they would hold their deathly grip.

The posters on the wall screamed about positivity, but he was certain Clarice wouldn't feel positive. After roughly applying the gaffer tape to her mouth, he slapped her hard across the face, and smiled a lopsided smile as she groaned and opened her eyes. He watched as she registered she was tied and couldn't speak, and then, he leant forward.

'I've been watching you,' he said, smiling as panic overtook and Clarice began struggling against the ties that held her immobile, screaming through the tape.

'Struggle away, bitch. I'm here to teach you a lesson or two. And you will learn.'

16th June, 0205 hours – Sunderland Outreach Centre

Clarice had never been so afraid in her entire life. The taste of it settled on her tongue, and she felt like she could vomit at any moment. He had left the room a couple of minutes ago, to do what she didn't know, but she'd already found out that struggling was useless, and the loudest sound she could make was a grunt.

Tears had already streaked her mascara, and she could feel it starting to go crusty on the sides of her face.

What the hell is going on?

There was a faint glow coming through the window from the street lights outside, and she glanced around the room.

Holy shit. I'm in Gill's office. She's gonna kill me. Why the hell didn't I just go home. What does he want with me? Please, God, somebody. Help me!

She felt the tears start to fall again, and again she tried to struggle. The ties cut into her wrists painfully, but she continued.

His voice suddenly echoed round the small office.

'Stop struggling or you will be punished.'

His face appeared right in front of her, his words spoken softly but with loud threatening undertones, and the scar near his mouth glowed eerily in the dim light. His eyes were hard, calculating even. Clarice felt the scream well up from the depth of her lungs, but it failed to gather momentum and exited through the tape as a muffled grunt.

Suddenly seeing the knife in his hand, she mumbled 'No!' and tried to pull herself across the floor; anything to get away from him.

He grabbed her legs and pulled her back, the rough industrial carpet scraping harshly across her cheek as she twisted her body and tried to pull from his grasp. But she couldn't.

He's gonna kill me. What did I do to him? Why me?

He dragged her back to his position, and held her in place by sitting astride her. He watched as fear sparked in her brown eyes. She was petrified. Just how he liked it.

'I've been watching you.'

His voice was soft, and he stared at her as his admission sunk in. He saw the moment she registered he'd said it to her previously when she'd woken up.

'I had a camera in your bedroom. I've been watching you for weeks.'

A camera in her room? What the fuck?

He leaned over her, smiling that lopsided smile, and suddenly she knew for certain, he had no intention of letting her live. She felt the tears well up in her eyes again, her breath catching as her chest heaved in fear. The knife seemed to grow bigger before her eyes and she tried her best to let loose the next scream.

Oh God, I'm gonna die. He's gonna kill me.

She found herself shaking her head again, doing her best to say 'no' over and over in the hope that he would listen and let her go.

'You'll beg before the end. You'll beg me to kill you, to end it. They all did that.'

All? Realisation dawned. She wasn't the first.

He drew the blade down the front of her dress, splitting the material in two like it was butter, and sat back on his haunches as he took in the lacy bra. He knew she had put the pretty underwear on just for him.

Her eyes were wide with fear but he knew they lied. She couldn't be scared - he just knew she'd chosen it all for this special occasion. She'd expected it. She wanted him. And now, she'd teased him long enough.

It was time for her to have him. Or rather, for him to have her. He leaned over her and ran his tongue down the side of her face, tasting the makeup and faint tang of body butter.

Clarice froze in fear, feeling his slimy mouth on her face. Tears slid down her cheeks of their own accord. *Why didn't I go home? Oh God. I want my mum.*

16th June, 0230 hours –Sunderland Outreach Centre

He picked the blade up off the floor and watched her face as he pressed it into the side of her stomach, smiling his lopsided smile as she tried to scream in pain. Drawing it out slowly allowed the blood to bubble past the blade and run gently down her side to the floor. She was whimpering now, fresh tears falling down her already streaked face. Leaning over her, he let his tongue catch one, tasted the saltiness as she tried to pull her head away from him.

He was so hard it hurt.

He cut through her black lace edged, pink satin bra, freeing her mocha breasts. He gasped as he took in her darkened nipples, and couldn't help but lean over and bite one, hard.

Moving position, he knelt beside her, and drew the blade across her breasts, grinning as thick lines of blood appeared. He hadn't don't this since number four, had almost forgotten how good it felt. Sitting back, he noticed Clarice had wet herself.

'Who's a dirty girl then?' he whispered in her ear, before grabbing the top of her leggings and yanking them down her legs.

He felt impatient now. It was time for her to learn.

He unzipped his fly, applied his protection and knelt beside her. He watched her eyes widen in terror, felt her fear permeate the air around him. The whites of her eyes were visible in the dull light of the street lamp outside of the window, giving her the appearance of rabid dog. She shook her head again, whimpering as used his knees to widen her legs.

16th June, 0510 hours –Sunderland Outreach Centre

He grabbed a rag off the table and carefully wiped his blade. He would clean it with bleach later, but this would do for now. Glancing down, he took in Clarice's now pale features. Blood pooled beneath her naked body, her injuries stark against the glow of the lights.

The knife had sliced into her stomach like she was made of hot butter, and he loved the thrill it gave him. It had never been about the killing for him, more about the pain and satisfaction he got from it. And she had been very satisfying.

He walked back over to her, her face and body swollen and bruised from the beating. He had made sure she knew the reason why she had to be punished all the way through. *Women* shouldn't be allowed to tease men, to tempt them and then say no. *Women* were nothing but the crap on the bottom of his shoe. They didn't even deserve to be on the same planet. Men were far superior.

Reaching down he cut the cable ties that bound her hands, and carefully cut a section of her dark hair for his box. He made sure he picked up the spent condoms, and everything else he'd brought with him and placed everything inside his trusty black bag. He left through the back of the centre. It wouldn't do for some nosy neighbour to see him coming out at this time in the morning. He made sure he locked the door, then made his way round the corner to where his car was waiting.

Turning the key in the ignition, he cranked the stereo up and grinned.

He turned and took in one long-lasting gaze at the centre, before whistling softly to himself as he drove off.

Chapter Eighteen
16th June, 0800 hours – Thompson residence, Sunderland

Gill yawned and took the last sip of her morning tea. It was getting late; if Clarice didn't hurry up she'd end up being late for her class. Deciding it was time to intervene, she made her way to Clarice's room.

'Come on, lazy bones, time to get up,' she said as she entered. A puzzled look passed over her face as she registered the room was flooded with daylight, the curtains wide open. The bed was made and had not been slept in.

Worried now, Gill made her way to her own bedroom and picked up her mobile phone. The screen was blank, no messages from Clarice.

Where the hell is she? She'd text if she wasn't coming home. Unless her battery died – I'm gonna kill that girl when she gets home. Making me worry like this.

She was in two minds as to whether to ring around Clarice's friends like a paranoid mother hen, or whether to head to work and wait for Clarice to contact her. Deciding on the latter, she grabbed her handbag and left the house.

The drive to the centre was not a pleasant one. Gill didn't know if it was the unease at Clarice not contacting her, or whether the roads were just full of arseholes but she felt like she'd pipped her horn at more than enough people through the journey. One guy had cut her off, one woman overtook her on a normal town single carriageway and another almost went into the back of her whilst applying her lip gloss. Who on earth applies lip gloss when driving anyway? Surely there were laws against such things.

Gill felt pounding in her temples and groaned. *Not a migraine, please not a migraine.*

Glancing round the car park she realised she was the first to arrive. Part of her had hoped Stan or Brian would be there: opening all the window shutters was a nightmare. Half of them felt like they rusted shut every night. She found herself smiling as she got out of the car though, her keen eyes picking up Stan's form walking towards her from the little row of nearby shops.

Deciding to wait for him, she waved and paused at the door.

'Morning,' she said as he approached, her tone much chirpier than she felt. She wished she'd worn a different outfit that morning, maybe comfy joggers or something. Her usual bright tunic with leggings felt tight and uncomfortable today, her tummy bloated. *That bloody sandwich yesterday, knew I shouldn't have eaten the white bread.*

'Morning back. Another day, another dollar,' sighed Stan with a wink. He stood back as Gill turned her key in the lock and opened the front door.

She crinkled her nose as a metallic smell burst forth from the corridor.

'Yuck, what's that horrible smell?'

Stan placed a hand on her arm, his silence causing her to stop. She felt nerves flutter and her heartbeat increased. The daylight had flooded the corridor, and something wasn't right. The dark floor was shiny somehow, the corridor threatening as opposed to welcoming.

They stepped inside together, Stan holding Gill's arm as they made their way down the corridor.

'Hello?' yelled Stan suddenly, making Gill jump backwards, impacting with his chest.

'Damn it, Stan,' she hissed back at him.

They reached the door to her office and Gill pushed it open, and as she saw Clarice on the floor, covered in blood with her glassy eyes staring straight at her, she felt the scream begin from the depths of her toes and rise through her body. Stan pulled her out of the room forcefully, holding her head to his chest and she screamed again, her legs giving way under her. He sank to the floor with her, not having a choice, and held her as she screamed again. With the hand that was free, he dialled 999, and as the operator connected, he said, 'Police please,' his voice shaking as he said the words.

16th *June, 0810 hours – Major Incident Room, Sunderland City Centre Depot*

Ali felt like he hadn't slept in a week. One of the neighbours in their block, had seen fit to have music blasting until stupid o'clock. It had reached the point where he had seriously been considering going down the stairs, kicking the door in and ripping the plug off the damned stereo. He'd watched out of his window as the police had finally arrived just passed 2 a.m. and told them to turn it down. One of the other neighbours who'd had enough had phoned for the cavalry.

Then when he left home to get to work, he'd hit traffic on the Wear bridge, which, thanks to road-works on the Queen Alexandra bridge, had been about ten times busier than normal. He'd wanted to be in for half seven, having loads to catch up on from the day before.

He pulled into the rear yard, found a space and turned the engine off, before sighing deeply and running his hands over his eyes. He knew in his gut that something was going to happen today; that sixth sense that cops have was bringing a feeling of foreboding. He felt his mouth open in a long yawn, and got out of the car. Failing to see the slick of oil, he felt his foot slip away and before he knew it he was on the deck.

For Christ's sake, falling over? Really? What am I, five years old? He pulled himself back to his feet. His pristine trousers were now covered in mud, gravel and oil. He felt his leg burn a little and realised he'd took some skin off his knee. His only saving grace was that no one had seen him fall.

Or so he thought, until, after a quick change into his spare trousers, he entered the Major Incident Team Office.

'You fell over, you fell over,' chanted his smirking colleagues.

Accepting the jibes, he grinned back. 'Did someone put that oil there just for me?'

It was hard taking the ribbing today, though. All he wanted to do was shout 'Fuck off' at the top of his voice, which wasn't like him.

The shrill sound of his phone ringing cut through the remaining chuckles. He strode to his desk and answered.

'McKay.'

'DI McKay, this is Inspector Hewitt from the comms room. I need to give you some information in regards to a murder. The call has just come in now.'

Ali groaned silently. A murder was all he needed today, of all days.

16th June, 0840 hours –Sunderland Outreach Centre

Ben and Kevin pulled up in the van just as the Major Incident Team's car parked up on the road outside the centre. A uniformed cop had put tape over the closed front door and set up another cordon around the building.

'Where's the loggist?' Ali asked loudly as he looked around.

'Sorry, sir. I was single-crewed when I got here. Officers Sewell and Cambridge are over with the two people who found the body.'

'One of them is the guardian of the deceased, yes?'

'Yes, sir. I believe her name is Gill Thompson. She's hysterical, sir. Cambridge has phoned for an ambulance.'

'OK. Ben, Kevin, can you do a quick walk-through of the scene. I don't want too many boots trailing through there and messing up any evidence. So far the entry since the murder seems to have been minimal.'

At their nod, he strode off in the direction of Gill and Stan.

Ben and Kevin were dressed in white scene suits within minutes, the hoods up and a mask over their faces. They wore two pairs of nitrile gloves on their hands to prevent any contamination. Kevin pushed open the door, and both ducked under the police tape. Keeping to the outer edges of the corridor to avoid contaminating potential footwear evidence, they both made their way down the corridor. Ben knew the log had said the victim was in Gill's office and as they reached the door, she stopped Kevin. Using his foot, Kevin nudged the door open.

The blood was stark against the pale carpet, and it was immediately obvious that the victim was deceased. There was too much blood for her not to be. Ben grabbed hold of Kevin's shoulder to peer round. Seeing the criss-cross cuts across the girl's exposed breasts, the dark lines on her stomach where she had been stabbed, and the heavy bruising to her face and neck, she gasped.

In an instant she was taken back in time.

He had his hands round her throat and was squeezing hard. Why the hell had she stopped? She knew better than to approach a man on his own in the middle of nowhere, even if it did look like he'd had an accident and fell off his bike. She felt bile rise in her throat as she panicked, clawing at the man's hands. She heard him say 'I've been watching you,' and momentarily wondered what he meant. Darkness had been threatening to close in on her when he'd finally let go, and slammed his fist into her face. She'd felt a couple of teeth loosen, and the bitter metallic taste of blood had filled her mouth. She was gasping for breath, her stomach burning where he'd shoved the knife in. She knew he intended to kill her. She felt her hands pull as he dragged her by the ties that bound her, could feel stones and dirt scraping down her back, pulling her skin off. She tried to scream but the blood gurgled in her throat causing her to gag and cough. As the dragging stopped, and he dropped her arms, she tried to turn and crawl away. Blood spilled from her mouth and her throat was finally free to scream, and scream she did. Loudly, begging someone to help her. He grabbed her shoulders and roughly threw her on to her back. In a swift motion she felt him cut through her top, exposing her functional sports bra.

Within seconds that was cut through too and he sat astride her, staring at her breasts glowing in the moonlight.

In that instant she understood he wasn't just intending to kill her.

Caught in the memories, Ben stumbled against Kevin, her breathing shallow and laboured, her eyes wide in fear. Turning he caught her as her legs gave way, 'Ben? Ben you need to listen. Breathe slowly. It's a panic attack, that's all. Just breathe.'

He'd hit her numerous times now, she kept fighting to stay conscious but her mind was telling her to just give up. When he pulled at her leggings, she screamed again, tears of utter fear streaming down her face, asking him why, begging him to stop. She heard the rustle of paper being ripped and forced her eyes open, pleading with him to stop as he rolled the condom down his penis.

From there her memory blurred, the next few hours melding into a sea of pain and fading consciousness. She remembered him dragging his knife across her breasts, the pain as the skin separated and wept red tears of blood. She vaguely remembered him plunging the knife into her abdomen a couple of times, and the feel of his hands round her throat as he squeezed so hard that her hyoid bone cracked under the pressure. And she remembered lying still as he gathered his things to leave, trying to stay motionless so he thought she was dead. Knowing that dead was the only way he'd leave her there. And as he left, whistling an eerie tune that faded with each step, she finally succumbed to the darkness.

Kevin held Ben up, talking to her softly, trying to pull her out of wherever her mind had taken her. Eventually her eyes started to blink, bright with tears as they fluttered, trying to focus on him. This wasn't just a panic attack. She couldn't focus, was finding it hard to breathe. She was having trouble speaking too, couldn't seem to string a sentence together. Slowing her breathing purposefully, she gripped Kevin's arms, using the police insignia badge on his chest to hold her concentration.

'It was him,' she managed to whisper. Though she knew Kevin wouldn't know what she meant. She hadn't told anyone except Jacob. Suddenly she wanted Jacob there more than anything. 'I need Jacob Tulley here,' she added, gasping at the end of the sentence.

Kevin led her out of the building and to the crime scene van. She'd gone pale, her skin was clammy, and she was still struggling to breathe. She knew she had to say something, tell Ali and Kevin, but she couldn't. *It was him, he's back.*

'Everything OK?' asked Ali, coming to meet them at the cordon.

'Not really, Ben's had a panic attack. Can you take her to the van, please, Ali. I need to call someone, and get another CSI here. It'll mean the scene's held up for a while – they'll need to travel. But I'll crack on with the photography in the meantime.'

Ali took her by the arm and he led her to the CSI van.

Ben started to shake, shock setting in. Her mouth was set in a grim line, and she hadn't spoken a word since being led outside by Kevin. He'd phoned Jacob, explaining the situation and hanging up when Jacob had said he'd be right there, and had contacted Deena by radio, asking her to attend as soon as she was done at the job she was at currently.

Craig was at a cannabis farm with Faith, a large one, exterior, too, so it wasn't like they could just up and leave it for another day, and they'd both be tied up for a while. Sue was up at court so couldn't attend, and Kevin's other staff member, Kimberley, had phoned in sick the day before. It meant they were thin on the ground. As he headed back into the building with his camera, he spoke with Jeremy Black, the CSM who ran the volume crime team, and made sure he was OK to pick up the slack. If anything else major happened, it would mean phoning in staff off rest days, not something the force liked to do as it ate rapidly into the already stretched budgets.

Ali sat Ben inside the cab to the van and handed her a water bottle. 'Ben, you need to take a few sips of this. It's only water.' Ali kept his tone even, wondering what had been so bad. Ben had seen murders before. He was certain it wasn't just the body that was bothering her.

16th June, 0905 hours –Sunderland Outreach Centre

Jacob hadn't needed to think twice when he'd heard from Kevin. He'd told Ed he had to leave for a family emergency, jumped in his car and hared it over to the scene. Parking his car at the rendezvous point, he signed in with the loggist, and made his way through.

He waved at Kevin who raised his hand in acknowledgement.

Jacob caught sight of Ali standing beside the CSI van and made his way over. Seeing him approach, Ali stepped back and motioned him to the side of the van.

'I'm tempted to call an ambulance to be honest. She's really pale and not responding very well to my attempts at small talk. I don't know what spooked her in there but whatever it was, it's bothered her big-style. You have any idea what it could be?'

'Maybe. Hold off on the ambulance for now, I'll get back to you in a sec when I've spoken to her.' Jacob was worried - he'd felt it take hold at the station, a vicious gnawing that was eating at his insides. He'd felt it the moment he'd been told TJ was in hospital too.

Stepping around Ali, he bent at the doorway and faced Ben.

'Ben. It's me,' he said quietly, taking hold of her face and gently manoeuvring her around to face him. Her eyes had a haunted look, but recognition quickly replaced it. Tears threatened to spill down her cheeks, and for a moment he felt like she'd punched him in the gut. She looked so scared he could almost taste it.

Silently he pulled her into his arms, her head resting on his shoulder, and he let her cry for a moment. 'Shhh, it's OK. Everything is going to be just fine.'

Ben stopped herself crying after a couple of minutes, a look of determination passing over her features. Now she was ready to speak.

'I'm sorry for making Kevin call you. I just...' she paused not quite knowing how to put into words what she felt, 'I just needed you here.'

'I'm here,' he replied, holding her hand and pulling back to look at her.

'It's him. The ... man that raped me. This is him.'

Carefully, Jacob said, 'How do you know that?'

'I'm not fantasising, Jacob. This isn't a case of misguided recognition or whatever the hell else you wanna call it. The body in that room has the same wounds he did to me, the same wounds in the same places. She's been raped, and she was strangled. It's him.' Ben's voice turned fierce on the last sentence, fiercer than she felt. She actually thought she might break apart. She'd had years of knowing the day would come when she'd have to face her demons, but it hadn't prepared her adequately for the flood of emotion. She knew in her heart that this was the same person, the same man that had tortured her and left her for dead.

'Then you need to tell Ali and Kevin,' replied Jacob, squeezing her hand, letting her know, without speaking, that he believed her. She'd been there, lived through it. If she thought it was the same person then that was all he needed. He watched as she breathed deeply, and plucked her radio from its holder on the side of her trousers.

Depressing the button, she said, 'Kev, can you come out for a second, I need to speak with you and Ali.'

Within seconds, both of them were by the van.

'This is hard, so bear with me OK. Eight years ago I worked for the police in Durham City, back before they amalgamated all the forces into one. There was a case that fit the

MO of this one exactly. The victim was beaten, raped repeatedly, strangled, stabbed and left for dead. The police never caught the guy responsible.'

Ben paused, more to steady herself than anything else. Before she could open her mouth though, Jacob interrupted, giving her hand another squeeze in support. 'Ben was the victim. She thinks the person who attacked her is responsible for this attack also.'

Ben flashed him a thankful glance.

'You mind me asking what makes you think this is the same guy? I'm sorry I have to ask. I get that some of the MO must match, but is it not possible that this is just a similar case?' Ali's voice was calm, he didn't *not* believe her, but he had to have the facts before he could think realistically that this might be the same person. Eight years was a long time.

Ben took in a deep breath. Even Jacob didn't know this part. Her voice was quiet and shaky as she replied, 'The victim has criss-cross cuts across her breasts and so did I. I haven't seen but she will have bite marks to her shoulders, possibly even around her nipples. If you swab both her cheeks, the killer will have licked down the sides of her face. There'll be a chunk of hair missing: he cuts it with a knife. And there won't be any semen inside the vaginal cavity: he wears a condom.'

Kevin looked at Ali, his face paling. 'She's right about the breasts and bite marks. Our vic has those wounds. Jesus.'

Ali stayed silent for a moment, letting the information sink in. His mind echoed Kevin's last word, but more blasphemous. *Jesus fucking Christ. Another serial killer in Sunderland? Second one in eighteen months? What is this place, a bloody shit magnet?* Then felt instantly ashamed of his thoughts. He was busy thinking of having another killer, when Ben was stood in front of him, telling him the horrible things that had happened to her.

'Ben, you're off the case. Conflict of interests. I need you to sit down with one of my detectives and go over everything.' His expression softening, he took hold of Ben's hand. 'I'm so sorry this happened to you, love. And sorry that I'm making you relive it all. But we need all the information we can get so we can catch this guy. You're in the prime position to help us do that. Will you help me, Ben?'

Ben just nodded, her voice suddenly overcome with emotion.

'I'll take her back to the nick,' said Jacob. 'Who do you want her to sit down with?'

'Charlie. I'll ring her now and give her the heads up.'

Kevin couldn't speak. *Poor kid. All she's been through and we didn't have a clue.* Before he could change his mind, he pulled her into a quick hug. He was close to all of his staff but to realise one of them had been through something so traumatic and still ended up in the police doing a role that helped others; it was an eye-opener.

'Look after her,' said Kevin to Jacob as he released his hold on Ben.

16th June, 0940 hours –Sunderland Outreach Centre

Stan watched from the semi-comfort of the police car he was sitting in. He'd grinned as the scene investigators had entered the scene in their white suits. They wouldn't find anything. He was too good. He hadn't left them anything that would point to him. The over-teeth dental casts he used during his teachings meant that he could attend the dentist when needed like a normal person. The bite marks would make them think they had a lead when in reality it would lead to nothing. And he always used a wipe over the mark afterwards to remove any DNA.

Seeing Gill carted off in an ambulance had pleased him. It had been a stroke of luck that it was her and not Brian who had gotten to the centre first, and even luckier that he'd been there when she found the body of someone she had cared about so much. He'd felt the power and held her as she screamed, all the while thinking that it was his handiwork and she didn't have a clue. He wondered what she'd have done differently if she had known. Would she have kicked out, biting, screaming, scratching? Or would she have backed away in terror, afraid the same fate awaited her?

He'd watched with interest as the female CSI had been walked from the scene, and placed in the van. There was a reason women shouldn't get involved in that kind of work. They didn't have the stomach. It was best to leave it to the men. Men could stomach pretty much anything. Well real men could, men like him.

Stan wished he was closer as they'd been talking near the van, wished he could hear what they'd said. They seemed concerned for her, the red-head.

Suddenly his cogs started turning, his senses kicking into overdrive as he processed the thoughts that were just on the periphery of his mind. It couldn't be. There was no way he was that lucky.

The frown was slow passing over his features. If it is her, then she'd have told them things. They might know things that no one was ever meant to know. Or find. He realised he hadn't wiped her cheek where he'd tasted the saltiness of her tears. He never did. But the police would never have cause to look for it. Not unless *she* told them.

Bree was alive, he knew this. But it couldn't be that she just happened to show up here. Could it? He had to find out where she was, what she was doing, whether there was any remote possibility that this red-head at the outreach centre was her. Tonight. He would do that tonight. Right now, he was too busy sat in the police car watching, waiting to be spoken to as a potential witness. But the seed of doubt began to grow in his mind. What if ...

Chapter Nineteen
16th June, 1420 hours – Tunstall, Sunderland City Centre Depot

Ben felt drained. She'd sat in the interview room and explained to Charlie what had happened to her in great detail. It had made her feel all the things she'd felt back when it had happened. The shame, the guilt, the fear.

It was awful knowing he was back, just being aware that what he'd done to her had happened to someone else who hadn't survived. Ben couldn't shake the cold feeling that seeped into her very soul. Was anywhere safe? She'd moved from Durham to get away from the nagging thought that he was always just around the corner, that he could strike again at any moment, that he would know she was alive and come looking. It had taken years for her to be able to function in society without looking over her shoulder constantly.

When she'd requested the transfer to the Sunderland section of North East Police, the chief himself had phoned ahead and put in a recommendation. The job on front office had been offered instantly: there'd just been a recruitment drive for the position.

It wasn't favouritism that got her the job, it was her need to work in a place she felt safe, and despite everything that had happened, that had still been the police force. And let's face it; the police force takes care of its own. When she'd needed stability and shielding the front office had provided that, a nice glass screen separating her from the world. Her new colleagues hadn't known what had happened. She'd been lucky really, the rumour mill hadn't started up, no-one at the Sunderland office had even known where she'd come from. *Now that's going to change. They'll all find out, look at me like I'm some kind of freak. Or worse, look at me in pity. 'There's the girl that was raped. The one that got away.'*

Jacob had sat with her the entire time, holding her hand, not speaking as she went through the whole thing from start to finish, handing her tissues when the emotion got too much. He'd nipped out and phoned Aoife to tell her what was happening.

All Ben wanted to do now was go home, lock the doors, and hide under a duvet to keep the monsters at bay. She'd thought she might have another panic attack but to her surprise, she'd kept it together through the interview with Charlie. Jacob had taken her to the canteen when they'd finished, but she was under orders not to leave the station yet. They'd been sat in silence in the canteen, Jacob automatically understanding that she needed to process her thoughts.

After an hour though, it was too much.

'How're you holding up?' he asked, looking up from his now cold coffee.

'I honestly don't know. It wasn't as hard as I thought it would be, telling them. I thought I'd fall apart, not be able to. Maybe even have to be sedated.' A faint rueful grin flittered over her lips. 'But it was OK.'

'You're incredibly brave, Ben. You know that, right?'

'I don't know if it's brave,' she replied. 'They needed to know. Hopefully they'll get evidence at the scene and catch the sonofabitch.'

'What's Ben short for? Benjamina?'

Jacob's sudden question threw her momentarily, and then she stared at him in horror. 'Benjamina? Oh God no.'

The smile faded as she went on to explain. 'He used my name. When he was... you know, he said my name over and over. Afterwards I couldn't bear to hear it. It made me cringe. I actually screamed at Aoife in the hospital when she called me it one day. It was awful. But I needed a name. My first name is Bree. It means strong and honourable. But it didn't feel either after he'd finished. Elizabeth was my gran's name and Nicole was my mum's best friend. I put the initials together and changed it by deed poll. Bree was who I was before the rape. Ben is who I've grown to be since.'

'Ben suits you. Still strong and honouring your family at the same time,' said Jacob.

Not quite knowing how to respond, she smiled back at him.

'I should ring Aoife. She'll be worried.'

'She is, but she knows you're safe with me. I said I'd get you home as soon as I could.'

'I bet she loved that. She's got this spidey sense where you're concerned. She's convinced there's something between us,' Ben's cheeks coloured as she realised what she'd said.

Jacob couldn't stop his eyes smouldering in reaction to her comments. All he'd wanted to do all day was tear her away from the police station and take her somewhere he could keep her safe. It was an urge so strong he'd had to physically stop himself. There was definitely something between them: Aoife's spidey sense was right.

'There is.' His reply was short and to the point, and Ben looked up, seeing the desire flash in his eyes even though he tried hard to hide it. 'I know,' she replied simply.

'TJ said the same. She's home now, you know. Did I tell you? She's staying at my place for a few nights and isn't allowed back to work just yet, but she's going to be OK.'

'I like your sis. She's very, erm, to the point.' Ben was reflecting on the exchange at the hospital when she'd taken TJ's injury photos.

'What did she say?' He felt a moment of panic. *What exactly did she say?*

'She warned me not to hurt you. I have no intention of doing that, by the way.'

Jacob groaned, 'She's such a mother hen, has been ever since our parents passed away.'

'She loves you, is all, same as Aoife loves me. They both just want what's best I guess.'

'True enough. Another coffee?'

At her nod, Jacob grabbed his stick and made his way to the coffee machine. *She feels it, too.* He hadn't wanted to seem like a teenager grinning from ear to ear at the knowledge that she liked him. Pouring the coffee, he composed himself and headed back over.

16th June, 1920 hours – Tunstall, Sunderland City Centre

Stan's anger had started burning the minute he'd been taken into the interview room. He knew the police had a job to do, but they'd almost made him feel like a suspect. Wanting to know the ins and outs of how he'd come to work at the centre, how many people had keys, where he'd been last night, whether he knew Clarice and so on.

He couldn't be seen as a suspect. He'd settled in Sunderland, didn't want to leave, but he would have to if this kept on.

And to top it off they'd had a woman interviewing him. A trumped up little school-girl playing cop: she couldn't have been more than twenty-five years old. He'd wanted to leap from his seat and slam her against the wall, show her that little girls should stick to the things they did best, like cleaning and cooking, though even that wasn't done to a high standard most of the time.

Disdain burned in his gut.

He needed to keep on top of what was happening with the investigation, needed to know if it got to the point when he would have to leave.

For now though, they didn't suspect. He was safe.

He reached to the shelf above his computer screens and took down the cardboard box. Unlike the other trinkets in the house, this one was pristine. There was no dust covering the top. He kept it clean.

The cops hadn't even searched him. It had given him a thrill having Clarice's hair in his pocket the whole time he'd been with the cops. And the fact he'd managed to see the delectable young girl again after ending her life just hours before only increased his pleasure. Frowning, he wrote her name on the back of the envelope, *13. Clarice Johnson.* Thinking for a second, he placed 8/10 beside her name. He'd started scoring after his first kill, his own little twist on the competition that was murder. Only one had ever scored ten out of ten.

He pushed the box to one side and hit the power button on the keyboard, smiling as his computer droned to life in seconds. This latest processor was great: it had cut his load time by more than half. It wanted to, for the price, but it pleased him that his computer was more responsive because of it. Hitting the search engines not used by the general public, those hidden where only certain people knew where to find them, he typed in what he knew about Bree. Seconds later the information he needed appeared before him. Scanning the document, he found what he was looking for. Bree Elizabeth Nicole O'Byrne changed her name by deed poll on 12th March 2009 to Ben Cassidy. She'd remained in Durham for two years before moving to Sunderland to live with her only living relative, an aunt, Aoife O'Byrne. She had a daughter, Grace Cassidy, almost five years old, born six months after moving back in with her aunt.

Sitting back in his chair, Stan grinned widely, the scar at the side of his mouth stretching his bottom lip awkwardly, making his smile more of a grimace. Glancing back at the screen he accessed her National Insurance information and found her place of employment: North East Police.

It *had* been her.

Deep down he'd known it the moment he'd seen her hair. Blazing red like a field of flaming poppies. *Shit, the bitch could have told them anything by now. It's definitely going to be time to move on. This is all her fault! How dare she survive. BITCH!*

His anger spurred him into action, but wary of destroying more computer hardware this time, he leapt up and slammed his fist into the wall to his side. He didn't feel the pain as he slammed it again and again into the wall, the plaster cracking and mingling with splat marks from his bloodied knuckles.

She would pay; this wasn't how it was supposed to be. The police might have evidence now. Evidence they wouldn't have had if *she* hadn't told them. Evidence that would point to him. He didn't know how much she remembered, didn't care if the truth be known. All that mattered was that she had survived, had told her tale. After suspecting for a while, even having it confirmed, finding out where she was and that she was linked to this case caused the niggle in the back of his mind to grow.

Stan strode into the kitchen, turned the tap on and placed his left hand underneath, calming as he watched the cold water wash over the cuts, letting the flow take his anger with it. He needed to remain calm, figure out a plan. Hell he needed to figure out where he was going now. Another city, maybe London this time. It was big, anonymous. A person could stay lost there for a very long time.

But first he would get rid of her once and for all. Never again would she be able to tell a soul about him. And he'd take care of the daughter and aunt too. Before she died she would understand that this entire situation could have been avoided if she'd just died when she was meant to. Plainly, she hadn't learned her lessons properly. He would make sure she did this time. All links to him would be extinguished, and when he finished there would be no-one left to stop him.

16th June, 2240 hours – O'Byrne residence, Sunderland
Jacob was sitting in the car outside Ben's house. He'd actually been there for almost twenty minutes, wanting to get home to TJ but not quite being able to pull away. He'd finally been allowed to take Ben home and he'd held on to her arm as she walked up the path to the front door, a small part of him afraid she might collapse without him to hold her up.

Her eyes had become haunted sitting in the station. He knew it was a relief to her that everyone knew, but there was still the stigma that *everyone knew*. All of a sudden her whole life was on show for all of her colleagues, her innermost fears coming to the surface as the day had progressed.

They'd been sitting in the office when Ali had entered and given them the brief lowdown on Clarice's injuries, how they believed she had been raped multiple times before finally succumbing to death.

Jacob knew what had happened to Ben. She'd told him, but the pure evilness of it hadn't sunk in. Until Ali had gone over everything with him, it had been a small part of Ben's history. Now it was a visual, a 3D movie with a killer shrouded in a dark shadow. He could almost hear her screams and pleas in his mind. Even more than ever, he wanted to hurt the man that had tried to break Ben, wanted to make him pay for what he'd put her through. What kind of a man did that anyway? He'd seen abuse on women on his tours abroad, women stoned in the square when they had broken whatever law the men had set, women beaten and forced to walk ten steps behind their male counterparts. Those men had hidden behind religion, excusing their actions with quotes from the Quran. Misguided? Definitely. But taking a girl hostage, hurting her, forcing her to have sex multiple times, then killing her. These actions he didn't understand.

They hadn't even made it up the three steps to the house when Aoife had flung the door open, grabbed hold of Ben and held her so tightly that for a moment, he'd thought she might break.

Aoife had looked at him with gratitude, her eyes filling with tears. And before he realised what had happened, she'd pulled him into the hug also. The three had stood there in the doorway for what seemed like an eternity, holding on to each other like they were safety buoys in a swirling ocean. For the first time in a lot of years, Jacob had actually felt at peace, and un-judged by his actions and injuries. He'd wanted to stay there forever, wrapped in the embrace of a woman so accepting of him, seeing him as a man and not a broken piece of one, and the equally strong motherly embrace of her aunt.

It was only now, some twenty minutes later that he realised the feeling was one of safety. It has been six years since his last tour, six years of pain and recovery, six years where he had never quite felt like he fitted anywhere.

In a sudden flash while standing on Ben's doorstep, he'd realised that it had been six years of focussing on himself. He'd never once in that time told TJ he appreciated everything she'd done. He'd sat and wallowed with an 'oh woe is me' attitude and struggled through each day.

Today had been like an eye opener. A young girl was dead, killed by the same man who had hurt Ben. He felt a little ashamed, if he was honest, here he was moaning about a gammy leg when she'd endured such horror and survived.

OK, the things he'd seen he wouldn't have wished on anyone, but there were a lot of people worse off than him.

A new determined look in his eyes, or rather the old determined look of who he had been before Afghanistan flickered brightly. No more feeling sorry. *So I have scars. So do a lot of people. Deal with it.* Finally feeling more at peace, he started the engine and pulled away.

16th June, 2320 hours – O'Byrne residence, Sunderland

Ben was sitting on the armchair with her legs pulled up under her bum, staring into space. Aoife had talked to her for a while after Jacob had dropped her off, telling her several times that everything was going to be OK. Eventually she'd realised Ben needed time with her thoughts, time to process having to expose herself to everyone she worked with, and time to realise that it wasn't as a big a deal as she thought it was. She had *survived* and that's what was important, Aoife had said, kissing her on the head and leaving her on the chair.

But Ben had her doubts.

Telling the people she worked with meant that the stares she'd had from the staff at Durham would return, those stares that said 'I can't believe she went through that, the poor thing', the stares that screamed 'Why's she still at work after an ordeal like that'; the stares that yelled 'I don't understand you any more'. That was how she'd seen them, at least. She'd noticed that people stopped speaking when she walked in the room, heard hushed whispers that hung in the corridors like accusations, and saw the looks of utter pity on the faces of her colleagues.

None of them understood.

You didn't give anyone chance to understand. You just turned tail and ran for the hills. The niggling voice in the back of her head could have been right she supposed, her mouth turning downwards in a slight frown. *I don't actually give people chance to understand, 'cos I've never actually told them or talked about it.*

It had been really tough today, telling her story over and over, trying not to let the emotion take over, but failing. People deal with horrific experiences in different ways, and after spending a couple of years living in paranoia, getting drunk and generally not *living*, Ben had pulled herself together when she'd found out she was pregnant. That after all the horror, that through both the physical and mental scars, her body could still carry the wonder of a new life had felt like a miracle. There was one moment she considered aborting the baby. It had been a turning point.

A lot of people didn't get that option. After the rape, they lived forever with the fear and paranoia, the emotional trauma itself, the feelings of not being worthy, the thoughts that somehow they were to blame.

A surge of anger flew through Ben's veins. *They're not to blame, none of them. No-one asks for that to happen. I'm not to blame. He is!*

She'd told other victims that often enough. The website she administrated gave her a forum to help where she could, but deep inside she knew she'd never believed it until just now. It was *his* choice to do what he did. She had no control over him. She didn't even know him. *But I know you now, you bastard. And I will do whatever I can to catch you so you never do this to another woman again.*

The haunted look finally left her eyes; tonight she would write it all down. Every little thing she remembered about that night, no matter how small. And tomorrow she would give it to Ali, and talk to Jacob. She knew that if he hadn't showed up at the scene of the murder, she might never have opened up as she had.

She at least owed him for the millions of coffees he'd bought throughout the day. Aoife was right, there was something about Jacob. She wanted to make sure he was OK.

Picking up her mobile, she sent him a quick text telling him she was thinking about him and saying thank you. Her mind now on a more even keel, she held her phone as she waited for his reply, but within seconds the device fell on to her lap as her head lolled and she fell straight into a deep sleep.

For the first time in eight years, she'd fallen asleep naturally, without any panic that she hadn't checked the windows and doors. If she'd realised she might have checked out of habit, and if she had, she might have seen something.

Stan stood outside the window, his eyes virtually burning holes in the glass as he stared at her. *You're going to pay for this. It's going to take some planning, but soon, you won't be telling anyone anything. You've fucked it all up. I have to move again and it's all your fault. I'm going to make you wish you were never born.* He stood there for several minutes, staring through the glass as his breath settled on the window pane. Now he knew everything he needed to, it was time to start laying the ground work.

He placed the pre-prepared letter in the letterbox, barely making a sound; the letter said there was water works in the area the next day, and that an engineer may need to attend to check the water pressure hadn't been affected. He would use his ruse to gain entry to the house, and fit what he needed to ensure he could see and hear everything, and then, when the time was right, he would strike.

Chapter Twenty
17th June, 1020 hours – O'Byrne residence, Sunderland

Aoife clicked the washing machine shut and set the load away. She'd been slowly increasing the usage of her arm since the operation, and figured she was now OK to do some washing. Ben would probably object but she wasn't here now.

Ben had left for work that morning, dropping Grace at school en route, and leaving Aoife at home with her thoughts.

She was worried. Ben had seemed so low the night before, and she understood why. Ben had never found it easy to open up about anything. Even when her parents had died and she'd wound up living with her aunt miles from her former home, Ben had hidden behind her shell and not shown much emotion. It had taken months for her to learn to trust Aoife, to open up and express her emotion.

The turning point had been when Ben had caught flu the winter after arriving. It was a pandemic at the time, a virulent strain that lasted a good couple of weeks. Ben had been laid up with fever, her head pounding, her temperature sky-rocketing, and she'd been afraid. Aoife had sat with her all night, stroking her hand soothingly, helping her drink fluids and generally just being there. She'd woken in the middle of the night to the sound of Ben screaming, tears running down her flushed cheeks, sweat plastering hair to her head. Aoife had held her tightly until the tears stopped, her heart overflowing with love as Ben had cried over the loss of her parents, months of pent up emotion released in a flood. As the tears petered out, Ben had whispered, 'Please don't leave me, Aunty Aoife, I don't want to be alone.'

And Aoife had promised she would never leave.

Pulling herself from the thoughts, she grabbed a cloth. There was only one thing to do when one had worries weighing them down, and that was to clean. She was just about to spray the bleach, when a sudden knock at the door made her jump.

Opening the door a crack, she peered round the side. Seeing his uniform, she opened the door further.

'Sorry to bother you, ma'am. I'm from the water board. We sent letters out advising of on-going work in the area this morning. I just need to check that your water pressure hasn't been affected. The works have been completed with a temporary fix. We'll be looking to get the permanent fix installed in the next month or two.'

He smiled at her reassuringly, his water-board ID card hanging from his neck by an insignia coated lanyard. Aoife barely even noticed his overalls. Her focus caught by the scar on his face.

'I wasn't informed of any on-going water works.'

Frowning, the man checked his clipboard. This is number forty-three, right? It's definitely on the list. The letters were hand-delivered yesterday evening. Normally we send them in the post 'cos there's time but this was an emergency repair. I apologise if you haven't received it. If you would like I can give you the contact number for the control room and you can double-check I'm supposed to be here.'

As Stan said the words, his hand closed round the knife in his pocket. *Damn it, don't make me use this. Not yet. The timing isn't right.*

'Let me see your ID closer.' Aoife was aware she sounded suspicious, but she didn't let people in her house unless she was certain they posed no threat. Deciding his ID looked real, she granted him access.

'Stop cock is in the kitchen under the sink.'

'Great thanks, busy morning today. Weather seems to be holding out nice though.'

'A little sunshine is cheering,' admitted Aoife with a small smile. 'Coffee?'

'Do you know, love, I'd kill for a cuppa right now. White with two if that's OK?'

'No problem.'

Busying herself she popped the kettle on. She didn't quite feel comfortable though. There was something about this man that set her neck alight and shivers of awareness tingled down her spine as she poured him his hot drink.

Just as she handed it over, the phone rang.

'O'Byrne residence, Sunderland.'

'Ms O'Byrne, Doctor Carmichael here. I'm sending a letter with the full results, but I just wanted to give you a quick ring. The results are back from your lumpectomy. The flesh margin is clear of cancer cells: it hasn't spread. I want to look at getting you booked in for a course of chemotherapy within the next month. The course will give fortnightly treatments over a period of a few months. I'm confident we've caught this in time. This treatment will ensure that any remaining cancer cells are eradicated completely.'

The man from the water-board was pointing to the ceiling and the front door. He mouthed that he needed to check the pressure upstairs and grab something from the van, and left the kitchen.

Aoife had almost convinced herself that surgery was all she would need. Unable to hide her disappointment, she said, 'Well, if you think it's necessary, Doctor, I understand.'

'I wouldn't recommend it if it wasn't. I know this is difficult, but trust me, you're in good hands.'

'You're right, I'm sorry. Thank you.'

'There are some things we will need to discuss. Can you come in for a chat next week? Say Thursday morning at 10 a.m.?'

'Of course. Thank you, Doctor Carmichael. I do appreciate everything you're doing.'

He clicked off the line, and Aoife replaced the handset on to the holder by the microwave. *Every couple of weeks for a few months. Boy, that's going to be fun.*

Noticing that the kitchen was empty and the man hadn't returned, Aoife made her way into the hall. He stepped off the bottom step of the staircase as she approached.

'Pressure seems fine upstairs, downstairs is a little low so I'll need to run some tests at the mid-station. Hopefully I can solve the problem from there and not have to bother you again. If I need to though, is it OK just to pop back?'

'Yes of course, no problem.'

She didn't know why she felt uneasy. It wasn't like she hadn't checked his ID. Maybe she would give the water-board a ring just to confirm once he'd left. She watched as he drained his coffee in one gulp and handed her the mug.

'Just what the doctor ordered that. You'd be surprised how many people don't offer refreshments, not that I'd ask mind you, but it's nice to be offered. Much appreciated, love.'

17th June, 1030 hours, O'Byrne residence, Sunderland

Stan couldn't believe his luck. That doctor had rung at just the right time. He'd already been pondering on how to gain access to the rest of the house. A moment in the living room to plant a sound bug on the table lamp, and two minutes for upstairs was all he needed though. He'd picked the right bedroom on the first try, fitting the tiny camera and turning the signal on. It had been easy to pick a spot too; the number of trinkets lying around had made choosing a hiding place easy.

He wanted to know what the phone call had been about, had actually been tempted to stop and listen outside the kitchen door, but getting his tools fitted was more important. He'd almost baulked as he took a mouthful of the coffee she'd made, whatever it was, it wasn't his favourite brand. Whilst upstairs he'd poured most of it down the sink, only drinking the last mouthful before handing her the mug back.

You'd have thought at her age she would know how to make coffee. All those years staying home and looking after her niece had not taught her properly. His mouth twisted in disdain; it was because there was no man in the house. This he'd ascertained from his quick glance around. How was a woman supposed to learn to act properly when not guided by a man? He would take great pleasure in showing her what he expected. He'd never tried teaching more than one student at a time. It would be interesting to say the least. He would need a good plan, and better yet, a good location.

Pulling away from the kerb, he decided it was time to check out some of the abandoned properties he had a list of. Places that had been closed so long people didn't even remember what they used to be. Places still in the city but secluded and forgotten. With so many likely spots available, perhaps his teachings could be done here without him living in the area. His job at the centre had given him the opening he needed: part-time hours suited and provided him with ample free time.

He would regret moving this time though. The kids at the centre needed a good male role model. And he knew he provided that. Better than wimpy Brian at any rate. The man was permanently staring into space these days, had been ever since his wife had been murdered eighteen months before. From what he heard, she deserved to die. No woman had ever cheated on him, he'd never given them the opportunity, but Brian's wife had. And if the rumours heard were believed to be true, she'd been pregnant with the bastard child of her killer too. And Gill, well she was OK he supposed, a bit exuberant for his liking, but she wasn't a man. She couldn't teach the kids like he could. Besides, she'd be too wrapped up in her own problems for a long time now. He doubted she would be at work for a while. Brian would have to get cover in, and who knew who that would be. Yes, the kids needed him. If he didn't have to move he wouldn't. It would all depend on what Bree had said.

The more he thought about her, the more he couldn't wait to have her again. She had been haunting his thoughts since he'd seen her, all trussed up in her white suit at the centre.

He had visions of her being pleased to see him, being submissive and allowing him to teach her without saying no. His mind had even ventured into the field that maybe he wouldn't have to kill her, maybe she would just do as he asked without question. He could see her breasts in his mind, big, beautiful and covered in his marks. She belonged to him, she always had.

He was starting to understand there may have been a reason she had survived, and that reason was to be there for him.

The others were almost like a compulsion, the act itself something he couldn't help but do. None had ever compared to her, though. It was almost as if he had been travelling the long road around the country just to get back to her.

Stan's focus had shifted, quite suddenly really. It wasn't about women in general but about *her*. And he would make sure she understood that when his plan was complete and he had her again. He had the knowledge he needed to control her. He knew exactly what to do to lure her to him. And soon he would have the perfect location too.

17th June, 1405 hours – Major Incident Room, Sunderland City Centre Depot

Ali reread Ben's statement with tired eyes. He'd been there until late last night; it had been around 2 a.m. when he'd finally crawled to the flat and into his bed, setting his alarm for six to get back to work. He couldn't believe she'd been through all that and survived.

He'd been surprised when he'd seen her earlier today, part of him expecting her to need time off. She'd been picking up the slack in the office, choosing to work the jobs to free up the other CSIs to deal with the murder. He knew Deena was at Clarice's home with Jacob, dismantling the girls computer while he sat there putting his files together and passing them to the girls to load on to the Holmes systems.

He'd rang the DNA Submissions company earlier too, trying to push the swabs from Clarice's cheeks through. DNA would be a good lead. This guy had to be on file somewhere for something. One didn't just wake up and decide to rape and murder women. There had to be something somewhere that would show him who this guy was.

For a moment, his thoughts went to Alex, his brother. Alex had been the DCI of the Major Incident Team for about four years now. He'd seen more than his share of horrors. Ali wanted to ask him how he coped with it, ask him how he stopped the dreams coming. But he knew he wouldn't. Asking Alex would be like admitting he couldn't cope.

The things that people did to each other never failed to amaze him. Maybe he had chosen the wrong career. He'd worked his arse off getting to where he was now, accepting the secondment with North East Police when it came up on Alex's recommendation. But he missed being in Edinburgh with his family, missed the banter and the fact he knew he could always go to his mum's and find cake, comfort and love. The flat was stifling, empty. Lonely. He hated it.

As the phone rang on his desk, he pulled his head back in the game.

'McKay.'

'DI McKay, this is Marie Smithson from the DNA lab. Do you have a moment?'

'Sure, go ahead, Marie.'

'We ran the swabs you sent through the database this morning. There appears to be some kind of anomaly. The sample you sent matches that of a John Whitworth. His file lists him as recently deceased.'

'What? You're kidding. Whitworth died last week whilst in police custody. How can his saliva be on the cheek of our victim?'

'I'd probably suggest that somehow the samples may have gotten mixed up. We tested both swabs just to be certain. Sorry, Detective.'

He heard the receiver click down in his ear. *What the hell? The shit's gonna hit the fan here. How the hell could the samples have been mixed up?*

Putting the receiver back in its cradle, he got to his feet. It was time to speak to Kevin and find out how the hell this could have happened.

17th June, 1415 hours - CSI Department, Sunderland City Centre Depot
'I'm telling you, Ali, there is no way those samples could have been mixed up, and frankly, I resent the implication that my staff would make a mistake like that.' Kevin's voice was calm as he reacted to the news.

'There isn't another explanation, Kev. Obviously Whitworth didn't kill Clarice - he was already dead at the time of the murder. The samples are stored in the same freezer downstairs in the hold. The only explanation is that they were mixed up!'

'Ali, my staff aren't stupid. They deal with this stuff all the time. If you truly believe the samples were mixed up, then let me take you downstairs and show you the swabs taken from Whitworth when he was booked through custody. If this isn't another bloody obvious reason why cops should store their own samples, I don't know what is.' Kevin walked out of his office and strode purposefully down the stairs.

He'd been campaigning for years to have the freezers in the hold solely for the use of the CSIs and not the cops. The CSIs monitored it and booked the samples in and out, but it created extra work and took time. He'd gone right up the chain to the Chief who now had it under advisement. The sooner the better as far as he was concerned.

They reached the hold and Kevin unlocked the door with the keys only the CSIs had. Keeping the keys in-house helped prevent issues arising with people not knowing the procedure. Inside the hold were numerous freezers, all labelled with a month. The samples were held either until needed or for the period of one year when they were moved to the central store at HQ. He pulled out the file and checked the entry log.

Going to the freezer for this year, he pulled open the door, opened the drawer labelled June, and pulled a large box from shelf two. It took him a minute to go through the samples but he found what he was looking for. With a triumphant smile, he waved the sample at Ali.

'This is the sample taken by custody when Whitworth was arrested. All swabs are present and correct, and labelled appropriately. The sample sent to the lab was definitely taken from Clarice's cheek.'

Silence reined as he placed the swabs back in the box, and put the box back on the shelf. Closing the door he turned to face Ali, his head cocked to one side thoughtfully.

'Have you checked Whitworth's family history, Ali?'

Ali nodded his head slowly, 'Of course. He grew up in foster care, pushed from pillar to post. Married his wife Eve in his late twenties, and they had their son Matthew a few years later. Why?'

'Is it possible he could have an identical twin? Identical twins have the same DNA sequence. It's the only other explanation I can think of to explain how the same DNA could have been found.'

'A twin? I suppose that could be possible, though surely both kids would have ended up in foster care? I need to go have this looked into properly. I'll speak to you later, Kev. Oh, and I'm sorry for sounding so bull-headed. It bugs me when stuff like this happens, but I shouldn't have been throwing it around accusing your staff. Thanks for helping clear it up.'

Ali left the hold and headed back up the stairs to the MIT office. He had research to do.

17th June, 1845 hours – Tunstall, Sunderland City Centre

Stan watched as Ben filled the screen in front of him. She'd just gotten out of the shower and was drying herself with an oversized peach towel. Her daughter was sitting on the bed chatting as she played with a teddy. The child's hair was damp, and she was dressed in her pyjamas. He assumed she had just gotten out of the bath before Ben had jumped in.

Maybe he wouldn't kill the child. He could take her with him, raise her and train her to be the subservient woman he knew he deserved. She was young yet, but she could learn.

He felt his tongue dip out and moisten his lips with a quick swipe as Ben undid the towel and moved it side to side across her back. When the towel fell to the floor it was like a bolt of lightning shot through him. He was instantly hard, painfully so in fact. Ben was stood with her back facing the camera. He knew if she'd been facing him, showing him *his* marks on her breasts, then he would've lost all control.

She leant across the bed and grabbed her pyjamas off the pillow. Within seconds her ivory skin was hidden behind the folds of the thin cotton night clothes. He sighed to himself. Next time. Next time, he would get to see his handiwork again. From the bug he'd planted in the living room, he heard the older woman call the two down, listened as she said she'd made cocoa with marshmallows. His mother had never made him cocoa with marshmallows. He didn't even remember ever having drunk it.

Suddenly a male voice sounded through the speaker, pulling his attention back to the present.

'Sorry if I'm intruding, I just wanted to check on Ben.'

'That's fine, Jacob. I've just made cocoa. I'll go pour you a cup. Ben and Grace will be down soon.'

He felt anger burn deep inside his stomach. *Who the fuck is that? There was no man living there! I checked, damn it!* He sat up straighter, and pulled his chair closer to the speaker system. He wouldn't miss a word of this conversation.

17th June, 1855 hours – O'Byrne residence, Sunderland

'Come on, pumpkin. Head into the living room to see Aunty Aoife. I heard her say she might have made cocoa.' Ben's voice was playful out in the hall as she pushed open the living room door. Not expecting to see Jacob, she jumped when she noticed him.

'Jacob, erm hi.' She tugged at the vest top she had on self-consciously. *Damn I knew I should've put a dressing gown on. He must think I'm some kind of freak. In my PJs before 7 p.m.*

He hid a grin, blatantly watching as she tugged at her top. 'Just wanted to check you were OK. Deena said you were back to work today.' At Ben's puzzled look, he added, 'I was at Clarice's house with her, dismantling the computer. She mentioned it. It's a shame, I knew the kid from college. Briefly anyway. She seemed nice.'

Ben nodded silently, suddenly remembered the comments Deena had made when she came back in the office. Ben had presumed she had been talking about a cop when she'd mentioned there had been a good view at the house. For a millisecond she burned with jealousy that someone else was looking at Jacob, and then realised how ridiculous she was being. She sat in the armchair in the corner, curled her legs up underneath her and reached for the cushion, hugging it to her chest. Grace on the other hand, was not quite so reserved. She clambered up on the couch beside Jacob, and happily threw her arms around his neck, pulling herself into him.

'Have you come to read me a story?'

Jacob grinned, and tapped her on the nose with his finger. 'That depends on whether mummy says you've been a good girl. If you have been a good girl, maybe mummy will also let me give you the pressie I have in my pocket.'

'You got me a present? Mummy, I have been a good girl haven't I? Can I please have my present?' Grace clambered off the couch and stood in front of Jacob, looking at Ben with hope.

She couldn't have said no if she'd tried, and nodded. 'You've been very good. Tell Jacob about the award you got at school today, and then he can give you the present.'

'I got an 'ward for reading. I stood up in class and read a whole story all by myself. Aunty Aoife and mummy helped me learn the big words.'

'Wow, that's fantastic. Well done, sweetpea. I suppose I'll have to give you your present then. Here you go.'

Jacob reached behind his back and pulled out an elephant soft toy. 'Elephants never forget anything. You can tell your elephant anything and he'll always remember what you said.'

Grace took hold of the toy gently, smiling at Jacob widely. 'Thank you. Do you want to pick a name for him?'

Jacob didn't have time to consider the vice-like feeling round his heart. The feeling that any walls he had built up were coming tumbling down with a few sentences from the innocent mouth of a child. He swallowed the lump in his throat and answered, 'How about Ernest?'

A flash of pain passed through his eyes, but Grace didn't notice. She nodded happily, 'I'm gonna go show Aunty Aoife my new el'phant.' She whirled away from Jacob and out into the hall, shouting at the top of her lungs.

Ben had noticed the pain though, the same as she picked up on his contemplative silence. 'Who was Ernest?'

Taking a breath, Jacob replied. 'Ernest was actually a lad in my old regiment. His real name was Stephen Watson. He got the nickname from constantly having his head in a book. His favourite was *A Farewell to Arms*.'

'By Ernest Hemingway,' interrupted Ben with a grin.

'Yeah. He loved the classics, Hemingway, Verne and all the rest. He must've spent half his wages every month on buying books. Ernest just kinda stuck.'

'What happened?'

'He was with my team when the IED went off. He didn't make it.'

'I'm sorry,' said Ben simply. When the silence stretched, she added, 'Thanks for getting Grace the elephant. She loves cuddly toys.'

'I guessed. When I took her up the other night I noticed them all around her room. I saw the elephant today and thought she would like it.'

The door pushed open and Grace leaned against it, keeping it open while Aoife entered with a tray of steaming mugs of chocolate with pink and white marshmallows melting on the top.

17th June, 2310 hours – Tunstall, Sunderland City Centre
'Jacob.'

Stan almost spat the word from his mouth. Who the hell did he think he was, coming in and staking a claim on *his* woman. Sitting there in the living room, flirting and chatting as if Stan didn't even exist.

Plainly the lessons he had taught Bree hadn't worked. She was definitely in need of further tutoring.

But first, though, he would find out more about this Jacob, and take care of business. A man took care of his own problems. Another snippet of truth from his pain-in-the-arse father.

He wished he'd placed a camera in the living room now, wanted to be able to see them sitting closely next to each other on the couch, canoodling as they chatted. He wanted to see them so he could then swipe them both from the face of the earth. He'd kill Jacob first, making Bree watch. Then he'd kill her slowly, telling her over and over that her daughter would be his next student.

Bree would die knowing he had Grace, and that he was raising her to be a proper young lady.

The anger was so strong; it felt like the worst case of acid indigestion ever, burning his insides and creating a red hue around his field of vision. *Damn it, I need to see them together. Who the hell does he think he is? She's mine!*

Grabbing his coat, he headed for the door.

17th June, 2335 hours – O'Byrne residence, Sunderland
Jacob didn't want to leave. But it was late and he'd been watching Ben struggle not to fall asleep for the last twenty minutes, her eyes closing slowly then opening as she fought to stay awake. She'd moved over to the couch when Aoife had taken Grace up to bed, not wanting Jacob to feel like he was sitting ten miles from her. It had been uncomfortable at first, for both of them. Neither was used to having someone else in close proximity. As the movie

progressed though the tension had eased, and now Ben's head rested on his shoulder as the film came to a close. Jacob's arm curled around her waist, his fingers resting lightly on the curve of her hip.

He heard her sigh softly against his shoulder, and snuggle in a millimetre more. Breathing in he smelled the scent of her shampoo, apples with a hint of mint. It smelled clean, fresh, and he inhaled again, aware that if she was awake she might think he was some kind of freak. He really didn't want to move.

Would it be so bad to stay?

He argued with himself, torn between leaving, which would wake her up, and staying still, which is what his heart wanted to do.

Ben's hand dropped from his arm to the top of his leg, and he was lost. Gently he manoeuvred them both so that he could lift his feet on to the footstool at the edge of the sofa, pulled the tattered blanket off the back of the couch and placed it around Ben's shoulders, and rested his head on the pillow. Tomorrow, he could argue with his head, tonight his heart had won.

He would stay.

Within seconds, his eyes closed of their own accord and he fell into a deep sleep.

18th June, 0005 hours – O'Byrne residence, Sunderland

Stan stood outside the window looking in. They hadn't even had the decency to close the curtains, laying there together for the world to see. Well OK, not exactly the world. It was a detached house after all with large fencing surrounding it. But it was the principle. She was *his*, and Jacob had no right trying to stake a claim.

He stood watching them sleep for some time, so long that his feet actually went a little numb from standing. The weather had been fair when he had arrived, but as time progressed clouds rolled in covering the faint light from the stars, and he felt the first droplets start to fall.

It was time to leave.

Not caring if anyone saw now, he strode back round to the front of the house, and paused as he saw the cars on the driveway. He didn't know whose was whose, and frankly he didn't care. He pulled the knife from his pocket and pressed the button, ejecting the sharpened blade, and methodically sliced into all four tyres on each car. *See how you both like that. You'll both learn.*

Walking round the cars had shown him which was Ben's: it was the one with the child's seat in the back. Deciding to make his point even more obvious, he etched the words 'I've been watching you' into the bonnet. He needed to remind her of her lessons, show her that he was disappointed she hadn't learned.

Appeased now, if only momentarily, he left the driveway, got back into his car, and drove off.

Chapter Twenty-one
18th June, 0625 hours – O'Byrne residence, Sunderland

Ben didn't want to wake up. She was warm, and comfortable and sleep was calling her back. Suddenly she heard the soft sound of breathing coming from beneath her and her eyes flung open. Her mouth dropped into a soft 'o' shape as she realised it was Jacob.

He looked so peaceful, his breathing deep and regulated, his face completely untroubled. She found herself drawn, and unable to stop herself, she gently traced his face with the tip of her finger.

Jacob was awake in an instant, his senses kicking into overdrive and making him sit up, disorientated. The movement jolted Ben off the couch and she landed on the carpet with a loud 'Oomph!'

'Shit, sorry. Are you OK?' Jacob grabbed his leg and swung it over the edge so that he was sitting up, and leant down. 'Ben, are you OK? I'm sorry, I was startled.'

He watched as her shoulders started shaking. 'Ben, please don't cry, I said I'm sorry. I didn't mean –' Ben looked up, interrupting him, her eyes sparkling with laughter. 'I've never seen anyone move so fast! I didn't even notice you were awake `til I ended up on my arse.' A giggle escaped, and before she knew it, she couldn't stop. Tears sprung into her eyes, and Jacob couldn't help but smile back. Her laughter was infectious, and within seconds they were both giggling hysterically.

Eventually, the giggling eased to smiles.

'I'll go make some coffee,' said Ben, kneeling in front of him, intending to use the edge of the couch to pull herself up. But something made her pause. Jacob's mirth had eased, and his eyes were full of something else. Something she hadn't seen for a long time, it took her a moment to recognise it as desire.

She felt like a deer caught in the headlights again, half-wanting to move but mesmerised. She didn't register him moving closer, not until she felt his breath softly touching her lips. *Shit, he's gonna kiss me. What do I do?* 'Kiss him back,' the voice in her head said. 'You know you want to.'

His lips were soft as they touched hers, and she wasn't prepared for the bolt of lightning that flew between them. He deepened the kiss a little, his hands gentle on the back of her head. Ben couldn't have pulled back if she wanted to. Her arms snaked up his back, her fingers caressing him, and he groaned into her mouth. Pulling back, he stared at her, almost as if he needed confirmation that it was alright to kiss her. She leaned forward and kissed him, tentatively, her movements a little shy.

Suddenly the door opened, and they jerked apart, looking guilty.

Grace wandered inside, rubbing her eyes.

'Mammy, is it time to get up now?'

Ben glanced at Jacob, a little pleased that he looked as flustered as she felt, and got to her feet. Picking Grace up, she hugged her daughter tightly. 'It's a little early, pumpkin, but that's no problem. Shall we go and see what we have in for breakfast? Maybe Jacob would like to join us in the kitchen, too?'

He nodded silently, watching as Grace laid her head on Ben's shoulder in contentment. He pulled himself up from the couch and for the first time in years, his leg didn't seize up. Stretching, he took hold of his cane and followed the pair through the doors.

The breakfast passed with ease, Grace not even thinking to question why Jacob was still there. When Aoife had entered the kitchen, she had shown mild surprise but it was disguised by a knowing smirk. The two were as awkward around each other as a wolf meeting a bear in the woods. But beneath the surface there was a comfort that they didn't even realise was there. They'd survived their first night together. It was a huge step. Aoife was pleased. She patted Ben on the back as she took her coffee and sat down next to Jacob.

He didn't quite know what to say to her, had gone to start a couple of sentences but realised how stupid they would sound. So he stayed silent, holding his coffee and just watching the interaction at the table.

Before he knew it, it was time to leave for work; they'd both showered as if it was any normal morning. As they walked to the front door, Aoife gave Ben a push towards him.
'Jacob can take you to work today; I need the car for an appointment at the hospital. You don't mind do you, Jacob?'

He could barely contain his grin as he shook his head. Ben just groaned quietly. Aoife just couldn't stop herself interfering. She was incorrigible!

She followed Jacob out to the car, and bumped into his back as he stilled suddenly.

'What is it?' she asked, her voice turning wary at his silence. He turned to her with a frown. 'Someone's slashed the tyres on both the cars.'

'What? Are you sure? Maybe we just ran over glass or something ...' Ben manoeuvred around him, and paused as she realised he meant all the tyres. Her eyes focussed on the words etched into her bonnet she felt the blood drain from her face. The world went off-kilter, and she felt herself start to fall.

Realising what was happening, Jacob dropped his stick and caught her before she hit the floor. The added weight caused his leg to give way and he only just managed to move himself under her to break her fall. 'Crap,' he muttered before raising his voice and shouting for Aoife through the open front door.

Ben had barely lost consciousness and could hear Grace telling her to wake up, and slowly she fluttered her eyes open. She saw the sky above and realised she was outside. Her senses went into overdrive and she realised Jacob was caught beneath her. Realising she had passed out again, she groaned and swore at herself softly.

'Mammy, that's a naughty word. Jacob said you fell asleep on him. Are you awake now?'

'Yes, pumpkin, I'm awake.' Embarrassed, she pulled herself to her feet and stretched a hand out to help Jacob to his feet. His face was twisted in a grimace and he tried to hide the pain that was shooting through his leg, but failed. Accepting her hand, he was surprised at the strength with which she tugged him to his feet. He leaned into her shoulder as Grace handed him his stick.

'Sorry,' whispered Ben into his ear, fear causing her voice to shake. 'It's him. He was here. I need to get Aoife and Grace away from here. I can't let them be here when he's out there and knows where I live. Will you help me?'

Jacob nodded, 'I know just the place. Leave it to me. You phone the police.'

18th June, 0810 hours – O'Byrne residence, Sunderland

Ali pulled on to the driveway of Ben's house. He'd literally walked into the office when comms had told him about the damage to Ben's car. He needed to see about getting her away from the house, putting her somewhere safe, but first he had to speak to her. How the hell had this guy known where to find her?

'Ben, Jacob,' he acknowledged as he strode into the living room. He'd glanced at the cars on the way past. This was getting personal. This guy knew where she lived, and had no qualms about letting her know he had visited. *What's so different about Ben though? Why is he focussing on her now, after all this time?* The question kept popping into his head, had been since he'd set off from the nick. Ali knew the answer was in there somewhere, and pushed it to the back of his mind as he sat down.

Ben and Jacob were sat next to each other on the couch, Jacob's hand resting softly on Ben's knee. She was leaning into him, their body language practically screaming there was something between them. Ali wasn't surprised; he thought Ben was enigmatic and appealing, had done since he'd first time he'd seen her. She was strong, but today her vulnerability was showing through, slight cracks appearing in her strong façade. She was tapping her foot softly against the carpet, nibbling at the inside of her bottom lip, and her eyes were haunted.

'I've read the report you gave to Charlie, Ben. You said he whispered those words to you during the attack. Is it possible that that sentence could have been found out somehow, either through the news or you telling someone, and this could just be someone playing silly beggars?'

Ben pondered his question. 'No. The police didn't release any of the identifiable facts about the rape. They didn't mention the words he said, and they didn't mention my ... scars. The news was generic. And until now I've never told anyone else except my aunt, about what happened. This is *him*, Ali. I'm sure of it. I don't know why he's come back, but he has.'

Ali nodded. He already knew that, but he needed to hear that she hadn't told anyone. His gut already told him she hadn't and that this was indeed the same guy, but the confirmation proved it. He felt a lead weight in his stomach. *Damn, I need some antacid. I've got a bad feeling about this.*

'I need to put you and your family somewhere safe. He knows where you live. We have a safe house we'd like to use outside of the city centre. I'll assign two cops to be with you at all times. It'll mean taking your daughter out of school for a little while.'

'They're safe, Ali. I've already sent them somewhere that nobody would look for them. Jacob knew a place.'

'Will you tell me where? I'd like to assign officers to them.'

'It's OK,' said Jacob quietly, 'They're staying with a friend of mine from my time in the service. No-one will get near them.'

Ali nodded silently. It hadn't escaped him that Ben and Jacob were keeping schtum on purpose. Understandable, he supposed. He couldn't say he wouldn't do the same in their situation.

'So just you and Jacob then.' He paused gauging Ben's reaction. Before she even spoke, he knew she wasn't going to let him put her in the safe house.

'If he thinks he can run me out of my home, and make me hide away like the scared girl I was after he attacked me, then he's dead wrong. I refuse to be driven out. When I moved back in with Aoife, we had state-of-the-art alarm systems installed. We've not really used them the last couple of years, but they will keep him out. I'm not going to the safe house. Feel free to assign cops outside, but I will not let this monster ruin my life again.'

'I'll be staying with her too. My boss has already given me permission to work from home for a while. I need to pick my kit up but otherwise I'll be here.' Jacob's voice was calm.

'OK. I'm going to have one of the PCSOs come and install a Tunstall alarm in the premises. You know how they work, right? Anything happens, and I mean anything, you press the button and it connects to the control room and results in an immediate response. I've got Kevin coming down here to examine the vehicles, see if the offender left anything behind that we could use. There'll be two officers outside the address in an unmarked pool car 24/7 until this guy is caught. We won't let him near you, Ben.'

'I know, thanks, Ali. Have you mentioned anything to Cass? I wouldn't want her to worry.'

'Yeah, I've told her. Only because I was discussing it with Alex, though. She said to tell you she's there if you need her.'

'I'll give her a ring tonight and put her mind at ease. She has enough on her plate right now.'

'Yeah, you're not wrong. OK, Ben. I'm going to head back to the office, see if we can't make some headway on who the hell this guy is. You've got my number. You need anything, day or night, you call me.'

Ali stood and left the living room. Pausing at the front door, he rested his head on the frame, just for a second. He felt a little sick, bile sitting in his oesophagus as he considered all the things that could potentially happen. Whitworth's wife had known she married a monster, and she hadn't reported him, but at least he was known. This killer was like a ghost, he could pretty much pass through walls. How the hell did one live under the radar in this day and age? Lifting his head slowly, his eyes narrowed as he thought about his silent question. The only way people could live under the radar, was if they were homeless and didn't claim dole which was unlikely, or if they knew how to navigate the system and use it to their benefit.

It gave him an idea, and jumping in the car, he sped back to the nick.

18th June, 1030 hours – Boxmania Gymnasium, Sunderland

Stan was in the gym, throwing punches at the large bag that hung from the ceiling. One of the young lads, a new-comer to the boxing world, was holding the bag and grimacing whenever the punch connected. Stan wasn't holding back.

He felt each impact shudder up his arm and into the muscles at the top - could feel the tension in his shoulders as he drew back and released in a steady rhythm. He was focussed, concentrating hard on his work-out. A lot of it was second nature now, twenty from the left, twenty from the right, ten from each knee, ten spinning kicks, and then repeat using upper-cuts instead. Sweat was beading on his forehead, dripping down on to the black sweat band he wore. For the time he worked out, his mind was a blank canvas.

He'd needed the workout today, wanted the challenge of kicking the hell out of something. He'd been listening that morning when Ali had turned up. *What kind of name was Ali anyway? What self-respecting man would let himself be called a girl's name?* He faltered as the errant thought entered his mind and threw off his rhythm.

Coming back to earth momentarily, he registered the burn in his muscles, smelled the sickly scent of sweat as it congregated in the curves of his armpits, and ran down the small of his back into the top of his shorts. His body was telling him he'd done enough. Glancing at the clock he realised he'd been working out for well over an hour. *Best not overdo it. I have planning to do.*

'Jacko,' he yelled suddenly, 'Come hold the bag for Ricky here, he's held it for long enough.' Jacko strode over, flexing his arm muscles. His wide chest caused his narrow hips to sway as he walked. *Now that's taking things to the extreme. Wonder if he realises how ridiculous he looks. Arms the size of tree trunks and I could still take him down in one move.* Luckily for Jacko though, that wasn't Stan's intent. He moved to the locker room at the side of the boxing ring, grabbed his bag, and left.

Getting back to the apartment, he dumped his bag at the door and sat down in his computer room. *I bet she's hiding out in the bedroom with Jacob. Stupid bitch. Does she really think two cops sat outside, and a stupid alarm system will stop me?*

He'd clocked the alarms when he visited last night. It *was* a sophisticated system, but it was also several years out of date. He had software that would reset the code remotely and allow him easy access. The two cops sat outside would pose little problem. He knew what cops were like. The slightest sniff of doughnuts and they'd be out of the car faster than daft mick. If he did it right, their deaths would be quick and painless. Well, relatively painless anyway. Then he would be able to finish his teachings. He intended to show Bree that she should never have survived in the first place.

Ideally, he wanted to find Grace and the aunt and use them as his bargaining chip, but he knew nothing about Jacob that would indicate who he had placed the old woman and kid with. That was what he needed to do now; go through the data and see what he could find on the guy who thought he could swoop in and take Bree from him.

Plugging in his search terms, he pushed his chair back and went to make a brew. This could take a while.

18th June, 1340 hours – O'Byrne residence, Sunderland

I am actually going nuts. Ben had been sitting in relative silence watching as Jacob set up the equipment he needed to work from home. Her home. Not his.

Realising her thoughts were petty, she headed into the kitchen. It wasn't Jacob's fault they were stuck inside. She didn't mind his company, in fact she actually thought it was sweet that he was refusing to leave her side. Last night had meant a lot. More than she could express in words to be honest. Since the attack, she had never spent the whole night in a man's company. The night Grace had been conceived, she'd been drunk. Another attempt at trying to drown out the screaming voice in her head shouting 'why me'.

She didn't remember a whole lot about the evening. She knew she'd been downing vodka, anything to try and numb the pain she felt in her heart, the feeling of utter desolation and worthlessness. She was already far gone when the guy had approached her in the bar, bought her a glass of cheap wine and reeled her in with his cheesy lines. What they were she couldn't recall. The rest of the evening passed in flashes. She had vague recollection of him telling her he worked in London and was visiting on business. She didn't know his name, hadn't cared enough to ask. He'd held her up as he took her to his hotel room. She'd gone into the bathroom and thrown up. And then she must've blacked out, that or the drink really had addled her brain because when she had woken up he'd been on top of her, his pelvis grinding into hers as he grunted in her ear. She'd tried to push him off at that point, bile rising into her throat, fear stopping her being able to say the word no. He'd just shuddered above her then rolled off, kissing her sloppily on the cheek and turning over.

She'd been aware enough to get herself dressed, or rather, put right her clothing that he hadn't even bothered removing. She'd swung her legs round off the bed, and promptly thrown up again on the carpet. She'd called a cab and made her way home. The thought of being pregnant hadn't even crossed her mind - she was more worried about the chance of STDs, and the fact she'd put herself in the position where she became a target again. She blamed herself – if she hadn't got so drunk, then she would never have been in the position where he could take advantage of her. She knew she'd implied no – he should have stopped. But the guilt stopped her reporting it to the police. She was certain they'd have hinted it was her fault – that she'd 'asked' for it. Now she knew differently – she'd been vulnerable, wanting to feel normal. She'd made a mistake getting so drunk, but he had taken advantage of the situation too.

She'd gone to the clinic the next day and they'd given her antibiotics as a precaution. The whole experience made her retreat into her shell.

Aoife had rung her several times trying to pull her out but she wasn't ready. She just went through the motions: work, then home, then bed. Ben didn't even realise she'd missed her period at first, going in for shifts at work and enduring the sympathetic stares from her colleagues. When she'd felt sick for the fourth time in a week, one of the other girls had said as a joke 'You're not pregnant are you?' and that was it. Ben bought a test and saw two pink lines. It was only down to Aoife's support that she'd decided to keep the baby.

Having Grace had been the one shining light in an otherwise dark time. She didn't remember the man, he had no idea who she was, and whilst he had taken advantage of her, he hadn't had a clue about Grace. Ben had left the father slot on the birth certificate blank, and the moment the tiny baby was placed in her arms, she'd known that no matter what anyone did to her, she would protect this child and raise her to be a good, kind human being. The rush of love she'd felt at that moment had been healing. She'd stopped living in the shadow of the rape, and started *living*.

Ben frowned as she stirred the coffee mindlessly. *All those years of doing what I needed to raise Grace, trying to forget what happened, and learning not be threatened by every little hiccup … But now he's back invading my life and he's a threat to my child and my family.*

There's no way in hell he is getting his hands on my child. I'll kill him before he gets that close.

Any remnants of fear she'd had over facing her nemesis again started to shrivel. He would not win. She had beaten him last time by surviving, and she'd damn well do the same again this time.

He didn't know what he was getting himself in for. She'd had almost seven years of self-defence training and martial arts, seven years of preparing herself for the moment she had to protect herself. And even as the niggling voice in the back of her mind started screaming that she wasn't ready, that she couldn't do it, she knew in her heart she could, if she had to.

Hopefully it wouldn't come to that. Ali was on the case, even as she stood there stirring coffee.

18th June, 1435 hours – Major Incident Room, Sunderland City Centre Depot

'So what've we got?' asked Ali, standing at the end of the desk with his hands resting lightly as he glanced round his team. 'Danny?'

Danny White had been responsible for the POLSA search once the CSIs were done with the murder scene. He ran a tight ship, but even with the best will in the world some searches aren't successful.

'It's a centre for troubled kids,' he said with a sigh. 'There's rubbish everywhere. The emergency exit at the back was wiped clean, though that's definitely the way the footwear marks went down the corridor. It's a good job the cleaners had chosen to polish the floor the night before. Kevin will tell you better, but I think the CSIs got some good prints. The rear yard was in the same state, empty crisp packets and bottles, smoked fag butts and chewing gum all over the place. It was all collected by the CSI and there was nothing else of note.'

'The centre's in the middle of the community. I think we can safely assume he left by the back to avoid being seen by the early risers. The pathologist has put the time of death at around

5.00 a.m. Kevin, can you update on the forensics, please.' Ali moved position and sat down on the chair. He took a moment to glance around. His staff looked tired. Murders mean long hours and little sleep for the people determined to get the offender locked up.

He wondered if this is how they'd looked when Cass had been taken. There was still a smell of determination though: they hadn't given up. Appeased, he leaned back and waited for Kevin to finish. He already knew about the forensics: he'd read the report just before he'd gone into the meeting.

'...and that's it. Footwear marks with decent detail but there're no hits on the database. Get me a shoe to compare to and they'll be as good as fingerprints though. This guy is good; he takes what he needs to the scene and takes it with him when he leaves. Even the post-mortem hasn't brought much evidence to the forefront. Dr Evans thinks the guy shaves his bits: there wasn't even a stray pubic hair when he combed the victim.' Kevin held his hands out in frustration. 'Sorry, Ali. Wish there was more I could tell you.'

'Me too,' replied Ali. 'Charlie, are we any further forward on why the DNA from her cheek matched our dead prisoner?'

'Actually, boss, I might have something. I was waiting for the registrar to confirm, but I've been over to social services and looked at the files they had on Whitworth. There're some inconsistencies at the start, at one point they actually thought there was two boys in the house. I've spoken to Kevin about it, and I've rang that woman at the DNA lab, Marie something-or-other. I think Whitworth had an identical twin, boss. It's the only thing that could account for the same DNA being on our vic's cheek. After the first few months the social services files become convoluted and they turn their attention to Whitworth, believing him to be the only child. I think it's highly probable there was another child there, and that that child was left behind to be raised by an abusive father. Unfortunately, there's no mention of the child anywhere else, I've requested birth certificates but they're not here yet. Whitworth's father died of an overdose back in the early nineties. I've not been able to trace anything further without a name though. As soon as I hear from the registrar, I'll let you know.'

'OK, great. Most of you will now be aware that one of the CSIs, Ben Cassidy, was a victim of this particular killer eight years ago. You may or may not be aware that for whatever reason the killer has chosen to refocus on her. Now whether this is just a passing infatuation, or whether he tries something remains to be seen. He left her a message on her car this morning and slashed all the tyres. She's currently under protection at her home. It is our priority to get this guy, folks. He's not a nice man, has killed people up and down the country, but now he's here, in our town. I want to do everything in our power to make sure it ends here. Any questions?'

As they shook their heads and filtered out of the room, Ali hung back, taking a moment to himself. The idea he'd had when leaving Ben's house that morning was that there would be a digital footprint to follow. He would call up Ed at digital forensics and get things moving.

Chapter Twenty-two
18ᵗʰ June, 1805 hours – O'Byrne residence, Sunderland

'Really? That's great, sweetheart... OK, you be good for Aunty Aoife and give her lots of cuddles from me.' Ben hung up the phone, and realised she had tears in her eyes. This was the first night Grace had been away from home without her, and she missed her. That coupled with the fact there was a murderous monster after her for the second time had made her emotions go up and down like a rollercoaster. One minute she was afraid, then she was determined, then she was sad. Hell, she'd even experienced mild jealousy as she'd watched Jacob focus intently on a piece of work he was doing. His face had been calm but he'd been sizzling with anticipation as he'd methodically worked his way through the copy hard-drive he'd brought with him.

Sighing in frustration, Ben swiped at her eyes. An eyelash dislodged fixed itself to her iris and her eye began streaming.

'Ow, crap,' she muttered, turning to go to the sink intending to rinse it under running water. She didn't even know Jacob was there until she smacked into his chest. He steadied her and looked at her with concern as she blinked furiously, trying to control the latest tear threatening to run down her cheek.

'Let me see,' said Jacob, removing her hand from her face and leaning forward. Carefully, he held her eye lids open and saw the problem. 'You trust me, right?'

His voice was soft, and his breath floated across the skin on her face like silk. She nodded, not trusting herself to speak. Jacob raised his hand and used his little finger, gently swiping the very end over the outer surface of her eye and catching the stray eyelash on the first try.

Ben didn't even feel it, didn't notice as it stopped watering. She was too caught up looking at Jacob.

He recognised the look now darkening her eyes from the colour of fresh grass to the green of forest pines. Unable to stop himself, he touched her face. Her tongue nervously dipped onto her bottom lip, making it sheen with moisture. The voice in the back of his mind telling him to stop and that she was vulnerable faded into nothing as he leaned in towards her, hovering millimetres from her mouth with his. He heard her breath catch but she didn't move. Lost, he allowed his lips to connect to hers, tasting the saltiness of the tears from her cheek. Ben moaned into his mouth, her body leaning forward and finding his as if it were the most natural thing in the world. He could've sworn his body was on fire, thousands of hot needles piercing his skin at every point she touched him. Her hands snaked up his back, lightly scratching at him through his t-shirt, and he heard himself groan. Stepping into her, he kept her moving until her lower back impacted with the kitchen side.

Whoa, you can't do this. Not now, this isn't right. She's vulnerable. Pull away.

The voice in his head got louder until finally, he broke the kiss and pulled his head back. 'We can't do this, Ben. You're scared, I'd be taking advantage.'

Ben understood what he was saying, and she appreciated it, but she was squirming where she stood at the thought of him leaving her like this. For once in her life, she needed something, and that something was Jacob.

She pressed in close to him, placing her lips to his neck. And alternated between planting kisses and whispering, 'Do ... you ... think ... I'd ... let ... you ... do ... anything ... I ... didn't ... want?'

Jacob felt his resolve slipping, she had a point, he couldn't imagine her letting him do anything she didn't want. And goodness knew, he wanted her. She carried on kissing his neck, and suddenly he felt her grate her teeth across lightly. A bolt of lightning ran through him, and that was it. The voice in his head was no more.

Bending his head, he captured her mouth, harder this time, his hips grinding into hers.

Ben had never felt anything like this before; she felt that if she didn't have him right now, she might actually die. She felt wild, her common sense abandoning her completely as the kiss deepened further. When his hand brushed over her breast, she pulled back and gasped. *Jesus! So this is what it's like.* Now it was his mouth on her neck, trailing kisses towards her neck line. Ben felt her hands sneak into his hair as he paused and flicked open the first button on her shirt, and suddenly she froze. *My scars! He can't see my scars, he'll hate me.*

Jacob sensed the change in her, felt her pull back as the connection ceased. Confused he looked at her. Her cheeks were flushed, desire yes, but there was something else. It took a second for him to register it as apprehension.

'Tell me what's the matter.'

'My scars,' she whispered, new tears springing to her eyes. 'They're horrible, you'll see them and run a mile.'

Incredulous, he gazed at her. 'Your scars are your battle wounds. You went through something horrific and you survived, those scars are proof of that. I would be the last person on earth to run from scars, trust me.' At that moment his words registered with him also, all those months of the therapists telling him they were just marks of battle and they didn't define who he was came flooding back. And for the first time in his life, he felt the spark of belief.

He leaned back towards Ben and kissed her lightly. 'This goes at your speed, Ben. But I'm not going anywhere. Besides, my trainers are by the front door.' He waggled his eyebrows in comedy, and Ben smiled back. Realising she wasn't convinced, Jacob did the most drastic thing he could think of. Slowly he released his belt, his eyes maintaining contact with hers, and unbuttoned his jeans. Ben's mouth fell open into a small 'o' as he pushed them over his hips and let them fall to the ground.

Now he was nervous. *Maybe this wasn't such a good idea.* He felt his own cheeks flush with embarrassment. His own scars were now on view, out in the open for her to see. She was the first woman who had. Self-conscious now, he stepped back and went to bend to pull his jeans back up. *This was a bad idea. You're an idiot.*

He felt her hand on his harm, stopping him, and pulling him back up.

Without saying a word, she gathered her strength and popped the next button on her shirt. If he could do it, when it obviously hurt him to show his scars, she was sure she could. Once all the buttons were undone, and the shirt sides were hanging loosely, she took a deep breath.

Seeing how nervous she was, Jacob stepped forward to help. He cupped his hands to her face, and captured her mouth in a deep kiss again. He felt her pulse quicken through her fingers which had migrated up his chest to his shoulders. They stood there for several minutes.

Ben gasped as his mouth left hers and closed swiftly around the tip of one of her breasts, and she knew she couldn't stop, didn't want to. Any stray thoughts about her scars vanished and her head tipped backwards, her eyes closed. Her hands linked through his hair and she felt his hands slide up her back and release the clasp on her bra.

In a deft movement, Jacob lowered her to the floor and resumed kissing her, his hand curled around her breast as his other cupped her cheek. Nothing had ever felt so right.

18th June, 1830 hours – O'Byrne residence, Sunderland

Ben laid her head on his chest, unable to stop the grin spreading as she felt his fingers draw shapes on her shoulder. 'Next time though, maybe we should at least try to make it upstairs?'

Jacob kissed her head, and teased. 'Next time huh, once not enough for you?'

'Don't think I'll ever get enough. You'll just have to stay a while.' Her tone was light, but he read between the lines. Right now she was vulnerable, exposed.

'I'm not going anywhere.' He kissed her head again, then pushed her so he could turn on his side and look at her. 'Seriously, I have no intention of going anywhere. Even before ... this' he gently ran his hand down her side causing her skin to prickle, 'I knew we had something special. It doesn't come along every day. You're the only woman who has ever seen my scars, accepted me for who I am without question, and hasn't tried to avoid touching me. I am not going anywhere.'

Ben smiled at his words. They were exactly what she needed to hear. 'Maybe we should get dressed, I'll make some dinner and maybe we can snuggle up on the couch and watch a movie?'

'Don't know that we'll get much watching done, but sure,' he replied, his voice a little husky as he ran his eyes down her body.

18th June, 2340 hours – O'Byrne residence, Sunderland

Stan stood in the shadows of the rhododendron bushes in the corner of the back garden. Climbing into the garden over the fence that separated the nearest neighbour from Ben's house had been easy. He'd already scoped the area out; knew that the old woman would be in bed fast asleep, as most old people were at this time of night.

He knew the cops were positioned right outside the front gates, and that they were closed. He was only there to look though, he would kill them when the time was right but that wasn't this evening. Tonight the desire to see her had been too strong for him to deny. He'd managed to find a lot of information relating to *him*, Jacob, before he left though. Much of his service record was sealed, and there were too many people he stayed in contact with for Stan to ascertain which one had the aunt and child.

Hate for the man who had stolen his student burned in his gut – he would make him wish he'd never been born. He'd seen Jacobs honourable discharge from service due to injuries received, and read about the Military Cross Jacob had been presented with on his return to the UK - if he hadn't used the hand sign many more of his men would have died, the paperwork said. Stan had even managed to hack into Jacob's medical files, had read about his injuries and extensive surgery and rehab. He would make him pay for stealing Ben. What gave him the right to encroach on another man's territory?

Stan had sat in his computer room, listening to the pair canoodle on the sofa. It had almost made him feel sick. When he'd left his house half an hour ago, he knew he just had to see her. Just a glimpse.

He felt his heart quicken as the kitchen light turned on and suddenly she was there. He wanted to step out from behind the bushes and go to her, start teaching her that she should never have survived, teach her that she should have obeyed him and died as ordered, but he didn't. Exposing himself now would be foolhardy.

After all the research he had done on places to take her to resume his work, he had finally realised that this was the perfect location. He would come back in a couple of days, when everyone was in bed. He would disable the two police officers, and disarm the alarm system, and he would resume the lessons she should have learned all those years ago.

Silently he climbed back over the fence and made his way to his car. A shiver of anticipation made its way down his spine. He'd been searching all along for one to be just like her. Now he had the opportunity to be with her again. This was going to be the best yet.

Chapter Twenty-three
19th June, 0805 hours – O'Byrne residence, Sunderland

Jacob didn't want to wake up. He was warm and comfortable. Surely it was Saturday and he could just turn over? He opened his eye a crack and suddenly felt the weight of someone sleeping on top of him. Memories came flooding back, and he blushed. He lowered his lips and kissed the top of her head gently.

She groaned beneath him and snuggled in tighter to his chest, her legs entwined with his. The DVD start screen to Die Hard was repeating quietly on the TV and he had a vague recollection of turning the volume down about half way through when she had fallen asleep. He didn't remember much of the movie after that so he can't have been far behind her.

When Ben lifted her head and smiled at him sleepily, he knew his words from last night were even truer. He wasn't going anywhere. This, right here, was what he'd been waiting for his entire life. He knew it was too soon to be thinking far ahead, and that Ben may not want a serious addition to her life, but he was here now, and that was enough.

'Morning,' he said, moving his head and brushing her lips with his.

'I can't believe we fell asleep in the middle of Die Hard. Who does that? Bruce Willis isn't exactly quiet when he kicks arse.' She coughed a little, ridding her voice of the morning hoarseness.

'I thought the same thing. Coffee?'

'Oh God yes, I can't go through the morning without my morning shot.'

'You stay here and laze, I'll make it.'

Ben moved and he swung his legs over the edge of the sofa. He managed to stand without grimacing, despite the shooting pain down his leg. The fall when he'd caught her fainting, coupled with their love-making on the kitchen floor had made his leg seize up. He registered her looking at him in concern and realised he'd failed to hide his discomfort.

'It's fine, just twinging. Next time though, definitely the bed.' He leaned forward and kissed her again, rescued his stick from its resting place half under the sofa and left the room.

19th June, 1005 hours –Major Incident Room, Sunderland City Centre Depot

'Ed, I understand what you're saying. But this guy must have a digital footprint. He's avoided being caught all these years because he does *something*, manipulates the system somehow, I dunno. You're seriously telling me that until we have more information you can't trace him?' Ali's frustration came through as he spoke to Jacob's boss on the phone.

'Ali, it's not that I don't want to help. We have cases spanning the last year backed up in here waiting to be dealt with. This one will be put to the top of the list as soon as I have something definite to go on. You don't even have the guy's name. Call me as soon as you have information I can work with.'

Ali sighed as he replaced the receiver carefully. Carefully because if he didn't check his temper he might well have smashed it right through the desk.

He knew this guy was closing in and was doing something that hid his identity, but he'd be darned if he had the knowhow to stop him.

He didn't want this to be one of those cases where the facts weren't known until it was too late. It was his responsibility to save Ben, and right now he had jack shit with which to do it.

Pushing back his chair, he stood, intending to go downstairs to speak with Kevin. The crime scene was due to be handed back over today. The clean-up crew was already making the centre look as if nothing had ever happened. But it had. Surely Clarice would provide something else. She had to. He also knew the CSIs had recovered some fingerprints from Jacob and Ben's cars. Hopefully they'd have come back from the submissions team.

He was lost in thought as he made his way towards the door, and didn't see Charlie heading towards him purposefully until she was under his nose.

'Boss. I have the birth certificates. Our guy was named Mitchell Gordon Brown, twin to John Francis Brown who later changed his name to Whitworth. I've already checked with social and they have no trace of Mitchell claiming benefits or paying national insurance since he turned twenty one – I haven't managed to trace anything since but it's not exactly my forte. Maybe that techy guy, Ed what-his-name, can work his magic now?'

Ali couldn't stop the smile. 'You are a bloody genius. Well done, Charlie.'

'I'm heading over to Clarice's house with Jason now. We'll have a chat with Gill, go over her bedroom with a tooth comb, see if there's anything that would indicate why she was targeted. It's my gut feeling she knew the guy, but without proof that's just a thought.'

'OK, great. Thanks, Charlie.' He took the slip of paper and put it in his pocket. He would head over to HQ the second he had finished talking to Kevin.

He still hadn't managed to erase the smile when he walked into the Supervisors office in the CSI corridor.

'Hey, boss,' greeted Kevin, waving his arm towards the vacant seat. 'Take a load off. Just give me a sec to finish this statement paragraph and I'll be with you.'

Tapping away slowly on the keyboard, he held his lower lip between his teeth in concentration. He hated statements. There had been a time when prosecutors and the CPS hadn't needed the ins and outs of a fart to get the job done. Now they did, and it made his statements even more time consuming.

Finally though, he looked up at Ali. 'How can I help you?'

'Just checking in really. The clean-up crew are at the centre today. I wanted to say good job to your staff: if they hadn't been as thorough then we may have needed the scene for longer. Any additional evidence come to light yet? I'm heading over to see her mother and guardian later today. I want to be able to say "we'll get the guy."'

'Nothing as yet. I was going to phone the fingerprint lab later and see if anything's pinged from the prints lifted from the wing of Jacob's car. They said they'd rush it through but it was waiting on quality checking at close of play last night. Is Ben OK?'

'She's holding up. Can't say many other people would be as calm in her position. Jacob's staying with her at her aunts. We've got two guys stationed outside 24/7. I've got a lead on a potential name so I'm heading over the HQ now to see what Ed can do.'

'Well a name's a good start. We'll catch up later today.'

19th June, 1120 hours – Digital Forensics Lab, Sunderland HQ

'Brown, you said his surname was, right?' asked Ed as he looked up from his computer momentarily. At Ali's nod, he turned back to the screen and frowned. 'Nothing immediate popping. This is going to take some time. I'll get back to you when I've looked into it further. Jacob's great at this kind of stuff but with what's happened at his new girlfriends house, him working on it could potentially be damaging court wise. I know a guy from way back when who might be able to help though, he's the best there is. Legit too, obviously. I'll get back to you when I have more.'

Ali said thanks quietly and left the office. He'd been lost when Ed had started what looked like symbols on to the black computer screens. *That's why he does digital forensics and I don't.*

Deciding to check in with the officers outside Ben's, he made his way over and parked behind the marked car.

'Everything OK, lads?' he asked after tapping on the window.

'Yeah, all quiet on the Western Front, sir. An old lady reported seeing a man in her garden last night when she went to the can, but there's nothing obvious. We had a look in her garden. She was possibly just imagining it. You know how these old birds can be. Couple of handsome coppers and they'll keep you chatting all day.'

Ali narrowed his eyes at the cop. He was a joker, this one. Ali wasn't familiar with him, and the other cop in the passenger seat was obviously relatively new, the sheen of enthusiasm not even dulled by the mundane task of essentially babysitting.

'Nice woman that,' said the first cop, nodding his head towards the house. 'Keeps us supplied with coffee. Nice and easy on the eyes too. That red hair ... Mmm.'

Ali was not impressed, and it showed. He glared at the cop, and bent so he was on eye level. 'That red hair is off limits. She is one of our own, in danger from a killer. Just keep your eyes on what's going on out here, and try and keep your mind out of the gutter. Now, where did the old lady live? I think I'd like to have a chat with her.'

'Sorry, boss. She lives in the house directly behind this one - the gardens adjoin via the rear fence.'

Nodding once, Ali straightened and made his way round the corner to speak with the woman. He couldn't afford to make any mistakes. He didn't rate that cheeky cop's opinion and felt the need to verify the neighbour's story for himself. He'd committed the guy's collar number to memory when he'd leaned forward: words would be had with his sergeant.

He knocked at the door and waited patiently for a reply.

Several minutes passed before it finally opened a crack, the safety chain firmly in place as a frail voice filtered through the gap. 'If you're selling, you've come to the wrong address. I'm old and don't have money to buy.'

'Not selling, ma'am. My name is Detective Inspector Alistair McKay from North East Police. I believe you had a word with my colleagues in the next street over about someone who was in your garden?'

'ID, sonny. I'll not be letting you in without it.'

Smiling, he held his warrant card up to the gap for her to see. He didn't see her nod in satisfaction, but he heard her slip the chain and open the door further.

'Come on in, I'll put the kettle on.'

Ali followed her through the neat living room and into the kitchen. She gestured to the chairs around the table and he sat patiently whilst she efficiently made a pot of hot tea. Noting the milk and sugar were already on the table, he accepted the tea cup with a grin. It had been years since he'd drunk from a proper tea cup. It reminded him of his own gran.

'Those other officers didn't believe me you know. They thought I was some senile old bat. But I know what I saw. Name's Agnes Wright by the way.'

'I apologise for them. I believe you. Tell me what you saw, Agnes.'

'A man, maybe late thirties, balding on the top. He was in dark clothes. I only saw him a moment, he'd climbed into my garden from the one straight behind mine. Nice old woman who lives there, with her nieces, I think. Always asks if I want milk getting. Not that I accept mind you, I get myself out to the shop every other day. Keeps my legs from seizing up with this darn rheumatism.'

'Can you remember what time this was?'

'Must've been around midnight or so. I went to bed straight after the nine o'clock news like always. Always get up around the same time, body doesn't work like it used to.'

'Did he do anything else?'

'He did look up at my window. He didn't see me though; I always go to the bathroom in the dark so as not to wake my eyes up. I was stood on the landing looking straight at him. The security light was on at the side of the house, that's how I remember what he looked like. Creepy man though, very much doubt he was up to anything above board. Are the folks over the way having a problem?'

'Possibly. Would you mind if I have a look in your garden?'

'You wanna see if there's footprints or the like. I watch that CSI show on the TV. American trash, really, but I do like that Grissom man. You fill your boots, sonny. The door's unlocked.'

Ali got to his feet and walked down the overgrown path to the fence at the back. He could clearly see where the vegetation was trampled in places. It was completely obvious that someone had been in the garden. He knew in his gut it had been the guy they were looking for. Unfortunately, though, due to the overgrowth, there was no visible footwear marks. The fence showed scuff marks on this side: he'd climbed over the fence into Ben's garden. Heading back into the kitchen, he found Agnes where he had left her.

'Agnes, it looks like the man climbed over your fence into the garden behind, then climbed back over and into yours which is when you saw him. Would you recognise him again do you think?'

'Well it was dark. But I might. Is this man dangerous, Inspector? Should I be worried?'

'He could be dangerous, we're not sure yet. But if you see him again would you be able to give me a call? I'll leave you my personal number?'

'I will indeed. And I'll make sure all my doors are locked at night. You tell that woman and her nieces to be careful. He didn't strike me as a very nice man at all.'

Agnes pushed out her chair and got to her feet. She was a prime example of the body failing but the mind remaining intact, and he was again reminded of his gran. She'd died years before, when he was a teenager, but he remembered her sparkling eyes, so mischievous; the cackle of her laugh – and she had laughed often. He was a little surprised to feel such overwhelming emotion. Occasionally in the job he came across people who felt familiar, but it had never been this strong before.

'Agnes if you're ever worried, or you need anything I want you to ring me, OK?'

'I'll be fine, sonny,' she replied softly, patting his arm gently. 'Don't you worry about an old bat like me. You just keep those women safe.'

Ali waited as she closed the door behind him, and smiled as he heard the click of the lock. He knew Agnes would be checking the garden every night now. It made him feel more at ease knowing someone else had Ben's back also.

He couldn't stop the frown though as he approached the cops again.

'For info, there is evidence in the garden that indicates someone has been in there. That old lady is as sharp as they come and it would pay you next time to listen when someone is trying to tell you about a potential killer. Don't expect to be given this duty again, I want people here I can rely on to protect Ben, not dick around taking the piss. I'm going in to see Ben now. I expect by the time I come back out, that you'll have your head back in the game until you're relief turns up just after 2 p.m.'

The chastisement was felt by both of them, and the driver had the graciousness to blush. A slating by one of the bosses was never a good thing.

19th June, 1420 hours – Major Incident Room, Sunderland City Centre Depot

'Boss, have you got a minute?' Charlie's voice cut through Ali's concentration and he looked up from his policy book. The policy book was essential to every murder. It held all his notes, points of investigation and all the other information required for the enquiries to commence.

'Sure, what's up?'

'We found something at the house. I wanted to speak with you first before we send the CSI in.' Charlie took a breath, obviously whatever it was, it was big. Ali leaned forward and pulled her a chair over.

'It was well hidden. We almost missed it, to be honest. It was only 'cos the screen reflected off my torch light that we saw it at all. Inside the window vent above Clarice's computer desk was a small camera, boss. We think he may have been watching her for some time before killing her. She may even have known him. We've left the camera where it is, didn't want to potentially destroy evidence.'

'A camera? Well that's a game changer. I knew this guy had technical knowhow, I just knew it. I'll call Ed to have one of his guys attend with a CSI later. See if he can't track down an IP address for where the signal was going to. Well done for finding it. This proves that he's organised, and of above average intelligence. Hopefully this will lead us straight to him. Charlie, put this case in your personal development record, OK? And next time the sergeants exams come up I want to see your name on the list. There's not a lot of cops that would have seen something so discreet as a hidden camera. I'll endorse your application and give you coaching for your interview if you need it.'

Charlie grinned at him widely, 'Thanks, boss. I will.'

Before she'd even stood, Ali was punching in the number for the digital forensics team.

After explaining the situation, he rang Kevin and arranged for a CSI to meet him and one of Ed's team at the house at 3 p.m. Finally he felt like he had a break in the case: something that might well help him ascertain where Mitchell lived. It was a rush; he wasn't there yet but he was a huge step closer.

19th June, 1500 hours – Thompson residence, Sunderland

Ali took a deep breath before knocking on the front door. Deena and Max, the technician from Ed's team, stood a few steps behind him. He'd already phoned and spoken to Gill to advise her that he needed to attend.

When she opened the door, he was surprised to see her with full make-up on and dressed to kill in dark green. Her green glasses had white dots on them and her hair had been styled in a fashionable up do. But behind all of the exterior primping, her eyes were red and bloodshot. She'd obviously been crying not long before they'd arrived.

'Ms Thompson, my name's Ali. We spoke on the phone earlier?'

'Just Gill is fine. Please, come through. Clarice's ...' she paused and coughed, trying to rectify the hitch of grief, 'Clarice's room is the second on the left down that hall. I haven't been inside as per the request from your officer earlier.'

Max and Deena made their way silently down the corridor, both uncomfortable. The cops dealt with family in grief. It wasn't normal that the CSIs and technicians had that much interaction after the fact. What did one say to the people left behind anyway? It wasn't a job they envied Ali.

Gill led Ali to the right and into the living room. It was spick and span, nothing out of place. Clarice's mum, Bernice sat on one end of the sofa, silently wringing her hands together. She looked like her daughter, and for a moment Ali was taken aback by the similarities. Sitting in the chair opposite the sofa, he waited a moment while Gill poured what looked suspiciously like home-made lemonade and handed him the glass before sitting beside her friend and putting a hand on her knee.

Ali inhaled slowly. He hated this part of the job, knew his brother Alex did too. There was nothing right in talking to parents whose children had died before them. Or anyone else touched by such horror for that matter.

'As I explained on the phone to Gill, when my officers were visiting this morning they have found a hidden camera in Clarice's room that may help us with the investigation. Can you tell me who has had access to the house over the last few months, Gill?'

'Nobody really. I work day shifts, and Clarice is - was at school. With the exception of her friends, there's no one really that I recall.'

'No workmen of any kind, or engineers?'

Gill cocked her head to one side, thinking. Suddenly her eyes widened. 'Actually there was a guy from Northumbrian Water about six weeks ago. I thought it was odd 'cos he knocked at like half past six. He said there was a leak somewhere and he had to check the water pressure.'

'Was he left unattended at any point?'

'Not unattended, exactly, but I was on my way out of the door so Clarice said she'd deal with it. She told me he went to the bathroom while she made her tea... Oh my God. It was him wasn't it? That man is the one who hid the camera and killed Clarice?' Gill's face went ashen as tears filled her eyes.

'We don't know that yet. Even if it was you weren't to know, Gill.'

Bernice interrupted now, her voice monotone as she glared at her friend. 'You let that monster in the house with my girl? You let him in and left him with her, and now my baby is dead?' Her voice broke and she got to her feet and walked out. When the front door slammed a second later, Gill winced. She didn't move, her silent tears falling onto the carpet as she replayed her friends words over in her mind.

'She's right, this is my fault.' Her whisper was horrified,

Ali got to his feet, and sat beside her. 'This is not your fault. Bernice is upset and looking for someone to blame. You just happened to be the closest person. She'll come around. You had no way of knowing that he was doing anything untoward. I'm guessing he was in uniform and showed you ID?'

Gill nodded, but Ali could see she was barely holding it together. It didn't matter what he said now. In her mind, she let the killer inside her home.

'Can you tell me what the man looked like?'

She closed her eyes trying to remember. Later she could beat herself up all she wanted over letting him get close to Clarice, but she knew the information Ali wanted might help catch him.

'Not really, we literally crossed paths on the doorstep. He was white, wearing uniform but he had a cap pulled right down over his face. I think he had a beard but I may be wrong. I'm sorry.' Gill's voice finally broke and she started to cry softly.

Ali handed her a tissue from the box on the table. 'I'll give you a couple of minutes.'

Making his way down the hallway towards Clarice's room, he wondered about Bernice's reaction. He knew that Clarice lived with Gill after getting involved with drugs in the past. Hell, he knew the whole history. But Bernice's behaviour had thrown him off balance a little. He'd half-expected to have to break the pair apart when Bernice lost it, but she'd just stormed out. He shrugged his shoulders as he reached the bedroom door. Grief was a funny thing. Sometimes there were just no explanations.

'Hey guys, what've we got?'

Max placed a tiny screwdriver back in his toolkit. 'The camera was turned off, but from what I can see he was using her own internet signal to bounce the footage to his location. We're taking the lot back to the lab and I'll try and trace back from there.'

Deena chimed in, 'The camera will be sent off for chemical enhancement, it's small and fiddly and I don't want to ruin any potential prints. The chem lab will be able to do it better based on the multiple surface types. While Max was looking at the laptop, I had a look through her bedside drawer. She keeps a journal but the last entry has been ripped out. I'm going to send the journal off for ESDA analysis. It should highlight the indentations on the next page which may show us what she'd written,' added Deena. She referred to the electrostatic detection analysis that could be used to highlight indentations on flat surfaces like paper.

'Great, thank you.' Ali made his way back into the living room. Gill was still sitting where he had left her.

'They're just about done in there. Can I call anyone to come and sit with you?'

'No thank you, Inspector. I'll call Bernice later and make peace. Though she has every reason to hate me. I think a little of it is blaming herself. She couldn't cope when Clarice turned to drugs, with the other three kids only young she panicked. Didn't want trouble in the house I suppose. But she loved her daughter dearly. And now she's gone. And whilst I know you're doing everything you can to find the man who did this, it won't bring her back, will it?'

'You did a good thing, Gill. You took Clarice in and helped her turn her life around. What happened isn't your fault. Clarice was a very bright young lady. She was doing well at college. I know because we spoke to her tutors. None of that would have happened if you hadn't taken her in. Try not to blame yourself. It seems to me you did a lot more for Clarice than you've been given credit for. It can't have been easy getting her off drugs and away from that life.'

'No I suppose it wasn't. I love that girl like she's my own. She was always a good girl who just got led astray. I wish I knew who her boyfriend was. She'd said she was seeing a man, but I didn't get any details. He won't even know what's happened.'

'How long had they been together?'

'Oh I don't know, a couple of weeks maybe. Not long. She seemed quite smitten though. I think I'd like to take a rest now, do you mind?'

'Not at all. I'll be in touch with you and Bernice shortly, OK?'

He stood to leave just as Bernice walked back in the door, tears streaking her face. 'I'm sorry, I didn't mean ...' Gill jumped to her feet and pulled her friend into a tight hug as Bernice started sobbing.

Taking his leave by patting Gill's arm, he left the two of them holding each other. He was glad Bernice had come back - the pair needed each other right now.

Noticing his vehicle was the only one present, he realised Deena and Max had already left. He climbed into the car and rubbed his hands over his face. Damn he was tired, it felt like forever since he'd slept. He felt like there was something he had missed, something obvious he needed to know. But it wouldn't come. With a sigh, he started the car and headed back to the nick.

Chapter Twenty-four
19th June, 1615 hours – O'Byrne residence, Sunderland

'I swear I'm going nuts being cooped up in here. I can't do this anymore.' Ben was on the phone to Cass and felt the need to vent.

'Listen to me, you need to stay there. Grace and Aoife are safe, and you need to be too. You can't go about your normal daily duties until this nut job is caught, do you understand me? This guy is dangerous, Ben. The last thing anyone wants is for him to get his mitts on you because you were too damn stubborn to listen to advice. I'm coming over tonight. Me and Alex, we'll bring Isobel.'

'No! You can't bring the baby here. Hell, you can't even come here, Cass. If this monster is watching and sees you guys, he might decide to hurt you, too. You've been through enough.'

'But I'm worried about you. I know how hard it was for you to tell me everything that happened. This guy is gunning for you. I need to know you're safe.'

'Look, I promise I will not go back to work or even leave the house without a cop with me. But there's nothing in the fridge for a start, I need to go get some food. And I haven't seen Grace in two days. I'm honestly going stir crazy in here. How long does it take for Ali to catch this guy?'

'Alex has said he's going back to work to help. Jacob's team are working on all the digital angles and Kevin has all the other stuff under control. All you need to do is stay safe so that beautiful little girl keeps her mum. I know it's not easy, but I know first-hand what happens when someone bad gets their mucky mitts on you. You're my friend, Ben. I don't want anything to happen to you.'

'I know. I'm sorry, you're right. I'll stay inside.' Ben said the words but she still wasn't quite sure she believed them herself yet. Saying her goodbyes, she hung up the phone.

Jacob had been listening from the kitchen table. 'She's right you know. You should stay inside. But I know what you mean, it's tough. Why don't I phone Ali and say we're both going out, me and you? I'll drive us to Asda, we can have a wander, get the bits you need and maybe have a coffee in the café You can ring Grace. At least it's a slip of normalcy? And nothing would happen in a crowded supermarket.'

Ben walked over and put her arms around his neck from behind. He kissed her forearm and placed his hand over her arm. They stood for a moment, and when Ben released him, he grabbed his mobile and spoke to Ali. It took some persuading, but eventually he agreed. The cops would stay outside the home, and Jacob had to check back in as soon as they returned. But they had permission to go out. It felt oddly liberating. Like a couple of school kids flouting the rules they jumped into Jacob's car and drove off.

19th June, 1905 hours – O'Byrne residence, Sunderland
The trip to Asda had been worthwhile.

Ben had put the shepherd's pie in the oven and was heading down the hall to the stairs when a loud bang came from upstairs. She heard Jacob cry out in pain, and realised he had hurt himself.

She took the stairs two at a time, and slammed open the door to the bathroom. 'Jacob, you OK?'

He was sprawled in the bath, his face contorted in pain.

'Slipped,' he said through gritted teeth.

'If I help you, can you get up do you think?'

He nodded and Ben moved to the side of the bath. He grunted as he pulled himself up, using the wall behind him to support for his weight.

Ben stood sideways, bending her knees slightly, as he leaned on her shoulder and gingerly manoeuvred his bad leg over the edge of the bath and onto the floor. He grunted again as his leg took his weight momentarily while he got his other leg out. His face was still twisted in a grimace, and Ben knew it was bad.

She helped him hobble to the bedroom, grabbing his stick from where it rested by the sink as she passed. As Jacob lowered himself onto the bed, she left his side and grabbed his wash bag.

He kept his tablets there – she knew as she'd seen him take them that morning.

'I'll need the oramorph.'

She opened the child-proof top and handed him the bottle, watching as he took an unmeasured swig.

After a couple of minutes, the look on his face eased.

'I'm sorry. I slipped on some soap and went down like a ton of bricks. It'll ease off in a couple of minutes. I owe you a shower rail.'

'Don't worry about the rail – we needed a new one anyway. You just gunna sit here for a bit 'til the drugs kick in? I can help you downstairs if you like.'

'No, I'm good. I'll get dressed in a sec and meet you downstairs. Honest, I'll be fine, it'll ease off.'

Ben nodded. She knew how embarrassed he must feel right now, he didn't need to be but she'd be the same in his situation. She leaned across him and kissed him gently on the lips before leaving the room.

19th June, 2005 hours –Tunstall, Sunderland City Centre
Stan could barely contain his anger. Why the hell hadn't he placed a camera or mic in the kitchen? The pair seemed to spend more time in there than anywhere else and he was missing conversations that could have been important. He considered going back to the address in his disguise, but discarded the idea as soon as it occurred. It wouldn't be long now anyway. And what information could have possibly been that vital that he needed to hear it?

He knew he couldn't wait much longer, though. She filled his every waking thought. His dreams were filled with images of him having her again and again, teaching her she shouldn't have lived because she couldn't obey. Even if she did obey this time, he knew she was dead. There was no way he'd make the same mistake twice.

The news had been full of Clarice's murder for days, but now it was petering out to the third and fourth pages in the papers. More important matters were taking the front page like a politician's latest indiscretion, and another Hollywood star dying of an overdose. All just crap really, nothing that interested him. He grabbed the Echo and scanned it, noting nothing new.

He felt frustrated; at least he thought it was frustration. He couldn't focus on anything but her, felt the need growing inside him. He couldn't wait a few more days. Stan knew he had to do it tonight. Then it would be time to move to another city, take yet another name and start over again. He'd done it so many times now he could barely remember his own name.

Maybe it's time to stop, retire. Learn to garden or something. But he knew he'd miss the hunt too much, miss the taste of their fear as they learned what they should already know about their place. He knew he couldn't stop.

Jumping to his feet suddenly, Stan cracked his leg off the edge of the table. It stung but it also felt good, made him feel alive. Without even thinking, he grabbed the metal ruler from his pen holder, and smacked himself hard across the back of the hand. As it smarted and changed colour, he smiled. Yes he was still alive, and tonight would prove just how alive he felt. He would have her again, and he would eliminate the cripple that had tried to claim her. Today would be a good day.

Chapter Twenty-five
20th June, 0100 hours – O'Byrne residence, Sunderland

Stan was more than ready for this. He'd checked on the cops waiting outside; one was old, maybe in his late forties and had the stomach to prove he was one for the clichéd doughnuts. He wouldn't be any trouble at all. The other cop was younger, stronger. He was the one to watch. Setting his panicked face in place, he ran up behind the car and rapped on the window.

'Help,' he rasped as the older cop cracked open the door. 'There was a man with a knife, he's just attacked me and nicked my wallet. I thought I was going to die.'

His story had the required effect and both cops jumped out of the car.

'Which way?' asked the younger one.

'He ducked into a garden round the corner, if you're quiet he won't hear you coming. He's got my phone, too. Tall lad, about thirty, with bald head and tattoos on his neck.'

The younger cop ran round the corner, and the older one leant into the vehicle to retrieve something. With the officers back turned, Stan knew this was the perfect time to strike. He pulled the shiny blade from the back of his trousers, and in one movement reached around the cop and drew the blade across his throat.

The cop fell forward, a gurgling sound coming from his neck as he put his hands to his throat. Stan was pleased. The cop's body was pretty much all in the car. Hoisting his legs in too, he closed the door with a quiet click, standing back and watching as the cop stopped grabbing at his throat and his eyes turned glassy and still. And then he waited for the other one to come back.

A few minutes later, the young lad made his way back up the street. Stan had hidden himself behind a hedge near the back of the car, wanting to surprise the cop before he got to the car and called for help. He knew the cop might have already called his communications department, but it was unlikely. With adrenaline pumping, it wouldn't have been the first thought in his head.

The cop strode past him, looking around for his colleague and Stan. In an equally swift movement, Stan had sliced through his throat like it was nothing more than butter and watched as the cop fell to his knees. He grabbed the back door of the panda and opened it, pulled the cop to his feet and bundled him into the back seat.

The cop was getting weaker by the second, but he made an attempt to reach his radio. If he could just press the orange button help would come. Stan leaned in and twisted it, removing it from the top of the cops vest. He threw it into the front of the car, and stood back with a smile.

'Sorry, son, bad day to be a cop.'

Resignation passed over the cops face, and the last speck of light faded from his eyes as he slipped into oblivion.

Stan closed the door with a click, there was nothing he could do about the blood on the pavement or the car, but it was late and it was the middle of the week. All he could do was hope no one walked past.

He retrieved his bag from the garden he'd left it in and made his way round the corner to the old woman's house. He knew the route now and went to the rear of the garden, nimbly jumping the fence. Ensuring he was hidden behind the rhododendron bush, he lit up his tablet and prepared his software.

Once he was satisfied, he made his way to the kitchen window. It was old and the putty had already been crumbling. Over the last week he had been picking at it slowly and now the window was barely held in place. It would be quick and easy to remove completely.

The alarm was motion sensitive, but the panel was in the kitchen while the motion sensors were in the hall, living room and at the top of the stairs. It wouldn't have a chance to pick him up as he'd have it deactivated before he entered one of the hot zones.

He double-checked the video feed from the camera in the bedroom, and saw that both Ben and Jacob were sound asleep.

Anger pulsed through him as he put his tablet away. With gloved hands, he carefully pulled the window from its frame and set it down on the ground nearby. Stealthily, he climbed up and silently moved the items from the windowsill.

He stepped onto the edge of the sink and lowered himself into the kitchen. Checking his tablet again, he was confident they had heard nothing. He pulled the fascia from the alarm and worked to wire it to his tablet. The code sequencer started whizzing through numbers and within a couple of minutes the code was displayed. He held his breath as he punched in the numbers on the alarm keypad, and watched as the light turned from red to green.

Packing his tablet away, he pulled out two sets of cable ties and a hammer. He needed to incapacitate the cripple first, he wanted Jacob to live as he taught Bree her lessons, watch and see the cost of trying to steal her away. Once he'd taught her he would kill her in front of her lover. She would be easy to control too, all he would have to do is hurt the cripple on occasion and she would do anything he wanted. Navigating the stairs with ease, he paused at the bedroom door and stood, just watching the pair sleep for a moment. *I wonder why she obeys him when she didn't obey me. I'll make her obey me.*

He entered the bedroom and raised the hammer above his head. It crashed down onto Jacob's skull without waking him. Blood started to dribble across his face and on to the pillow. Stan grabbed his hands and secured them with cable ties. He'd get control of Ben then come back and rouse Jacob.

Silently he made his way around the bed and looked at Ben. Her red hair was spread around her head, almost like a halo but he knew she wasn't an angel. He felt the anger ebb back to a controlled rage - it was definitely time for the lessons to begin.

20th June, 0115 hours – O'Byrne residence, Sunderland

Ben lay still under the duvet, her eyes closed. She had no idea what had woken her but her senses were on overdrive. Her skin prickled with fear and she almost felt frozen to the spot. She wanted to open her eyes, she really did, but she was petrified of what she would see. She felt Jacob beside her, felt his warmth, but still she couldn't open her eyes. It was like one of those waking dreams that people have, her mind was wide awake, screaming even, but her body wouldn't respond.

Forcing herself, she opened her eyes.

As her vision adjusted to the darkness, she moved her eyes round the room. Jacob was facing the other way, but he seemed deep asleep, his breathing steady. She spanned the room in a few seconds and let out the breath that she hadn't even realised she was holding. *Stupid bugger, there's nothing there. It's just your mind playing tricks.*

Deciding now she was awake she might as well go for a wee, she stood and padded over the landing to the bathroom. Her heart was still pounding and she felt uneasy, but she pushed the feeling to one side. Plainly she'd been having a nightmare and had felt the effects when she woke up. She felt a shiver pass down her spine; it seemed chilly for the time of year. Ben flushed and pulled open the bathroom door to head back to the bedroom.

As she walked out of the room, she felt sudden certainty that she wasn't alone. Spinning round towards the stairs, she found herself face-to-face with *him*. Fear clawed at her insides, all her training flew out of the window and she felt a whimper escape.

He was really there. He had found her and somehow gotten into her house. She backed away, a tear winding its way down her cheek.

'Hello, Bree. I've been watching you.'

Finding herself at the entrance to the bedroom, she turned and ran to the bed.

'Jacob, please, baby, wake up! He's here, Jacob!' her voice rose a few octaves higher as she shook his shoulders.

'Pull the duvet down,' said Stan from behind her, his voice completely even and calm.

Ben felt dread replace fear, albeit temporarily. She pulled the duvet down and saw the streaks of red across Jacob's face. Panic was threatening to overwhelm her but somehow she kept a grip on reality. She placed a hand in front of his face, and felt the soft whisper of his breath on her skin. *Thank God, he's not dead. What the fuck am I going to do?*

She turned to face her nemesis, trying so hard not to show fear, but she couldn't stop herself from shaking. Her mind flashed back to the field when he'd tricked her, she recalled every little thing he'd done to her in the blink of an eye, and slowly she remembered something else.

Grace. I'm so glad she went away. She'll never know about this. Ben felt a sudden rush of determination. *Who the hell does this guy think he is, breaking into my house, hurting Jacob?*

Stan saw the change in her. Her body language changed from terrified to more confident in the space of a few seconds. It threw him. He needed her to be afraid, she had to be afraid or she wouldn't learn. He needed to get that back.

As he took a step towards her, he heard Jacob groan loudly. *Damn it, he was supposed to be out longer than this.*

Ben half turned and touched Jacob's face softly, and Stan took advantage of her distraction. He crossed the space to the bed in a flash and grabbed her by the hair, yanking her hard towards the door.

She couldn't help but let out a loud scream as her hands instinctively moved to his and she grabbed them, trying not to let him pull her, but she had no choice. He had complete control of her movements and he dragged her out onto the landing. Turning suddenly, he slammed his other fist into the side of her face with such force that she saw stars instantly. Her knees gave, and he let her fall, releasing her hair. Working now, he pulled the cable ties from his pocket and secured her hands together. Then he ripped a piece of silver gaffer tape off the roll and placed it over her mouth.

Leaning down to her ear, he said, 'don't worry, I'll take it off later. That pretty mouth was made to take a real man, not some cripple who didn't even wake up when someone broke into the house.'

Stan was lucky, he didn't know it, but usually Jacob would have woken at a mouse crossing the floor. The pain killers he'd taken earlier though were strong enough to keep him asleep.

Chapter Twenty-six
20th June, 0120 hours – McKay residence, Sunderland

Ali had finished work hours ago, been for a run and grabbed a takeout on his way back to the flat. He now sat on the couch flicking through the channels on the TV but nothing grabbed his eye. The run and takeout food had done nothing for the gnawing stress monster in his gut, it had been growing since he'd left Clarice's home earlier, and whatever was causing it was just on the verge of his thoughts. He knew whatever it was would be important and it had been bugging him all day that he couldn't see it.

Flicking through the movie channels, he found a classic Stallone movie and put the remote on the table in front of him, pulling his legs up to the couch and settling his head on a cushion. He barely even saw five minutes of the movie before he was sound asleep.

He awoke some time later, disorientated and with his neck aching. Light filtered through the window from the street lights outside and somewhere in the distance a siren wailed. He groaned and sat up, rubbing his eyes. Reaching for his phone he checked the time, the illuminated screen told him it was twenty to two and he groaned again. *Wish I hadn't seen that.*

He froze, contemplating his own thoughts. 'Seen? What was seen? Clarice was seen by the killer because he had planted a bloody camera. He's gunning for Ben. That bloody bastard, he's watching her!'

As the last sentence escaped loudly into the silence of the flat, he jumped to his feet and grabbed his car keys. As he sped down the stairs, his phone started ringing. Hitting the right buttons on his mobile for once, he held it to his ear.

'DI McKay, it's Agnes Wright. You said to ring if I saw that man again. He was in their kitchen. Should I go round?'

Ali paled at her words, his feet pounding even faster. 'No. I'm on my way. Stay inside.'

He ended the call without saying goodbye, and quickly plugged the number in for his superintendent.

20th June, 0120 hours – O'Byrne residence, Sunderland

Jacob felt the pull of consciousness but tried to resist. He heard himself groan, and then felt the explosion of pain in his head. *Christ that feels like I've been drinking for a solid weekend.*

He went to lift a hand to his head, and suddenly became fully conscious as he realised his hands were tied. He pulled himself round onto his back to check for Ben, but her side of the bed was empty.

He paled as he heard a scream from the hallway outside the bedroom.

Jacob took a breath to calm himself, and reaching past the lamp on the bedside table he grabbed his mobile phone. He lit the screen by touching the button at the bottom and scrolled to the dial pad and entered 999. He strained to listen to the call being answered, and then whispered, 'I can't speak louder. My name is Jacob Tulley. I work in the digital forensics lab. I am at the house of Ben Cassidy. The killer is here. You need to ring Ali McKay.'

With that he put the phone on the bed, leaving the line open.

He got to his feet and felt a wave of dizziness as his head wound protested.

Shuffling without his stick, he walked to the bedroom door.

20th June, 0125 hours – O'Byrne residence, Sunderland

When he'd hit Ben she'd seen stars and fallen to her knees. Stan had taken advantage and grabbed her hands, securing them with more cable ties. *What the hell is this guys' obsession with cable ties? Can't he just use rope like normal nut jobs?* Ben felt a faint giggle try to escape at her thought – was there such a thing as a normal nut job?

She knew from experience it was pointless struggling against the plastic ties, without a blade they wouldn't be stretched or loosened. She calmed her breathing, trying not to let the panic envelop her. Ben was afraid, but she found herself more afraid for Jacob than she was for herself this time round. No matter what happened, she had to survive and save him. He hadn't asked to be a part of this messed up thing she called life. He'd come in charming her, accepting Grace and protecting her and Aoife, and hadn't asked a thing in return. It was no wonder Ben was falling for him.

When Stan suddenly appeared before her, she stopped herself from portraying her fear. *What the hell did Ali say this guy's name was?*

'Look, Mitchell, isn't it? You don't have to do this.'

Stan stilled, his face going pale. He knelt down beside her, 'What did you call me?'

'Mitchell. That's your name isn't it?'

Rage suddenly blinded him. How the hell did she know his given name? It had been so long since anyone had called him that, he'd all but forgotten it. Memories flooded his mind: his father sneering his name as he administered the latest beating, shouting it from the bottom of the stairs, and how, after he'd killed his father, he'd finally decided to change his name. His temper got the better of him, and he lost it completely, his fists flailing towards Ben's face in repeated motions.

He didn't even notice Jacob behind him until his tied hands appeared round his neck from behind and tightened, cutting off his air supply. He roared feebly, and pushed himself to his feet, throwing himself backwards. Jacob hit the wall behind with such force a crack appeared in the plaster covering the brickwork. He tried to keep his hands taut, but Stan swivelled and pulled himself free.

Jacob had never seen such hate in anyone before. The killer stood before him with eyes sparkling with anger. He was getting off on the violence of it all, and Jacob just managed to raise his arms in time to block the first punch from the large man. Stan's build was stockier than his own, but Jacob had fought bigger. His military training kicked in, and he leaned on the wall whilst using his good leg to swipe Stan's feet from under him so that he hit the deck with a curse.

Jacob didn't want him to get back up though; pulling back he kicked Stan in the stomach with as much force as he could muster. He heard the man grunt as his breath left him.

The movement caused his bad leg to give way, and Jacob fell heavily, landing beside Stan. Jacob pulled himself to his knees, but Stan threw a punch, connecting hard with the side of Jacob's nose which started pouring blood. While Jacob struggled to regain his feet, Stan connected another punch, and Jacob flew sideways, his head hitting the solid pine chest on the landing. Black curtains were closing in on his vision from both sides, but he knew if he passed out he and Ben would be dead. He groaned, blinking rapidly as he tried to stay conscious.

Stan advanced again, and knowing how to incapacitate the man before him, he raised his leg high and slammed his boot down on to Jacob's thigh. Jacob screamed, and unable to keep the darkness at bay, he passed out.

Stan turned back to Ben. She was still in the position he had left her, her face bloodied and swollen from the rain of punches. *How does she know my name?*

He slapped her across the face hard, smiling as she moaned in response. He watched as she tried to open her eyes.

He wasn't expecting her foot to hit his groin with such force.

Stan fell to his knees, his hands cupping his privates as pain coursed through him and he struggled to breathe.

Ben had got to her feet and now her training finally kicked in. She connected her foot with his jaw using a roundhouse kick, then kicked him again in the stomach.

She wanted to hurt him. Hell, she wanted to kill him for all he'd done to her. Her leg seemed to have a mind of its own as she kept kicking. She didn't register the tears streaming down her face, the groan behind her or even the sudden commotion on the stairs.

The first she knew of Ali's presence was when he firmly placed his arms around her and pulled her away from her task of destroying the man who had almost destroyed her. She felt herself go weightless as he lifted her and turned her from Stan's inert body. Several cops were already holding him immobile as one applied the cuffs to his wrists and read him his rights.

Ben finally saw the uniforms, heard the cop-speak through the haze of her fear-fuelled rage, and slumped in Ali's arms, her adrenaline finally spent.

'It's OK, Ben. I've got you,' said Ali softly, turning her around to face him.

He watched her composure slip, and instinctively knew she wouldn't want Stan to see her cry. Leading her, he took her into the bedroom and sat her on the bed.

But Ben's tears didn't arrive. A sudden look of horror flashed over her face, 'Jacob!' She got to her feet and tried to run past Ali onto the landing. He was going to stop her, but realising she needed to see Jacob for herself, he let her go. Stan had already been removed from the landing, and two cops were knelt beside Jacob. He'd woken moments ago, just in time to see the cops cuffing Stan, and his face was panicked as he looked around for Ben.

When his eyes finally settled on her face, his expression eased.

'Help me up?' he asked the cop beside him.

Ben watched as he held the cops shoulder and stood. She knew his leg would be agony, could still hear his scream in the back of her mind. She wasn't surprised when he grimaced, leaning back against the wall, his face turning ashen.

'Jesus,' he said through gritted teeth.

'Lean on me,' she said softly, positioning her shoulder under his so she could take his weight. Her ribs were throbbing and when she took his weight they started pounding with pain. But she ignored it, she could check them later.

Ali followed them downstairs to the living room.

'I've got ambulance crew en route to check you both out. We can take your statements a little later.'

'How did you know?' asked Ben, suddenly curious.

'Charlie found cameras in Clarice's house and it came to me suddenly that he had to have placed cameras here, too. I didn't know he was going to be here. I was coming to alert you to the cameras. Then Mrs Wright to the back of you phoned me to say he was in your kitchen.'

'Mrs Wright? Oh, you mean Agnes. She had your number? I'll pop over in a couple of days and thank her.'

The conversation was progressing with normalcy, something that both Ben and Jacob didn't feel. She suddenly wanted to be alone with him, and instinctively leaned into him for comfort. He placed his hand at the base of her spine and stroked lightly, picking up on how she felt.

Ali also noticed the movement. 'I'll let the crew check you out. If you don't need to go to hospital we'll be booking a room in a hotel for you. This house is a crime scene, at least for now.'

Within an hour both Ben and Jacob were wearing hospital scrubs and had been allocated a private room together on the trauma ward. Jacob had phoned TJ and updated her, and despite her wanting to come straight down, he had asked her to wait until the next day. Ben had decided not to wake Aoife and Grace, despite needing to hear their voices. Tomorrow would be soon enough.

For now, they both lay in separate beds, their wounds treated

'Hell of a night. It's nice to finally have some peace and quiet.'

'I miss Grace, but I'm so glad she wasn't here. Remind me to get your friend the biggest bottle of whiskey I can find as a thank you.'

Jacob smiled, 'He'll love that. This bed feels awfully big.' He glanced at her hopefully.

She grinned back. 'Thought you'd never ask.'

She got onto his bed and positioned herself in the crook of his shoulder, her head resting on him lightly. The only sound in the room was their breathing, at least until Ben gave a slight hiccup. Jacob had already felt her tears wetting the top of the scrubs he wore, and he pulled her tightly to him, kissed her on the head, and whispered, 'It's OK. We're OK. You cry if you want to.'

He almost felt like crying himself to be fair, but he didn't. He just held Ben with the silent promise that he'd never let her go.

Epilogue

Mitchell Brown lay in the small cot bed in a quiet corner of the hospital. It turned out the rumours that you hear about prisoners not liking rapists were true.

The attack had happened a couple of days previously, on his fourth day since the court appearance that sent him down for life. Even with all his fighting skills, he hadn't stood a chance. They'd pounded his ribs until one had splintered, puncturing his lung. His face was a mass of cuts and stitches, swollen and discoloured with bruising. And he could hardly see anything out of his left eye; the doctors had said they didn't think his sight would recover. His right hand had been placed on a pillow, the pins sticking out at odd angles, after it had been mangled as one of the prisoners methodically broke every bone, the damage injuring the nerves in his hand.

Currently he was in the room alone, staring at the grey walls and wondering how he could get out of this. He'd started refusing pain medication yesterday, wanting to be more alert in case an opportunity arose that he could take advantage of. Not that he really believed one would. The two prison guards outside the only entrance to the room would stop him if he tried and he was in no condition to take on both of them.

The doctor had made the decision not to allow him to be cuffed to the bed though, allowing him unrestricted movement, well as unrestricted one could be with chest injuries and a hand and eye that no longer worked.

Still, at least he was ready. At first the pain had been unbearable; he'd actually thought he was going to die as he was transported to the hospital, gasping for breath and in a sea of pain. He vaguely remembered being wheeled down to surgery, but when he'd awoken the pain had eased. The doctor had no idea of his childhood, didn't know he could take a lot more pain that most people could. The doctor had been nice to him, she'd spoken to him like a human being, and he'd played the part well, a solitary tear confirming to her that he wasn't strong enough to stroke a kitten, let alone escape.

Yesterday, he'd stood for a minute, feeling waves of pain and dizziness drift over him as he held the side of the bed for support. He needed to be able to handle it, able to react if an escape appeared. It was this hope that was keeping him strong. He'd stood several times after that, and today had walked round the entire room.

He heard the door open with a click and closed his undamaged eye to a slit, watching as three people entered. The nurse efficiently checked his vitals then went to the chart at the end of the room. The prison guard was young, still green. He hadn't been in the job two minutes and it showed. The older ones would have been stood next to Mitchell, not trusting that he looked asleep.

Mitchell felt a fold of hope unfurl.

The third person was a handyman of sorts. He was in his fifties with a paunch belly, and was wearing overalls and carrying a toolbox. He set it down on the floor to Mitchell's left and pulled the shelves apart, removed a wrench and spanner and set to work on the oxygen supply pipe in the next bay along. His back was turned, concentrating on the task at hand.

The guard was flirting with the nurse, and she was smiling back, both totally engrossed in each other.

Without a sound, Mitchell reached down into the toolbox and liberated a tool. He had no idea what it was when he grabbed it, but the metal was cold in his hand as he slid it underneath his body so it was hidden under the curve of his back. He gave a groan to cover any noise that might have been noticed, and the nurse hurried over in response.

'Mr Brown,' she said coolly. 'Do you want something?' Her attitude had changed; normally the nurses and doctors didn't get to know what the crimes of the patients were from the prison. He'd bet his hat that the youthful guard had just spilled the beans and told her everything.

'Water,' he croaked, wanting the pretence to continue. He couldn't take three people out in his condition. Silently she held a cup to his mouth and he took a few sips. The water was tepid, metallic, but what more could he expect?

He replaced his head on the pillow and closed his eyes.

When they all left the room a short time later, he pulled the tool out from under his back. He smiled as he realised he'd pulled out a Stanley knife. Perfect.

It seemed like hours before anyone else came in the room, but the nurse entered to check him followed by the young guard. As they entered the older guard followed.

'Am gonna go take a leak and get a coffee from the café. You want anything, Billy?'

'No, I'm good thanks.' Billy was already focussed on the nurse, watching as she checked Mitchell's dressings and vitals. It was the worst thing about being in hospital he had to acknowledge, being woken every two hours so someone could check blood pressure with a beeping machine was definitely not fun.

The nurse walked to the chart, signed it off and left the room. Mitchell waited until the guard followed then slowly he got to his feet. His body screamed at him to lie back down as he stood. He was surprised to find himself a little unsteady on his feet. Moving as quietly as he could, he made his way to the door and peeked out through the window.

The older guard was nowhere in sight, the young one was sitting on the chair outside looking bored.

Positioning himself behind the door, he yelled out, knowing the guard would come running.

Billy didn't disappoint, running inside, and then stopping in confusion as he realised the bed was empty. It was long enough though - there was a flash as the blade moved across the front of Billy's neck, and he gurgled as he fell to his knees, his hands grabbing desperately at his neck as his life left him floating in an ocean of red.

Mitchell stood over him and looked down in satisfaction; that was definitely the easiest way to kill someone. Checking the pockets on Billy's stab vest, he removed his baton and pulled out the little money the lad had on his person.

First he needed to find somewhere to rest up, recover from his wounds, then it would be time to start planning what he would do next. He couldn't stay in Sunderland, he knew that. He'd thought of London before - that would do. For now. One day he would come back for Ben Cassidy, and next time he wouldn't fail. The eye he could see out of squinted with determination.

He opened the hospital door, slipped into the corridor, and left.

THE END.

Acknowledgements

I'd like to say a massive thank you to the team at Bloodhound Books
– particularly Betsy and Fred for believing in me and this novel
enough to give me a contract. Also thanks to the lovely editor and
cover designer – they make working a pleasure.

To the Crime Scene personnel and police officers who have put up
with me constantly double checking facts, thanks for the unwavering
belief in my writing, and for regaling me with endless tales of crime
scene gallows humour. To the lovely Inspector Caroline, I give thanks
for answering the numerous questions asked about the police side of
a crime novel.

Special thanks to my amazing family – Peter, Jeannet, Derek, Michael,
Mary and Harry -without them writing just wouldn't be possible. The
support they provide is unwavering and constant. They all make me
so proud every single day. They make me strive to be a better person
and push me to believe in myself.

My close friends are my rocks – constant support through good and
bad, and not being too shy to tell me when I'm doing something I
shouldn't be! You know who you are – but to mention a few names
(by no means all) Claire, Angela, Dionne, Rachel, Vicky, Eileen,
Michelle and Char. Keep shining like the stars you are.

Finally, I'd like to thank YOU, the reader. Writing really wouldn't be
as pleasurable without each and every one of you, whether I know you
or not, you make my dreams a reality. It makes me very proud to
admit I'm a member of THE Book Club, UK Crime Book Club,
Crime Book Club and Crime Fiction Addict on Facebook – these
clubs make speaking to readers simple and I thoroughly enjoy the
interaction, banter, and suggestions for books to read, characters and
plots to write. I look forward to meeting more of you at the various
events planned in the near future.

.